*Well-behaved Women
seldom make History...*

Laurel Thatcher Ulrich

Project: <u>FEMME</u>

PROLOGUE

Baltimore, Maryland
September 14, 2015

The plasma television set glowed in the corner of the laboratory, its volume lowered enough so that the two men huddled in front of it could listen and still speak privately. The facility was deserted, save for the nightshift security and a janitor making the rounds with his trusty mop and bucket, the latest Top 100 Billboard Hits booming from his headphones as he danced from floor to floor.

They watched the election coverage with mild disinterest, concentrated on the mission at hand and debated the merits of the program that would be 5initiated with the new administration.

"Is it wise to wait until the second term? How can we be sure they won't use their leverage to just control us?"

He was tall and lanky, his long fingers constantly reaching for his tortoise-rimmed eyeglasses, cleaning them haphazardly and returning them to his worried face. He did this after every question and seemed to never be satisfied with their cleanliness.

His partner, colleague or co-conspirator, as it were, ignored him. As irritating as it was to figure out the scientific specs of the plan alone, it would have been worse to work solo than just entertain a worrywart, so he reluctantly replied for the umpteenth time, "Relax. We've got it all figured out."

Another question, again with the glasses off and on.

"But how can you be sure?"

"This program has been tested and proven effective time and again. This wasn't an overnight decision. It is certain to work."

Glasses off.

"But they're mobilizing troops. Generating a militia. Its only a matter of time. If we are going to implement a defense we have to start now."

This time the glasses stayed in his hand, suffering the exertion as they wrung endlessly, no doubt clammy with the sweat of preoccupation.

His partner raised a salt and pepper eyebrow, but never took his eyes off of the television screen.

"How the hell do they even stand a chance? We're talking about the greatest military force on the planet. It's the United goddamn States of America."

"In a couple of months, it won't be the USA any longer. We have to strike now!" he exclaimed, his already large eyes growing wider.

"No!"

His voice boomed through the lab, immediately silencing any doubts waiting to be voiced. "We wait. We finalize the program. Perfect it. And then we implement it at the right time."

"The president will never back that. He'll appear weak."

"The president has been briefed. He's received the proper recommendation. The program moves forward."

"And how will we know that it'll even get to this? They're just rebel forces."

"A rebel command that combined with ours will be larger than any Russian, Japanese or Chinese forces. Don't be fooled."

"If you're so sure they're that powerful, how will we be able to win?"

"We'll have the secret weapon."

"A group of women is now a secret weapon?"

He reminded himself, again, how much harder things would be without his worrisome friend.

"A group? Try half the population of this country."

"How do you plan on controlling a subject that size?"

"Think logically. How did plantation owners keep slaves in check when they were outnumbered twenty to one? Fear. Plain and simple. Scare them into submission. Scare them into staying."

He seemed to calm slightly. "Okay. So they stay. That's the easy part. The question is, how do you get them to fight?"

"Well, that's the beauty of it. You give anybody a righteous cause and they'll do just about anything for you. And what's a nobler cause than motherhood?"

PART ONE

Chapter I

On the day Paul Ryan Yenmor was elected President, internet search engines all over the United States of America stalled and crashed. Reminiscent of the way cell phone companies collapsed on September 11, 2001 under the weight of their customers' frantic calls, so too were Google, Bing and Yahoo crippled. Computer techs and geeks from every major facet of the world wide web scrambled to get their websites back online before their competitors. The Dow Jones dropped further than it had since the days following 9/11, and before the day was through, November 8, 2016 would become known as the beginning of the end.

The internet bounced back right away. By midnight everything was back to normal, and by 6am on the 9th, thousands of travel companies reported a massive hike in relocation searches, particularly into Canada. By Thanksgiving, popular tourist locations like Toronto and Montreal were reporting an expected jump in revenue for the following year; and by Christmas, Canadian provinces in lesser known regions too, had more visits than ever before.

After his inauguration, the migration began. Spring Break, 2017, saw flights through Air Canada at an all-time high. Schools throughout the continental U.S. reported more withdrawals of students that June than combined throughout their respective existences. Immigration into the US came to a virtual halt. The people were speaking; at least the ones who didn't vote for Yenmor.

Things calmed down for awhile. President Yenmor laid low, simply kept with the policies of the previous administration and barely made any waves. Though as Senator of Wisconsin he had stood strong against abortion and favored the standing on Proposition 8, he didn't force the issue once elected, and instead, worked to preserve Obama's previous work. The rate of employment continued to rise, jobs opened and the economy moved upward in furtherance of Obama's eight prior years. So the migration stopped. Democrats and independents alike chalked their original fear up to paranoia and began to accept Yenmor as a docile leader, someone interested in propelling the United States forward, despite some of his political stances.

So his reelection on November 1, 2016 came as no surprise.

What followed however, did…

~

Delilah Cordero adjusted her White House ID badge and moved down the corridor, gripping the stack of documents in her hands and hugging them to her chest.

As she passed Milton, the press secretary to President Yenmor, she offered a smile in his general direction and without waiting for reciprocation, picked up speed and turned the corner of the large hallway, grateful that no one had yet approached her.

She had been an aide at the White House now for three years, having started as an intern on Yenmor's campaign and then moved up to intern for his administration. By day she was a lowly gopher, delegated to fetching files, fielding calls and running errands. By day she went virtually unseen, unnoticed and unbothered. By day she passed President Yenmor and stood at attention like everyone else at 1600 Pennsylvania Avenue, addressed him as Mr. President and cast her eyes downward. Just like everyone else.

But by night, she roamed an unknown part of the White House, a secret passageway used by former presidents during times of crises; now used by President Yenmor for his lackeys, she being one.

By night, she ran his errands, did his bidding. No questions asked.

When the most powerful man on the planet came inquiring about her ability to keep a secret, Delilah jumped at the chance. Deliver messages, run confidential files from the Oval Office to the Department of Defense, provide Senate members with classified information. She did it all, no questions asked. In turn, Yenmor promised her status and power. As long as she did as he asked and stayed quiet, all would be hers. Everything else that came with their little arrangement was a perk, a highlight.

The First Lady was a flake, a trophy wife who spent more time on committees and as chair of so many charities, she and Yenmor were rarely alone together without some form of press or photographer in the room. Their two sons were away at West Point and there was nothing between them but convenience and photo ops. Delilah knew the First Lady would never leave Yenmor and didn't quite care about his many trysts, so she had no remorse about her questionable relationship with the President of the United States.

She had plans, goals. And what better way to achieve them than underneath the world's most influential politician?

She reached the main office for the President's staffers and taking caution to ensure she was alone, plugged in the correct code into the panel against the wall and waited for the click of the lock opening. It did so quickly and she opened the door, slipped through it, and shut it behind her.

Her orders were always the same. Deliver the files to the room, leave them on the gray marble slab in the center and retreat immediately. She followed her orders, as she always did, and as she made her way back to the door through which she'd entered, she felt a pinch on the right side of her neck.

Instinctively her hand flew to the spot but before she could decipher whether she had been bit by anything, she suddenly lost all feeling in her hand.

Delilah looked up, confused, and her eyes met with Niall, the Director of the Secret Service that served Yenmor's administration. She opened her mouth to speak her surprise, but nothing came out.

Immediately, a crippling pain coursed through her midsection, into her chest, causing Delilah to double over in pain. She screamed, but still no sound emerged from her parted lips. Tears formed in the corners of her eyes and spilled over, but she felt nothing on her face. Nothing but the agony gripping her as she collapsed on the floor at Niall's feet, silently pleading for his help.

He watched, detached, as her body twitched in convulsions, and a thin sliver of blood poured out of each eye.

When it was over, approximately thirty seconds after it had begun, Niall pulled Delilah into another room by her feet, dragging her past a secret door she knew nothing about, and into an unmarked government van waiting outside.

Just as quickly as he'd appeared in the corner of that secret room she had thought she knew so well, Niall picked up the files she'd left on the table and left silently.

~

President Yenmor didn't play by the rules or rather, he opted to play by a different set of rules. In the world he'd envisioned upon setting out to become President of the United States, he wouldn't be answering to any branches of government created to minimize the chance of a dictatorship. He wouldn't be at the mercy of the Senate of lobbyists out to get their own agendas met. That was not what he signed up for.

He used Delilah Cordero, and others like her, as a means to an end. He needed backing to get from A to B and the only way to do it quietly, was by using the gophers and interns that ran the hallways of the White House. So he did. They delivered plans and messages, ideas and drafts, back and forth between him and other like-minded individuals in Congress. In turn, he was able to see his plans come to life.

In order for a bill to be written into law, it has to pass a series of stages. Or at least this is how things were done, before what would become known as the Yenmor Era. First, a representative of the State would sponsor a bill, which would then be assigned to be studied by a committee. If released, it would be put on a calendar to be voted on and would need to pass by simple majority (218 of 435) in order to move to the Senate. In the Senate, it would move to another committee and, if released, voted on again to pass. After discussion, debate and various clever ways Congress could spend taxpayer dollars, the revised bill would then return to the House and Senate for final approval. It would then be printed, enrolled and presented to the big guy himself. The President would then have ten days to sign or veto the enrolled bill.

This part of the American legislative system didn't fit in to Yenmor's plans, so he found a way around it.

He had his flunkies pass a series of bills into laws and when finalized in the dark confines of the Oval Office, he had completely reconfigured the United States government.

First came the elimination of the whole legislative process. No more days of an animated rolled up document sitting on the steps of Capitol Hill and singing about becoming a law. And in order to keep things simple, a complete disbandment of the Supreme Court and Judicial Branch of the government followed immediately.

Then came his new rules.

Restrictive laws against voting that required so much procedure to be met, after the red-tape was funneled through, women and minorities were all but banned from the voting booths; a complete nationwide ban on abortion so severe, that within 72 hours all providers were arrested, any women seeking an abortion was hauled to jail on the spot, and all clinics and hospitals offering the service were shut down, locked up and boarded shut; and a nationwide ban on all contraception and all preventative care. Pharmacies were raided and medical records were seized to determine who was using birth control. Those found to have any type of contraception in their system or on their person, arrested.

When revealed to the public, it seemed as though it happened overnight. But in reality, it was a long time coming. Yenmor had begun setting the wheels in motion upon his second inauguration in 2017. Slowly but surely, the road was paved in private. Secret meetings, codes only deciphered by a chosen few and conspiracies that rivaled that in any Hollywood film were par for the course, and had he not eliminated the Legislative branch following the passing of his new laws, Yenmor would not just have been impeached, but tried for crimes of treason. Chaos colored the events to come and on the shoulders of a majority of American voters rested the guilt for having had elected him into office.

Had network television not been destroyed and Freedom of Speech and Press remained in tact, the American public might have weighed in on events and noticed Yenmor's approval ratings weren't exactly appealing. But network television was gone, along with newspapers, radio broadcasts and internet activity. The Bill of Rights ceased to exist and Yenmor wouldn't have cared even if it did.

Yenmor was neither racist nor a mysogynist. He was not a bigot or prejudiced against minorities or any ethnicity. He did not care about skin color, education, status or class. He was after more than just a cleansing. He wanted a revitalization of the United States. A new world order run by the military of a super power. It wasn't enough for the United States to be respected, a status which had long since been lost in much of the world. He wanted the globe to fear it, tremble at the mere mention of this once great country. He wanted complete control. And to get there, he had to get rid of some collateral damage.

Chapter II

Washington, D.C.

When the ground shook at approximately 5:39 a.m. on the morning of March 25, 2017, the majority of the coastal population in the East barely noticed. The death of Osama Bin Laden during the Obama administration and the lack of any terrorist activity since had allowed for the return of complacency and comfort in the United States. Even the jaded citizens of the city that never sleeps, who had not yet forgotten 9/11 but who had long since forgotten the fear of its successor, were content with the status quo.

The first reports that poured in were scoffed at. The Pentagon staffers didn't even get up from their seats when the phones started ringing. But like all pressing matters made all the more urgent in the age of technology, the suspicions of a tiny tremor off the coast of Africa snowballed into a crisis. The President's advisors finally consulted with him after more urgent notes came in from all over the globe.

President Yenmor only offered an undecipherable smirk and went back to working on his golf swing.

New York City, NY

It was a particularly warm day in October when President Paul Yenmor's lackeys implemented the second phase of his master plan.

Dixon Milian kissed his sleeping son's forehead and tiptoed out of his room, careful to leave the door open just a crack. The four-year old was still adjusting to his big boy status and not yet entirely comfortable with a closed door in a dark room.

He made his way down the long hallway of his cozy coop apartment and crept through the kitchen, grabbing his briefcase and gym bag on his way out. Locking up behind him he jogged down twenty flights of stairs instead of taking the elevator and made his way to his brand new Acura in the residential parking lot underneath the building. Inside the car, Dixon adjusted his mirrors and checked behind him for pedestrians before putting the car in gear and reversing out of his spot.

After putting in an hour at the gym, Dixon showered, changed and grabbed a quick breakfast on his way into school. He had a big day planned for his fourth-graders: it would be their first field trip of the year and they had tickets to see a new reptile exhibit at the Bronx Zoo in preparation for their winter projects on animal species. The kids had been talking about it all week and were uncontrollably excited.

After the first bell sounded, he walked his kids into their classroom and tried his best to patiently keep them calm while they waited for the school bus to arrive. They played 7-Up and told jokes until a faint rumbling could be heard outside the window. His most rambunctious student, Oliver Duran, popped up from his seat and ran to the window to announce the arrival of their transportation. Dixon didn't bother admonishing him, knowing the kids were simply combustible with excitement.

"Hey, Mr. M, are we going to the zoo in a army jeep?"

"'An' army jeep, Oliver. 'An'," he replied, getting up from his chair and walking around his desk to have a look.

The explosion ripped through the wall first, seemingly seconds before the glass shattered and the windows imploded. Little Oliver's body was pushed back through the air and crashed against the wooden closets behind him, landing lifelessly on the carpeted floor. The last row of kids closest to the windows were all gone. Their desks were completely covered with rubble and shards of glass. Dixon shook the shock out of his head and looked around, unsure of how he ended up on the floor behind his desk, his briefcase beside him and all of his paperwork scattered. He crawled to Jessica Adelia's desk still hoping for their safety for the sake of his kids but freezing when his eyes landed on her tiny hand exposed from under a wall of cement, a thin line of blood darkening the taupe carpeting underneath them.

The sounds of screaming and crying tore him out of his daze. Dixon rose and looked to his right, through the gaping hole that was once a classroom wall. Military jeeps lined the streets outside.

He breathed a sigh of relief. Whatever had just happened would be quickly solved.

He helped several children up and coaxed several others out from under the desks, where they cowered in fear. He urged them to cover their eyes and look away from the lifeless bodies of their friends. Another explosion and another earth-shattering shake of the building knocked Dixon and his seventeen surviving students off of their feet. He rose quicker this time and looked outside again, his eyes landing on the men scattered on the school grounds, one of which was holding a bazooka aimed at the school.

David Texeira tugged on his shirtsleeve and Dixon looked down at him.

"Why are the police shooting at us?"

He sniffled and blinked his big brown eyes at Dixon, who could offer no response. He simply picked David up and holding him with one arm, ushered the children through the classroom door and into the hallway, where they met up with several other teachers and students, all as disoriented and confused as he felt.

Above the crying children and panicked voices, Dixon heard the pounding of boot-clad feet coming through the stairs on both ends of the hallway. Several men in army fatigues appeared from the stairwells brandishing automatic weapons. To the rest of the student body and administration it was a welcomed sight, but to his class it meant more explosions and death, so Dixon's kids screamed. He tried to calm them and quiet them down and with the help of other teachers, got them under control as the men waved them all down the hallway and out of the building.

Outside, Dixon helped all of the children into military vans. The officers were silent and rough, showing little patience for the crying kids. When all kids were accounted for, Dixon went back into the school to make sure everyone was out, and to deal with the aftermath of the tiny bodies in his classroom. Behind him, teachers and administrative staff followed him inside at the urging of the officers, and as he shifted around the corner of the second floor hallway and turned to look behind him, he was hit with two bullets in his chest.

The force propelled him backward and he fell, hitting the floor with a louder thud than had little Oliver Duran. The last thing he saw before everything went black was the sight of his fellow colleagues and superiors hitting the ground all around him in a shower of blood and bullet casings.

Bronx, NY

It started as a simple plan to meet up, and snowballed from there. Henry Waterstone, the red-headed kid from Sister Francis' class had a crush on the new girl, Jianna Moreno. So he called her and asked her if she wanted to meet up at Van Cortlandt Park. After a lengthy conversation with her older cousin and best friend, wherein they dissected every word exchanged between Jianna and Henry, they agreed. Henry called his friends, Jianna called hers, and on a beautiful Fall day in October, they converged at the park.

It was one of those days that would have gone down in the record books as perfect. Two pick up games of basketball, another soccer game played boys vs girls, and everyone riding their bikes in random relay races that ended in gasps for breath and the red faces of overexerted childhood. They mapped out plays for a game of touch football, called themselves the 'Bomb Squad' and celebrated a win as though it were bigger than the Superbowl. Mr. Softie came around for the first time in weeks due to the mild weather and they ransacked the truck like looters. An African cricket team showed them some moves on the grass and stood back and watched the kids play, a sense of peace coming over all of them in reminder of the value of youth.

As they tired, Henry moved in closer to Jianna, summoned the courage to make his move, and got as far as a quick peck on the cheek before his friends taunted him until he was red in the face.

It was one of those days that definitely would have gone down in the record books as perfect.

Almost.

Two kids made it home, out of the thirteen that had gathered. Henry died with his arms wrapped around Jianna in a desperate but futile attempt to protect her from the onslaught of bullets. Their friends lay by them, some caught off guard, others hiding behind benches that didn't provide sufficient cover against the gunfire that had erupted.

Four African cricket players lay dead beside the children having bravely tried to shield them when danger arose. But they had been no match against the future that lay ahead.

Chapter III

Despite his meticulous planning, Yenmor's new policies and laws took some time to implement onto the American public and for the rest of society to subsequently collapse, but to Shane Milian, it was as though things had changed overnight. One minute she was a career woman, married to a loving husband and mother to the greatest four-year old on the planet; and the next, she was a widow in hiding with her son avoiding capture by the militia. All around her there was death, chaos and destruction and there was literally nothing she could do about it. Her only hope for survival and for the life of her son was to follow the new rules and keep her head down.

Business as usual had become anything but.

When it had begun and all of the able-bodied men in the general vicinity of New York City had been executed, all that remained were women- mothers, daughters, even the elderly. And there was no information, no more media or social networks spreading news like wildfire. Just millions of women scared and alone, wondering why they'd been allowed to live when it seemed the rest of mankind was being systematically wiped out. What they hadn't known at the time, Shane included, was that it wasn't annihilation of mankind, but instead an overhaul of civilization in the manner Yenmor saw fit. Men were not needed so they were eliminated and woman of a certain pedigree were allowed to remain because inevitably, they would serve a purpose.

After her husband's death, Shane began the short-lived process of mourning by hiding from the newly formed militia under the Yenmor regime in her home. She'd received the phone call while she was at work, told to turn on the television set and watch the News 12 Broadcast about a shooting at her husband's place of employment. She'd caught about ten seconds of the report before the screen went black and though she didn't know it at the time, that was the last television program she'd ever see.

Her car at the time, an Infiniti GX model of the year, didn't disappoint and helped her get from her office in Scarsdale to her late husband's job in Harlem in less than fifteen minutes. But the ride had proven fruitless and she'd run into a barricade of army jeeps and armed soldiers guarding the area. Seconds from parking and exiting the vehicle in an attempt to get past the guards, Shane watched in horror as everyone who got close to the guarded perimeter was mowed down with bullets. Right in front of her eyes, dozens of people were murdered in a hail of gunfire. Terrified, she'd fled as quickly as she could and made her way back uptown to their Riverdale neighborhood to pick her son up from daycare.

The days that followed were a sick and twisted blur. She heard gunshots from the inside of her coop apartment in a usually quiet and safe neighborhood. Screams and cries for help became commonplace outside and she hid with Silas, her four-year old son, in fear. There was no television, no radio broadcasts, no internet. Cell phones and even landlines were useless. Periodically, a large vehicle would drive up and down the streets blasting pre-recorded messages of statuses or instructions on a loudspeaker. Otherwise, there was absolutely no contact with the outside world that could provide insight or answers.

Shane hid for almost a week, barricaded inside her apartment, trying her best to act as though nothing were wrong and daddy would be home any minute.

Then she began to watch. To learn. She'd follow them, learn their patterns and habits, and prepare herself and her son for the worst.

On the day she was finally put out of her home, Shane woke up with a start. She hadn't allowed herself to become accustomed to sleeping in ever since the world had erupted, but a late night of rocking Silas to sleep while he cried out for his father left her feeling groggier than usual and she'd overslept well past the usual hour she preferred.

For the past two months she'd gone to great lengths to ensure being awake before the sun came up over the Palisades. Though the city was policed at night by the militia, it was fairly quiet nonetheless and by dawn, most of the stragglers were passed out elsewhere. This allowed her the opportunity to move around without alerting anyone to life behind the walls of her boarded up apartment.

So she would rise at 5am on the dot and after freshening up and doing a quick round of strength training, all with her ears trained on the front door for the slightest suspicious sound, Shane would take her usual spot by the window that faced Riverdale Avenue and with an old but trusty pair of binoculars, she'd stay out of eyesight and map the entirety of the West Bronx from Westchester into Manhattan. As far as her extended eyes could see, Shane would painstakingly document every man with a weapon, every wandering sicko using the end of civilization to live out his twisted fantasies, and every military vehicle. She documented it all in one of Silas' small notebooks and though she wasn't quite sure how it would help her in the long run, just the process of spying and itemizing made her feel a little more in control in a new world where women no longer held any.

Once the rest of the city would begin to come to life, Shane would wake Silas, dress him and along with a backpack full of emergency provisions, she'd lock him in the closet of their spare bedroom right next to a private dumbwaiter behind a hidden panel as she foraged the building for supplies and food. When she'd purchased the coop unit in the prestigious Skyview buildings, the realtor had whispered it to her as a selling point- the room was intended to be maid's quarters and the dumbwaiter added to that particular line of units extending from the basement to the top floor. It was controlled manually and could stop on any floor chosen by the inhabitant of the 4x4 container.

Though Silas was only four years old, still a baby by most standards, it was no longer an average world where a little boy would spend more time worried about what toy to utilize next rather than survival. So Shane had trained him, had used the past two months preparing him meticulously until Silas' brain was so ingrained with the habits she's made that he could enter the closet at his mother's prodding, curl up with his favorite stuffed animal and go right back to sleep until his mother returned for him. If for any reason she could not, Silas also knew how to serve himself dry Cheerios from a plastic bag inside of his book bag and hold his bladder until she could return to him. He also had with him his father's digital Swatch watch that would tell him the date and time. Shane would synchronize the watch with hers each day before she closed the closet door and Silas knew if she was not back by a certain time, he was to follow their evacuation plan and make it to a safe location until they were reunited again.

This particular morning, she'd overslept and as the commotion began outside of her door, Shane's eyes snapped open and an overpowering feeling of dread came over her. Their safety had been compromised.

She heard the pounding on each apartment door as it made its way to hers at the end of the corridor. She knew she didn't have much time so she jumped out of bed, already fully dressed since they no longer slept comfortably anymore. She grabbed Silas' backpack and her own emergency pack and scooped up her still sleeping son into her arms.

Silently, as she had practiced many times before, Shane moved quickly down the hall of her coop apartment which was once airy and spacious and inviting to all who entered. She moved hurriedly past the pictures on the wall of a happy family, just beginning their journey, all smiles and tender hugs. She passed the open space of the living room where she had sat many a night curled up on the couch with her loving husband and watched movies, had laughs and just existed. She said goodbye for one last time to the life she had created, nurtured, loved and known for so long and entered the spare bedroom, shutting the door softly behind her.

With Silas still safe in her arms, Shane opened the closet and walked in, moving the clothing hanging on the pole out of the way and closing the door. Silently, she moved a panel against the back wall whose grooves were perfectly lined up and hidden to the outside world and she gently nudged Silas awake, ushering him inside the dumbwaiter. Silas did as instructed and sat against the far corner, curling his knees close to him and smiling brightly when he realized his mom would be coming along for the ride. Shane curled her long body into a tight ball and before entering completely inside the tiny box that would save their lives, returned the clothes on the hangers to an unbothered and haphazard mess, making extra sure they did not rock. She slid the panel back softly and satisfied when she heard the clicking of the grooves snapping back in place, closed the door of the dumbwaiter and began the descent to the basement just as she heard her front door get kicked in.

Shane had investigated the sound the dumbwaiter made as its dials and mechanical wiring functioned and pulled the box up and down within the walls of the building. She'd tested it with a television set, heavy pots and pans and on occasion, with Silas, just to see if the sound could be heard from the hallways. Now using it for real, she was confident it was silent enough to avoid detection, but she nonetheless stopped it every five floors and listened as she made her way from the twentieth to the basement.

During her months investigating the events transpiring in the outside world, Shane had picked up on a couple of tricks. She knew to stick to the yards and alleys between houses and buildings; the main street was where everyone got caught, killed or worse. She knew that silence truly was golden- chaos attracted them, brought them in droves and once there, they spread out and looked for more chaos off of which to feed. And most importantly, she knew which apartments were safe inside of the building, and what was safe outside of it.

Right now, she could not afford to bring her son into broad daylight, across a large intersection like Riverdale Avenue, and past the militia that likely lay hidden and waiting for their prey. So she settled on implementing her back-up plan and as she made her way to the basement, she tightened her grip on Silas and waited with bated breath for whatever she would come in contact with on the other end of their little dumbwaiter.

Silas, trained well, was completely silent.

Shane waited five minutes after landing to ensure there wasn't a soul on the other side of their door and even then, she held her breath and noticed her hand shaking slightly when she finally opened it.

Careful to not call any attention to their arrival, Shane worked as quickly as she could. The dumbwaiter opened to a hole in the wall behind the line of dryers on the far side of the laundry room. The dryers were stacked two at a time, one on top of the other, and stood about eight feet tall so they remained out of eyeshot to anyone in the room.

Shane unwrapped her long body and crawled out of the tiny box, putting her backpack back on and reaching back inside for Silas. He entered her arms quickly and she pulled him out, setting him softly on the linoleum floor, shutting the door behind them. To anyone not looking for it, the grooves of the door in the wall were almost nonexistent.

She grabbed Silas' little hand and with a finger to her lips reminding him once again of the importance of silence, ushered him around the dryers and out of the laundry room.

Listening closely, she heard nothing and confirmed her belief that the men were inside the building on the upper floors, going door to door looking for women in hiding. Though she didn't wish their presence on her neighbors, she did however say a quick prayer of thanks that they were steering clear of the basement.

They moved through the corridor stealthily and quickly, pausing long enough to listen for militia before opening the door leading to the underground garage.

There, Shane made her way as fast as Silas' little legs could shuffle towards the far end of the massive garage until she reached the secondary vehicles belonging to renters. Ten cars in and only eight cars from the exit of the garage, Shane reached the black GMC Suburban with the tinted windows that had belonged to the police officer in 6C that had been killed when the first wave had hit. And as quietly as she could, she opened the back driver side door and lifted Silas up in the air and into the SUV's back seat. She pushed him in further and climbed in too, closing the door softly behind her. She locked all of the doors and climbed over the back of the seat and into the truck's bed, pulling Silas up and over with her.

Shane looked out through the windows of the vehicle for roaming visitors, windows which had been tinted to almost complete blackness at the request of its prior owner, despite New York City law prohibiting same; windows which, after spending weeks looking for the perfect place to hide out should their location be compromised,

Shane had finally found and after swiping the keys from 6C upon his untimely death, had covered with aluminum foil from the inside so as not to give themselves away.

Satisfied that they were safe for now, she expertly stretched the accordion truck bed cover over their heads, turned on the timer of her now useless cell phone to 1:00am and settled in.

Chapter IV

One month later, Shane and Silas had become accustomed to an entirely different routine than their previous solitary one. They now shared a safe house with four women and six other children on the outskirts of the Washington Heights section of Manhattan. There, they had a pile of blankets on and with which to sleep, a roof over their heads and a stipend for daily food to pick up outside from the militia handout.

After escaping the garage undetected that night, Shane had driven through empty side streets down to Kingsbridge, where she and Silas slept another eight nights in the trunk bed of that stolen Suburban. Fearing capture by the wandering militia patrolling up and down Broadway, Shane abandoned the truck and made her way on foot further downtown, blending into crowds and hauling her tiny son in a large backpack to keep him out of sight. Eventually she'd stumbled into a childhood friend who was looting the Target on West 225th Street and under her guidance, Shane and Silas became the newest squatters at an abandoned townhouse unit on 158th Street.

Now, they would rise every morning at 6am to the sound of horns playing up and down Broadway. They'd wash up in the bathroom shared by all occupants of the townhouse and then they would walk thirty blocks to 125th Street for the distribution of meals to the remaining inhabitants of the city. There, Shane and Silas would stand on line, hoping to not be selected by random passersby for their own sanctioned whims or by militia for capture, and would wait to be given three plates of pre-packaged food. The food was Yenmor's way of keeping the hordes of surviving women under control. He had power over every single infrastructure, including agriculture, and he subsequently controlled the food being made, processed and distributed. At his word, they could all starve to death, so he easily kept his subjects in line by making them believe his generosity was keeping them alive.

Shane had never been one for the flock mentality and as such, didn't use the food for her own consumption. She had a hard time believing that the same maniac that had obliterated a world power, shipped off its troops to die overseas, murdered half of the citizens of this once great country and enslaved the remaining half was making food for the masses that was actually edible. And instead of waiting for the day they would all find out they had been consuming what she suspected could be anything, she would instead trade it. Long after leaving 125th Street and making their way back uptown towards the Heights, Shane and Silas would walk in the shadows, taking care to not call attention to themselves, and in the back alleys of abandoned apartment buildings, she would trade their packages for anything- blankets, bread, cash, water, even candy. Anything to feed her son, keep him healthy and keep them moving for as long as possible.

Shane stayed on the sidelines, careful to watch it all from behind the scenes. If an altercation broke out on Broadway, she and Silas would quickly make their way to the back streets by cutting through empty bodegas and former beauty salons.

Several times during distributions in the city, Shane stood on line next to women she'd once known in passing. A couple of attorneys she'd known from the bar association or had encountered in court had made it out of the first and second wave and stood there alongside Shane, waiting for the scraps of food to be bestowed upon them. Officers from the Bronx and New York county courthouses and their children, a couple of old chums from elementary school and even her high school principal, who Shane watched in horror as she was taken off the line by militia and shot once in the head for simply being too old. Nadia Vostowsky, a prominent Appellate Court Magistrate for the third division of New York State tried to cut in front of her once. Shane had locked eyes with her and for a split second, couldn't hold the smile on her face as the irony of their situation kicked in. This same judge had once ridiculed an attorney in open court because he worked for pennies in Legal Aid and couldn't afford a new car. And there she had been, dressed in rags and cutting in line to get a free meal. At that moment, their status and social standings made no difference between them- they were women and were therefore, expendable.

Shane and Silas managed to keep to themselves for three months. Three months sleeping on a hard floor with only blankets between them and the wood beneath them; three months spent standing on food lines like obedient servants waiting for a hand out; three months spent walking and running through allies and darkened corridors trading for scraps to keep her son alive; three months spent keeping their heads down and staying out of trouble to avoid capture.

On four separate occasions, Shane had had to ignore the cries for help she'd heard in the distance in order to keep her son safe. And once she had braved capture to save a teenage girl from three men that had pounced on her, had beaten her and were in the process of trying to rape her. Shane and Silas had barely made it out alive when the militia had shown up to help the men and kill the girl. Everywhere around her women were openly assaulted, raped in the street, beaten and killed and there wasn't a damn thing she could do about it but continue to keep her head down and keep her son safe.

Three months she spent in the same torturous routine, until the day one of the women she was hiding out with had become stir crazy, left the house and killed an attacker on the street. Instead of running the other way when the militia arrived, she'd led them right to Shane and the others, and that night, as one of the worst storms to hit New York City since Superstorm Sandy raged outside, the militia came into the house where they were staying and dragged them outside.

It was there that Shane had been caught off guard and as she had tried to run with her son in her arms and escape the raid, they'd caught her. Around her women were being shot and killed, their children taken from them and loaded onto another large van. She tried to run but there were too many and as she felt a large hand pull her back as another tried to break the grip she had on her son and separate them, Shane fought. She struggled against them and more and more of them piled on, trying to wrestle Silas free from her grasp.

Shane fought against them and screamed, an inhuman wail rising from deep within her as her greatest fear played out before her eyes. Holding Silas' wrist so tightly a small part of her worried she'd rip his tiny hand clear off, Shane refused to let go, kicking, scratching, punching and biting at the five men it took to pull them apart. Her right hand held strong while the left waved wildly, landing anywhere it could. Multiple jabs to her face and torso winded her, but she would not let go and met Silas' tear-filled eyes, hearing him screech, "*Momma!*" for the last time before the butt of a gun to her temple finally knocked her unconscious.

PART TWO

Chapter V

Shane looked back at the driver of her jeep when she felt the vehicle turn sharply onto the street where a Burger King once stood.

Five minutes out.

She turned back towards the window of her passenger seat and watched the scenery, glimpses of snow covering the tree-lined sidewalk of what was. Two and a half years after a near genocide of the population and an all-out attack on the people of the United States, the world inhabited by those left behind had become very different. It was ugly, dystopian even. A cruel place where Shane had to learn how to survive, adapt and eventually, fight back.

After they had taken Silas, ripped him from her arms and forced them apart in what would become the source of her most frightening nightmares, Shane had spent a torturous and agonizing eighteen months on the inside, in a prisoner of war camp of sorts. Subjected to brutality on a daily basis, beatings, rape and savagery were the norm. She lived because she was tough, smart and above all, had always had an affliction to authority, that this time, had served her well. Her son had been taken, but was alive and at the first opportunity, Shane broke free. With a group of like-minded women who also raged with the fire of a mother's hope, Shane and her newly formed army tore through their camp, eliminating anyone who had anything to do with the abduction of so many young children for the shits and giggles of a psychopath.

There were various camps all over the country, or so she'd deduced after stealing their records once she'd been freed. Each facility was run by doctors, or some medical variation thereof, and served a purpose towards their ultimate goal. What that goal was, Shane could not answer, but she had kept the location of each camp within the documents she had kept from the camp in which they had been held. Though she could not rescue thousands of women all across the continent on her own, she had vowed that one day, after finding and rescuing her own son, she would begin the trek to free every woman held captive, just as she had been for so long.

They pulled into the college campus and the large wrought iron gate closed behind their jeep silently. Shane watched the white blanketed quad roll past them as the jeep entered the grounds of what was once Manhattan College in the Riverdale section of the Bronx. Another security checkpoint passed them by and Shane nodded to Julie Challaw, a high school friend she had found during her time inside who was now the head of security for their camp.

The jeep had barely come to a stop when Shane opened the passenger door and jumped out, immediately joining Julie as they walked towards what used to be the cafeteria in Seton Hall.

"Anything?" she asked, always with a glimmer of hope in her hazel eyes, something Shane dreaded having to disappoint time and time again.

"Not today. Ran into an abandoned base under the Cloisters, though. Got a couple of finds in the back. Have Carina and Danielle empty it out and bring it inside."

Wordlessly they split, Julie off to delegate the usual list of orders and Shane inside to map another run the following day.

After escaping, Shane, Julie and dozens of the other women had overrun the institution and searched tirelessly for any clue to their missing children. They had managed to free themselves but they were too late and could only watch helplessly as their kids were choppered away, up into the air and out of their reach. After days of searching relentlessly for any information, finding some of their people, the so-called scientists, in hiding, torturing them and getting nothing, they finally moved on. With one final flick of her wrist, Shane dropped the match that lit the place up in flames and blew it sky-high as she and the rest of the women made their way out of the camp in the cars and jeeps stored there.

They had wandered aimlessly, picking off any random militia that had attempted to attack them, block their path or had so much as breathed in their direction. Using the meticulous training they'd received inside, they were now more than just a group of women, some mothers looking for their kids, some aimless survivors; they were lethal.

Eventually they had travelled north, made their way past Manhattan, into the Bronx and came across the now abandoned college campus. Shane had known it, had grown up in that neighborhood before college and eventually marriage had moved her into the city and then brought her and her new family back again. She knew the area well and immediately claimed it as their domain. A quick sweep getting rid of squatters and loose members of the militia proved simple and after properly securing the perimeter with weapons and manning the watch towers with guards, soon enough the place was theirs.

Shane normally operated out of the cafeteria in the center of the quad. She was the reticent leader but not by choice. The other women just naturally flocked to her, followed her and took direction easily. She was particular and detail-oriented: two things that made the organization and set-up of a female civilization possible. They looked to her for strategy to defend themselves against the occasional intruder, for guidance in the ongoing search for their kidnapped children and ultimately for the likemindedness that she provided each and every one of them.

The women set themselves up as a fully functional community and moved easily inside the corridors from one hall to another. Each section of the campus served a purpose and utilized its functionality efficiently. Obviously, they continued use of the dormitories. The science lab became their medical facility and was run by an army medic and two registered nurses. Each woman, having had come from some sort of professional background or another, used their abilities to help the community survive and eventually, thrive.

Every couple of days they left the premises for one reason or another. They never ran too low on food and supplies because the institution had come well-equipped when they'd found it and therefore could go some time before restocking any shelves. Some days their mission was one-sided- a search for their missing kids. Shane and most of the other women with her had had their children taken from them: some as old as teenagers, some still infants. That was the shared bond that kept them moving forward, always searching, always looking for a clue or sign as to the whereabouts of their kids.

Thus far they had been unsuccessful but with each encounter with the militia, Shane felt one step closer to eventually getting her son back.

In the distance, an owl shrieked and Shane turned to face east, watching the sky for inhabitants. Before Yenmor had destroyed and dismantled every city agency and government body in the former United States, the animals in New York were kept controlled. With no more zookeepers, park rangers and animal control to secure the masses, the animals were on their own. Many kept in captivity in the zoos died of starvation at first, some of loneliness. All the aquatic animals immediately perished when their handlers abandoned them. A few bleeding-hearts around the city took pity on the survivors and made the decision to free them in the interest of returning them to the wild. Their mistake came in thinking their good deeds would go unpunished and when the lions and wolves of the Central Park Zoo and the Bronx Zoo were released after weeks of hunger had made them wild with frenzy, they immediately thanked their rescuers by eating them.

It turned out that animals raised in captivity their whole lives and then unleashed on the streets of New York City procreate at an alarming rate. Lions, wolves and bears found mates, made babies and created whole families who went off to live among the woods in Central Park. Some came upon militia occasionally, sometimes getting a meal out of it, sometimes getting themselves killed. Though big cats like lions and even wolves tended to steer clear of humans because of their scarce meat, the animals overtaking New York were a little different and knowing their instinctual prey were lacking on the mean streets of Manhattan, they turned instead to human beings.

Because it was so dangerous to cross into the city and for fear of Manhattan's newest inhabitants gentrifying other boroughs, when Shane and the women had escaped the camps and made their way into the Bronx, they had destroyed the bridges and major highways connecting the city behind them. Broadway and other borough crossing intersections however, remained unmanned and too exposed for them to destroy. A few stragglers had eventually made their way inside, now taking up residence amongst the trees and forests in various parks. After many close calls, Shane and her army carefully guarded the perimeter of their college and at the first opportunity, they had set up a siege at random cross points from Manhattan into the Bronx, fooling the militia into blowing up targets of their choosing. It took some time and the loss of some of their own, but eventually almost every access point into their borough had been completely neutralized.

Keeping within the city limits, their runs, whether for food, supplies or information, were never planned too meticulously because Shane feared saboteurs. She knew too many women were desperate to find their kids as well and could very easily be turned given the right offer. She knew what she was capable of when it came to her son so she would not put it past any other female to infiltrate their sanctum and destroy them from the inside. So they maintained a very strict set of rules when bringing in new women from the outside. They had not yet been discovered by the government officials that orchestrated the revolution and wanted very much to keep it that way. So they trusted only themselves. Because men were no longer seen on the streets, any member of the male species was considered the enemy and either interrogated or killed instantly.

Shane always took a group of women with her on their runs, never the same ones. They switched it up in case they were being followed, something they worked very hard to prevent. Their headquarters had been attacked on four occasions, and each time it had resulted in the loss of life on their side, albeit overall victory. Shane took her role in the new world they inhabited very seriously and as such, though she was not well-versed in military warfare and strategic planning, she was nonetheless a quick learner. So Shane led them, reluctantly but effectively.

As such, the women often regarded her as unapproachable. She had her confidants, the few that she kept in the know and bounced ideas and plans off of them, but mainly she kept to herself. No one knew of her past, where she'd come from and the life she'd lived before the revolution. They did not ask and she did not offer. Shane played it close to the vest and could be found more often than not, bent over blueprints of various city buildings, plotting their next steps.

Shane continued on to the grounds after separating from Julie and walked through the snow towards the dormitories. She usually updated the women in the cafeteria with any news from their daily runs. Most days yielded nothing more than extra bins and boxes of food taken from abandoned supermarkets, empty grocery stores and homes that had long since been left by their previous tenants. The more interesting days brought action the likes of which Shane wanted no part of but to which she was becoming quickly accustomed. Her only enjoyment came from the militia that they came upon and were able to kill.

As her feet crunched the snow, its top layer frozen by the one-digit temperature outside, Shane tucked her hands in her pockets and slowed down. She was reluctant to run into Marianna, one of the women who always stopped her at the college entrance and waited, breath held, for news on her daughter. But the desire to not be alone in her room outweighed the discomfort of disappointing an anxious mother and Shane pulled the hat she was wearing down low and walked along the edge of quad, past the dormitories and towards the registrar's office.

Each crunch below her feet chilled her, not because of the weather, but the reminder of that sound. That crunch that she'd heard when she'd lain on the cement floor of the camp and had been beaten by multiple men until her clavicle had all but caved in. That crunch she'd heard when the five men on top of her, trying to rip her apart from her son had hit her hand over and over again, breaking her knuckles in countless places so she would let go. That crunch that echoed in the back of her mind with countless memories of the torture she had endured since being separated from her son.

Shane stared at the white snow on the lawn, virginal and untouched by humanity and thought of her son, tried desperately to remember his smile and his smell. Every so often she found herself struggling to recollect what it felt like to hold him in her arms, the way his hair smelled when she would snuggle her face against him, the way it felt to hold his tiny hand and know that she had someone she would love and whom would love her unconditionally for all of time.

Her eyes watered and she quickly wiped them away as she heard the sound of footsteps pounding behind her. Irritated, she spun around and met Julie's worried face reaching her and quickly blurting out, "We just found a man outside."

Chapter VI

Approximately eighteen months after Yenmor began his one-sided war against the United States, Lieutenant Commander Steven S. Bernchal stepped foot on American soil for the first time in three years. It was a different world than he'd remembered.

He was unaware of the carnage and devastation that had taken place in his homeland during his absence save for speculation and rumors that had been fed to the him and his soldiers during their tour in North Africa and he barely had time to look around at the ruin surrounding him when he landed in what used to be North Carolina before his unit came under militia attack, got captured and were sent to a makeshift POW camp. After six months in captivity, he and a small group of soldiers managed to escape but were immediately pinned under heavy fire and forced to split up.

On his own though the Blue Ridge Mountain Range during an excruciatingly frigid winter, Bernchal moved as far north as he could go, confused, frightened and utterly alone. He was outmanned, outgunned and outmaneuvered by the militia around him, so he hid as best he could along the riverbanks in the woods, just west of I95. Along the way he picked up whatever scraps he could find- weapons off of bodies, loose ammunition among what remained after random gun fights, half-starved squirrels that he ate raw.

After nine weeks on foot, he cleared the New York state line and dragged himself across the George Washington Bridge into Manhattan, or what remained of it. Pushing himself as far as physically possible he made it another ten miles before finally collapsing on an overpass above the Saw Mill River Road in the Bronx.

He was drifting in and out of consciousness when they found him, half frozen, half starved. He'd landed with an inaudible thud on the unbothered snow and lay there until two women from the institution stumbled upon him. Guns drawn, they had approached him cautiously, tapping him with the toe of their boots when he didn't respond to their verbal commands. A quick search to determine he was not militia and a few minutes later, he was loaded onto the backseat of their jeep and driven back into the college grounds for presentation to Shane.

She walked quickly back towards the cafeteria, hurriedly past it and into the south wing of the main building. The other women were gathered around him, gawking as though they had never seen a living, breathing male before and though she understood their amazement, she nonetheless shooed them away and approached the man, who was at this point on his knees, dazed but coming to.

Hat pulled low, wearing a thick coat and high combat boots, Commander Bernchal could barely see anyone around him in the darkened lobby. The sun was almost set and the navy blues preparing the sky for dusk barely lit the confined space. He rubbed the exhaustion from his eyes, looked up and came face to face with Shane.

She eyed him, immediately on the defensive. He was weak, propped up by Julie and Shilan on either side of him and could barely stand on his feet. His skin was a sickly shade of gray and his lips were almost blue. Every other second he would shiver violently and his eyes would flutter uncontrollably. She wondered if he even knew what was happening.

With one glance to Julie and Shilan, Shane ordered them to drop him and they did. He crashed to the floor and suddenly looked up, alert, as though he were present for the first time and just now seeing a group of curious women surrounding him and one mean one staring him in the face.

"You're one of them?" she asked matter-of-factly.

He shook the cobwebs from his brain.

"Them who?"

"The men. The company. The ones that orchestrated this whole thing. Are you one of them?"

He coughed, spurted some phlegm around and rolled his eyes.

"Look lady, I have no fucking clue-"

Shane looked at Julie with a raised eyebrow and nonchalantly ordered "Kill him."

Commander Bernchal suddenly woke up.

"What!?"

"Kill him. Now."

Julie took her gun out and held it at her side. The blonde curls and oversized hazel eyes hid an almost expert marksman who never hesitated to pull the trigger when necessary.

"Wait! What the fuck did I do?"

"You know what?" Shane bent at the waist and brought her face close to his, mockingly.

"You were born a man, that's what you did. Sucks for you, but those are the cards you've been dealt."

"Wait! Wait, wait wait wait! Listen, what do you want?"

She chuckled, derisively. "What I want, you don't have."

"Look, I'm not part of this company, this group you're referring to. I have nothing to do with that."

"Then who are you?"

"Why does it-"

She finally lost her cool and screamed.

"Who are you?!"

He sigh, defeated. His one wild card was that they didn't know who he was, but if he wanted to live, he'd have to play his hand.

"My name is Lieutenant Commander Steven S. Bernchal, United States Navy, Special Warfare Command."

Shane paused a moment, letting the information sink in. She took a deep and shaky breath and he could almost see the boiling rage rising inside of her.

With an unsteady and almost inaudible voice, she asked slowly, "You're a SEAL?"

"Yes, ma'am."

"A SEAL?"

"Yes."

In a split second, she pulled a gun from her waistband and pointed it at his head. He immediately dropped to his haunches and put his hands up.

"Whoa!"

"All military is gone!" she screamed. "All SEALs are gone! How the fuck are you still breathing?"

"We're not gone!" he answered, desperately. He kept his eyes trained on her trigger finger and responded hurriedly.

"There are still soldiers left. Cops. Fucking C.O.s! We're still alive."

Shane shook her head stubbornly.

"They're gone. All divisions. The national guard was the first to be taken out; the Marines the last."

Commander Bernchal gulped and answered her, his tone measured.

"There are soldiers all over the place. Given the current state of affairs we're not exactly advertising for jobs. But we're out there."

"No," she answered defiantly like a petulant child refusing the approach of bedtime. She looked almost beaten down, as though he had told her everything that had happened had yet to happen.

"Yes. Our military is broken... But still alive."

"How?"

He shook his head and shrugged. "I don't even know what you're asking about..."

"How many?"

"What?"

"How many soldiers?"

"Enough."

Shane put the gun down at her side and he relaxed a little.

"This doesn't make any sense." She spoke quietly, almost to herself. "Why would they enlist new soldiers? Why would they train and teach and and and go through all that trouble if there were still soldiers left?"

He wanted out of his predicament, but she looked like she needed answers and he hoped that honesty was the way to keep her from shooting him. "Lady, I don't know what's going on. And I especially don't know where you've been getting your information, but think about it. What kind of force do you think it takes to wipe out the entire United States military?"

Unsatisfied, she glared at him.

"So then what were you, huh?" she asked, her voice rising dangerously. "What part did you play?" she asked, lifting the gun again and aiming it at his head.

"What the fuck are you talking about!?"

"Were you a part of it?"

"A part of what?" Confused and angry, he screamed in response, his body tense and rigid as he waited on his knees with a gun aimed at his head.

"I'm a fucking SEAL! I was deployed before the shit hit the fan, gone before the fucking National Guard was bulldozed during the first wave. They sent us out, overseas. Conflicts in South Africa. We spent twelve months abroad, another fourteen in combat and I barely made it out alive. Had to go through hell to get back to the U.S., illegally might I add. We come back and suddenly, the country's gone to shit. Our president is holed up in some bunker and there are no fucking men on the streets. Women are carrying bazookas like they're handbags and we have to hide in the woods and keep our service under wraps."

He took a deep and trembling breath.

"Look lady, I have no fucking clue what's going on, but I sure as shit know this- I ain't part of a goddamn thing having to do with this unholy madness. So unless you plan to fucking shoot me today, let me go. Trust me when I tell you, I don't want to be here any more than you want me here."

She eyed him a moment longer and finally, dropped the gun to her side wordlessly. He sighed and dropped to the floor.

"Thank you."

She gave him her back, returning the gun to her belt clip and walking away, while replying, "Save your gratitude. I didn't want to waste a bullet."

He watched her walk away and his breathing returned to normal. Though he had tried his best to not let on, he'd come close to staining his drawers. Coming out of the hellhole he'd survived in Africa, a prisoner camp and being shot down over the east coast hadn't prepared him for the face-to-face he had just had. Somehow he'd survived war, combat and being on the run for weeks alone in the wilderness, yet he almost lost his life at the hand of some quasi-soldier psycho.

The same two women that had apparently found him outside and brought him in were at each side of him and they ushered him up. He stood without their help however, and kept his eyes on their leader's back until she turned the corner and was out of his sight.

Shane whipped around the corner of the corridor, fired up. She was pissed, had been about a second away from blowing that guy's brains out all over the linoleum floor of the college lobby.

Law enforcement? Military? How could they be alive, roaming the streets of New York or the United States in general when everyone left behind had been led to believe there was no help available, no one left to protect them from what had befallen them? How was it possible that there were soldiers around who could have helped them, saved them?

Shane didn't want to think about it, didn't want to dwell on what he had said and implied. Living military meant military that didn't help. It meant military that didn't save her son, keep him safe and keep him with her.

She stopped in the middle of the hallway and looked up, taking a second to breathe and control the rage rising inside of her at the moment. Her eyes traveled to the hanging portraits of past Deans, all of them towering above her and looking down on her as if to say, *You fool, no law enforcement? Really?*"

She closed her eyes and almost didn't hear the heavy footsteps approaching from behind. Julie tapped her on the shoulder and she took a deep breath before responding, taking extra care to curb her annoyance.

"What do we do with him?"

"I don't even know at this point. Where the hell can we stick a damn man in this place?"

"It *is* a huge facility. I'm sure we can find a spot for him."

Shane nodded, reluctantly agreeing.

Julie lingered, pulling at her strawberry blonde ponytail and Shane immediately knew she was fishing for information.

"What is it?"

"Do you think he's right? That there have been others? Other military and law enforcement- alive?"

Wanting to dismiss the questions, Shane hesitated and finally gave in. She couldn't blame Julie for asking- she too was desperate for answers, desperate from some inkling of information or more importantly, some goddamn help out there.

"I don't know. I... part of me wants to believe it's true. That there are people out there who can help. But at this point, how we can we trust anything he has to say? Anything any of *them* have to say? We don't know him. And literally everyone has been against us - who can we possibly trust?"

Julie nodded acceptingly and waited for further instructions.

Shane considered the schematics of their headquarters and finally, just pointed back towards the soldier still waiting for news of his fate.

"Have Magda set him up in the other dorm. Make sure he doesn't have any weapons."

Julie nodded and wordlessly turned and started back towards the lobby. Shane turned to continue further down the corridor towards the old dean's office for some review of blueprints. As an afterthought she turned her head back towards Julie and called after her.

"And take his ass to the lab for some medical help. He looks half dead."

Chapter VII

"Keep up."

The purple-haired lunch lady glared over her shoulder and Commander Bernchal sped up, shuffling behind her. His leg hurt like hell- he could barely feel the ground under his feet and knew that had he stayed out there any longer he'd have surely been frostbitten.

She turned a sharp corner and he struggled to keep pace, holding his right side gingerly as the cramping worsened. She was making a series of twist and turns through hallways and old classrooms, directing him around the institution. Behind him, two of the leader's henchmen followed, their eyes on him every time he turned to scope them out. Clearly, he was untrustworthy but they had decided to let him live and stay, for now apparently.

They walked through a set of large revolving doors and into an open space with tables and chairs that he guessed to be a cafeteria, or what once was. Women were moving around, unpacking some boxes and loading others. Some were seated, drinking tea and chatting and when he walked in, they stopped what they were doing and stared.

"Everybody pulls their own weight. This isn't charity."

He turned back towards his guide and nodded.

"Okay."

She pointed to the women who resumed their work.

"You find some way to help out. While you're injured you can cook, clean. Anything. If you're not the domestic type, then you can help with inventory, supplies. You look strong. Once you're back to good health you'll have no reason to not participate."

"Alright."

She turned back around and led him back through the revolving doors and down another hallway. The henchmen continued to follow.

"We use all of the school's resources. Cafeteria serves food 'round the clock. We make runs at all times, depending on what we need, so food's gotta be ready. As you can see there's a shortage of men here."

"Shortage?"

"Shortage as in you're the only one. So showers are coed, but seeing as how we've never needed to implement that before, hold off on that 'till we check with the boss."

"The boss," he repeated sarcastically.

She ignored him and led him to another newer section, pointing towards the closed doors ahead. Stained-glass windows looked back at him.

"We use the attached wing of the convent for the dorms. It houses all of us so we split tours. Eyes everywhere, cover at every point, perimeter manned always."

He turned to look at her and was surprised to see such a dark expression on her face. "Seriously?" he asked mockingly.

"Yes," she glared at him, angrily. "We are under constant attack when we leave these grounds. Most of the militia have tried more than once to get our location. Being cautious is what's kept us alive."

He nodded, admonished. "Got it."

"You'll be assigned a dorm room. Like I said, having a man around is unprecedented. So we can't just shove you in anywhere, all willy nilly. Your anatomy complicates things."

"Well, don't sugarcoat it for my sake."

Again she ignored his retort and led him though a doorway and up a flight of stairs, talking the whole way.

"Two of the women that found refuge here used to be doctors and one was an army medic, so compared to the rest of the world, we have a fully functioning hospital. We base it out of the chem lab and it's kept as sterile as possible. They'll take a look at you and patch you right up. They're miracle workers over there."

"Working miracles against what- a cold?" He chuckled to himself and gripped his right side hard when it hurt.

Without breaking stride, she led him towards the science building and opened the door for him. In front of the chemistry lab, she stopped abruptly and turned to face him.

"My eight-year old daughter had AML-M7. Cancer of the blood and bone marrow. It went untreated under this regime that took her from me for nine months. She was on her way out when I finally got her back. These women made her as comfortable as possible, eased the pain and kept her with me for five extra pain-free months. That's five additional months that she lived and I almost didn't have with her. That was a miracle."

With that, she turned on her heel and walked away from him, leaving him to look at the unimpressed faces of his two guards.

After being warmed down with some pretty high-tech heating supplies and having been fed a couple of bowls of the blandest but most gloriously hot canned soup, Commander Bernchal asked to be brought to where the action was. The two guards, who had yet to leave his side, patted him down for the umpteenth time and satisfied he couldn't possibly be hiding any weapons, brought him back to the cafeteria. There, he looked around and not seeing the leader from earlier, turned to one of the henchmen and asked for her.

"I want to talk to her."

Joyce stared at him and asked, "Who?"

"The scary bitch that aimed a fucking gun at my head before."

"Oh, you mean her?" she asked, smiling. She pointed her chin in the direction of the work going on at the far end of the cafeteria towards Shane.

He squinted, waiting for his vision to adjust to the fading light coming from the gas-lit lanterns encircling the cafeteria. Gone were the fatigues and oversized parka and now, undone and unbothered, he noticed how non-intimidating he found her to be. Yes, she was tall, imposing even, but at 6'4 he stood at about half a foot taller. And she was in great shape yet she was now so different from the towering amazon he'd knelt in front of only a few hours prior.

Holding a tattered shoebox filled with oranges and quietly whispering with another woman at her side, she was no longer as unapproachable as she had been.

Bernchal eased over to her, struggling to curb the limp he'd developed after his muscles began the long and painful process of defrosting, and cleared his throat. Shane barely glanced up and when she met his eyes, one quick nod sent the other woman away and she set to work, speaking quickly while she packed up another box on the table in front of them.

"You look decidedly less pale."

"And you look different when I'm not staring down the barrel of a loaded weapon."

Not wasting any time, she asked quickly, "What do you want, soldier?"

"Commander."

"Excuse me?"

"Commander. Lieutenant Commander, actually, but just 'Commander' will do. You see, it's a title I earned and of which I was once immensely proud. I don't refer to you as 'girl.' I'd appreciate it if you'd return the courtesy."

She eyed him for a second and then looked back down at the box again.

"What do you want, *Commander*?"

"Intel."

"What makes you think I have any?"

"I know that you know a helluva lot more than I do right now. Consider me an empty slate."

Without missing a beat, she replied, "Shouldn't be too hard. You are male, after all."

He didn't respond so she ordered him to have a seat and walked towards another group of women who had just entered with several crates.

His eyes followed her as she moved around the cafeteria, barking orders. It wasn't so much an air of superiority that enveloped her; it was more like the natural poise of a leader. Almost as though she were the de facto president, the other women looked to her for directions, guidance and even discipline. And she led with a reluctant ease, as though she were born into the responsibility and understood its necessity rather than having had chosen it for herself.

Bernchal pulled out a chair at the nearest table and struggled to sit down, painfully readjusting himself until his ass was numb. He waited, patiently, until she had wrapped up her duties and returned to him with a cup in her hand. He thought she was bringing him some tea and eyed the smoking mug but when she sat down in front of him and took a sip, he couldn't hide his chagrin.

"So what is it exactly that you're looking for here?" she asked.

She took another sip and Bernchal rolled his eyes in annoyance.

"May I remind you that I did not request to be brought here? Your two little security goons dragged me here."

"Half-dead. Yes, I remember. I also recall that you did not protest as they saved your life. Nor have you complained once about the medicine or food you have been provided."

After a moment, his eyes crinkled in amusement. "Touché."

"So again, what do you want?"

"Information. I was in the dark all this time. Now I'm back and it's a different country."

"It's a different world."

He looked around the cafeteria, taking it all in. Glass windows at the top of all four walls did nothing to light the room under the darkness of night. It seemed to Bernchal as though even the moon had ceased to shine after everything went to hell.

He turned back to Shane and rubbed his mouth, considering his next question. She didn't appear to be particularly forthcoming, so he had to work his way to a real interrogation.

"I've never seen an American university boarded up behind gates."

"It wasn't, not originally anyway. You're not from this neighborhood, huh?"

"Brooklyn boy," he replied, hooking a thumb in the direction of his chest.

She nodded her head and continued.

"It was once Manhattan College. Open campus, had security but very lax. It was a really good neighborhood so even with rowdy college kids, it was safe. They had started to go green- it went under a huge reconstruction around 2015. Solar-powered panels on the roof, an eco-based sewage system- hence the running water. Full sustainability. Then when everything started going to shit, the college gated it up, I guess in an attempt to continue to teach the kids in a safe place. After it got really bad, they closed up shop. Don't know what happened to the kids. I like to think they all got out, got home, spread out far and wide and anywhere else but this fucking hellhole."

"Hellhole... How did this thing shift like this overnight?"

She took a long sip of her tea and kept her eyes trained on him, searching for the root of his questions.

"What do you mean?"

"I mean, one minute I'm in the reserves, living a pretty normal life here in the good ole' U.S. of A. Then war breaks out, soldiers get drafted like its 1963 and I'm off to battle for my life in Africa of all places. I come back and everything is..."

"Everything is what?"

"Fucking backwards. And I keep hearing women talking about missing kids, stolen kids. What the fuck is that about? How was all of this even possible?"

"How do you not know? Everyone who okayed it had a penis, so...."

He shot her a look of contempt. "So all men are evil now?"

"Not all of them, Commander," she answered matter-of-factly. "Just the ones that kidnapped hundreds of kids and want every woman dead."

He opened his mouth to reply and was interrupted by a woman he hadn't seen during his tour of the facility.

"There was a regiment truck spotted past the expressway," she whispered to Shane, breathlessly. "Ginny says it was alone."

Shane positioned herself to rise from the chair and asked, "When?"

The woman looked at Bernchal suspiciously and answered. "Just now. Headin' southbound."

Shane offered a quick nod of her head to one of her sidekicks at other side of the cafeteria, behind an open space where it looked like the food was made. She shot up from her seat and started walking away quickly.

Bernchal, not willing to accept more time without answers, followed her, questioning.

"What's going on?"

"None of your concern. Let us handle it."

"Hey lady, I can help."

"You're useless right now, or did you forget you almost died out there?"

"You need me."

She laughed aloud and shot him a condescending look of humor.

Bernchal ignored her and prodded. "I'm a soldier."

"I don't care if you're Jesus Christ resurrected. You're not coming."

"Are you fucking kidding me?"

At the entrance to the cafeteria, she stopped in her tracks and swiveled around. Face to face she replied to him, all business. Her dark eyes bore into his and she raised one perfectly sculpted eyebrow and spoke.

"Do I look like I'm joking?"

Bernchal knew to back down and keep from overstepping his boundaries. But he couldn't keep quiet about his frustration.

"This is bullshit…"

"So's your use of our roof, bed and food. Want that to last? Do what you're told and get back inside."

She turned on her heel and walked through the double doors of the cafeteria, leaving him both dejected and disappointed.

Is this what chicks used to feel like? he thought to himself, frustrated. *'Cause it fucking sucks...*

Angry, he kicked over a crate and immediately regretted it when simultaneously his foot started throbbing and the gray-haired guide from earlier cleared her throat and eyed him. Embarrassed, he picked up the crate and placed it where it had been, and sulking, walked back to his place at the table in the center of the cafeteria.

Four hours passed as he waited for her to return from whatever the hell it was she ran out to do. In that time, he watched women come and go from the cafeteria, some with clear chores to handle, others just roaming and seemingly bored. A few came over and poked around, asked him harmless questions as though he were the freak on display for their curiosity. He didn't mind much, just passed the time by watching their habits, their routine, and hoping to get some inkling of information to no avail.

He started nodding off somewhere around 4am and just before dawn, she returned with a small group of women. She was covered in snow, shivering and blowing on her hands for warmth. If she was surprised to find him waiting in the same spot she'd left him, she hid it well and continued inside towards the cooking area.

The moment her presence became known, Bernchal watched as all of the women who were lazily cleaning or cooking in the now almost empty cafeteria scrambled to her for news.

Did they have the kids with them?

Did you see anything?

Do you know where they are?

Did you see Timothy?

Are the kids safe?

Can we get them back?

She warded off the questions with both palms in the air, a solemn look on her face.

"We haven't found them yet. It was just a shipment of fruit from the Hudson Valley. They were alone and didn't know anything."

"How do you know?" pled one woman Bernchal recognized as one he'd seen during his tour. He remembered the forlorn look on her face as she'd watched him walk by with his guide.

"We asked, Mariana. Trust me, they didn't know anything."

The women begin to disperse, visibly disappointed.

Shane watched them walk away from her, their shoulders slumped from the lack of news, and took a deep breath. Shaking it off she walked over to where Bernchal sat quietly and pulled out the same chair she'd sat in earlier and removed her coat and sweater. His less-than-hospitable tour guide, named Sulieka he would later learn, wordlessly brought her a steaming cup of hot cocoa and left them at the table to unload the boxes being brought in by the rest of the women.

Shane rubbed her hands together and warmed them over the steam of the cocoa. He waited for her to volunteer information but when she barely acknowledged him, he finally broke the silence and spoke.

"So you hijacked a shipment of fruit? That was the top secret mission I couldn't be a part of?"

"It wasn't a top secret mission. It was a run."

"No, that was a recon mission," he replied, leveling her with his eyes. "You went after that truck to see if it could lead you to those kids. Am I right?"

She met his stare momentarily and finally answered. "Yes.'

"Dead end?"

"We have enough fruit for a lifetime of smoothies," she replied, deadpan.

He quickly realized that there were no corners to be cut here. If he wanted information he would have to be direct with her. So he stared at her until she relented and answered truthfully.

"Yeah. They didn't know anything."

"How do you know?"

"I asked them."

"As nicely as you asked me when I got here?"

She didn't respond, only eyed him for a moment longer. Her stare was both shallow and deep at the same time, somehow managing to penetrate through him with little effort. He couldn't read the blank expression on her face and guessed that she was either very annoyed with him or very tired and wanted to go to bed.

After a few seconds of awkwardly uncomfortable silence, Shane got up abruptly and pushed her chair in. Bernchal watched her as she grabbed her cup and walked out of the cafeteria, leaving him alone once again in the now empty room.

Chapter VIII

He slept fitfully and when his body finally adjusted to the warmth of the comfortable bed in the small dorm room he'd been given, Bernchal rolled over and felt a presence lingering next to him. He begrudgingly opened his eyes and was surprised to find Shane sitting in a chair across from him.

"What the f-"

"Wake up."

He sat up, rubbing his eyes. "What?"

"Get up. You have all these pressing questions about what goes on around here, don't you? So come on and get some answers."

She was sitting in the only chair provided to him, one leg crossed over the other, tall winter boots bouncing up and down. Her dark brown curls were pulled back into a severe bun and though she looked more awake and refreshed than how he'd seen her at dawn, she certainly looked meaner.

Bernchal sighed and looked around the empty room, confused.

"Now?"

"No, later. I'm just sitting here because it's comfy. Yes, *now*, moron. Let's go."

He was not accustomed to sarcasm after only two hours of sleep and did little to hide his anger.

"Can I get dressed first? I doubt you want me to join this quest without any drawers on."

"I saw you while you slept, Commander. Nobody would notice."

With a smirk, she got up and walked to the door, calling back over her shoulder, "Be at the main doors in ten."

As he dressed in the same clothes he'd been found wearing since he had been told- on more than one occasion in a ten-hour span- that his presence was both unprecedented and barely tolerated and therefore would not yield any extra clothing for him to utilize, Bernchal considered making Shane wait past the ten-minute deadline she'd issued. Ultimately, he decided against it and hurried over to the main lobby as quickly as he could. The last thing he needed was to be left behind once again while the leader went off on an adventure without him.

He was good with directions and even better with navigation so despite the size of the college and its overwhelming twists and turns, he found the lobby easily and made it through the double doors of the entrance just as she was buttoning up her coat.

Dressed again in the same gear in which he'd first seen her, she was back to her scary look and when he entered, only shot him a look of inexplicable surprise before barking yet another order to some poor gopher.

Snapping her fingers in his general direction, she took off through the doors and into the cold. Bernchal, again reminded by the weather that he was grossly underdressed in nothing but a sweater and a down vest, took a deep breath and fell into step behind her. Among the many things he was learning as the only male in an all-female community of alpha women, being at someone's beck and call was something to which he did not plan to become accustomed.

He followed her outside trying his best to not appear cold, though the first hint of winter slapped him hard as a reminder that it had made him its bitch only hours prior.

"You ride with me," she shouted above the howling wind and he complied without protest. Anything to be inside of a vehicle and out of the cold.

Across the newest layer of snow, Bernchal followed her into a forest green Jeep Grand Cherokee and seated himself in the front passenger seat. He ignored the stare he received from the woman he remembered called Mariana and buckled in as she begrudgingly got into the back seat. In the driver's seat, Shane buckled up and with a quick look in the rearview mirror, pulled out past the security booth and through the metal gate surrounding the property.

They drove in silence for almost a half hour and Bernchal was surprised to find himself crossing what used to be the Tappan Zee Bridge towards the Palisades.

Beside them, remnants of the abandoned project to build a new bridge hung hundreds of feet above the Hudson River, icicles dangling from the incomplete steel pieces.

"Where're we headed?"

He wasn't expecting an answer that wasn't laced with venom.

"Nanuet. The truck we saw last night was headed there."

"You're hoping to get some information?"

From the backseat, Mariana spoke up.

"We want our kids."

Bernchal snuck a look at her through the mirror in the visor he'd lowered to block the early morning sunlight. Her black hair matted against her face by melting snow, she was staring out of the passenger window, watching without emotion as the snow-covered hills of the Palisades got closer as they crossed the long bridge. Behind them, the city skyline was completely obliterated by the fog hanging over the previous night's snowfall. He watched her, the way her dark eyes looked lifeless and lost, waiting for more than those four words, but she offered none and instead went back to ignoring him as though he didn't exist.

He looked to his left and watched the leader drive, her jaw clenching as she maneuvered the large truck across unplowed snow and abandoned vehicles strewn haphazardly about. The not-quite blackness of her eyes matched the darkness of her eyebrows and hair, but offset the severity of her features. He knew he was staring but her face was appealing, not exactly stunning, yet unconventionally beautiful at the same time, and he was enjoying himself.

"What do they call you?"

"Excuse me?" she asked, her eyes still on the road ahead.

"I don't know your name. You know mine, but no one's told me what they call you."

She considered for a moment and apparently, not seeing the harm in sharing, replied. "Shane."

"Shane? Last name?"

"Nope."

Sensing the bitter end of their dialogue, Bernchal nodded and sat back, momentarily satisfied.

"Cool."

When the bridge shifted south, another car appeared on the eastbound lanes suddenly, bearing down on them from the other side of the medium. Shane fingered the gun on her lap, her left hand tightening against the steering wheel. As it neared, an American flag hanging out of the passenger window flapped in the wind and the driver, an older male wearing camouflage, nodded to Shane. She reciprocated and the cars passed each other without incident.

Bernchal sat back in his seat, interested.

"Does that happen a lot?"

Shane shook her head, surprisingly explanatory.

"Most days are empty. Not a soul in sight. People have learned to blend in, men and women. Some guys, Americans... Not all bad. They turn a blind eye to a lot, but they patrol the streets sometimes. Help when they can. Or are willing. Mainly though, it's quiet. I think a city like this gets abandoned really fast. Not much left but those that have a different agenda than just hiding."

Fifteen silent minutes later, they arrived at their destination. In what appeared to once be a strip mall, Shane drove into a large parking lot and came to rest in front of a large arts and crafts store called Michael's, though most of the sign's letters were either broken or missing and now boasted the name "Icel's."

He unclipped his seatbelt when she shut the ignition off and waited for further instruction. Throughout, he evaluated their every move and took mental notes to run down later.

Following Shane's cue, he exited the vehicle and looked around the empty parking lot. It looked as though no one had inhabited the space for years. Some of the store fronts were blown in, glass still on the ground outside where it had likely landed upon impact of whatever it was that blew holes across the mall. Off in the distance he saw a body slumped over the front display of what was once a jewelry store. Bernchal guessed that animals hadn't ventured out of the woods and across state highways yet because it was spookily silent all around them and that corpse did look intact. He guessed however that it would just be a matter of time for that to change. Spring was around the corner and the hot weather would undoubtedly give way for any combination of odors to fill the air and create a map for any furry visitors to grab a meal.

He was about to ask her for the details of what had happened there when Shane started moving forward into Micheal's, motioning for him to follow. He complied and together with Mariana and two women from the other vehicle that had been driving behind them, they entered the front doors of the store.

It was sunny outside, blinding as the sun reflected off of the snow covering everything, but inside the store it was dark, as though the sunlight purposely ended at the doorway and didn't dare follow them inside. Narrow traces of it snuck in through randomly placed crevices in the cement walls that perplexed Bernchal, until he realized they were bullet holes.

Looking around, he noticed the tall aisles of homemade items and craft supplies were predominantly untouched save for the occasional bullet riddled corner here and there. As they walked further in, the shattered glass of the entranceway crackling under their weight and breaking the silence, Shane made some hand signals to the other two women and they split up, each with a firearm poised and ready. They turned left and continued further into the store towards home decor and Bernchal followed Shane deeper towards the wedding section.

Mariana trailed them, gripping her small pistol and watching their six o'clock disinterestedly.

Past aisles of stencils and ribbons, easels and markers, Bernchal followed in eerie silence, creeped out that he was the only one unarmed among them. They reached the "Employee's Only" door at the same time as the other two women and again, Shane directed them wordlessly. Mariana and the redhead split back towards the entrance to presumably cover the front of the door and the brunette stayed with he and Shane at the back. Gingerly, Shane pushed open the swinging door with the toe of her boot and ducked down a little, going into the darkened stockroom first.

Bernchal had yet to become accustomed to their style of working, their manner of doing things. Shane was abrupt and abrasive and on most occasions, extremely condescending. But trailing behind these women as he watched them, armed and expertly handling their weapons, cautious and very clearly well-versed in staking out a location and picking up hidden supplies, he couldn't help but admit he was impressed.

The brunette flipped a switch and when the light failed to come on, Bernchal looked inquisitively at Shane who answered, "No power."

He pondered it for a moment and realized that he had yet to see a light switch or lamp being utilized. The women at the college worked in the cafeteria by gaslight and lanterns and even when he'd been brought in and presented to Shane, the lobby has been lit by only the natural and fading light of the sun setting outside.

"Everywhere?" he asked.

She nodded and pointed to the open back door with her chin. They could see clear outside, around the back of the strip mall, and into the half-empty truck parked outside, backed up onto the ramp leading from the door down to the ground. He looked to Shane and winked, indicating that her intel had been correct.

Awkwardly, Shane shot him a look of confusion and pushed past him, walking through the doorway and outside to the look in the truck. The brunette followed and Bernchal brought up the rear. A click, several meters away, caught his attention and he stopped, looking past the truck. Shane and the brunette bent at the waist, looking into the truck bed and fishing around the boxes thrown inside. He heard the whispering to each other, commenting on the find, but his attention was elsewhere.

Past the covered lot where the truck was rested was another deserted parking lot. Save for a few abandoned cars and an RV, it was empty. Beyond that were the trees surrounding the main road. He strained his eyes and watched the open space, waiting and listening. He was certain he'd heard something though he was unsure exactly what it had been. He knew Mariana and the redhead were in the front of the store, keeping an eye out and though he had spent weeks on the run, paranoid and fearful of everything outside, he was certain he had heard something.

Bernchal watched, still and didn't hear Shane call to him to help empty the truck and bring the boxes to their vehicles. He didn't hear the brunette make a wisecrack about him and didn't see Shane turn to eye him in annoyance.

Instead, he saw movement from his peripheral vision. A dart among the trees, fast enough to look like a blur, but within view long enough to note it ran on two legs, not four.

They were not alone.

"Somebody's here," he whispered, his eyes still trained on the woods beyond the parking lot.

Another brazen dash, this time from the trees to the parking lot, behind the massive RV at the far end with the tires flat and sunken in the snow.

Shane looked up from the truck and watched Bernchal.

"What?"

"Somebody's here," he repeated, this time breaking his stare and meeting her eyes.

Though she did not come from a military background, Shane knew to trust her own gut and at the moment, her gut was telling her that his gut was warning them.

"Where?"

Bernchal responded by diving into the truck bed as the first round of bullets whizzed past him and landed inside the stock room they'd just exited.

Chapter IX

Shane ducked low and made her way to the edge of the truck frame, peering around. Bullets continued to fly, some penetrating the truck cab and narrowly missing Shane as it pierced straight through. She extended her arm around the frame and popped off a few shots. Bernchal covered his head and shouted at Shane, in disbelief that he was unarmed in a gunfight.

"Can I get a fucking gun?"

She hesitated and he yelled louder, his voice barely audible above the hail of gunfire that was getting louder with every second that passed.

"A gun! A gun! Give me a goddamn gun before they blow my fucking head off!"

Shane exchanged a look with the brunette who pulled a .45 from the back of her pants and tossed it to Bernchal. Despite his desire to criticize their nonchalance, he shook it off and stood, aiming around the other end of the frame and shooting at one of the militia soldiers that had begun to creep up towards them. He caught him three times in the chest and watched him hit the floor before setting his sights on another soldier approaching. Another five rounds, two of which made contact on the man's torso before he too slumped to the floor.

The .45's chamber was empty and Bernchal looked back at Shane, bewildered. "Did you bring me here to kill me?"

She yelled back at him, screaming above the noise surrounding the truck bed.

"What?"

"One gun, no ammo. What the fuck am I doing here?"

Shane took one hand off of her own .45 and fished around in the pocket of her cargo pants.

"Look man, *you* demanded to be here. *You* harassed and *you* begged to be a part of this. So here you are," she replied, tossing him a magazine clip. "Sack up. Stop whining like a little bitch and get fucking involved."

"Seriously?"

"There's another clip," she added, turning back to her end of the frame, where she reached around and shot twice at an unseen body who landed almost at her feet. "There're the bad guys," she said, pointing around the truck towards the shooters with her chin. "Aim and shoot."

He shook it off angrily and got up on one knee, shooting around the corner again and hitting two more men.

The gunfire stopped as soon as Bernchal's bullets made contact and they took the opportunity to book for their cars.

He grabbed a box on the way out and Shane grabbed another. They ran back through the stock room which now looked war-torn, through the store back to the front, where they met up with Mariana and the red head.

"We got three in the front."

Shane nodded and passed the box to the redhead, took her gun back out and led the way to their vehicles. Bernchal shot his last six rounds at a car coming at them full speed, taking out the driver with a neck shot and the front tires. The car barely missed them and veered to the left as the driver's lifeless body slumped over. It ran a while longer in a semi-circle until it came to stop against a tree at the far end of the parking lot.

They continued running and the redhead tripped and fell hard, sending the contents of the box scattering all along the parking lot. Bernchal looked to Shane who kept going and was already halfway into their Jeep. Mariana and the brunette were opening their car's doors, so he turned back and ran to her, helping her up and carrying her the rest of the way as she hobbled alongside him. He didn't see the soldier behind them until he looked up to see Shane aiming her gun his way. She shot and he ducked instinctively, looking behind him when the sound of contact reached him. One clean shot to the forehead and the guy went down. Shane didn't even say a word, just got into the driver's seat and started the ignition.

Bernchal and the redhead reached the jeep and he helped her into the backseat, closed the door behind her and hopped into the passenger seat, closing the door as the wheels screeched and they took off towards the main road.

When their breathing returned to normal, he turned around towards the backseat and asked the redhead if she was okay.

She nodded and gripped her ankle, grimacing. "Thank you for coming back."

Bernchal offered a small smile and turned back to Shane, who looked unimpressed with the ordeal. He in turn was bothered. Shane had gotten out of the car and shot the soldier approaching him and the redhead, essentially saving their lives. Yet she had seen the redhead fall and had left her without a second thought. He ignored the burning questions and instead looked out of the window and at the side mirror, keeping an eye out for any tails.

They made it back to the college without any further incident, the sun already high in the sky above them. Behind them the gates of the perimeter closed and the cars came to a stop in the quad in front of the lobby. Shane wordlessly got out of the car and tossed the keys to the brunette that had traveled with them, already waiting.

"Do me a favor, Cristela, and park it behind the math lab. Yours too. I don't want them to be seen from the outside."

The brunette, Cristela, nodded and took off back towards her own jeep to park it. Bernchal looked back to the redhead who struggled to get out of he car and instead of helping her, ran after Shane.

"You wanna talk about that?"

"What?" she asked, impatiently when she realized he was following her.

"What happened?" he repeated. "You left her in the parking lot, that's what happened."

"And you helped her. Your point?"

He stopped and grabbed her by the elbow, turning her towards him forcefully.

"Why did you leave her?"

She pulled loose angrily and he expected her to berate him for putting his hands on her. Instead, she licked her lips and summoned him to follow her towards the gymnasium.

Silently they walked, Shane in front, Bernchal closely behind. They passed the gym and entered the women's locker room. There, Shane stopped in front of a dry erase board that had dozens of pictures of kids held up by magnets.

She pointed to the board and spoke unemotionally.

"This Commander, is what we do. Every day. From the minute we wake up until we go to sleep at night. It's not a top-secret mission and it's not some crazy chicks playing Rambo for the hell of it. We have lost lives in our pursuit of these kids and even if you think it's insane or cruel, we cannot stop. Ever. If someone falls or slows us down, we have to keep going. If I can save your life with a bullet, I'll do it. But if you slow me down at all, I will leave you. It is that simple."

She paused, breathing deeply and he stared at all of the pictures of smiling kids, seemingly happy long before the world went to hell.

He turned back to face her and Shane looked into his eyes and spoke again, decidedly less angry.

"And the absolute worst part of it, the part you have yet to comprehend, isn't just opening every door and not seeing those kids safely on the other side, but knowing that I have to look into the faces of each and every mother out there and tell them I still haven't found our kids."

Bernchal shot her a look and asked, slowly. "*Our* kids?"

"That's right. My son, Commander. Also taken."

Shane turned her back to him and walked towards the door, opening it. When she was half-way through the doorway, he called after her, hoping for clarity after her revelation.

"Does this mean you trust me now?"

She didn't turn around. Instead, she replied over her shoulder "You're alive, aren't you?" and walking through the locker room door, let it slam shut behind her.

Chapter X

Time passed. Bernchal did not know how much time, only noticed that the snow melted and the trees came to life again. Days blurred as the sun stayed with them longer and the hours on the clock became a thing of distant memory to him. He became one of the group with the women who'd saved him, or at least as comfortable as one could be as the only man among them. He learned their names, some of their children's names or at least those of the women who shared them, even their movements. Some of the women made him feel at home, others jumped and cringed whenever he came near. He kept to himself, talked with Shane whenever he could and simply sat back and watched them exist as a functioning society, hidden away from the rest of the world.

He got a firearm and trained with them. When he'd first arrived he wondered where Shane disappeared to every day, gone for hours at a time somewhere in the facility. Now that the snow had melted and it was warming up outside, he'd found out. She used the track at the bottom of the school property to work out. Every day she was off, running up and down the field, stretching against the fallen trees or the reinforced fence surrounding the massive space. She always had a holster at her waist, always at the ready against an inevitable attack and the first day he followed her, she scoffed, huffed and puffed her disapproval. But eventually she relented and he began to run alongside her, sometimes teasing her to a race, sometimes taking the hint that she wanted to be left alone and just jogging quietly behind her.

Eventually he began to engage her in conversation. Slowly at first, just a question or two here and there until it was almost an expected part of their daily routine. Working out, target practice, making runs, planning outings- he became an integral part of their operation. Ingratiating himself into their lives he replaced the men he had lost out in Africa with a hundred crazy women and became just as important to them as they were to him.

Shane seemed to keep to herself as much as possible. She directed the women to their duties and delegated others, chewed one out on occasion for committing errors and even had a sporadic chat with those whose company she preferred here and there.

But she remained standoffish for the most part, particularly with Bernchal. He would make it a point to talk anyway and would often rattle on so much that she eventually began replying to his soliloquies without even noticing.

Four months after his arrival, Bernchal approached Shane as she took a break from planning the evening's run and sat across from her in the cafeteria, straddling his chair and smiling widely.

She rarely acknowledged his presence save for the occasional groan or scoff in his direction.

"Can I help you?"

Luckily Bernchal had thick skin and shook off her coarseness, much to her dismay.

"Talks. I'm bored."

"Only boring people get bored. Make yourself useful; go do something."

"I can't."

"Can't or won't?"

"Literally can't. No one will let me do anything. I try to help unpack yet another goddamn box and purple-hair over there shoos me away," he whined, referring to Suleika, the usual source of his complaints. "I try to clean up the grounds and your friends run away from me. I can't even walk the halls without getting some side-eyed remark about my fucking penis. My penis, Shane. No one here has seen my penis; why are they so afraid of it?"

Shane held back a smile and continued pouring over the maps in front of her. "If its so unbelievably horrible, then why are you here, Commander? You must like something about this place to endure the abuse."

"You think I'm happy around a bunch of man-hating drama queens?" he asked, annoyed.

"We don't hate men. We just don't trust them."

He looked taken aback, insulted almost. "I've never given any of you a reason not to trust me."

Shane put her pencil down and sighed. She wanted to shake him, slap him around and drill into him what life was like while he was overseas. But she reminded herself that he did not know it all, had not yet learned everything that had happened while he'd been gone and instead gave him a small, matronly smile.

"But you haven't given them one in favor of trusting you, either. So what choice do they have?"

Bernchal considered what she said for a moment and realized that if he was to be trusted and in turn trust them, he had to know more.

"Then show me how. What happened, Shane? While I was gone, while we were fighting in Africa. What the hell happened over here?"

It was Shane's turn to be surprised. She eyed him, startled as though it were the first time she'd thought about the reason for the events of days past. In reality, she thought about it everyday. But thinking about it and talking about it were two different things entirely. And truth be told, she and Bernchal hadn't discussed in detail anything at all really, so she decided to act against her usual isolated manner in the hopes that he could shed some light on some of her questions that needed answering.

"What do you wanna know?"

He rubbed his chin, the stubble on his face sounding like sandpaper as his calloused hands moved along it. There were over a dozen women in the cafeteria, each roaming around working on some predetermined project, but Shane suddenly and unexpectedly found herself in a sound vacuum and all she heard was Bernchal.

"How…how did it lead to all of this? I mean, I know what happened up to deploying, how it all started to fall apart. But I didn't think it would get to this. Fucking Thunderdome."

"Fucking Thunderdome…" she repeated.

"We had rules. Laws. Suddenly sixteen-year old kids are fighting next to me in a war that isn't even ours to fight telling me they got drafted like it's the goddamn sixties."

"Well, to answer that you have to know how it all went to hell over here after you guys all left."

"So tell me. Please," he asked, his large hazel eyes imploring her. "I got nothing."

Taking a deep breath, Shane put down the pencil she didn't realize she'd been gripping so hard until that moment and locked eyes with him, beginning the sordid tale of demise she had dissected more than once herself.

"Yenmor apparently created some sort of dual attack, like a one-two punch on the United States. The first part, the part that got all of you guys out apparently, most of us had no clue about. I mean, we didn't really know much about the war in Africa. It was always such a tumultuous place and I'm sure because of how things used to be, it wasn't covered as extensively as Kim Kardashian's ass."

Bernchal chuckled and she continued.

"Somehow, he rearranged Congress. Hell, he rearranged the country. No one knew what was happening until it happened. He implemented his new laws overnight. Stripped *everyone* of their basic civil rights. There were demonstrations, protests. Riots that made L.A. and Baltimore look like a playground. But those all ended in bloodshed. It was useless. So there was nothing to do but comply and plot. Underground rebels rose, but he had a plan. He countered insurgents with an attack on U.S. soil. You guys were all gone and the few pieces of news that were leaked said there was no law enforcement left. He controlled the media, which had been reduced by that point to radio broadcasts and an occasional flash across a television screen. Because he *wanted* everyone to see what was happening, to see it unfold and shit their pants in fear. So he made sure we knew there was no one left to help. No one. The world started to crumble and there was no one here to protect us.

They killed…. millions. Swept through the country starting with the big cities- New York, L.A., Chicago- and killed without prejudice. All the men. *All* of them. Women without kids. It was fucking chaos. We didn't know why they were letting certain women live, leaving certain kids alone. We didn't know there was criteria for death and survival…"

She kept her eyes trained on him but Bernchal could see Shane's mind had gone elsewhere, possibly back to that time seemingly so long ago.

"I kept my son close to me, ran and eventually found a safe place to stay with other women, mothers and their kids. We hid. They found us. They took our kids from us and began this insane crusade to train us. For what, I couldn't tell you. They never told us, kept us in the dark. We had to learn but we didn't even know why. Our only incentive was keeping our kids alive, getting them back. So we survived. Did exactly as we were told. It was like a concentration boot camp by day. We'd train like the goddamned gestapo. Weights, guns, knives. If you couldn't disarm and overpower an opponent in five seconds, they would drag your kid in and execute him in front of you. Then lock you up 'till the grief made you utterly useless. These were what our days were like. Our nights? A horror show. Sick bastards studying live human subjects. Experiments. Torture. Day in, day out; everywhere some variation of our fucking prison existed. He was building an army with us. All spearheaded by some fucking four-eyed psychopath living out his sickest fantasies on living, breathing women.

This went on, oh, I'd say about eighteen months. 'Till someone fucked up and said something out loud. A rumor spread and finally hit us."

"What was it?"

"That they'd killed our kids."

"Holy shit."

"Yeah," she replied with a wry smile. "See, at first, to get us docile and manageable, they told us our kids were dead. Naturally, most of us shut down. Just laid down and waited to die. Took whatever they gave without any struggle. What's the point of fighting, of living at all if your kid is dead? So it got dark. Then the hope came. 'We lied! Here are your kids, alive and well. Fight, train, do what you're told and maybe, *maybe* you'll be reunited!' We complied, of course. For an inhumane year and a half.

Then they slipped. One of the women who was basically used as a maid overheard some talk. Our kids were pawns, nothing more. Some of them were still alive, *some* of them. But the rest would be killed the minute we had completed training. When that rumor spread, some of the women just… they couldn't handle it. Some went crazy, literally bat shit crazy. A lot of women killed themselves. Took it as a way out of the pain of losing their kids, out of the torture in the camps. Hell, a lot of people did it as soon as things started going bad. Hopelessness is just as toxic as torture.

The rest of us, well, we waited. It's not like they had a great track record for truth-telling. We waited and did our best to get information. Our kids were alive. Still being held captive somewhere by our institution- but alive. We fucking lost it; I know I did. Basically took the whole establishment down. Killed anyone and everyone who couldn't or wouldn't lead us to our kids. Got close enough to see them loaded on a helicopter and Bam! Gone. All tracks and traces of my son and all those other kids just gone.

We didn't even give ourselves a chance to cry about it. Moved out, picked up what we could to survive along the way. We found this place as refuge and set it up. As soon as we could, we started searching for our kids. And here we are."

Shell-shocked, he eyed her. "Are there other…camps?"

She nodded, noticing but disregarding the look on his face, that sad look of utter disbelief. She recognized it because she had seen several women in and around New York City wearing the same look, and she was sure she had worn it herself more than once.

"There are. I don't know where, though. Honestly, I could barely tell you where the ones I was in are at. Your location is not exactly high on the list of things to figure out when you are the subject of some twisted science experiment. I wish I knew where other women are being held, though I can't imagine adding more to our already-growing list of things to do. We have to find the kids that were taken before we can begin a new quest."

Finally releasing the breath he had been holding, Bernchal broke his stare and closed his eyes tight. Seeing the devastation in his homeland when he'd returned, witnessing that his country had become nothing more than a war-torn shell of what it once was hadn't prepared him for what he'd just heard. Even until this moment he had hoped, somewhat naively, that everything that had been done could somehow be undone. That some sick tyrant from another country hell-bent on destruction had caused their downfall and rebuilding would eventually commence once the bad guys could be taken down. He had hoped, the way a poverty-stricken child who had never gleefully opened a gift on Christmas morning still waited up at night, eyes wide open with bated breath, in the hopes of hearing Santa Claus make his way into the home he'd never found before.

Shaking his head, he pried open his eyes again and discovered her attention already returned to the map in front of her.

"That's… quite a history lesson."

"Quid pro quo, Commander," she answered without looking up. Business as usual.

"Ah, you mean I show you mine, you show me yours?"

Ignoring him, Shane sat up again and held the pencil with both hands, arms outstretched before her.

"I mean, I answered your questions and hopefully filled in some blanks for you. Now you do the same for me."

"What do you want to know, Shane? Who I voted for? 'Cause it definitely wasn't that asshole."

The steel expression barely budged. "How did he get you guys out of here? How did he get the entire United States military out of the country? How did he destroy all law enforcement? I mean street cops, NYPD, corrections officers, border patrol, port authority- everybody! How the hell-"

"Whoa, whoa! Let's start simply, okay?"

She nodded, embarrassed. "Why did you leave?"

It was a simple question, four words directly stated. But to Bernchal, it sounded like a plea, a desperate and devastating appeal that reminded him, lest he forget, that he was thousands of miles away as his home was ravaged and his people massacred.

He cleared his throat and began.

"We didn't... we didn't leave. We were deployed. *I* was deployed."

Admonished, Shane lowered her eyes and he was surprised to hear an apology from her, of all people.

"I know. I'm sorry. I meant-"

"I know what you meant, Shane, but excuse me while I take a second to focus on the fact that you actually apologized. To me. For something *you* did. This is amazing..."

"Commander-"

"I know, I know. Our daily four seconds of fun are over. Back to business."

She stifled a laugh and struggled to shoot him a dirty look but he ignored it and started again.

"So, we were deployed. They didn't tell us anything. I didn't even know where I was going. My team and I got shipped to South Africa, right around Cape Town. Or at least that's where they put us en route to. We found out on the way there that there was a war breaking out in this tiny province inland. The Bakari Republic. Apparently North Korea had attacked."

"Genocide. We saw that, on the news. They actually aired all of that before it started."

"I'm surprised. It must have been a scare tactic, because we knew nothing of what was happening here. And the rest of the world seemed to be operating perfectly fine."

She nodded, somewhat enthused that someone was finally filling in some of the gaps of information after all of this time. "I had friends and family around the world- Dominican Republic, Argentina, London. They all knew what was happening here, but not Africa. No one did. The news was deliberately vague so all we heard was that it was genocide. And sadly, war and turmoil were so common there that-"

"That no one cared," he finished bluntly. "Yeah, it was genocide. North Koreans were slaughtering these people by the hundreds. A tiny village of people who hadn't been corrupted by technology in centuries. They were sold out by another village to the North Koreans over some land dispute. They didn't even tell us any of that. This is all intel we learned after spending almost two years among the survivors. There was no communication whatsoever. They told us Cape Town and we shipped off to Cape Town. Somewhere outside of Saldanha, just northwest of our point of drop, we got attacked. From there on in, it was chaos. I lost almost all of my men in the ensuing battle. Do you know what it's like to shoot back at teenagers holding Uzis? Half of their damn armies are filled with kids. It was… insane. Between the country's own rebels and the North Koreans massacring everyone else, somehow we survived long enough for the remaining half of us to die of various diseases. Good times."

Shane continued staring at her hands, fumbling with the same pencil. She had listened closely to his version of events and noticed that his voice never wavered. He never changed tone, instead kept it cool, disconnected and even. Anytime she spoke of the past or even thought about it, she felt as though her insides were catching fire, quickly becoming enflamed until it threatened to consume her and she had to focus on something, anything else. With Bernchal, it was the opposite. He seemed to have made peace with the events of his past and Shane guessed enviously that it was because a piece of his heart had not been ripped out the way it had with hers.

"What I don't get is how Yenmor's goons managed to completely take over like that. How did they eliminate our entire military defense?"

"First, you have to understand something. The United States military doesn't blindly follow orders from one man, commander-in chief or not. We make an oath to uphold the Constitution. That's it. Our job is to serve our country and if our country sends us to save innocent people being slaughtered, then you don't question that. You follow the orders given by your commanding officer and when those orders come from the Commander in Chief of the United States, you put on your uniform and go where you're told. So we didn't question any of it at first. But a president that makes unlawful orders and expects them to be carried out without question is a dictator, and that's what Yenmor was. He needed us gone so he could carry out his plan without interference. Sure you have soldiers that do as told but for the most part, no soldier would have abandoned his home had we known what was happening here, regardless of the orders."

Though his eyes remained crisp and no-nonsense, his tone was slightly clipped, an edge of defense audible in his words. She put one hand up to stop him from continuing and shaking her head, replied adamantly.

"I don't blame you. At all. I'm sure *no one* blames the military for what happened, especially now knowing what you went through-"

He stopped her midsentence with a soft smile.

"I know."

Flustered, Shane quickly looked away and turned her attention back to the pencil in her hand. She tapped it a few times on the linoleum table for good measure as the silence between them got heavier. He watched her, intrigued by her discomfort.

He cleared his throat and got back on track. "Anyway, with the military gone, he did whatever the hell he wanted. Yenmor orchestrated this whole thing. This was his plan from the beginning, and that motherfucker carried it out like a goddamn chess match. Precision, strategy and enforcement. Perfectly executed."

"All branches? Fucking NORAD?"

"NORAD. All of it. Air travel was suspended immediately and anybody who came within an inch of our airspace was shot down, commuter planes and all. We didn't stand a fucking chance."

She eyed him, silent. He knew her wheels were turning, trying to decipher how the events unfolded to lead them there.

"I know the politics behind it. I was lucky enough to be here for that," she added sarcastically. "But the technicalities behind everything…"

"First wave that rode out with the National Guard never made it out the sidelines. Their air support was unbeatable."

She eyed him and asked incredulously, "How?

"Again, I learned all this the hard way. Before the internet, before social media, we'd have bounced back. Hell, we'd have wiped our asses with them and kept it moving. But we made it too easy. Put our shit out there, put our secrets at the fingertips of any hacker worth his salt. Left everything in the open as long as you had the right code. And they cracked it. Cracked our codes, learned our secrets. Disabling our military forces was a walk in the park. Then they hit us with the cyber invasion. Ever seen Independence Day? They followed it like a goddamn playbook. Basically used our own satellites against us. Ultimately, our hubris was our downfall. Not to mention that the leader of this fucking country was standing behind everything, twirling the strings like a puppeteer. This was a coup, orchestrated from inside the White House and planned for God knows how long. This was all a means to an end. He wanted to turn this country into exactly what he envisioned, and he did it."

"And all these weapons of mass destruction we spent years searching for, the ones we had on standby- we couldn't use that?"

"On who- ourselves? They literally disarmed us with the flick of a wrist. They dismantled our nuclear warheads while they were still in the goddamn silos. Knocked our own B-2 bombers out of the sky without batting an eyelash. We didn't stand a fucking chance. Not with half the military overseas and the other half murdered."

Unsatisfied with the details, she shook her head like a child unwilling to accept the word 'no.' "But why didn't anybody help us?"

"Why would they? Huh, Shane? We criticized everyone and called the rest of the free world savages, but look at how we treated our own people. We chased down terrorists but grew our own here. We were no better than anyone else yet we preached freedom and equality. What equality? We alienated the rest of the planet, a planet which we primarily destroyed. Why would anyone help us? They all just sat back and watched us kill ourselves. Probably eating popcorn while they did it."

"Jesus Christ…"

"Yeah, that guy wasn't exactly around, either. Probably vacationing in Canada."

Chapter XI

Shane patted the sheets on her bed and straightened out the creases until there were none. Her hand smoothed over the drab gray blanket and out of the corner of eye she caught the matching curtain on the window shift slightly with the breeze coming in through the crack in the window. Her hand froze midair and her breath caught in her throat.

Suddenly she was back in her bedroom, back in her cozy apartment before the world had ceased to exist. Back when her husband was in the kitchen, making breakfast for his family as she lay in bed, entwined with her son.

He was resting on her chest, listening to her heart beat slowly as she traced circles in the soft brown curls on his head. She was sniffing his scent, smelling that intoxicating aroma of baby mixed with growing boy while he lingered somewhere between slumber and lucidity.

The sheer white curtains of her bay windows danced as the wind reaching the twentieth floor whipped around her bedroom. She didn't turn her head, didn't dare move a muscle for fear of shifting Silas' position and waking him, ruining that amazing moment of peace.

"Shane?"

Shane sucked in a mouthful of air and blinked, immediately back in the present. Gone were the curtains, the beautiful windows with the breathtaking view.

Gone was her son, no longer nestled safely in her arms.

"*Shane?*"

She looked up and saw Bernchal in the doorway of her room, a half-eaten apple in his left hand, his brow creased with concern.

"You okay?"

She cleared her throat and nodded quickly, immediately turning her attention back to making her bed.

"Yeah. I'm fine."

Bernchal nodded, nonplussed. "You went away there for a second."

She straightened up and dropped her hands to her sides, but couldn't bring her eyes up to meet his.

"I'm back."

He hadn't known her long at all but given the current state of their lives, Bernchal felt that a few months was now equivalent to several years and he considered himself a burgeoning expert on all things Shane. So he took the hint exactly how it was given and dropped the issue immediately.

"Wanna get a work out in before the madness?"

She nodded, words suddenly caught in her throat. Bernchal was annoying and intrusive and bold, qualities she normally hated. But he was clever and compassionate, and those were two things she desperately needed. And try as she might to resist, he was working his way into her psyche and leaving an indelible impression. So instead of rebuffing him and pushing him away, Shane uncharacteristically did the opposite.

Clearing her throat, she turned her back to him and patted the mattress, smoothing out the already perfect sheets again.

"I'll meet you downstairs."

He turned and walked away munching on the apple.

Ten minutes later, Shane met Bernchal in the same lobby where she'd held him at gunpoint several months beforehand. The irony wasn't lost on her, or him either evidently, because he threw his arms up in the air when she entered and screamed, "Don't shoot!"

Ignoring him, Shane zipped up her pullover and walked past him through the double oak doors of the entrance. Shooting a quick wink back at the other women working in the lobby watching their exchange, Bernchal followed.

Outside, they ran down a couple of blocks to the track of the old Gaelic Park in silence. Though they jogged at a steady pace, neither was unaware of their surroundings and kept a close hand to the guns in their holsters. The streets were quiet however, and they arrived a few minutes after leaving without incident.

The field was situated adjacent to Broadway and across from Van Cortlandt Park, what used to be one of the largest and loveliest parks in New York City. It was now nothing more than straggling patches of dirt across blown up minefields with the occasional dead body thrown in for good measure.

Upon the first attacks, the North Korean forces that had backed Yenmor obliterated all of the parks across the city and the only ones left untouched for the most part were small, private plots such as Gaelic Park, mostly because it was small enough to have escaped the damage unnoticed.

They crept in through a hole in the perimeter fence and took to the track immediately. After two laps around making approximately a half mile, Shane slowed to a walk and Bernchal followed her lead. He never said it out loud but he admired her stamina and her resiliency in general. After that day she'd told him the ins and outs of what had occurred during his absence, she never again mentioned what exactly had happened to her during her imprisonment. Some of the women around her had made comments here and there and he'd picked up on it all, but never anything specific. And though he knew she trusted him to a certain extent, he accepted that it would be some time before she would be comfortable enough to tell him everything.

So instead he discussed their plans and mission and even with all of his prodding and insipid need for conversation, Shane acknowledged that Bernchal recognized her desire to keep some details to herself, thankfully. So in gratitude, she answered most of his generic questions.

"So, tell me- how haven't they found you?"

"They?"

"Bad guys. Terrorists. They."

"Oh. Well, we're well hidden."

"Yeah, but this was a school, a college. It has to be in some record somewhere."

"What we are working with Commander, is evil. Not so much intelligence. They destroyed the only source of information themselves."

He stopped short and put his hands on his hips to take a breath. "Why?"

"Who knows why?" she replied impatiently. She barely slowed and continued walking and he caught up quickly while she spoke. "Because they were afraid to educate women as though this were the 1500's? Because they wanted to scare us into submission as though this were the 1800's? I don't know. But they bombed all the libraries almost immediately."

"All of them?"

"Every single one, starting with the biggest and the best."

"The lions?" he asked incredulously, referring to the infamous New York Public Library on 42nd Street.

She nodded. "Yup. First one to go."

"No…"

Shane looked over at the shock on Bernchal's face and softened her tone. "Yes."

"Jesus. That place was beautiful…"

"That it was. Gone now. No books left anywhere. They ignored the smaller universities and colleges and as big as this place is, it isn't the most well-known school in New York City, so it survived. We still have the library in tact, luckily. But they got to all of the other places and when there's no internet, there's no information."

Bernchal shook his head, dumbfounded. He still had so much to take in about this new world in which he'd found himself. It felt like every day there was more information, more devastation around which he had no choice but to wrap his brain.

"Anyway, with the internet gone and us finally free, we did the next logical thing and took out all of the Building and Land development offices around the city and Westchester."

"So you became invisible?" he asked, impressed.

"Yup. But not before grabbing every goddamn blueprint we could get our hands on. So now we can plan better more coordinated attacked using the subways and pathways nobody even knew about."

She paused again and looked up at the blaring sun. The summer had been brutal and despite the beginning of a new season, didn't appear to want to leave.

"That's how it started, actually. Subterranean tunnels we dug if there was no access. We moved throughout the city this way and within the subways, always back here without detection. They found some of them and smoked us out, tried to use them for themselves. We collapsed the few we had at the time and moved above ground for the most part. A couple of women that used to live with us were city engineers- we got very lucky when they were alive."

"But how can you move around freely in loud ass trucks? I would assume they'd kill on sight."

"They normally do. But they are easy to spot. They all wear their military uniforms, they use automatic weapons that can be heard for miles and they shoot at anything. They are confident in their takeover so they don't bother to look hard. It's actually pretty funny. Here is this military power that helped stage a coup and completely destroy our government and democracy. They killed half of our population and enslaved the other half. So they're cocky. They think they got everybody so they don't bother to do sweeps for stragglers or search abandoned properties. There are thousands of women all around the city still in hiding and they don't even know. Every once in awhile you'll hear or see something but usually, it's quiet."

"So you guys can move in and out without trouble."

She started walking again at a much slower pace.

"For the most part. Sometimes we stumble on a group of them and take them out, always leaving one alive for information. We've gotten details on movement of other kidnapped kids, other women being held. Delivery of supplies from God knows where. We've hijacked ammo, food, weapons, artillery. Always coming in hard undetected, always quick and simple."

He nodded and considered his next question carefully.

"With this many soldiers, how do you-"

"We're not soldiers."

"Excuse me?" He slowed again and this time, she slowed with him.

"We are not soldiers."

In his best attempt to not sound patronizing, Bernchal smiled sincerely. "You behave as though you are."

Shane tightened her mouth for one second and then answered quickly, her words more hurried than usual.

"Because we have no choice if we want to survive and get our children back. But please don't be misled, Commander. You and your brethren, your men- *you* are soldiers. You signed up for battle. Willingly volunteered to defend your country, pick up a weapon and lay down your life for the man next to you. We did not. We were enslaved, forced into servitude after our children were taken from us. We yield weapons because without them our children will die. This is not a choice. We are not soldiers."

Admonished, he nodded. "Sorry."

Shane released an awkward giggle that caught them both off guard and tried to lighten the suddenly tense atmosphere. If she and Bernchal were to get along she would have to learn how to interact with people, namely men, again.

"No apology necessary. I was just making a distinction. Please continue."

He cleared his throat, shot her a quick and puzzled look, and started walking faster again, continuing with his line of questioning.

They seemed to play this game of Frogger, always one pausing and slowing down, the other playing catch-up. Everywhere they went together, one was always following the other, feeding off of the other's knowledge as they handed it out like charity, tiny little morsels at a time.

"Ahem… Well, with this many… this many women, how do you control the element of surprise?"

"They don't know where we are."

"But your attacks- how are they implemented?"

"We plan," she answered, matter-of-factly. "Strategically."

He wondered if his questions were too ambiguous or she was purposely avoiding them.

"But how do they not hear you coming?"

Shane stopped again and he almost ran into her. Her dark eyes looked overcast with confusion and she hesitated before answering curtly, "I don't know."

He couldn't help himself, and chuckled.

"You don't know?"

More honestly, she answered, her voice low and measured. "I don't know."

Bernchal tilted his head and stared at her, his mouth open to speak but no words coming forth yet. She stared right back but he could tell she was not lying, that she literally could not answer the question. Shocked, he asked again, "You seriously don't know?"

Visibly frustrated, Shane started on the track again, this time headed back towards the way they entered. She rolled her eyes as she passed him and replied tightly.

"You wanna know what I know, Commander? A bullet is four times faster than the speed of sound. That's what I know."

The sound of footsteps on the dying leaves just beyond their perimeter fence stopped them and they eyed each other, waiting. Two women, one much older, the other barely in her twenties, stepped out from behind a large tree and while Bernchal reached for the gun on his belt, he noticed Shane's was already out and aimed.

Silently, the women made eye contact and hesitated. Shane watched them, weapon drawn but hand relaxed. The older of the two gave a subtle nod of her head and they were off, disappearing into the dense forest just as quickly as they'd emerged. Shane said nothing, just returned her gun to its holster and moved ahead again.

Bernchal caught up to her and tapped her shoulder, asking, "How do you know they were friendlies?"

"I don't," she replied politely. "But they had no guns, and by the looks of their clothes, nowhere to go."

"Why didn't you offer the school?"

Her tone shifted, her voice suddenly more direct and condescending. "I'm not in the business of recruiting," she answered bluntly. "Someone wants in, they can plead their case. Otherwise, you go your way, I go mine."

He nodded, satisfied.

"Fair enough."

Chapter XII

The deafening boom of the explosion rattled the dormitory and woke everyone from their sleep. It was right before dusk and was close enough to feel like it came from inside the institution.

Shane had sentries set up all over the perimeter of the school and everyone took shifts and reported in every hour on the hour. Though they had had their fair share of incidents involving militia in the past, up until recently things had been quiet and they had all become, for the most part, quite complacent.

All except Shane, who woke up with a start when the sound hit her bedroom. She reached for the gun she kept under her pillow and jumped out of bed. It took less than thirty seconds for her eyes to adjust to the gaslight coming from the corridor, jump into a pair of leggings and shove her feet into her boots.

She met Bernchal in the hallway and stopped short inches from him. He was shirtless, wearing only a pair of pants and holding his semi-automatic weapon in his right hand, his left extended in front of him and hanging precariously close to her breasts.

"What was it?" he asked, quietly, his eyes darting around the corridor looking for any unwanted guests.

Shane wondered where he'd been when he heard the explosion to have found his way to her room so quickly. She wondered why he had found his way to her room so quickly in the midst of some strange explosion happening around them. And she wondered why in the hell she was wondering these things about Bernchal when there was an explosion happening around them.

All business, she balanced her weapon in front of her and indicated for Bernchal to follow her as she began to make her way down the hallway towards the main staircase.

The inside of the main office of the school housed what was once the Bursar's and Registrar's offices, as well as the Dean and the Assistant Dean, and led into several hallways and sections that split off like small tributaries. Each tunnel, whether having been built alongside the school or added later on, was connected with each portion of the school, including the dormitories. The dorms used to be its own faction and as the population of the school had grown back in the early 2000's, empty lots in the neighborhood were bought by the college and used to expand the dorms for students, so there had been buildings all throughout Riverdale housing Manhattan College kids. When Shane and the other women had taken ownership of the institution, they set up direct access by expanding the underground tunnels they'd discovered on the property blueprints. The dormitory where they all slept was now the only one connected directly to the rest of the school and because it was the only dormitory attached to the main office, they occupied that one for their own use and left the other buildings abandoned and blocked off.

With Bernchal in tow, Shane reached one of the tunnels and hearing movement on the other end of it, blew out the gas-lamp used to light it. In the darkness, she felt Bernchal inch closer to her and despite the sudden awkward awareness of his presence, began making her way further into the tunnel.

Behind her, Bernchal maintained a close proximity to Shane while his eyes struggled to adjust to the blinding darkness enveloping them. The shuffling sound they'd heard upon their entrance was quieted and now short of his own heart thumping loudly in his chest, he heard nothing.

For all of her quirks and annoying habits, which were plenty, Bernchal hated to admit to himself that she knew what she was doing. More and more he felt like just another follower in her little rag-tag group of soldiers and though he contributed as much as he could in any way that he could, he could not deny that the power balance had not and probably would never shift.

A loud shuffle stopped them and Shane pushed Bernchal back against the wall with her arm, her hand landing on his chest. They waited with their breaths held for further indication that whoever had joined them in the dark tunnel knew they'd arrived. Bernchal tried his best for as long as he could but the weight of Shane's hand on his chest was too much to ignore and he finally gave in, letting his pecs give one good flex for her enjoyment.

Shane felt the move and dropped her hand, irritated.

"Shane?"

Her attention was diverted and she froze. A beam of light temporarily blinded them and Bernchal covered his eyes until it moved, down and to the left.

"Julie," he heard Shane whisper.

The light had a source and Julie's strawberry blonde hair spiraled wildly as she turned her flashlight on to her own face and smiled at Shane.

"Why are we whispering?"

They all turned to face Bernchal and he offered a weak smile.

Turning her attention back to Julie, Shane pushed past him and continued down the same direction, towards the main office. Save for their light footsteps and soft whispering, the tunnel was silent.

"Has anyone breached the perimeter?"

"Mariana reported no breaches." Shilan answered quickly and turned to face him as she walked beside Shane, shooting him a quick glance that reminded him he was the only one of the four half naked.

"Where did the explosion come from?" he offered, suddenly self-conscious and began to shrug into the t-shirt he had grabbed on his way out of his room and palmed on the way to Shane's.

Julie walked alongside him and replied. "Mariana said it came from the north, past the stables. So far nothing's come our way."

They continued silently until they reached the main building. Shane led the women with Bernchal bringing up the rear and one by one they climbed the narrow staircase and crossed into the Dean's old office. There Shane listened at the large wooden door and satisfied that nothing was happening on the other end, opened it and walked out with the rest of the group following. There, they were met with more beams of light trailing across the floor and some of the other women gathered, weapons drawn.

"Shane!" Their surprised faces when the four of them emerged from the Dean's office would have been amusing were in not for the stream of questions that began pouring out of them. Thankfully, Shane had little patience above all else and quickly silenced them with an immediate palm in the air.

"I need seven of you, *now*."

Julie and Shilan automatically pushed back against the crowd of women and stood close to Shane indicating their intention to be among the seven chosen. Bernchal, noticing that other women were also coming forward, pushed his way through and stood behind Shane, Julie and Shilan like an eager puppy. Before the world went to shit he'd have never shoved a group of women out of the way for any reason, but since residing with over a hundred of them for almost a year and being treated like nothing short of a pariah, he had no problem with it now.

She pointed to Mariana, Joyce, a quiet girl named Megan and a tiny brunette named Betzaida, creating her group. Turning to walk out of the front doors of the lobby, she ran into Bernchal who had squeezed his way through Shilan and Julie to the front spot. He smiled brightly and she rolled her eyes, pushed past him and barked some more orders.

"Check every hallway, every corridor, every fucking bed. Make sure nothing and no one is here without me knowing. We're gonna go check things out outside."

They streamed out the front double doors of the lobby and quietly into the night. The usual gaslights that could be spotted occasionally around the quad were all off and it was dark enough to cover them as they made their way through the college's front to the wrought iron gate. There, Adenelly and Maura silently opened the gates to let them through and returned to their positions guarding the entrance of the school once the gates closed behind them.

"The Leo Building is secure. Jessica said the explosion likely game from the north, past the Saw Mill."

Bernchal recognized Julie's voice but could barely see her light-colored curls as he followed her, could barely see two feet in front of his face. The sky was blacker than he'd ever seen it. At least he'd had the moonlight to guide him during his nights in the woods as he'd traveled up the east coast. There seemed to be no moon tonight, or stars for that matter, and though they claimed the explosion was about two miles away at the very least, the air was already thick with smoke and making it even more difficult to see.

He squinted and found Shane ahead of the group. Her dark hair was haphazardly pulled back now in a ponytail, very different than it had been when she'd emerged from her room earlier with a wild mane of curly hair. Now that they were quiet, each lost in their own thoughts as they concentrated on making their way through the forest connecting the school grounds with Broadway, he thought back to the moments after the explosion.

He'd jumped up, startled and confused. Up until that second he'd been deep in slumber, comfortable on his bed and nestled in, dreaming of the old days of bachelor fun- women, sun and drinks- something which now seemed so long ago. The sound of the explosion and the way the entire building where the dormitory was housed seemed to rattle and vibrate woke him with a start and he'd flown out of bed immediately. Grabbing a pair of cargo pants given to him by Shilan when he'd first arrived and presumably taken from the closet of a former student, Bernchal had made his way out of the room, gun and t-shirt in hand. Not knowing the standard emergency procedure someone like Shane had undoubtedly set in place, he immediately had made his way to her.

Holding the same gun she'd reluctantly given him on his first run with her, he had startled her outside of the door to her room. It was pitch-black save for the gas lamp propped up in the corner and he knew he'd scared the shit out of her, but as always, she was calm and collected and hid it. Her demeanor remained professional- always stiff and composed.

But her eyes- her eyes told a different story. They were wide, alarmed even. The usual darkness and suspicious stare were gone and replaced by a brightness he'd never seen. As though she'd forgotten, however temporarily, about the matter at hand and instead were seeing him for the first time.

It was… interesting, to say the least.

He jogged a little quicker to catch up to her, disregarding the crackling of the dying leaves under his clumsy feet and when he stumbled up to her side, she shot him a look of annoyance and continued forward.

"What's the plan?" he asked her breathlessly. She shushed him and tossed an elbow in his direction, narrowly missing him when he dodged her blow.

"Did you bring a flare gun, or are you just gonna yell our arrival for the world to know?"

"And I have a question for you, if you can take a break from the never-ending onslaught of sarcasm you seem to replenish every day. How do you live every single second of the day with this much hostility? It seems exhausting."

He couldn't read her face in the darkness, though truth be told he couldn't get much of a read of her face on a regular day. She played it close to the vest at all times and this would probably be no different, but when he heard a slight change in the pitch of her voice, he was pleasantly surprised.

"It's not exhausting, really. It's quite easy. Or rather, *you* make it quite easy."

He chuckled as he worked to keep up with her. "I try." Their steady back and forth clearly knew no bounds and as they trekked through the backwoods of the institution and cut through the alley between an abandoned apartment building and an old Planet Wings, a faint light reflected off the broken window of the restaurant and Bernchal could have sworn he caught the hint of a smile on Shane's face.

They reached Broadway and Bernchal took lead. That move had cost him a pretty penny- an hour long argument about his training and how he was best equipped to lead the women in strategical planning and even then, Shane had barely budged. Bernchal had spent weeks alone in the open space struggling to survive, months in a prisoner-of-war camp, three years abroad in combat and over two decades in service and at the end, only his promise to teach her how to properly fasten a tourniquet had finally prompted her to concede.

He flashed some of his military hand signals and looked back at Shane, smiling to himself when she met his eyes with irritation. Bernchal knew Shane didn't know the signals and ignored him whenever used, so he finally motioned with his chin for the rest of them to follow and together, they slowly they made their way out from between the buildings and onto the deserted street.

The smoke was thicker there but still scarce enough to indicate they had further to go. The loss of electricity nationwide meant no streetlamp and if they thought the woods were black, the street was even worse.

Shane and the other women knew the woods well, had used them almost on a daily basis in and out of the institution, so running in the dark on uneven ground was not a problem for them. But on the street, sidestepping broken glass and litter, garbage strewn and other items indicative of a world that once was, they had to move much slower.

Shane kept close to Bernchal and Julie was right behind her. Shilan, Betzaida, Megan and Mariana followed with Joyce holding up the rear. The stifling summer night was quiet and could barely be heard above the sound of crickets and various other insects searching for food. With woods behind them and the park to their right, they were surrounded by nocturnal creatures whose noises thankfully drowned out their footsteps.

He led them closer to the edge of the park, off of Broadway to avoid detection but close enough to keep out of the park grounds. Without policing and the occasional hit and run, the population of the coyotes and foxes in New York City had gotten uncontrollably large and they were now fearless. Caution for humanity was a thing of the past and Bernchal had encountered plenty on his journey north and had luckily survived, unbitten and without contracting rabies.

They shuffled along at a quicker pace, the sound of their feet masked by the occasional howling inside the park. A broken twig nearby caused Shane to involuntarily inch a little closer to Bernchal and though he didn't mention it then, he made a mental note to bring it up later to torture her.

The night, once lit by streetlights, life behind the walls of apartment units and stores bustling with business sales, was now nothing but the bleak blackness of an endless abyss. On the occasion they were lucky enough to see the stars because the smoke usually coming from explosions and gunfire dissipated, Shane and her group used the light to creep among the shadows, the way nocturnal animals hunted. But when the moon hid behind the dark, the once great city was nothing more than a wasteland, quiet but for the occasional appearance of militia or random citizens. For the most part, it was desolate and silent, as though someone had literally turned off New York City.

They reached the overpass of the Saw Mill River Road and saw the flames in the distance. Joyce recognized the building right away.

"That's the Russian Embassy," she whispered in awe.

Shilan furrowed her brow in confusion and looked to Shane. "I thought that was gone."

She shook her head and bit her lip for a second in thought. "Me too…"

The smoke was thicker and the fire was visible from where they stood less than a half mile away. It was just up the hill and in the dead of night the crackling of the embers could be heard clearly. Every so often something would pop loudly, indicating that the fire was still very much alive and had engulfed something else inside of the embassy.

The sound of voices, faraway chatter, traveled through the silence and though largely inaudible, a few words carried over the crackling of the flames, indicating the language spoken was english. Undeterred, they continued forward, knowing it was likely a group of passersby investigating the explosion.

Wordlessly, they turned onto West 256th Street and climbed the hill to the city steps. Littered with dying leaves and remnants of explosions and bullet casings, the steps were crumbling and difficult to navigate, but luckily there were few. On Sylvan Avenue they turned right and cut through several backyards, careful to not alert any residue residents to their arrival. On Fieldston Road, they hopped a fence behind the Russian property and made their way towards the Embassy, already feeling the heat emanating from the burning building.

Shane had seen a lot of random fires and explosions after society had imploded but none up close and this mesmerizing. The flames had engulfed the entire top half of the multi-story building and even as they stood below it a hundred yards away, the intensity was enough that beads of sweat were already forming on her forehead. Random licks of fire dropped from the sky and landed on the dry grass at their feet, embers igniting immediately and starting small fires around them that Bernchal began stomping away with his feet.

Another loud pop and they froze as several windows on one of the middle floors blew out and rained glass in front of them. Bernchal reached out an arm, pushing Shane and the other women back just as shattered glass landed inches from where they had stood. The ground below them rumbled and shook and they all looked at each other for a split second before Bernchal yelled, "Run!" He grabbed Shane by the wrist and they took off just as the Embassy started to crumble.

Chapter XIII

Shane followed Bernchal, not much by choice, towards Mosholu Avenue as fast as her boot clad feet would run but her head remained turned back as she watched the building collapse and come down behind them. It felt with every step as though the ground underneath them was going to split open and Shane couldn't figure out how such a narrow building could make the world move so.

Bernchal led them past what was once P.S. 81 and up the hill until the smoke that was billowing at warp speed from the destruction no longer looked like it would envelope them whole. They stopped, all taking a break to catch their breaths and look around. Barely anything was visible through the thick smoke and debris surrounding them. Shane looked up and down the block for some indication as to what still stood and her eyes landed on the edifice rising above the hilltop ahead of them.

The onyx colored sky behind Skyview didn't do much for its silhouette and had she not lived there for over a decade, Shane might not have recognized it. But she did and immediately, her demeanor changed. Gone was the headstrong, decisive leader that had survived up until now and she was replaced by a broken woman.

Gulping a mouthful of the foul air brought about a wave of coughs that shook her body and surprised them all. Shilan patted her roughly on the back until it passed and when it did, Shane just looked again towards the tall building, her eyes brimming over with sweat and tears from the choking and from the emotion she was trying to keep hidden.

"Do you know where we are?"

Betzaida asked the question aloud, but Shane was the only one who nodded. She knew the air was too thick to navigate through and would remain that way for at least an hour or so. They needed a place to hunker down and refuel. They were all coughing, covered in soot and ash and out of breath from running and narrowly escaping with their lives. And she knew that the only place she could bring them with the least chance of detection was her old stomping grounds.

"There's a building up the block. We can... we can go in."

They followed her wordlessly as she turned and started up the steep hill towards Skyview. As they neared, the other two buildings in the set became visible, looming over them. The last one of the trio, 5900, was missing its entire top portion in the smoke and fog and Shane couldn't tell if it was the atmosphere or if half of the building were really gone.

They walked down the circular driveway and entered 5700 through what used to be sliding glass doors but were now just a metal shell devoid of glass. Mariana offered to stay outside and keep watch and Shane nodded her approval as the rest of them stepped over the closed frame and tried to avoid the broken shards of glass on the linoleum floor. The silence inside of the building was deafening. The crystal chandelier above them swung back and forth indicating that the tremor from the collapsed Embassy was felt up on the hill.

Shane led them past the concierge desk and around the ornate decorative wall indicating that this building had at one time been particularly luxurious. At the elevators, she opened the door to one of the staircases and listening long enough to determine it was all clear, began to lead them upstairs.

The climb to the twentieth floor was silent, with only heavy breathing after the first few floors and some under-the-breath complaining audible among them. When they finally reached their destination, Shane took a deep breath and opened the stairway door, turning right and leading them down the hall to the last door on the corner.

No one questioned her or commented on the lavishness of the surroundings. It was obvious Shane knew where she was going and at one point in their established sisterhood, all of the women had made a wordless pact of sorts, the kind where they didn't question each other of their old lives and recognized that there wasn't ever a need to discuss the past in this new world. So though they knew this place meant something to Shane and was the reason behind her sudden pale complexion and haunted expression, Bernchal did not.

He watched her, enthralled. She looked like a complete stranger and he couldn't quite place what the difference was. Her eyes, barely visible in the darkened corridor, shone with a light he hadn't seen before and he hardly noticed Julie's quiet voice reading the name of the occupant in front of whose door they now stood.

Milian.

Bernchal looked to Shane and as she felt the knob and turned it with a look of surprise on her face, he finally recognized the foreign expression written all over her.

It was sadness.

They filed in after her and immediately noticed the pictures hanging on the wall, undisturbed. A family- mother, father and young son. A little boy with dark eyes like his mother and a toothless grin that stretched across his whole face. White sand beaches and a man throwing a baby high in the air, the picture snapped at the perfect moment to capture unbridled joy.

Shane walked lifelessly down the corridor and stopped at the entrance to a large living room. Large sofas adorned the open space and save for a thick layer of dust that covered everything inside the apartment, nothing had been touched. No broken glass. No overturned tables or emptied drawers. No broken furniture or ripped out television sets. It was as though the owner had abandoned the place and never looked back. And she had.

Julie had grown quite fond of Shane and considered themselves friends, so she immediately knew where she was and what was happening, as did Bernchal. Joyce and Betzaida however, did not, so they made their way to the kitchen in search of food and supplies to either eat now or take back to the institution. Shilan and Megan found the guest bathroom just past Shane's son's old room and used the remaining water in the toilet bowl to wash their hands and wet a towel to remove some of the black soot from their faces. Bernchal stayed near Shane who remained frozen, stuck to the ground staring at a picture of her son.

He took a step towards her and when he neared he noticed solemnly that she did not tense up as she always did when he got too close.

Her voice, haunting and more despondent than he'd ever heard, crept out and towards him, pulling at his heart before he knew what was happening.

"I haven't been back. Since we left. Since we escaped."

She paused, vaguely aware that he was behind her and hanging on her every word.

"I thought it would be… different, you know?" Shane turned slightly and met his eyes, his concerned and inquiring, hers black as the sky outside.

"I thought they attacked. That's why we left, that's why I took him and ran. But…"

She looked around the apartment, pointed at nothing in particular and continued.

"But it's fine. Everything is perfect. Everything is exactly the same. They never came."

Bernchal knew where she was headed and knew the dangerous road she was about to travel but could do nothing to detour her.

"They never came," she repeated, the anger in her belly rising steadily. "I left for nothing. I took him out of here for *nothing*. If I would have stayed-"

He stopped her, his hands gripping her shoulders before either of them knew what was happening.

"If you would have stayed, things could have been much worse. Just because this place looks untouched doesn't mean no one came, Shane. They came, didn't see anyone and *left*. You saw what it looked like downstairs," he reasoned. "They came…"

She nodded, hearing the words, understanding the logic and trying her best to accept them.

Swallowing hard, she gave herself a little shake, barely felt as his hands still gripped her shoulders. And just as quickly as she'd gone from alpha to distraught, she bounced back, her jaw tightening and her chin pointing upward.

"I'm fine."

He felt her stiffen under his touch and lingered, not breaking their eye contact. She blinked and waited, watching him to see if he'd get the hint and let go.

Faintly, in the back of their minds and in another world they heard Julie's voice asking calmly, "Did anyone hear that?"

The question and any offered answer did not register because the door leading to the terrace blew open and gunshots erupted.

They ducked immediately and scrambled out of the living room and towards the foyer behind the protection of the corridor wall. Shilan and Megan walked out of the bathroom closest to them and onto oncoming bullets, Shilan's body landing at their feet and knocking Megan back to the ground. It was fast and clean- two shots to her forehead and her eyes still open when she hit the floor. Megan scrambled around Shilan's body and crawled towards the front door.

Betzaida screamed and Julie pulled her down at the kitchen doorway, narrowly escaping a shot that tore through the sheet rock wall and hit the freezer door of the fridge. Shane didn't have a chance to say good bye to her apartment or her memories, or grab a picture of her son or late husband. The rain of gunfire began to shatter everything around them as they crawled out, including the picture frames above their heads. Julie pushed Betzaida and Megan forward and they crawled towards the entrance. Bernchal and Shane followed, with Joyce far behind them. Scuffles on the terrace indicated more arrivals and Shane took lead, pulling them out of the apartment and into the hallway.

More glass broke inside of the apartment and they heard Joyce scream as they opened the door to the stairway and began to make their way down to the lobby. Moving dangerously fast, they descended, one by one and floor by floor in a desperate attempt to escape their followers. The heavy door of the stairwell above them burst open, boot clad feet hitting the linoleum a second later and filling the narrow hallways with the thundering sound of footsteps. They turned another corner, another floor behind them and kept moving, down the staircase as fast as they could go.

Bernchal led the race, always faster than each of them, and grabbed Shane's hand to force her speed. Her feet moved faster than she thought possible and somehow, she kept his pace. Julie was a foot or two behind, with Betzaida at her heels. Behind them, Megan tripped and went down, her shoulder banging against the rail and sending her tumbling, head over heels. Militia feet bounded down above her landing, stopping at her sprawled body. Betzaida made eye contact a second before turning to the next landing and Megan nodded, a knowing look passing between them before Betzaida was gone behind the others down another staircase.

Before they got to the next landing, a scuffle and some yelling was followed by a gunshot. The women continued down as though they hadn't heard it but Bernchal paused, his face frozen in horror.

"They shot her!"

"No," whispered Shane, this time ahead of him, yanking at his hand as he stood, stunned.

"Not them..."

Confused, he allowed himself to be led away and they continued forward. At the fifteenth floor, Shane led them out and towards another staircase at the opposite end of the corridor.

"How the fuck did they come in?" whispered Julie, afraid to make noise in the empty hallway.

Shane shrugged and opened the door of the second stairway after checking it for militia. "Sometimes they man buildings and hang out on the balconies."

"Twenty stories up?" asked Bernchal, breathless and incredulously. They followed Shane into the stairwell and looked down at the fifteen stories of steps awaiting them.

"The terraces are connected, two by two. They must have been in the neighbor's apartment and heard us..." she offered with little conviction and she and Bernchal began descending.

Julie, pausing on the landing above them, tried to wrap her head around the events of the past few minutes.

"But who blew up the Embassy?"

Bernchal looked to Shane, who struggled with a response. *Who blew the Embassy? How did they find them? How did they know exactly which apartment to attack? Are they being followed?*

The unasked questions shot back and forth between their eyes. No answers, as usual, because the doors above them on a higher floor burst open and they took off down the stairs again. Shane fell behind Bernchal and when he passed her, he grabbed her wrist again and pulled her to speed up as Betzaida held up the rear.

Bernchal continued forward until they made it to the lobby and as he started to open the staircase door, they heard commotion behind it, immediately shutting it back up as quietly as possible. Shane elbowed his chest, ignored how hard it was, and motioned for them to continue down to the basement. Silently they descended one last floor and there, opened the door cautiously before stepping out. They ran past the laundry room and the parking garage door and emerged on West 259th Street, quickly turning left and making their way down to Riverdale Avenue, where they encountered Mariana ducking low behind an overturned SUV and she joined them as they continued down the hill.

Out of the corner of her eye Julie caught something on the grass as they ran past the property behind Skyview that covered the parking garage and as they neared the old shops on Riverdale Avenue, she realized it was Joyce's lifeless body.

Julie wiped the tear away and followed Shane, Bernchal, Mariana and Betzaida as they ran into the backyard of the SAR Academy and made their way silently down to Broadway to head back home.

Chapter XIV

A month had passed without incident. The institution and its residents were quiet and all surrounding areas were existing in harmony with Shane and the women around her.

An exhaustive search a week after the mayhem caused by the mysterious explosion brought no answers and Shane was no closer to figuring out who blew up the Embassy and who discovered them at Skyview than she had been while it was happening. The only benefit had been their ability to retrace their steps and retrieve Joyce's broken body from the grass below the twentieth floor window. Shilan and Megan however had been lost to them. The building was on lock down and too dangerous to enter to get her body back as well.

Joyce was buried in the Woodlawn Cemetery in the dead of night, with only Shane, Julie and Jolene present. Bernchal had stayed behind to keep an eye on things and comfort some of the women who were unable to say goodbye to Joyce and would never be able to say goodbye to Shilan or Megan.

From the moment the explosion had disrupted his sleep, Bernchal had felt increasingly uneasy. Something was in the air, something foul. He could not put his finger on it and unfortunately did not know all of the women well enough to discern any strange behavior, but he knew in his gut something was off.

He felt within him an unsettling of sorts that was getting worse as the days crept by. He kept himself busy accepting the orders Shane barked, running errands and doing what he was told for the most part. But the feeling was growing, surely and steadily inside of him. Every woman looked suspicious, every scenario was more farfetched than the last. He began to think he was going crazy and could no longer differentiate between reality and paranoia. Whenever he felt himself eyeing the women around him with questioning glares, he had to remind himself that he was only member of the institution not on a menstrual cycle.

Unable to bring his suspicions to Shane without concrete information, he opted instead to stick by her side. He rarely left her alone and when he did, he made sure she was surrounded by the only person he trusted lately- Julie.

Shane in turn, quick to anger and not slight of tongue, made them all aware of how bothered she was by the new entourage and tried her best to escape them at any given opportunity. But because their runs and outings were so well-coordinated, she had no choice but to be accompanied by either Bernchal or Julie everywhere she went.

It was Bernchal attached at the hip this time as they made their way through Wave Hill, looking for ammunition or supplies to take back with them. Since the Embassy explosion, they'd kept their scavengery pretty low-key and the fruit in the college was running low. Wave Hill had at one time maintained the most beautiful lemon trees in New York so they set out in the hopes of bringing back at least some edible lemons, if nothing else.

In truth, Shane was grateful for the distraction. The women had been different since the explosion, since Joyce, Megan and Shilan's deaths. They had lost women before, especially when they were first freed and just starting out on their own. But they'd gone incident-free for over a year and since then, the women had grown closer. Though she'd shied away from bonding with anyone, she felt the loss of her two friends and was thankful for something to keep her mind off of them.

Bernchal tossed a pine cone at her, hitting her in the chest and ripping her out of her sad melancholia.

"What the fuck?"

He ignored her, walked ahead of her some more with his gun in his left hand, and his right hand pulling at the low hanging plants above them.

Wave Hill was immense, over twenty-eight acres of land that had once been meticulously kept and was now running rampant with weeds, bugs and God knew what else. The trees that were once manicured daily and kept in pristine condition are now jutting out of the ground and blocking the sky making a cavernous opening for any who dared enter.

Bernchal pushed a brush of weeds out of the way, making space for Shane to walk through behind him. When she caught up, he cleared his throat and faced forward, giving her his back and asking nonchalantly, "What was he like? Your husband, I mean."

Shane stuttered for a moment, both caught off guard by the question and the sudden onslaught of memories of her dead husband.

"Dixon? He was... I don't know. A good guy, I guess."

"Was he?"

"Yeah," she answered, reminding herself of the attributes she'd tried so hard to forget to ease the pain of his loss. "Yeah. He was. Kind. Mild-mannered."

"I think those are the exact words used to describe Clark Kent. Are you Superman's widow?" he joked.

She giggled quietly, realizing that was the first time she'd thought of her late husband and not cried.

"Widow..." he repeated to himself. Facing her, Bernchal smiled crookedly. "That sounds weird, don't you think? Widow. It kinda implies old age."

"So now you're calling me old?" she asked, eyebrows raised.

"Listen, I don't know your real age. You could be a really hot ninety-year old."

Barely ignoring the compliment, Shane replied matter-of-factly. "I'm 35."

"Sure."

"Younger than you," she pointed out, smirking.

"You don't know how old I am."

She stared at him with a mischievous gleam in her eye. "Did you think I would let you in and not know everything about you? You're 41."

Bernchal shook his head and muttered under his breath, "Damn. Bitches be crazy."

"Watch your mouth."

He laughed heartily. "Okay, so 35, huh?"

"Yup."

"Interesting."

They continued forward, lifting dead plants off the ground, picking old fruit long past their expiration dates. The only sound heard was the crackling of dead leaves under their footsteps for several minutes.

Finally, Bernchal broke the silence again.

"Something's been bugging me since the Embassy, Shane."

"What?" she asked, watching him as they moved; his eyes everywhere without looking worried, his arms flexed and weapon ready without looking tense. The ease with which he existed flummoxed her and she envied him that, envied that he could walk through the new world seemingly without a care while she felt as though every day the weight of the planet on her shoulders got heavier and heavier.

"What was the point of Mariana keeping watch if she didn't warn us?"

Shane looked at the ground as she walked behind him and answered, matter-of-factly.

"She says they were already inside. That no one approached while she waited."

"You asked her?"

She heard the change in his voice. From inquiring to skeptical. The tiny hairs on the back of her neck stood up. Something was off and he felt it, too.

"I did. She said she was alone."

After a long, contemplative pause, Shane asked quietly, "Why?"

Bernchal surprised her by swiveling suddenly and appearing inches from her face as she stopped short.

"I don't know yet, Shane."

She was silent as they stood toe to toe, both holding their weapons and eyeing each other, curiously. Shane waited and suddenly he spoke again, his voice hushed, his eyes questioning.

"You said they didn't kill Megan. How do you know?"

Shane broke eye contact and stepped around him, her feet landing on the ground and the sound shattering the short-lived silence.

"I know," she whispered as she walked forward.

Behind her, he caught up quickly and insisted, "How?"

Realizing immediately that he wasn't going to let this one go, Shame sighed heavily and looking up as they walked forward, finally met his inquiring eyes.

"We made a deal. When we first made the school a home, we all made a deal. No going back. No holding out torture from the ones that want to find us, stop us. If it looks bad..."

She paused and offered a sad smile before continuing. "If it looks bad, then we make the choice."

He held her gaze, pondering her words.

"The choice?"

"Yes. It's our choice. Only when it's hopeless. Only when there's nothing else. But it's *our* choice."

"But what about-"

"Her daughter?" she interrupted, knowingly. Another smile, sadder than the first. "We'll still look for her. We won't stop because she's gone. But Megan knew what would happen if they took her. There's only two options for any woman taken on the street. Death. Or something much, much worse."

He weighed her words for a moment, never taking his eyes off of her as they walked. Finally, he started, "What if they-"

But she knew what he was asking and beat him to the punch, laying to rest any fairytale notions of naiveté.

"No. You don't know, Steve, and that's okay. It's not your story," she added with a sympathetic little laugh. "But, no. There's no other way. Death or Hell. So we make a choice. For us. Megan made her choice."

He nodded and finally looked away, thoroughly tormented. That a woman, searching for her kidnapped child, would have to choose between death or God knew what else upon capture, was mindboggling. Even having to consider something like that meant that the world he had once known was truly and officially never coming back.

Taking a breath, he turned to face her again, surprised to see her watching him.

"Would *you*?"

Almost as though she'd known that would be his question, she shrugged, looking back down at the the ground and listening to the sound their boots made as they walked.

"I'm not much for ending things before they're through. I don't think I would but... I don't know. Who's to say, right?"

He nodded and watched her, wondering what exactly he would do with himself if she were ever placed in such a scenario and had to make her own choice, until he saw the conversation leave her. Shane was so expressive that even her desire to change the subject was visibly notable and as she sniffled, raised her chin and began to walk with a little more determination in her step, Bernchal knew right away she was done with that line of questioning and eager to discuss something else.

Obliging, he asked, "So, what did you do before the world was shot to shit?"

Alongside him, Shane did a 360 degree turn to watch their backs and replied quickly, "I was a lawyer."

He stopped suddenly and faced her. "Shut up."

Confused, Shane looked around, her gun raised in front of her. "What?"

"You?" Bernchal asked incredulously.

"Yes."

"Seriously?"

Annoyed, she blurted, "Yes! What's the big deal?"

He started walking again, shaking his head. Shrugging, he proceeded a few steps in front of her, downplaying his reaction. "Nothing. Nothing. I just... Just thought you were maybe a cop or something. Never figured you for the desk type."

"Why not?"

He stopped again and faced her, a sardonic smile on his handsome face.

"'Why not?' she asks while holding an assault rifle? Really?"

Shane hid a smile and turned away, passing him and moving forward. "Point taken."

"So, where'd you learn to shoot, Rambo?"

Since his arrival, Bernchal had dug deeper and deeper for information from her about her past post-disaster. She handed him little morsels of details here and there but for the most part, kept the ugliness to herself. So as usual, she responded with a short and sweet reply.

"I didn't. I picked up a gun and shot. If I didn't hit my target, I shot again. And again and again until I did hit the target."

"Is that why they recruited you?"

She tamed her sudden anger. *He doesn't know,* she reminded herself. *His questions are innocent because he doesn't know.*

"I wasn't recruited, Commander. I was enslaved. Big difference."

"You're smart, Shane. Crafty. Why didn't you escape?"

She resisted the urge to fire back and instead answered honestly, taking great care to rein in the venom in her tongue.

"My son was taken from me. I walk away and I never see him again. Escape was not an option; not without my son."

Bernchal nodded, clumsily tripped over a fallen branch and steadied himself. After a second, he prodded on, taking notice that she was actually answering his questions so he may as well keep asking them.

"When was the last time you spoke to anyone about your kids? Had any…"

She finished his sentence devoid of any emotion. "Proof they're alive?"

He hesitated and immediately regretted asking. Suddenly, the various brown and yellow leaves still hanging on to dear life from the trees were the most interesting things on the planet.

Sensing his discomfort, Shane addressed him, softer.

"It's okay. There's nothing wrong with that question. It's been ten months since we've had any real proof of life."

He whistled. "How do you-"

"He's alive," she interrupted, complete certainty in her voice. Bernchal said nothing in response, just nodded in feigned agreement, so she spoke up and answered his unasked questions.

"It's irrational. I know it is." Shane scoffed and shook her head at her own naivete. "I know that's what you're thinking. We're dealing with murderers and savages and here I am with no solid evidence, yet totally convinced my son is still alive. It is stupid. But... I *know* he's alive. I know he is."

At this point, he was genuinely enthralled, and was no longer staring at the ground in an awkward attempt to avoid eye contact and was instead turned, facing her. His dominant hand holding the weapon had fallen to his side and he was mesmerized by the sudden change in her voice- from playful to forlorn to vacant to hopeful all in one fluid motion.

"How?"

She hesitated for a moment; only for a moment. And then the words spilled out of her as though she had been waiting patiently for a reason to release them.

"I've seen what hell looks like," she said hurriedly, with a sad smile on her face. "If he were gone…"

She paused and started over. "When I thought he was gone- I saw what that looked like. I've seen it. And I wouldn't survive it again. I barely survived it the first time. But I'm ...alive. I'm still here, breathing, functioning. So... then so is he."

He stared at her with wide-eyed wonder and before he could respond, she spoke again, this time her voice so low he could barely hear her.

"That's the only thing that makes sense right now. In this whole fucked up horror movie of a world, that's the only thing that makes any sense to me right now…"

"Then he's alive," Bernchal replied, assuredly. "He's alive."

Chapter XV

Bernchal rounded the corner of the main lobby and walked into Julie and Wendalyn in deep conversation. They looked up at him, annoyed at the intrusion.

"Where's the she-devil?" he asked nonchalantly.

Of all of the women in the institution besides Shane, Julie was the best at ignoring him. She had it down to an art and had perfected the side glances thrown his way over time. But like a connoisseur, he had studied her looks and knew them to a tee. No matter the scenario, he could decipher Julie's mood and what kind of shade she was going to throw his way.

This time, it was irritation. Like an older sister trying to hang out with friends only to be constantly bombarded by the frustrations that come with babysitting a little brother, Julie rolled her hazel eyes upward and flared her nostrils. The shake of her head sent her strawberry blonde curls bounding back and forth and she fluttered her eyelids for what seemed like an eternity before replying, doing nothing to mask the disdain in her voice.

"She's in her room."

Without so much as a second glance, Julie returned to her conversation with Wendalyn as though Bernchal had disappeared as quickly as he had materialized.

He too, had mastered the art of ignoring some of the women and with Julie, it was simple. They spoke as little as possible and stayed out of each other's way. But truth be told, he liked her. She was tougher than she seemed, smarter than she let on, and ferociously loyal to Shane. Several close calls had her proving her worth time and again and Bernchal smirked as he turned and headed back into the main hallway towards Shane's room. Julie's demeanor towards him didn't dissuade him from making himself comfortable and he knew her treatment was more about his anatomy than it was about his personality.

He got to Shane's room and peeked in. She was sitting on the floor cross-legged, a large map sprawled out in front of her. Her dark brown hair was still wet from a shower and draped over her shoulders, droplets of water landing on the unfolded map.

Bernchal watched her for a moment as she squeezed her eyes shut tight and pushed her head back, stretching her neck. She made a soft moaning sound as she rolled her head back and forth, left and right, easing the tension from her neck and spine. His eyes traced the fabric of her t-shirt and how it fell against her and he noticed immediately she was bra-less. Her shorts, of the short and tight college coed variety, stopped high on her thighs and her legs folded before her seemed to go on for days.

He stared a moment longer, enjoying the view, and finally knocked on the open door, startling her. Shane glanced up and stiffened immediately.

Bernchal smiled widely and walked into her room without waiting for an invitation.

"What up, el capitán? I overheard some of your girls talking about moving out to intercept some intel."

She nodded knowingly. "Mariana wants another run out by the Cloisters. Swears she heard activity."

Bernchal felt the familiar stirrings of paranoia creep into him.

"Mariana, huh?"

She did not pick up on the subtlety behind his question and instead, cocked her head to the right and asked, "You're not going with them?"

"Trying to get rid of me so soon, Shane?"

She pursed her lips and turned away from him, looking back down to the map and replying, "Always."

He walked further into the room and stood above her and the map, purposely putting her below his line of sight.

"I see through you, you know. Keep using those walls to mask your true feelings for me."

"What true feelings would those be- disgust? Frustration? Intolerance? Pure hatred?"

He chuckled and shook his head. "Nobody believes these lies; least of all you."

She didn't reply so he squatted in front of her and pointed to the map.

"I see you've wisened up and implemented some of my ideas," he mentioned, referring to his suggestion that they begin to steer far from Broadway and the outlying streets and instead use the West Side Highway when venturing into Manhattan. She had, as with all things, fought him at first but his logic was too sound to protest: their enemies had begun to anticipate their moves. The element of surprise could only continue working for them if they changed things up.

"While I hate to boost that ever-expanding ego of yours, yes, some of your ideas were worth taking a look at."

After almost a year together trying to survive, he had come to know her facial expressions quite well and Shane was now trying to contain a smile that was slowly peeking throwing the almost permanent scowl she kept plastered on her face.

"And implementing, of course. Go ahead. You can admit it."

She continued fighting the smile and ignored his prodding.

He looked again to the map and noticed the size of the property they were to investigate.

"That's tomorrow's plan, right? Who's making the first run?"

"Same group," she offered without looking up at him. Her hands were gripping a pencil tightly and tracing a line perfectly adjacent to the Hudson River to plan their route.

Bernchal figured she had already taken his advice on a few occasions and would press his luck once more.

"I'd advise against that," he replied, suddenly serious. "This is a new route. It's unstudied."

She stopped mid-trace and looked up at him, her almond-shaped eyes questioning.

"It was *your* idea to use this route."

"Yes, but things have changed."

"What things?" A suspicious smile crept on her generous mouth and she waited patiently for the joke, pun or corny one-liner she had come to expect from him during their chats.

But Bernchal remained stoic and responded seriously. "Things. We can't afford to be blindsided again."

Sensing he was more concerned than he let on, Shane pushed for more from him.

"What do you mean 'again'?"

He shrugged his shoulders and hesitated for a moment, his mouth open to speak but nothing coming out. She waited and he finally shook his head, clearing his thoughts and answered her.

"The Embassy. That was reckless. You and I both know that. We had no business running out there like that investigating some explosion that didn't even affect us. We were unprepared."

For the first time he was exhibiting some vulnerability and Shane was taken aback. She had for all of the time he'd been at the institution, taken him for a johnny-come-lately. Though he'd proven his worth and his expertise in all things military and war-related, Bernchal nonetheless gave off an air of complacency. As though he didn't care enough to really want it, but stuck around for the shelter and food. He pulled his weight, certainly, but Shane had always suspected that he might be biding his time and would abandon them the moment he had a better opportunity.

Now, seeing the crease of his brow and the worry written all over his face; hearing his tone of voice change from light to heavy and listening to him using the word 'we' where a couple of months ago only a 'you crazy bitches' had been used, Shane realized he might actually be more invested than she'd originally suspected.

"It *was* reckless. Yes. But we had to see what happened."

"At the cost of three girls?"

"Women," she corrected him.

He adjusted his statement, his voice hushed. "Women…"

Sensing his concern, Shane countered. "But we lived to see another day."

"Yeah, but there's gotta be more to it than that. How will we get anywhere if all we're doing is surviving? We've got to hit 'em where it hurts. Beat them at their own game."

"That requires more manpower than we have."

"First of all, its woman-power. Secondly, are you freaking kidding me? We have an army here. We just have to work out some kinks. Our greatest weapon is our numbers and the element of surprise. They don't know where we are, where we're holed up or when we're coming. We have to use that to our advantage. If you know where they're going next-"

"We'll know what to hit," she finished.

He was right.

"Exactly. Strategy is about more than just surviving. It's a game of battleship. You learn to anticipate, then you win the war."

His eyes lit up in excitement and Shane couldn't help but smile. He looked like a kid planning an imaginary game of interstellar battle complete with the Star Wars light sabers and Jedi power.

She softened a bit and conceded. "So what do you recommend?"

"A solid group of four to recon. You, me and two others. One car, extra ammo. You and me walk the path with two following suit. In and out."

She eyed him for a moment, considering and then pointed to the map.

"Wouldn't some extra firepower be worth it to cover these corners here and here?"

He leaned over, studying the map. Close to her, he responded.

"Spoken like a true leader. That would work. But extra bodies only to maintain the perimeter while we move in. Absolutely no motor running once we're inside."

Shane nodded absentmindedly and continued staring at the map envisioning the area surrounding their routes and trying to recollect her brief time making her way back and forth with Silas those early days after fleeing Riverdale.

"Mmm hmmm…"

Bernchal looked up at her, watching her deep in thought. She felt his gaze on her and lifted her eyes, meeting his. His face was close enough to hers that she could feel the heat from his breath on her cheeks. She saw a quick flash in the yellow of his irises before he broke contact, her eyes still locked as his glanced quickly at her chest. She followed his gaze and realized that from his vantage point above her he could see clear down her oversized t-shirt as it hung loosely while she was hunched over the map.

After a solid five seconds, Bernchal nonchalantly trailed his eyes back to the map, smoothly and expertly making the transition from intense to business as usual without breaking his stride, leaving her silently stunned.

"When do you want to take off?"

"Huh?"

"When do we go? Morning?"

"Oh," she managed, stuttering. *What the hell?* she asked herself, wondering why she was suddenly so affected by him.

"Um, yeah. Early. Any ideas on the two accompanying or the two patrolling?" she attempted for the sake of her own sanity to keep things professional, or at the very least, civil.

"That's your call, chief. I'm just a lowly foot soldier in your war."

"A lowly foot soldier with an opinion on everything," she added.

He smiled at her and watched her squirm. "A wise and experienced foot soldier, then? I'll accept that."

Ignoring him, Shane started to roll up the map, expecting Bernchal to take the hint and rise to leave. But he stayed squatting next to her and when she looked up at him, she caught him staring at her chest again.

For almost three years, Shane's only experience with men had been one of indescribable fear. She had fought and survived but at the root of her survival had been utter fear of the opposite sex. Men had created the disaster that had occurred; men had raped and pillaged and destroyed everything they had come into contact with since; and men were the original creators of the misogyny that had led them into disaster in the first place. She'd had a good man, but he had been killed, along with so many others. And though she knew now, after long deliberation, that Bernchal was truly one of the good guys, she nonetheless felt the same indescribable fear whenever he came too close to her. Now that he had officially acknowledged her as a woman and more than just the mean sexless bitch that bossed him around, that old familiar sensation crept into her and her first and immediate instinct was to nip it in the bud.

Flustered, Shane quickly placed her hand against the neck of the t-shirt, pushing it back against her. His eyes shot up and met hers and a smirk appeared on his lips slowly. She knew him well enough by now to know he wasn't threatening her, but was purposely making her uncomfortable.

Eyes still locked, he spoke up as he unfolded his long legs and rose from the floor with ease.

"Lady chef made muffins. You coming?"

Shane uncrossed her legs and stood up, bending over to stuff the map into a sphere container that had been resting on the floor behind her.

"No. I'm gonna check on some more routes."

"All work and no play make Shane a dull dictator," he teased.

She glanced over at him long enough to offer an eye roll before giving him her back, returning the map to her desk while looking for another one among the pile.

Realizing she was done with the playful banter, Bernchal moved to the door but before leaving, turned back to her.

"Hey, Shane?"

She looked back up at him and met his gaze.

After a pause, he offered, "Keep your eyes on your team."

"Excuse me?"

"Keep your eyes on your team," he repeated, offering nothing else to elaborate.

She held his gaze and shook her head, quizzically. "Meaning…?"

"Meaning you never know who has a different agenda than you."

After a moment of hesitation wherein Shane tried to decipher his statement, she replied.

"We all have the same agenda- getting our kids back."

"It may just appear that way."

She tried to read the expression on his face but got nothing back. Again, she felt the same fear creep into her veins and this time, found herself getting angry. Was *she* becoming complacent, and not seeing the flashing neon "Danger' sign in front of her face? Was Bernchal threatening her? Or was he simply trying to tell her something and she was missing it, once again fearful of a man simply because other men had been so cruel?

"Commander, any one of these women would die for their kids."

"You said it, Shane. *Their* kids. I'm not arguing that. But would they die for you or your kid?"

When she didn't reply, he shrugged his shoulders and moved further through the doorway.

"Just... Keep safe is all I'm saying."

She watched him but said nothing.

He lingered a moment longer, seemingly waiting for a response, so she nodded her head. Satisfied, he gave her a quick smile and disappeared down the darkened hallway, leaving her to her thoughts.

Chapter XVI

Shane was the last one to hear the sound, the unmistakable 'click.' They were on the recon run that she and Bernchal had discussed the evening prior and they had brought with them Mariana and Jolene. Lately every location they made it to had either been wiped clean or was too dangerous to enter. They had opted for the northeast side of Fort Tryon Park at Mariana's urging to investigate the Cloisters and were slowly making their way through the overgrown grass and toppled trees.

The weather was picking up. Autumn was quickly approaching again and they were not dressed for the sudden onslaught of frigid air surrounding them that deep into the woods of the park.

The four of them had entered together but split slightly to cover more ground. Shane was close to Jolene throughout and stayed at her three o'clock, knowing Bernchal was manning the other side and had his eye on things. Mariana had drifted off again and everything around them was quiet. The woods surrounding them were so dense the interior blocked all the sunlight and created a canopy for them as they walked. Without the brutal assault from the ferocious wind, the trees still maintained the leaves, even the ones that were all but dead, so the ground below them was nothing but grass and dirt. It muffled their footsteps and allowed them to make it most of the way through with nary a sound.

A twig crackled to the far right and Shane, Jolene and Bernchal froze in place. Mariana reappeared in between some trees and pressed forward, her weapon in front of her. The three of them continued moving again and Shane noticed that Bernchal had retrieved his weapon in a split second and was now returning it to its holster.

One perimeter search later, they were relaxed, walking the edge of the property line once more at Shane's suggestion to evaluate the distance between the park and the neighboring Cloisters. This time, they went further inside, investigating the best route to cut through the woods and avoid the highway outright. Jolene led the group,

Shane followed behind and Bernchal a couple of steps behind her, with Mariana bringing up the rear.

Out of the woods and into a clearing they hadn't maneuvered through in their first search, Shane was a few paces behind Jolene, listening to her prattle on and on about her love of Winter. She was unconsciously focused on the crunching sound the dead leaves made under their footsteps, leaves that appeared suddenly though they were not under any trees. She stopped walking and though she heard Jolene's voice in a far off place, she glanced up at the sky, wondering if the wind could have carried the dead leaves so far to cover such an open area of grass.

Behind her she felt Bernchal stop short, his brow furrowed in concentration as he suddenly tensed up.

"What is it?" she asked him, annoyed for no particular reason.

She turned to face him confused, and watched as he spoke tenderly to Jolene.

"Don't move…"

She was mid-sentence, really, ready to offer a witty yet subtly insulting reason for his sudden concern. But he didn't give her the chance. By that point, Bernchal had heard the 'click,' as had Jolene. Shane had not and instead watched Bernchal's alarm-stricken expression with curiosity.

"Don't move…" he whispered, but Shane barely heard him and she wondered how Jolene would.

She turned towards her friend and in a split second, answered her own question.

All at once, she read the look of horror on Jolene's face, one that immediately changed to resignation when the foot she had midair landed softly on the hard ground below her. And as the IED released from the ground beneath the cover of the leaves and spun upward, Jolene's eyes connected with Shane's and finally, she understood.

Bernchal dove, wrapping his arm around Shane's chest and roughly pulled her down with him.

To the outside world, the explosion was muffled by the dense trees surrounding the park but in such close proximity to it, the sound was deafening to them. Shane tried to look up from the floor underneath the protective cover of Bernchal's body as he shielded her from the pieces of Jolene's remains that rained down on them like a special effects horror show.

The odor of charred human skin filled her nostrils and she choked back a gag. It was powerful and filled up her lungs. It combined with the smell of land, the dirt and soil beneath their feet with its distinctive scent; and covered the air immediately around them like a blanket.

There was no time to recover, no time to get her bearings. Bernchal was up, weapon out, hands motioning for her to follow.

"We have to go. They'll have heard the explosion. They'll be coming to investigate."

"Jolene…"

He was breathless, yanking at her hands, trying to get her to stand up. "Shane, we have to move *now*."

Shane was frozen on the hard ground, her eyes glued to where Jolene had stood only seconds before.

"Jolene…"

"Shane!"

She snapped out of it, meeting his eyes as he squatted in front of her, his hands on her elbow pulling at her.

"We have to move, *now*."

She shook her head violently. She knew what had happened, yet could not comprehend what it meant. All she could think of was bringing Jolene home.

"No," she whispered, choking up. "She needs help. We have to help her…"

Bernchal put his hands around her ribcage and in one motion, pulled her to a standing position, his lips close to her ear as he whispered, "It is a minefield, Shane. We have to leave. Now."

She shook her head and looked at him as though he just didn't understand. "I have to clean this up so no one else will trip."

She tried to walk back towards where Jolene had stood but he pulled her back roughly and she slammed against his hard chest.

"Listen to me! You'll kill yourself."

Still protesting, Shane shook her head like a spoiled child. "No. She was-"

"She is dead!" he yelled franticly, immediately controlling his voice and looking around for militia. Behind him, Mariana wordlessly bounced back and forth, her eyes darting around impatiently in search of an escape route while Bernchal tried to get Shane to leave Jolene behind.

"Look, I'm sorry. Okay? But *you* are still alive and so is your son. You die now and he has no one. Live another day and you can get him back."

Like a lightbulb going off, Shane's eyes finally focused on Bernchal's and she obliged. Doing as she was told, she reached her hand out and grabbed a hold of his extended one and allowed him to guide her back through the woods and towards their vehicle.

They drove back in silence and at the institution, Shane disappeared silently as Bernchal went in search of the shower to wash off the muck of the day's tragedy.

A couple of hours later, she was seated on the floor with her knees to her chest, her back against the foot of her bed. At her feet was a box with some of Jolene's things; pictures of her son, knickknacks and various other items she'd acquired since they'd found the college and created a life there.

Bernchal's knock on her open door surprised her and she looked up at him. He didn't wait to be invited in, as usual, and walked over to her. He pulled out the lawn chair at her desk and turned it around, straddling it. Placing his elbows on his knees, he faced her.

"Get some sleep."

"What?"

"You look exhausted."

She scoffed. "Thanks."

"Seriously," he pressed, genuinely concerned. "You need to sleep."

"I'll sleep when we're successful."

Bernchal shook his head, irritated at her stubbornness. Her behavior at the site of the explosion had been understandable, but since returning she'd been unstoppable and inexplicably fired up. He heard her through the hallways of the institution, barking demands and tearing Mariana's head off for disappearing in the woods; and now she appeared drained and out of it- like a kid crashing after coming off of a sugar high. He had seen that type of behavior during service from more than a few soldiers who feared the things that appeared in the dark more than they did what was really out there.

"You can't sleepwalk through life or death situations."

"I don't have much choice," she replied quietly. As she rubbed her eyes, attempting in vain to clear the exhaustion from her face, she took a deep and troubled breath. He expected her to blow him off but instead she relented, pinched the bridge of her nose and leaned back against the footboard.

"Every day we come back empty-handed stacks the odds of ever finding them more and more against us."

He welcomed her uncharacteristically candid reply. "Yes, but you cannot go out there without the proper training."

"How am I supposed to train everyone?" she asked, her questioning eyes meeting his. "How am I supposed to look for all these kids and protect their moms at the same time? I didn't even know what that was! I've never seen a goddamn minefield before. I only even heard of IED's from the movies..."

For the first time, he saw the worry in her face and resisted the urge to make a lighthearted joke to alleviate the heavy feeling hanging over them.

"You can't protect everyone."

"I have to."

"Shane..."

"If I'd taken better care today-"

"No," he interrupted her. "No, that's not your fault. You can't take that on. It's not your fault she's dead."

She held his gaze for a moment and then broke it abruptly, looking away to the far side of the room. Outside, women walked around in the hallway, quietly keeping busy, while in there, it felt as though the entirety of the world's dire situation was crashing down on her shoulders.

She turned back to Bernchal and spoke, her voice barely above a whisper.

"Jolene."

"What?"

"Her name. Her name was Jolene. Like the song."

She scoffed at a memory and continued. "You know that egotistical bitch used to sing that song every day? Cooking, showering, whatever. All day every day. Got to be that half of us wanted to murder her and the other half could sing that song backward and forward."

"You were close?" he asked in the hopes to keep her talking and out of the funk into which he'd seen too many soldiers fall.

"As close as these times would allow. No one's 100%. How close can you be when you can't even reveal all of yourself anymore?"

"But you bonded?"

"Bonded?" She snorted, derisively. "How? This world we're living in has pretty much eliminated any type of life span. Nowadays, you're lucky to even learn someone's name before you watch them die in front of you. No. There's no bonding here. We haven't made any attachments. And if you're smart, you won't either."

After a moment of hesitation, she spoke again, her voice significantly less angry.

"I know you question our intentions."

He shook his head and started to protest.

"I don't-"

Shane interrupted him with a sardonic smile, her eyes revealing the sorrow behind them.

"You do. You do. You question every move we make, every decision we make. As though we're the one's looking for trouble."

He hesitated and finally conjuring a decent response, answered her.

"I just... I guess I just don't understand this need to chase after them."

She nodded understandably. Satisfied that he was done, Shane locked eyes with him and spoke, her voice steady and measured.

"She had a thirteen-year old. Jolene did. He was one of the few older ones. So they thought it... 'interesting subject matter,' I think they called it. Because he wasn't a baby, you see. And they experimented on her. Sodomized her with all sorts of gadgets while her son watched, just to gather some data. I could hear her screams from down the hall where they kept us. I watched that kid slowly die seeing her suffer."

She paused, whether for dramatic effect or to gather her thoughts. In either case, Bernchal appreciated the break and finally released the breath he had been holding.

And just like that, she started again to speak, looking him in his eyes with a new and revived gleam in hers.

"That's what were dealing with here, Commander. Not humanity. I can't even call them animals because they're a lower form. Any normal situation and I'd be okay just getting my son back, getting all of our kids back and moving on. I'd be okay with that. But they won't be. And they're the ones that started this war, they opened these floodgates. And now they will reap what they have sown. They will suffer and they will pay for their sins. So please don't expect remorse from me when I gun them down. You'll be sourly disappointed. Because they deserve every damn bullet that's coming their way."

Chapter XVII

Shane leaned against the flag pole, bent at the waist and fumbling with the laces of her boots. Bernchal was having another go around the track through the deep snow and she was biding her time, catching a breather and waiting for him to finish his lap. He had been showing her some new workout routines, ones reserved solely for Navy SEALS and other people insane enough to attempt them. Shane was exhausted and beaten to the ground but the competitor inside of her didn't allow for surrender, especially not in front of him since he'd likely use it as an excuse to badger her for the rest of time; so she pretended to re-tie her shoelace and gave herself a couple of minutes to rest.

The flag above her, tattered and torn, colors faded from the elements, was flying in the severe wind. She pulled the zipper of her parka higher, covering her mouth and chin from the biting cold and looked up.

Somehow it still stood. They flew it half-mast if for no other reason than to avoid it behind spotted from a distance. But really it was in reverence of what it once represented and what they all hoped it would represent again.

The sound the flag made every time the wind whipped around and changed direction was familiar to Shane and she closed her eyes and leaned her head back, allowing her recollection to transfer her back to that summer she and her husband had vacationed in Costa Rica, before Silas had been born. The *flap flap* it made reminded her of the waves hitting the black sand beach of Guanacaste, where they had lain on lounge chairs for hours, sipping fruity drinks offered by the resort staff and dozing off.

Flap flap. They were in the water, her legs wrapped around his waist and arms extended, letting the motion of the tide move them back and forth. He held her and bounced with each passing wave, watching her relish the blinding sunlight like an escaped convict seeing the ocean for the first time.

Flap flap. Content to just groove with the movement of the water surrounding them, they had remained there for what felt like eternity.

"Flying away?"

Shane opened her eyes and turned to face Bernchal who was behind her, out of breath and watching her curiously. She looked down and noticed that her arms were extended as if preparing for flight and she quickly lowered them to her side.

With no discernible explanation available, she just shrugged and jogged away from him.

With his interest aroused, Bernchal sprinted to catch up to her. She had had an expression on her face he had not yet seen before, beautifully peculiar, as though she were thinking of something peaceful. And peace was such a rare commodity nowadays, he wanted to know more.

"Hey! What was all of that?"

"What?" she replied absentmindedly, feigning ignorance. She was embarrassed to be caught, and not for the first time, by him mid-daydream.

Somehow, he was able to regulate his breathing while they jogged so his words came out smooth and steady as he asked, "Back there. Were you dreaming?"

Shane could not ignore him. He was too much of a pest to leave anything alone, so she relented and with her own breathing now labored mid-run, she answered choppily.

"Daydreaming. Problem?"

"No," he offered. "You're entitled. I daydream all the time. Never that I'm gonna fly off like a unicorn, but I still daydream."

She ran on with him almost beside her. There was nothing to say at that point so they continued in silence for another lap around the track until they reached the same flag pole again. Shane slowed to a stop and Bernchal came up behind her, waiting for her to speak her mind.

Looking up at the top of the flag pole, Shane commented aloud, "I can't believe that all of this is going to be someone else's history."

"A new history," he replied, now next to her. "This flag might end up in a museum one day."

Shane glanced around the empty track, suddenly aware of what a different world it had become in so short a time. Strands of hair blew around her face and she brushed them away, annoyed.

"I wonder what it'll be like for kids in the future, if there are any. Reading about now, I mean. How everything went down."

Bernchal sneered at nothing in particular. "They'll probably react the same way we did when we read history books about slavery, the slaughtering of Native Americans, the Holocaust, civil rights. They'll be shocked, indignant. Embarrassed even. That we went from civilized to this so quickly."

Shane pursed her lips and tore her eyes away from the flag and towards Bernchal. He watched her and she opened her mouth to speak, her voice sad and forlorn.

"Can we really say we were civilized, though? Modernized, yes. Had all the trappings of a first world, futuristic society, but I wouldn't even call this country civilized. We went from Jim Crow laws against black people to practically the same shit against gay people. Civil rights systematically stripped from women by Republicans. 'Stand Your Ground' laws that executed teenagers and acquitted murderers. And a media frenzy that stirred up everything for ratings. Reality TV, internet facts that raised our kids for us. People who couldn't hold a conversation without being glued to their cell phones. All we did was prove that the only thing this country hated more than a black man was a woman. Civilized? No," she added, shaking her head and smiling ironically as she answered her own question. "We may have had our moments of peace and beauty and love. But really, what was truly civilized about our world then?"

Bernchal considered her words for a moment but before he could respond, she continued.

"There was this movie, a billion years ago, one of my favorites. *Begin Again.*"

"Never heard of it."

"Kiera Knightley. Mark Ruffalo."

"Who?"

"The Hulk."

"Oh, that guy! Okay."

Shaking her head, she looked again at the flag and seemed lost in its waving as she spoke.

"Anyway, this film had literally one of the greatest soundtracks ever. And in it was this one song, with this one ridiculously ambiguous and amazing line: '*Are we all lost stars trying to light up the dark?* '"

Bernchal growled, "What the hell does that mean?"

Tearing her eyes away from the flag, Shane looked at him and smiled.

"Hell if I know. I always thought it meant that all of us, we're all just these random, wandering souls clumped together in the galaxy, sort of surviving together."

He kicked at a patch of snow that didn't penetrate the ant hill on which it had rested and questioned, "Just surviving?"

With a look of resignation, Shane shrugged. "What else is there? Surviving is all there is now."

He shook his head, suddenly angered. He refused to believe that staying alive when all of his men had perished; that his finding the institution and the women and Shane and now joining a quest to rescue their children was nothing more than just going through the motions of life until death came knocking.

"Then what's the point? To spend the first half of your life sleepwalking though monotony and keeping your head down, and the second half of it trying to survive? Rolling the dice everytime you open your eyes in the morning?"

"What *is* the point, then?" she asked. "It can't be to do more than make it another day. Not anymore."

Bernchal looked back up at the flag, shielding his eyes from the sun, and rejected her answer.

"No. This can't be it. This can't be as good as it gets."

Softly, she retorted with, "Maybe it is. Maybe this is our hell on earth."

He turned away from the flag and looked at her again, this time his face so close to hers that the clouds of breath they released intertwined in the air before disappearing.

"If it is, it can't be any worse than the kids. You can't tell me we didn't at least get a few good years out of it. Some good times. Laughs. Friends. Adventures. Chaos. Trouble. Great sex," he added with a twinkle in his eyes that made her cheeks flush.

"But those kids? *Your* kids? What will they remember? The ones that survive- your son- what will they remember? Only this. Ask me, we're the lucky ones."

Shane mulled over his words as he continued to stare into her eyes. Increasingly uncomfortable, she broke the stare and stepped around him, back to the track, only this time at a slower pace. Bernchal followed and together they walked another lap around the track.

"It was like Soylent Green up in here, you know that?" she asked him. "Remember that flick? They had people rioting for food on the streets like animals. I think they rather enjoyed it. Watching us, like we were cattle, lined up waiting for a handout. Feeding into their perception of anyone beneath them. And you had the riots, the chaos. Those that perpetuate the very stereotypes assigned to us. It was... *That* was uncivilized."

He watched the perimeter of the fence surrounding the track as they walked on.

"Civility was never this country's strong suit."

She continued, fired up from remembering.

"You know who I found the funniest? The rich white women. The snobs. They were second in line behind only rich white men. Saw themselves as untouchable. Watched everything unfold from the safety of their Manhattan brownstones, behind their Prada shades, thinking it couldn't possibly affect them because of their status, their money. Well, guess what? No money in the world could separate them from us when the only deciding factor between life or death is what's between your legs. In that scenario, we all owned the same plumbing. Some of us just have cleaner pipes than others…"

He snickered and turned to look at her as they walked.

"How did they keep you in line?"

Shane shrugged off his question and watched her feet as they moved along the track.

"Seems to me you're unmanageable."

She shot her head up and looked at him, irritated. "Excuse me?"

"What?" he asked, genuinely surprised by her response. "What'd I say?"

Disbelievingly, Shane repeated, "Unmanageable? As in difficult to keep in line?"

He heard the resonance and back-peddled.

"Whoa! Let me reiterate."

"Please do."

"Unmanageable as in uncontrollable."

Shane raised her eyebrows and faced forward again as they walked.

"Not much better."

He threw his hands up in the air and conceded.

"Jesus. Okay, you're gonna make me dig deep? Fine. I'm saying you don't seem the type to be controlled, or kept down. Or managed. It seems like you are kind of… untameable."

After a long pause wherein they continued their walk in silence, Shane nodded and replied.

"While it seems you're complimenting me, you should know it feels like you're comparing me to a fucking horse."

Bernchal stifled a chuckle and nudged her with his elbow.

"But you admit there's a compliment somewhere in there, right? Good."

"Okay," she answered, nonplussed.

"So let me ask you a question, chief. What's the end game here?"

"What do you mean?"

"The plan," he pushed.

Shane tightened her lips and gave him a blank stare. "Not following you."

He scoffed and eyed her, somewhat thrown for a loop.

"Seriously? What's your goal, Shane?"

Clicking her tongue, Shane understood the question and faced forward again, watching their feet as they made new fresh footprints in the snow next to their last lap.

"Getting my kid back. Isn't it obvious?"

"Glaringly. But I mean the bigger picture. What comes after that?"

She shrugged her shoulders and threw him a questioning glance.

"How should I know?"

He stared at her, dumbfounded.

Realizing Bernchal had been hinging on her having more than one solid objective for the future of their little colony, Shane spoke, her voice dripping with sarcasm.

"What, you think I have all the answers? That's cute. Look, duke. I just want my son back. Beyond that, it's anybody's guess. The world's changed and I'm not gonna pretend to have any solutions. I wouldn't even know where to begin."

Bernchal appeared ready to offer some retort and instead opted to nod his head and continue along their path. Before they knew it, they'd walked two more laps when the silence was broken yet again.

"If I had to vote on all the things to end the world, this would definitely have been in last place."

Shane smiled and discreetly turned to face Bernchal, who was lost in thought. Interested, she prodded for more.

"Yeah?"

"Yup. My top pick would have been zombies."

"Zombies?" she asked incredulously.

"Yes, zombies. Dumb, brainless, slow-moving walking dead."

With a wide smile, Shane offered, "Greatest show ever."

"Yes!" he exclaimed, looking at her again. "I loved that show."

After a slight pause, he continued. "Zombies. At least we'd know the rules with walkers. *'Fight the Dead. Fear the Living.'*"

Shane replied halfheartedly, "Yeah, but only now its just *'Fear the Living.'*"

Bernchal said nothing, only walked further on with Shane by his side. After another couple of minutes with nothing but the sound of their steps on the slow-covered track audible, Shane nudged Bernchal with her elbow and motioned for them to head back towards the institution. He obliged and followed her as she made her way through the hole in the fence surrounding the track and into the wooded acre connecting them with headquarters.

"Though its quite the set-up we have going here, did you ever think about moving somewhere else?"

"From here?" she asked, surprised by the question. Their boots crunched loudly on the frozen snow and Shane ignored the chill that spiraled down her back every time the sound penetrated the density of the forest around them.

"Not really. At first we were mobile. But it gets hard to constantly keep that up with a hundred women, some of whom were so distraught over their kids they were practically catatonic."

Bernchal nodded knowingly but in truth, he could scarcely imagine what it had been like for Shane and the other women when their own country had turned on them.

"But now, staying in one place- you're never scared of what's out there?"

"I for one find it hard to believe what's out there could get any worse. I mean, don't get me wrong- it's still scary. But what can we do? Every decision has its consequence. We knew we could set up a sustainable life here, some roots, so we made the decision to do it. We have to make that choice work, because in our case, there's no right or wrong. In the alternative, we could have hopped from place to place, always one step ahead of the bad guys. The positive is that you move and move and move and never get stuck. Movement is life."

"Movimiento es vida," he translated. "*World War Z?*"

Shane smiled, a much larger and more earnest smile than he'd ever seen her offer. It was honest, indicative of her being genuinely amused.

"That's… that's funny. I haven't met anyone who can quote a movie anymore."

She continued staring at him, a silly grin on her face stuck until she realized her goofy smile and cleared her throat, breaking eye contact.

"Damn, Shane," he responded jokingly. "I'd have never guessed it but you actually have teeth. Never seen 'em. I always kinda thought you just swallowed your food whole."

Her laugh was cut short. Bernchal grabbed her roughly by the forearm and pulled her towards him, suddenly slamming her into the trunk of a tree, hard.

He pressed his body against her and before she could protest, his large hand covered her mouth and he stiffened, waiting.

Shane heard her heart hammering in her chest, the sound pounding in her ears despite its silence to the rest of the world. Instantaneously she was brought back to each attack, each violation of her body back when she existed solely for the whim of any random man's fancy.

She didn't resist and instead shut her eyes tight, controlling her breathing and forcing herself to read the obvious signs- Bernchal had heard a noise and was trying to keep them hidden.

Loose tendrils that had come undone from her ponytail blew around and around in the wind, tickling his face as they stood, still and silent. Finally, she felt the weight of his body ease and he moved his hand from her mouth. Shane cracked open her eyes and instantly trained them on him.

Bernchal was still pressed against her but now she could breathe easier and the rough grooves of the tree trunk were not stabbing at her back. Her chest heaved, up and down, against his and her breath made small circles in the cold air that evaporated in front of him. He watched her, his ears still listening for strange sounds but his eyes were locked with hers.

"I thought I heard something," he said sheepishly, his breath hot against her cheeks.

Shane said nothing. Only gently pushed him off of her and turning back towards the direction they had been traveling, started up the hill to make her way to headquarters. Bernchal simply looked around once more and satisfied they were alone, followed Shane towards the college.

Chapter XVIII

Another day, another run. Bernchal poked at the stiff carcass of a dead pigeon with the toe of his boot. The poor bastard toppled over onto its side and barely made a dent in the melting snow of Van Cortlandt Park.

He looked up and saw Shane reappear amongst the brushes a couple of yards ahead of him. She looked back and caught his eye, held it for a second and turned forward again.

He watched her ahead of him, walking lightly on the snow, careful to keep from making noise. The other women, Wendalyn and Mariana, had stayed back towards the vehicle and only he and Shane had continued onward in search of something, anything.

Lately he'd been wondering what their runs were yielding. They had not encountered any useful supplies in over two months, and they hadn't run into another living soul in ages. Even the militia had been quiet for a while and other than the Embassy explosion, hadn't done anything notable in months.

Add to this a growing frustration at the goings on of some of the women and Bernchal had been in rare form lately. Unable to conjure any civility for some of the women, namely Mariana, he had resigned to sulking quietly by himself and spending more time than usual with Shane. He followed her pretty much everywhere and smiling to himself, realized it was the first time in his life he'd ever had to follow a woman *anywhere*.

Bored and growing increasingly aggravated at the same unsuccessful routine as of late, Bernchal picked up his pace to catch up to Shane. She immediately felt him creep up behind her and continued forward, essentially ignoring his appearance as usual.

"Hey, Shane."

"Yeah."

"Question."

"Ask it."

She pulled at a hanging branch and yanked the rest of it off the rotting tree from which it emerged, bending over and gently placing it on the ground. Eyes on the snow beneath their feet, she studied a tiny set of prints for a quick second before discarding it as rabbit paws and moving onward. For all of her quirks, among which were included the inability to crack a smile, a patronizing nature and constant condescending commentary, the one thing he could never deny was her ability to track and search.

Bernchal walked alongside her and kept his eye on the edge of the treeline. The first light of dawn was creeping over the horizon and he could now see couple of crows flying overhead and circling the wooded area, returning to the same spot.

"What do you think your life would be like if this shit hadn't happened?"

"You know, you're real fucking philosophical in the mornings."

He turned to her, bewildered. "Huh?"

"You're all business at night making runs, but when the sun is shining, its like talking to a middle-aged psychology professor."

"Wow," he uttered. He would have stopped for dramatic effect but didn't want to call any attention to themselves.

Shane snorted and ignored his reaction, which he carried on further.

"Wow. Here I was just trying to make small talk."

She smiled despite herself and rolled her eyes. "Oh, please."

"No," he whispered loudly. "No, it's fine. I'll take the insults. We'll just walk in silence."

"Whatever, you big baby."

He stomped off dramatically, whispering "I didn't know I'd be surrounded by hurtful critics…"

"Lord help me…"

They continued ahead, walking in complete silence until Shane finally relented and broke it.

"The truth is I try really hard not to think about the 'what ifs.'"

Falling right back into chat mode, Bernchal replied, "There's more than one?"

She scoffed and looked at him, perplexed. "Are you kidding me? There's a million. What if this hadn't happened? What if my husband hadn't been killed? What if we would have seen this coming? What if I'd have run? Left the country? What if my son is dead, and all of this... All this is for nothing?"

After a pause, she whispered quietly, "Fucking 'what if's...'"

Bernchal whistled his astonishment and offered, "Here's an idea- how about we never play the 'what if' game again?"

Shane shook her head and moved to Bernchal's right side, scanning the woods around them. They had ventured deeper into the park, underneath what used to be the golf course alongside the Saw Mill River Parkway. The lake surrounding the property had run over without maintenance and had turned the surrounding land that connected the park with the old train tracks into a swamp. Bernchal and Shane kept their footsteps light and with the snow still on the ground, they remained, for the most part, undetectable.

"Do you have any 'what ifs'?" she asked, curious. He didn't really strike her as the silent type. After all, he badgered her almost daily for more and more information. But he rarely offered insight into his own past and she wondered if he carried half as many demons as she did.

"Me? Nope. I did it all. Literally. Tried everything."

"Death wish?" she asked, joking.

"More like... An intolerance to authority."

Shane didn't face him as they stepped gingerly along the train tracks, careful not to miss a step and wind up in the snowy marshland around them.

"So how does a smart ass with a so-called intolerance to authority end up in the military?"

"I needed authority."

"I see."

Bernchal followed her along the track and stepped off at the first chance, pulling her with him to the right and further into the park's wooded land.

"My mom was great, but I was difficult to rein in."

"Unmanageable?" she asked with a smile.

He chuckled, amused. "Yeah, that's one word for it. Anyway, I was a bit much for her. And I started seeing friends on the same path getting locked up, some of them dying. I knew I needed some sort of direction, if not for myself than at least for her sake. My old man had been a colonel, US Air Force. I decided to give it a shot."

Softly, she prodded. "A twenty-year career is more than just a shot."

Bernchal shrugged and replied, "I was good at it. Navy, Special Ops, then the SEALS. It came naturally. And I liked it. Seemed to develop a talent for target-range, sniper shots. Plus, I got into traveling, handling weapons, the comaraderie- it's a dream come true for any teenage boy."

"Ah, so you finally admit you are far from grown up?"

"I'm a kid at heart. Even after all this crap, I still try to enjoy life, or what's left if it. I like to laugh, joke around, pull pranks."

Shane nodded, knowingly. "Trust me, I know."

A step behind her, Bernchal watched how her dark brown curls moved under the black knit cap she wore despite trying to tuck it into her jacket. As odd as it was, even though they were both tense and on the look-out for enemies, it seemed to him that they did their best talking when they were alone in the woods together. Shane seemed to open up more, becoming significantly more comfortable in releasing details about herself she normally wouldn't and in turn, smiled and laughed more than she ever did back at the institution.

"As much as you try to hide it, seems like underneath all that, you do, too."

He saw her shrug and cock her head to the side as though she considered his words.

"Did. Very much so. But when the world hates you because of what's in between your legs and your son gets kidnapped and you're enslaved and tortured, it gets kind of hard to retain your sense of humor."

And back to the gloom and doom.

"Yeah, Shane. 'Cause that right there is a barrel of laughs."

He was going to poke her with his weapon and possibly illicit some sort of witty banter, though he knew it was taking a chance with her volatile mood, but instead he saw movement up ahead of them. The trees leading out of the swamp and back towards the artificial grass in the track stadium, shifted. Far beyond where they were, he heard the unmistakable *pop* of a gunshot.

Shane turned immediately at the sound of gunfire and faced him. She didn't speak but he read the worry in her eyes and shook his head, indicating the sound had not come from the location where Wendalyn and Mariana waited for them.

He pointed further into the swamp and motioned for her to hide. Shane obliged and ran into the tall brush of the marshland, her boots making soft squishing sounds as she landed on the wet, soggy snow.

When he was satisfied she was not visible from her position behind the tall plants, Bernchal backtracked to where they had come from and left Shane there to watch him disappear behind the trees.

Shane waited, patiently, silently cursing Bernchal for abandoning her and then cursing herself for both feeling abandoned and the temporary insanity involved with needing a man to keep her safe. Angrily she reminded herself of all of the work it took to survive and get to where she was, albeit hiding in a swamp. And, she reminded herself, she had gotten along quite fine without him up to that point, and though she didn't place all of her trust in him yet, she couldn't shake him either. Another person on their team- man or not- had proven too good to pass up.

Satisfied she was alone, Shane crept out of the clearing, her footsteps expertly light on the dead leaves below the snow. Scanning the area, she instantly knew where Bernchal was. They'd become masters at hiding, at laying in wait and watching the enemy. She didn't have to turn around to know that he was behind her, a couple dozen yards past the swamp. She cleared the wet area and moved into the woods, listening.

Shane caught movement out of her peripheral and stopped, watching. Her breath caught in her throat she felt the empty space behind her, knowing instinctively that Bernchal too, had stopped. She controlled her breathing so that her heaving chest wouldn't be visible and waited, as the sounds of twigs snapping broke the silence in the woods.

Her hand moved slowly to her holster and silently undid the safety, waiting. Marianna stepped into her line of vision and Shane calmed, allowing her heartbeat to return to normal. She picked up her left foot to take a step towards her but stopped midair when Marianna turned back east and her eyes darted back and forth nervously. She glanced around, as though she were ensuring no one had been following her, and when satisfied she was alone, Marianna dropped to her knees and began to dig a small hole in the ground. She reached into her coat pocket and removed something and looking around again, dropped it into the hole and covered it with some leaves.

Shane asked herself where Wendalyn was and why Mariana was not at the truck. But she knew the answer.

She watched Mariana squatted on the ground, hiding whatever had been in her pocket and her curiosity piqued, but deep down, low in the pit of her gut, she knew. She knew how the militia had found them in Skyview; how they'd lain the mine trap and from were they had heard that gunshot. And though she tried to convince herself in that millisecond that it wasn't real, she immediately knew how Jolene had been killed.

With a familiar mixture of sadness and anger bubbling inside of her, she moved towards Marianna silently.

Marianna didn't feel anyone behind her and rose, brushing off the wet dirt and frozen leaves from her knees. When she turned, she came face to face with Shane.

If Shane had had any doubt in her suspicions, the shock and guilt in Marianna's eyes dissuaded them immediately.

She said nothing. Shaking her head back and forth, she tried to run, swiveling around back towards the swamp. Shane grabbed her with one arm around her throat and pulled her back, slamming her back against her own chest. With the other hand, she raised up the hunting knife she had unsheathed from her belt, and when a little ray of sun creeping through the condensed foliage surrounding them reflected off of it, a sliver of light gleamed on Marianna's terrified face.

"I'm sorry," she pled, her voice caught in a choking gasp.

Shane swallowed the overwhelming guilt and emotion threatening to overcome her, whispering, "I'm sorry, too."

She plunged the knife into Marianna's throat, her lips close to her ear. The knife slid in easily and she moved it quickly from left to right, feeling the hot and gooey blood seeping out of the wound and onto her hand. Shushing her to sleep, Shane felt Marianna's life slip away and when her knees buckled, she caught her as she slid to the floor. Gently, she laid her on the ground and stood over her.

Though she tried to stifle them, a single tear escaped and she quickly wiped it away. Reaching for some leaves, she used them to clean her hands and knife and then dropped them back on the floor. She moved the twigs covering the makeshift hole Marianna had dug and retrieved a folded up piece of paper, shoving it into her jacket pocket without a second glance.

Some leaves crackled and her head snapped up, her eyes landing on Bernchal as he walked out from behind a tree. She was going ask him if he'd seen the events that had just unfolded, but his eyes burned through her. He had his firearm out and aimed at something past her, and Shane read the urgency in his stare. She felt the air change, sensed their arrival before she turned to see them coming and made a split-second decision. Motioning for Bernchal to get back and hide, she gave him a final indecipherable look and turned to face the four militia soldiers making their way into the clearing.

Chapter XIX

Bernchal, torn between the lesser of two evils, had to make a hasty decision. He didn't want to leave Shane but he knew he had a better chance of overpowering the soldiers if they thought she was alone, so he finally obliged and maneuvered behind the large trunk of a broken tree, hidden from view by the bushes surrounding it. He watched helplessly as they wordlessly pounced on her, three of them grabbing her and dragging her back into the thickness of the forest while a fourth one followed.

He waited for what seemed like hours, until he was sure they'd left and wouldn't hear him advancing and finally took off, retracing their steps.

Shane allowed herself to be led further into the woods, memorizing their exact route. She didn't know what they had planned. Rape wasn't a fear anymore; ever since the revolution, the remaining men were likeminded misogynists who had no interest in a vagina for anything other than experimentation. And if it was an execution they had planned, she wondered why they hadn't just put a bullet in her back in the clearing.

Her feet dragged against the floor of the woods, wet and half-frozen leaves sticking to her cargo pants. She wanted to pick her legs up and walk but the bitch within her refused to give in to what they wanted.

They stopped a few hundred years into the woods and miles from any camp she knew about. The two holding her arms shoved her roughly, pushing her to the ground and they crowded around her. They had not disarmed her or searched her for weapons so she waited, watching them as they decided their next move.

They were soldiers in the militia, not one of the few psychotic civilians that had joined the administration's cause back when it had all started. Most of those were no longer around. Their deluded self-aggrandizing behavior couldn't back up the training they didn't have and they were immediately cut down by the citizens and law enforcement that did take up arms and fight back.

These were North Korean soldiers, part of Yenmor's coup. Their faded and worn out uniforms were no longer the camouflage green they had started with but the patches on their shirts of their nation's flag were unmistakable. Shane had come to know it well in the camp where she had been kept.

They said nothing, just suddenly started kicking her. Shane curled into a ball and tightened her body, trying her best to keep from crying out.

Three pairs of boots pounded on her and she saw spots behind her closed lids. It must have only been seconds but it felt like hours. Over and over again they kicked and stomped, each blow making it harder and harder for her to not beg for an end.

The tip of one of their boots hit at the just the right spot, breaking through her hands covering her face and landing on her mouth, instantly splitting her upper lip. One of them stomped down hard and she felt an unbelievable burst of pain across her ribcage. It was becoming very hard to breathe.

They stopped just as suddenly as they had started.

Slowly, she peeled her eyes open and despite the agonizing pain across her torso, somehow Shane managed to uncurl herself and lift herself onto her hands and knees. She spit out a wad of blood and coughed, the pain it caused making her nauseous. Still, they said nothing, just watched her closely. She figured they were waiting for some tears, so she spoke up.

It hurt to open her mouth and the blood inside made her voice come out phlegmy and halted. "I'm not a 'beg for your life' kinda chick… so don't hold your breath."

It angered the one to her left and he pulled his weapon, aiming it at her. His long black hair fell over his forehead and into his dark eyes and he shouted something in Korean, jutting the gun towards her with each angry syllable.

Another one responded to him, this one to the right of her. He pointed at her as he reasoned with the first one. Though he had joined in on the kicking, his face was far kinder than the others.

She heard a sound back in the direction from where they had come but ignored it and kept her eyes on them. The one who hadn't touched her heard it. His ears perked up; he scanned the woods around them and reached his hand out to grasp the elbow of the angry one to her left. He said something and pointed to the woods.

The long-haired one with his gun aimed on her turned to his cohorts and answered them. He let his arm drop to his side.

That was all she needed so Shane took her chance.

She dropped on her haunches and pulled her gun from its holster. She popped off one shot at the long-haired one with the gun, hitting him an inch below his right eye before he could lift his arm back up and aim his gun at her again. In one movement she held her breath, steered herself against the pain, turned the gun and opened fire on the reasonable one with a kind face to her right, getting off four shots and landing them all in his chest before the first body had even hit the ground.

A round of gunfire erupted from the woods and hit the other two. They never saw it coming and dropped with tremendous speed. The one with the excellent hearing died instantly and the last quiet one fell next to her and still alive, scrambled to get his gun free. She wanted to leave him writhing in agony for what they'd done to her, not to mention her own pain was unbearable and she didn't want to move an inch. But she couldn't take the chance of letting him live, so grunting loudly, she put her gun up against his temple and turning away to avoid the splatter of his brain matter, pulled the trigger, the shot echoing loudly across the forest.

Shane let gravity pull her back down and she dropped hard on the ground, the vibration wreaking havoc in her ribcage.

It hurt to sit up straight, but it hurt to hunch over. She was about lay down, hoping that would ease the pain, and she heard the same sound again. A crackle, this time much closer. She lifted the gun back up, her arm shaking with pain. Bernchal appeared and made his way toward her, his gun out and aimed at the bodies. She breathed an ached sigh of relief, letting her arm drop to her side again, her gun involuntarily slipping from her fingers.

The adrenaline didn't just leave her body- it made a break for the fucking border. All at once, the little energy keeping her conscious seeped out of her and was instantly, cruelly, replaced by indescribable pain coursing through every inch of her battered body.

She heard Bernchal mutter, "Holy shit," before her body gave out and she slid back against the ground. Her head fell back on the soft mound of grass underneath her and she almost smiled.

Bernchal reached her and dropped to his knees, sliding the remaining distance to her like a runner making a play for a stolen base. Shane fluttered her eyelids as the consciousness tried to leaver her and exhaustion settled in its place.

"Shane! Hey! Hey, you okay?" he demanded. He tugged at her chin, his thumb sliding back and forth against her swollen lower lip, wiping away the blood that had started to dry.

Speaking hurt, so she nodded her head.

"Can you walk?"

She nodded again and tried sitting up. Unsuccessful, he helped her to her feet as she bit her lip hard to stop herself from crying. They hobbled back the way they came, Bernchal bearing most of her weight against him, Shane struggling to stay conscious and keep up.

They stopped twice to hide. He pushed her roughly against the nearest tree and shielded her with his body. Holding her up he covered her and waited, his breath hot against her neck. Shane could do nothing more than hold hers and count the agonizing seconds until she could breathe painlessly again.

"Stay with me, Shane. You hear me?"

She opened her eyes and met his, which were full of panic. "I hear you. So can everyone else," she added, her words slurred and spaced out.

"Everyone who? We're alone in these godforsaken woods."

She coughed and spit blood out on the ground. Without looking up, she asked, "Then why are we stopping… every two seconds to hide?"

Bernchal heard the difficulty she was having breathing and guessed her to have a couple of cracked or broken ribs. Careful to not jar her body, he pulled himself off of her and placed her arm over his shoulder, helping her walk. She gripped her ribcage and groaned as he started walking them out of the woods again.

"Can never be too careful. Know who taught me that?"

They respond simultaneously.

"Me?"

"Captain America."

Another crack of the leaves a dozen yards from the soccer field sent them running towards the thick trunk of an aging tree, Shane with her back pressed into the freezing wood and Bernchal leaned up against her. He waited, listening for the slightest of sounds when she went limp in his arms and he panicked, lowering her softly to the ground and trying to rouse her.

He shook her face back and forth, gripping her chin with his hand, squeezing hard and whispering as loudly as he could into her ear without compromising their location.

"Talk to me, Shane. Stay up, stay with me."

Her eyelids fluttered and he brushed her hair from her face, shaking her a little harder.

"Talk, come on. Talk to me!"

Her eyes finally opened and she focused on him, muttering angrily, "What?"

He smiled at her, relieved. "There she is."

She smiled back, exhausted.

"I'm here." After a pause she added, "And are we staying here?"

"And there it is, ladies and gentlemen," he replied. He helped her up, mumbling, "There's the sarcasm I've come to know and despise."

With her fully erect and his arm once again holding her up, he turned them towards the original path and started back again.

"Come on, smart ass."

He half-carried, half-held her the rest of the way back to their vehicle, which was tucked in behind the Van Cortlandt Manor. In the car, he picked her up and settled her in the passenger seat next to him. Buckled in, he peeled out of the long driveway that used to be reserved for Park & Recreation Rangers and took off towards the institution.

Halfway to the college, her head dropped to the right against the window and Bernchal reached out and pulled her back to a seated position, talking to her loudly to keep her awake.

They made it back to camp without further incident. Despite his better judgment, he leaned on the horn as he drove up Manhattan College Parkway and Julie ran out when alerted to their presence to help him carry Shane in.

When she was finally safe and secure in the infirmary, Bernchal stopped against an open doorway leading to the showers and allowed himself to slink to the floor, his own body spent.

Chapter XX

Carina and Julie bathed Shane, washing the crusted blood from her face, taking care to delicately clean around the ugly bruises already forming on her chest and back. She grimaced with each touch and swallowed her tears until it was blessedly over.

Bernchal had demanded to see Shane when she was dressed, believing himself to be the only one capable of addressing her injuries. She allowed him entry when he appeared at her door with bandages and was too exhausted to argue when he shooed the other women away.

Silently, he sat on the edge of her bed and helped her sit up, wrapping her hands around his neck and pulling her to a seated position, despite the excruciating pain. She was uncomfortable with his close proximity but couldn't do much more than avert her eyes.

"I took a bad spill in Afghanistan after 9/11 when our chopper was hit," he told her, his voice gratingly soft and patronizing. "Bruised three ribs, broke two more, one of which lacerated my liver. Luckily we had triage on the field. They kept me alive and then they set me up in a hospital in Germany so I was treated properly. You..." He paused, choosing his words carefully. "It seems you have a couple of broken ribs. Fortunately, it's an easy fix. Unfortunately for us, we don't have an X-ray machine or, more importantly, pain medication. So the best I can do for you is minimize your discomfort... a little."

She nodded slowly.

He leveled her with his eyes and continued. "I'm gonna wrap your chest. It's gonna hurt like hell, but you'll feel better when I'm done. Just promise me you won't take too many deep breaths and give yourself pneumonia, okay?"

Shane nodded again.

"So, I need to lift your shirt. Is... is that alright?"

She tried to breathe and felt her heartbeat quickening involuntarily. Nodding, she closed her eyes and let him touch her.

His hands felt warm against her skin and she shuddered roughly as he eased the oversized t-shirt up and tied it in a neat knot just below where her bra-strap would be, were she wearing one. Suddenly aware of her precarious position, Shane fidgeted.

"Hold still."

If he noticed she wasn't wearing a bra, he mercifully didn't let on. She opened her eyes and watched as he worked, unrolling the bandages and laying them out carefully over the quilt covering her extended legs. When he was done, he looked at her, catching her gaze and holding it.

"You have to put your arms up. This is gonna hurt…"

She nodded again, unable to form any real words.

His gaze never wavering, Bernchal reached for her hands and gripped them. With a gentle squeeze he lifted them up and extended them, stretching her torso in the process. The pain hit, like a tidal wave of torture starting at her chest and moving unbelievably fast through her body. Shane stifled a scream and buried her face in her right bicep, unwilling to let him see her cry. Every breath was agony and her chest was rapidly rising and falling as she involuntarily gasped for air.

Knowing there wasn't much he could do for her, he worked quickly, imploring her to slow her breathing. He put his face close to hers, his own rhythmic breath hot on her chest and working as a model for her to replicate.

"I know it hurts. I know it. But you have to relax your breathing. If you overload your lungs, you'll be susceptible to pneumonia. Slow down…"

She used the sound of his baritone voice as a guide and allowed herself to be calmed.

He wrapped the bandage snugly around her, the first tug agonizingly tight, but those that followed easing the pain. With such tightness around her ribcage it actually helped control her breathing and after a minute she relaxed somewhat, her heartbeat slowing and her chest rising and falling at a calmer pace. He noticed immediately when the worst of it had passed.

"How's that? Any better?"

She nodded. Clearing her throat, she pulled her face out from her behind her bicep and met his eyes.

"I'm good," she replied breathlessly.

"You're not good; you're hurt."

"I'm good."

He met her eyes and didn't try to hide the skepticism written all over his face.

"You're not used to being taken care of, are you, Shane?"

She watched him as he worked on her. Her breathing had slowed but was still labored and struggling.

"Not for a long time."

"There's nothing wrong with getting a helping hand now and again."

"Don't usually need it."

"I can tell," he answered, a small smile playing on the corner of his mouth.

She became annoyed and snapped, "Are you enjoying this?"

"I am. Your vulnerability is sexy."

Shane rolled her eyes and looked away. "There's nothing sexy... about vulnerability."

"I beg to differ. That all-go, no play tough chick is definitely intimidating, don't get me wrong. And not a little bit hot. But letting the guard down sometimes, sometimes... It's nice to see that there's a human underneath that tough exterior."

She flinched, his words cutting deeper than he intended. "I am human."

"I know you are."

He paused as he worked, the bandage getting shorter as he wrapped more of it around her, his face getting closer to hers as it wound around her.

"You lied about that, you know."

"Excuse me?" she asked, watching him again.

"You lied. You said there were no bonds, no attachments."

Shane looked away. With halted breath, she asked, "Jolene?"

"Marianna, too. I saw."

After a moment, she replied, breathlessly.

"What would you have rather... I'd said? That I care ...about everyone here? I worry ...about everybody? What's ...the point? It wont bring us ...any closer ...to our goal. Sentiment ...won't get us anything ...but captured ...or killed."

He knew her well enough to avoid eye contact and let her process her own emotions, so he kept bandaging her. Softly, he asked, "But that line of thinking doesn't work, does it? You still care about them."

She said nothing, only looked down at the fold of the bed sheets while he continued working.

After a moment's pause, Bernchal spoke up again.

"I think the thing about it is that there's no in-between in this new world. There's no getting to know someone or even searching for yourself. That's all whimsical shit that has no place here anymore. It's survival now. Kill or be killed. How do you take it slow in a world like this? When you don't even know if you'll still be alive tomorrow, much less an hour from now? How do you go slow?"

Without waiting for her to deliver a broken and choppy response, he kept going.

"You don't, that's how. You live each day like tomorrow isn't promised, because it isn't. So acquaintances become friends, friends become family and strangers become sex toys. What do you think about that?"

She didn't think she could respond without suffocating herself so Shane just closed her eyes and clenched her jaw, wondering how Bernchal's presence wasn't enough to make her forget the pain.

"You could have turned me in back there."

She opened her eyes and watched him deep in concentration, still bandaging her. She considered his words and replied softly.

"I could have."

"Why didn't you?"

"Why would I? You've helped us...Whether you believe ...in this... or not, you've ...helped us."

"Turning me in could have prevented all of this damage."

"It might have. Or... they might have just done... the same... to both of us... And then killed us.... Who knows?"

"That sounds like sentiment to me."

"Does it?"

He finally met her eyes as his pulled the bandage around her back, his lips dangerously close to hers.

"Regardless, thank you."

She looked away again, unable to hold his stare for too long. "No gratitude ...necessary. I don't like owing anyone anything. You saved ...my life in the minefield. This week... I returned the favor."

"I wonder what next week will have in store for us."

She didn't reply, only pursed her lips and kept eyeing him as he worked. Finally after a long pause, she whispered.

"Thank you."

He remained silent and finished, his hand smoothing out the creases of the bandages and touching her gently around her ribcage. He undid the knot of her t-shirt and let it fall around her waist, his hand brushing against her breast before sitting back. Making eye contact again he reached for her hands still extended over her head and pulled them down. She grimaced in pain but regained her composure, watching him as he pulled at the hem of her t-shirt and fixed it, his eyes traveling from her collarbone to her loose breasts under the thin fabric, and back up again. His hand wrapped around her to her back and the other slipped under her neck as he helped ease her back against the pillows, his grip making the pressure on her ribcage almost bearable.

He sat up straight and eyed her.

"All done."

She cleared her throat and pointed towards the chair in the far corner of the room with her coat draped over it.

"Would you mind grabbing ... something from the pocket... of my coat? I'd get it myself, but…"

"Sure," he joked as he rose from the bed and walked to the chair. "Use a broken rib or two as an excuse to be lazy."

He retrieved the folded up piece of paper and handed it to her. Then he surprised her by sitting back down on the edge of her bed, making himself quite comfortable as though it were the most normal thing in the world.

"Mariana?" he asked, knowingly.

She nodded, despite his hulking frame sitting beside her and serving no purpose other than unnerving her. She cleared her throat and finally gained the courage to ask him the question to which she already knew the answer.

"And Wendalyn?"

Bernchal tightened his lips and shook his head slowly. He spared her the details of having had found Wendalyn's body by the car with her throat slit.

Taking as deep a breath as she could physically muster, Shane unfolded the paper and scanned it, holding back a cry and failing miserably. She let the paper fall into Bernchal's awaiting hand and looked away, unable to wipe the falling tears and cursing the broken ribs for preventing her from doing so.

Bernchal didn't take long to read the crudely drawn map leading its reader to their sanctuary so he crumpled up the paper and shoved it into his pocket. Shane avoided his gaze until the awkwardness could no longer be ignored and sniffling, finally turned to face him.

Their eyes met and he reached for her face to move a strand of loose hair and tuck it behind her ear, but she flinched, a quick darkness appearing in her eyes suddenly.

Bernchal pulled back with a start and eyed her, now convinced more than ever that a lot more happened to all of the woman than any of them let on.

He got up from the edge of her bed and it strained and creaked when his weight lifted, as though it did not want him to go. He turned to leave and stopped at the door, sighing. Without turning to face her, he lowered his voice and spoke over his shoulder.

"I'm sorry I didn't get to you sooner."

Before she could respond, he was gone.

Chapter XXI

It took Shane almost six weeks to recover from her bruised and broken ribs. So much time immobile for someone like her was enough to drive everyone insane so at the first sign of healing when she insisted she be let loose to run a mile, Bernchal obliged and followed her out for a run around the perimeter of the track.

She was sitting on the edge of the track, her bottom on the dirt and her feet on the cold, dewy grass, tying her shoelaces. Bernchal was a few feet away, watching her. She was moving her lips slowly, reciting something he'd heard her saying in the past but had always brushed it off. Now, as she concentrated on getting herself back into fighting shape after more than five weeks of bedrest, he noticed it wasn't just a random prayer.

"What the hell are you saying to yourself?"

Shane looked up and squinted her eyes in the blinding sunlight. She'd forgotten he was there and furrowed her brow.

"Excuse me?"

"I've seen you saying something before. Working out, shooting targets, the like. And always your lips are moving like you're reciting some prayer. What is it?"

Shane groaned as she rose from her seated position, shooing away his offer of help. Standing upright, she stretched, still feeling the soreness from her fading bruises and replied.

"It's not a prayer. It's... They told us this speech, this mantra. During training. Had us outside in subzero temperatures running drills like the goddamn Marines. They'd play this speech on the loudspeaker system over and over, all day, every day. Nothing else. I guess they were trying really hard to make it stick."

"So you repeat it?" he asked, curiously. "Isn't that just doing what they wanted you to do? I thought you were dead set against conforming."

Shane laughed and said, "I am. But a good speech is a good speech. I think it was some coach, years ago. A pep talk for a football team. He convinces them they're champions."

They started walking down the track, Bernchal controlling the pace and not letting her strain herself, as she was likely to do because of her insane need to overdo it.

"Champions of what?"

She frowned, trying to remember the source of the speech she had come to both loathe and respect.

"The football field, I imagine."

"Football…" he responded, more to himself. "Jesus, it's been a long time since I've even seen a football, much less picked one up. Seems so long ago…"

Shane offered a sad smile. "It does, doesn't it? Seems like years ago. Everything is so ancient. Surreal. Things like the internet, Facebook, Twitter, Instagram- ten years before this all happened, those things weren't even in existence. Ten years later, no one can live without them and now ten years after that, there aren't even any computers left. It's insane. It feels like it's been years since I've done anything I used to normally do."

She took a deep breath and winced and he jumped to attention, his hands immediately pulling at her jacket to check her ribcage. Ignoring the impropriety of it, Bernchal fiddled with her undershirt and lifted everything up, and Shane could do nothing but stand there like an idiot and allow it to happen. Truthfully, she was grateful for the contact. It was cold as hell and she was tired of trying to see her own reflection in the mirror of the ladies' bathroom to investigate the healing of her injuries. So she closed her eyes and ignored the chills that ricocheted throughout her body as his warm hands touched her bare skin and examined her, dangerously close to her breasts, dangerously close to her heart.

"That's because there's no normal anymore," he replied to her, satisfied she had healed properly. He lowered her shirt first, then the hem of her jacket and tugged it downward as he faced her. He was close enough to her that she could have inhaled the puff of air he released when he spoke.

Facing the track again, he nudged her for them to continue forward and finished, "At least not in this home we've made ourselves."

Shane ignored the way her heart sped up a little whenever he used the word 'we.'

"You're a long way from home, Commander."

"We're all a long way from home nowadays, Shane."

She shrugged in agreement and trodded along the path beside him. Every so often, she would open and close her fists, stretching her hands in the cold. Eyes on her, he lost focus and almost tripped over a tangled set of weeds growing over the track. Catching himself before he took a spill, he straightened out and noticed that she had barely thrown a glance in his direction as she kept going.

"Well," he joked, back alongside her. "At least we know there's a silver lining to all this fuckery."

She scoffed and tossed him a disdainful glare over her shoulder.

"And what could possibly be a silver lining in this hellhole, Commander? Do tell."

"No more global warming."

She scoffed again, this time amused, and shook her head. Turning to face him, her eyes twinkling with laughter, she added, "And no traffic jams."

"Ah, yes! No traffic. God, I hated sitting in traffic."

"Me too…"

They walked further along the track. Winter had all but faded away once again and Spring was rearing its lion's mane with a roar. The buds were already forming on the trees and the ground, which had so recently been frozen over and all but dead, was now a rejuvenated shade of emerald green again.

Bernchal kept the conversation going, surprising himself with the number of things he was remembering and now missing.

"Jesus, now that I think of it, it's been years since I've watched a game on TV or drank a cold beer at the bar with my friends. Years since I've seen anybody I knew before the revolution. I don't even know if my family is still alive. My mom…"

His voice trailed off and Shane looked over at his face. With the common household items much of the world had taken for granted back when things had been normal lacking regularly, Bernchal's facial hair was thicker than usual. Oftentimes he had found a razor here and there after rummaging through empty dorm rooms, but it seemed lately he'd been coming up empty-handed and now his beard was coming in fuller, hiding his generous mouth. It lent him a much more mature look and with the pensive expression on his face, he walked along the track resembling a tortured artistic soul, deep in thought.

Careful to not dismiss his obvious worry, Shane tried to make him feel better.

"I don't know where my family is either. My mom left to the Dominican Republic the minute Yenmor got elected. Like she knew something like this was coming."

"Smart lady," he replied, slightly less troubled. "My mom is way more idealistic. Genuinely believed it wouldn't get so bad. Even when it did get that bad."

"A lot of people did. Myself included."

He turned to her, shocked. Shane did not seem the type to remain optimistic in the face of chaos.

"You didn't see it coming?"

She turned to him, answering honestly.

"This? Oppression? Slavery? Hell no. I knew he was a vagina-hater. I knew there was something evil in him. You could see it. The plastic smiles, the darkness in him when he talked about gays and women. I saw something, yeah. But I didn't think... I didn't think it would come to this. I honestly didn't think our own government would stand for it. This fucking place was built on the backs of foreigners and slaves. This country practically had a sandwich board advertising immigration. The goddamn symbol of our country asks for the huddled masses to be sent to us so we could shelter them. How do you then back an animal that deports everyone, rounds up all the gays into concentration camps and systematically strips away the rights of half its damn citizens? How do you turn your back on your own people?"

She shook her head as they walked, seemingly still in disbelief at the events that had brought them there.

"You know, I get him getting elected. I do. There'll always be the crazies that would back someone like him. And I get him laying low for the first term, planning, and then unleashing hell. I get it. The abandonment, though? The way Congress, all the elected officials, goddamn governors and mayors- how everybody turned a blind eye and let it get like this? Fuck them."

He eyed her, seeing the fury and rage quickly rising within her, threatening to boil over. It was fascinating to see her exude all of the emotions she kept bottled inside in one quick conversation- from casualness to ferocity in less than sixty seconds.

"Fuck them?"

Without making eye contact, she responded, her words rushing out of her. Her footsteps quickened and he doubted she even knew she was walking faster.

"Yeah. All of them. I was an American citizen. You know that? Born and raised here. As was my son. American citizens. Law abiding taxpayers. And not the Hispanic statistic they make us all out to be, either. No hand outs. No welfare. No fucking food stamps. A true blue citizen that saluted my flag every time I laid eyes on it. An American. Until they ripped my son from my arms and forced me into indentured servitude to get him back. Until they worked me to the bone against my will while my son is God knows where, without me. Wondering where I am, wondering why he keeps waking up without seeing me. Wondering if I've left him, if I don't love him anymore…"

The little control she had over her demeanor snapped and her face crumbled as the tears sprung up into her eyes. She looked to the right and hid her face as she broke down for a few seconds and then immediately shook it off. Wiping her eyes with the back of her hand, she quickly composed herself and finished.

"Yeah…" she said, facing forward again, her tone much less angry. "Fuck 'em."

It was the first time he'd seen her show any real emotion other than tenacity and a general disdain for the people around her. She had fought the urge to cry over three broken ribs and he respected her toughness, but this was something else. For the first time she was allowing him a glimpse into what it meant to have a child, love and adore them, and have him taken away, literally ripped from her arms. To feel like the world at large had painted her Public Enemy #1 despite her devotion to her homeland. To turn around and be left with nothing and no one and to have to claw her way to freedom for the sake of her missing child.

Shane was softening, albeit slowly and frustratingly haltingly. But she was softening nonetheless and he not only appreciated her ability to trust him enough to show it, he admired the shit out of her for it.

Breaking the rising tension, she started to pick up the pace and he admonished her immediately.

"I know you're used to doing what you want, but you can't strain yourself, Shane. Don't overdo it. Just a nice brisk walk for starters."

Rolling her eyes, Shane acquiesced and slowed to a crawl.

"Yes, sir."

He ignored her sarcasm and decided to keep the momentum going. Who knew when Shane Milian would bestow upon him some more valuable information? He decided to strike while the getting was good.

"How long has it been since you've seen your son?"

"Three years, six months, eight days. And counting."

"Jesus…"

She stopped suddenly, reflecting. Closing her eyes, she tilted her head up to the sky and paused, letting the warmth of the sun hit her face. Finally, she spoke again, once more moving along the track.

"It's funny. It feels unreal sometimes."

"What does?"

"This. Everything. I haven't seen or held my son in three and a half years and I just said it like its nothing. Like if you just asked me for the time. Sometimes I think becoming numb is a good thing…"

She moved towards the perimeter fence, in the direction of a fallen tree along the last leg of the track and picked up a foot, leaning back against the standing trunk. Bernchal followed suit and sat on the fallen section large enough for him to lay his long body on it and propped his head up on folded arms.

"But if you were numb, you wouldn't be trying this hard to get him back."

Without missing a beat, she responded. "Yeah, but if I were numb, I wouldn't feel like I'm dying a little bit more everyday."

Bernchal nodded without much more to offer. He wasn't usually one for optimism, but in this instance it seemed necessary.

"You'll get him back."

"I know…"

She sighed then, eager to change the subject.

"What'd you do in the Navy?"

"Marksman."

She nodded, unsurprised. "That's why you're such a great shot."

He chuckled and replied smoothly, "I'm a *good* shot; I'm just great at a lot of other things, too."

Shane sped up a bit then and Bernchal got the hint- another faux pas. She wanted to talk pleasantries, so he followed her lead.

"Some days I think I miss noise."

"Huh?"

"You know, like city noise. The trains, cars honking. Cop sirens. Even the damn car alarms. Anything. Used to hate it. Now sometimes in this damn silence I find myself wishing for something familiar."

She nodded her head and looked over at him, studying his face. Even with the beard, his lips were visible and spread in a constant smirk.

They moved and she almost didn't hear what came out of them.

"What do you miss the most?" he asked.

"Oh, that's hard. I'd have to say… cheesecake," she replied, smiling. "That's definitely at the top of the list. Movies, too. I loved going to the movies, or even curling up on the couch with a warm blanket to watch a movie at home. I could watch Pride & Prejudice every day. And the beach. I hated the sand back then, but now... And manicures. Definitely. Now I have man hands."

He opened his eyes, laughing at her. He sat up on the tree and innocently reached for her hand.

"No, you don't."

Shane, caught off guard, pulled her hand away abruptly and immediately realizing her overreaction to such an innocent gesture, cleared her throat uncomfortably.

He eyed her for a second and then quickly shook it off, presumably ignoring her lack of etiquette. Laying back against the fallen tree trunk, he crossed his arms behind his head and closed his eyes again.

"I miss sleeping in. Actually sleeping comfortably. Like a deep slumber and then waking up whenever I felt like it."

Still embarrassed, she relaxed somewhat and watched him resting on the trunk, his dark lashes fidgeting as his eyes moved under the lids.

"I never slept in," she offered.

"You don't seem the type," he replied, a smile already spreading on his mouth. "Let me guess- early bird?"

"Yes."

"I can tell…"

Shane watched him under the shade of the tree, his tousled hair moving in the soft breeze. It was obvious even with the thin jacket that his arms, relaxed behind his head, were well-defined and muscular. She saw him shudder when a slight chill went through him because of the cool crisp spring air and it made him smile again.

"And donuts, too."

His deep voice brought her back and she looked away, scanning the grounds for anything out of the ordinary.

The wind whipped around them, scattering twigs and dead leaves that remained on the ground. But other than the occasional gust, it was quiet and without the any sound in the background, the silence was overwhelming. Shane immediately understood why he said he missed noise.

After a moment of silence, her eyes moved back towards him, still at rest on the trunk. His lean body was haphazardly perched with nary a care and his chiseled face was peaceful, serene.

As though he could feel her eyes on him, he offered a smirk on his lips.

"And a nice, long, hot shower…"

Shane cleared her throat in discomfort, fighting and failing to manage the heat rising to her cheeks. Increasingly flustered, she looked around, her eyes darting back and forth between Bernchal on that damn tree trunk and the rest of the track, which suddenly held way too much interest for her.

Giving up, she stood up straight, moving backwards towards the path.

"I'm getting back on the track…"

Before he could open his eyes, she was gone, her ponytail bouncing behind her as she walked briskly away.

Bernchal propped himself up on one arm and watched her ass. When she was too far gone for him to get a good view he sighed heavily and flopped back onto the tree trunk, laying one forearm to rest over his face, covering his eyes. The other arm hung languidly at his side.

To no one in particular, he whispered lazily before dozing off in the spring shade.

"I miss sex…"

Chapter XXII

Bernchal walked into the cafeteria with an armload of ammunition to clean and the commotion in progress at the back of the room stopped him in his tracks.

Shane was leaning against the wall behind the cook station, with Julie in front of her yelling at Deirdre, one of the women that rarely made runs and instead was relegated to cleaning messes and handling household chores around the institution. She was a frail little thing, with little wisps of graying hair and narrow wrists that looked close to snapping whenever she picked up a box.

She wasn't intimidated by the death rays Julie was shooting from her hazel eyes however, and instead of backing down, took a step closer to her, rising on her tip toes and getting in Julie's face.

"We have a right to know if we are in danger!"

Shane shot back from behind Julie, her voice dripping with a dangerous level of sarcasm and impatience.

"We're always in danger! What the fuck do you think this place is- a vacation resort?"

Julie pushed Shane back against the wall with one hand, the other pointing in Deirdre's face, menacingly.

"Let it go," she warned. "Walk away."

Deirdre looked close to making the mistake of speaking when Shane beat her to the punch, peeling her long body off the wall and taking a step closer to her. Julie remained in between the two women, clearly using her body as a buffer should something more than words be thrown. More women gathered at the sounds of increasing tension and Bernchal spotted a couple of concerned faces in the growing group.

"I don't know what the fuck you are expecting here, but let me make it *really* simple for you. Mariana tried to deliver information, but she didn't get the chance. It was intercepted. So they got no information. Get it? *No information*," she repeated, condescendingly slow.

She took a short pause and continued, darting her eyes around the room as though there were enemies everywhere out to cut her throat.

"This is the last time I'm gong to address this issue, you understand me?" she asked, lips tight and jaw clenching. "You are no more or less safe than you were yesterday. They still don't know where we are, but if we aren't careful, they just might find out. So instead of standing here pissing me off, why don't you make yourself useful, get a goddamn weapon, stand on a fucking fence and keep an eye out so that maybe, just maybe, you won't feel it's quite so dangerous here. If you can't muster up the energy to do that, why don't you take your chances out there and see how long you fucking last? You just might end up like Mariana did..."

Any questions Deirdre and the other women that had gathered had in their minds about Mariana's fate or Shane's resolve were immediately erased by her thinly veiled threat.

With nothing clearly left to discuss and seeing herself as the loser in any further war of words, Deirdre did as she was told and turned on her heel, making her way to the end of the cafeteria silently. Most of the other women dispersed, some of them Shane's biggest fans with smiles on their faces.

Satisfied nothing was going to escalate, Julie turned to Shane and offered a sad smile.

"I think you made her piss on herself."

Shane chuckled and shook her head. She appeared over and past it, but Bernchal knew better; knew *her* better. He read the tension in her arms, the way her eyes still looked the way they had when she'd fired back at Deirdre, like she was ready for battle. Shane was wired like a powder keg and right now, she was close to exploding.

He dropped the guns on the table closest to the cook station and trotted over to them before they went their separate ways.

"Hey, Shane. I have some ideas about the sentries watching the Leo Building. Let me show you," he asked, already making his way towards the double doors of the exit.

Shane took a deep breath and looked at Julie, who nodded her head in an unspoken acknowledgment. Julie motioned to Bernchal as Shane turned and walked towards him and he expected the usual eye roll or look of disgust, but instead she offered an even stare. He guessed it to mean she was in agreement with his plan to remove Shane from the current environment and help her calm down, so he smiled at her. Julie, not one to break character, shot him a quick sneer and turned to clean the guns he left behind.

Wordlessly, Shane grabbed a thin jacket that was laying over the bannister of the staircase in the main lobby as they passed and led him outside of the building. As soon as they hit the brisk air outside, she stopped and closed her eyes, breathing it in. It was a cool fifty degrees in late March and though he felt the chill in his bones immediately, she seemed to enjoy it. Like a battery being recharged, Shane came back to life. Gone was the tension in her shoulders and arms. Her jaw unclenched, her fists opened up and she looked lighter, rejuvenated.

Shooting him a quick glance, she started for the perimeter fence, shouting, "Let's go!" as she jogged away.

Bernchal kept up her pace and side by side they made their way expertly through the forest separating the top of Riverdale with the bottom until they were at the city steps just behind the Leo Building. The facility housed the abandoned math lab and all of the computers and electronic gadgets once crucial to survival in the old world.

Shane kept the master keys for all of the buildings belonging to the college and revealed a huge set when they arrived, unlocking the back doors. Bernchal had his weapon drawn and watched their backs until they were inside. He suggested they get to the roof to get a better vantage point over the surrounding neighborhood and she complied. Once in, she locked the doors behind her and retrieved her own weapon and they made their way down the corridor and toward the stairs that would lead them to the top floor.

In the stairwell, Shane walked behind as Bernchal led the way. Despite everything inside of her fighting it, she eyed him going up the stairs, the way his muscles moved underneath his clothes and made the climbing of twenty staircases look simple.

He was quieter than usual, so she changed things up by being the one to initiate conversation.

"This is actually a good idea," she offered. "Using the cars from dealership across the street, I mean. We can always use more electrical supplies."

"Good, huh?" he responded as they continued climbing. "Just good? Are you incapable of paying me a decent compliment?"

"Jesus. fine. Wonderful. How's that?"

"Wonder- wonderful? Wait, did you just say I'm wonderful?" He stopped on the steps at the fifth floor landing turned to face her, pointing to his chest exaggeratedly with a twinkle of amusement brightening his eyes in the darkened staircase.

"Not you, dingus," she replied, making her way to the landing and passing him. "The idea."

"I'm wonderful?" he repeated, ignoring her candid reply. "Wow, well that's unexpected. Wonderful is usually one of those words that's severely overused, but I think in this case is perfectly appropriate, don't you?"

He fell into step alongside her and she rolled her eyes in response.

"This," she said, pointing to him, "this is why I don't pay you any compliments."

"Too late, Shane," he said to her, speeding up and passing her again. "You've admitted I'm wonderful. The damage has been done."

"Clearly."

They continued forward in silence until she spoke again.

"Don't think I don't know what you're trying to do here," she shot at him.

He didn't turn to look at her, just continued languidly up and up with her in tow.

"What?"

"This plan of yours, Commander. I'm not dumb. You could obviously tell I was going to flip my shit and you brought me out here to talk me down."

"What?" he asked, feigning ignorance. "Never that."

She shook her head, unable to conceal the smile on her face.

"Well, it didn't work. I was calm before you offered."

"I know."

They were on the eighth floor and she slowed to a stop, holding on to the rail and watching him continue climbing.

"So, then why are we out here?"

Bernchal stopped one flight above her and turned to look at her.

"Don't you listen, Shane? I wanted to show you my ideas about manning the Leo Building and the used car lot in front of it. I think we can use some of the parts from the vehicles, as well as create a shorter route from there to here without being detected."

She dropped her eyes and feeling the heat rise to her cheeks, immediately started up the staircase to join and then pass him. Quietly, she mumbled, "Oh."

As she started towards the ninth floor, he fell in behind her and whispered, "And to calm you down." Before she could respond, he sprinted up the rest of the way and left her to follow.

On the tenth and final floor, Bernchal opened the main door to the roof and they walked outside, taking in the surrounding land. Though they had a high vantage point, there were no chances to be taken, so they both hunched over and sprinted for the edge of the roof to take cover behind the waist-high wall.

After thirty minutes arguing over what to retrieve in the vacant dealership across the street, they sat with their backs against the wall for a quick break before heading back to the institution.

Sensing a lull and possible opportunity to talk, Bernchal began.

"So, that was *some* conversation."

Saying nothing, Shane just nodded and started fiddling with the link of tiny ivy growing from the concrete against the wall behind them.

He continued shamelessly. "I thought for a second you were gonna punch her."

She shrugged noncommittally. "Nah, I'd have shot her."

Familiar with her style of humor, he was not alarmed and instead, pushed further. "Did she blame you for Mariana?"

Bernchal had learned by now that with Shane, it was best to be direct and fire your biggest cannons first while the door was open. Once shut, it was difficult to pry open again unless she allowed it, which she rarely did.

Shane shrugged and replied softly. "I think it's more of a matter of why Mariana did it. We've been unsuccessful so far. So what's the point of trying? If it happened to Mariana, it can happen to any one of us."

"I think you're forgetting one very important detail here. Mariana didn't turn on you because you couldn't get her kid back. She turned because that's who she was. She was so desperate to get her kid back that she would have turned on anyone. And she did. It wasn't just you. She betrayed the whole place, every single person there. She didn't give a shit if they found us, came in the middle the night and shot us while we slept. She betrayed every woman and every child that is counting on this mission to work."

She swallowed and bit the inside of her cheek as she processed his words. She knew he was right, yet her guilt was still more powerful than his logic.

"Still. If I would have found her-"

"Shane," he interrupted, one hand landing soothingly on her knee. "She killed Wendalyn. There was nothing, literally nothing you could have done to prevent that. Mariana was not the same person that got here with you. The same hope, the same fire that drives you and everybody else in here to keep looking- she lost that a long time ago. And she ended up a ticking time bomb."

Shane took a deep breath and held back tears.

He was right. Bernchal was right. The Mariana that had sold them out, turned her backs on them and betrayed them to their enemies was not the same sweet, loving woman who believed in their cause. She had been lost.

She suddenly remembered their conversation a few weeks past wherein he had warned her to keep her eyes on the women.

"You knew," she said, her eyes small and dark as she finally turned to meet his gaze. It was more of a statement than a question and Bernchal immediately knew to what she was referring.

"I didn't know. But I… I suspected something."

"From her?

"Yes. No," he wavered, considering his next words. "I always felt there was something about her, something too volatile. The rest of you: you plan, you act, you move- day in and day out. She was… She was sadder. More lost. Almost as if she was just going along for the ride but she didn't really believe you'd ever be successful. She lost all hope, Shane. And that's a dangerous thing."

She nodded, still unsatisfied but willing to accept, for the time being, that he was right again. The difference between Mariana and the rest of them was that they were still hopeful of finding their kids safely. She had lost that.

Shane broke eye contact and looked down and realized, quite shockingly, that his hand was still on her knee. Because she had lost all ability to be subtle or even daresay, flirtatious, Shane did the only natural thing she could think of- she jerked her knee out from under his hand and very obviously stared at anything in the open space in front of her rather than him.

He stifled a laugh and resisted the urge to make fun of her reaction. He didn't dare question her apprehension around him, even after all the time they had spent together; he knew that there was so much more to her backstory than she'd likely ever let on. But he found it humorous that she was so uncomfortable with his attention. If it were innocent or casual, she seemed okay with it; but the second the air became thick with his desire and her cheeks became flushed with her hesitation, she bailed.

After a moment of very uncomfortable silence, Shane summoned the nerve to question him about his unnecessary touching and as she opened her mouth to speak, the radio at her feet crackled.

She picked it up immediately and turned it to the frequency most often used by Julie when checking in.

"Shane," she spoke into the walkie, keeping an eye on Bernchal in her peripheral. He was looking around the rooftop, his arm dangling at his side and almost touching hers.

Julie's voice came in loudly and Shane quickly turned the knob, lowering the volume.

"Carina spotted cars headed your way."

Chapter XXIII

"They don't look like militia, but she didn't recognize them. They circled us three times before heading down."

Shane looked to Bernchal who was already getting up and scanning the ground below them. He crouched at the edge of the roof wall, careful to stay out of the line of sight for random snipers. Shane started to get up as well but he pushed her gently back down with a hand on her left shoulder.

"Stay down. I see two jeeps coming on Corlear."

She silenced the walkie and put it down next to her feet, waiting. She hated to depend on Bernchal, or anyone for that matter, to be her eyes, but she couldn't risk being spotted because she'd been stubborn.

"What's happening?" she whispered.

He watched the two cars come to a stop at the intersection of 238th and Kingsbridge Avenue, feet from the entrance of an old Rite-Aid. The large jeep doors opened and he could see three men exit the vehicle, as another jeep pulled in next to the first, blocking his view. The second vehicle's doors opened and three more men climbed out. He lacked binoculars and the distance did not allow him to make out if they were militia, but he thought he saw a shock of red hair on one of the men.

"Bernchal?" Shane whispered, aggravated. "What the hell is going on?"

He smiled and continued watching the men enter the pharmacy in military formation. One of them stopped to admire a Dodge Charger abandoned in the Rite Aid parking lot before following the others inside, all carrying assault rifles.

"This is killing you, isn't it, Chief? Not knowing what's going on? Relying on someone else for information?"

Shane closed her eyes and prayed for patience.

Lying through gritted teeth, she shook it off. "Nope. I'm good."

"You're a filthy, filthy liar. You know that, Shane? A filthy liar. I can see right through you."

"No, you can't."

He dropped back on his haunches and was suddenly eye level with her, so close that he surprised her and her breath caught in her throat.

"Yes, I can."

His hazel eyes were almost translucent in the sunlight and she stared at him, involuntarily mesmerized. His tone had been light but his expression was dark, his handsome face masked with earnestness. He remained squatted in front of her, fixated on her eyes, one hand touching the roof wall for support. The muscle on his extended arm was flexed and taut and Shane noticed out of the corner of her eye how near it was to her, suddenly.

Everything with Bernchal seemed to have happened suddenly. His arrival, his closeness, his staring. Everything happened at a speed which she had yet to wrap her brain around and Shane was once again caught off guard with him, finding herself at a loss of everything- words, reasoning, functions. He induced in her this rapid fire heartbeat, like a bolt of lightening that fired directly into her chest and made its way through her blood stream, accelerating everything coursing through her veins. She was flushed and damn near hypertensive and she had ignored it up until now but it seemed he was now aware of what was happening inside of her.

Clearing her throat, Shane brushed it off, immediately reverting to the emotion than came easiest for her- anger.

"Goddamit, Bernchal. What did you see?"

He smiled, infuriating her further. He knew what he was doing to her, and her natural reaction to it. And he seemed to enjoy it a little too much.

"Two trucks; six guys. They went into Rite Aid."

Shane glared at him through narrow slits.

"Militia?"

He shook his head and straightened his legs out, keeping his back hunched low to avoid detection by anyone on the ground.

"I don't think so. Pretty sure they're American."

Still bent over, he eyed her, waiting for her next move. In the distance, they heard voices. It used to be that once upon a time that neighborhood had been alive and bustling with people- college kids on their way in and out of class, working folks climbing the elevated station to the train or driving below them on Broadway to work, stay-at-home moms on their way with their little ones to the park down the block.

Now, the air around them was still and silent, nothing heard for miles but the occasional howl or screech of an animal, gunfire or explosion. What was once normal had disappeared and in its absence, the unthinkable had become routine.

They were both deep in thought as the voices could be heard getting onto their vehicles. Car doors slammed and ignitions turned over. The squeal of tires indicated the departure of their guests and finally, Shane released the breath she had been holding.

"Think they're headed up our way?"

He held his hand out for her to grasp and pulled her to her feet.

"Come with me. I have an idea."

She jogged behind him, crouched low, pretending not to notice that her hand was still gripping his. At the roof door, he opened it gingerly, looking inside and around one last time to make sure no one was waiting on other side, and they walked through it, shutting it softly behind them.

In the stairwell, he got close to her and spoke excitedly while she berated herself for thinking about him when there was still a battle to be fought for her son and strangers on their way.

"The dealership across the street. We can gather them there and pin them down."

"Now?"

"No, next week," he replied, sarcastically. "Yes, now, Shane. Right now."

"It's just you and me."

"Yes, a winning combination. But we can radio Julie to bring some girls."

"Women."

"Women. She can bring three of them. Six on six. They're armed but if we surprise them, we can take 'em and no one has to die."

Shane considered his plan for a moment. He enticed her with some more bonuses in a sing-song voice.

"They have two jeeps and lots of guns…"

She smiled despite her attempt to appear pensive.

"And how do you suggest we'd get them there?" she asked.

"Oh, they'll follow the shiny toys. Trust me."

Relenting, Shane handed him the radio so he could call it in. When he reached for it, she realized she'd suddenly given him a lot more power than he'd ever received and she hoped it didn't backfire on her.

Bernchal took the radio and offered her a wink in return. He brought the box to his mouth and clicking the call button, radioed for Julie.

"Julie, this is Commander Bernchal."

After a moment of silence, Julie's voice crackled from the other end.

"Where's Shane?"

He rolled his eyes and watched the smug expression on Shane's face as he answered, "She's right here."

Another second of silence.

"Put her on."

Exasperated, Bernchal shoved the walkie back at Shane and she took it, biting her lip to keep from laughing.

"I'm here."

"Why is he talking to me?"

Stifling a giggle, she replied "Because he's setting something up and needs your help."

"Do I have to?"

"Julie, just give him what he wants. Okay?"

Julie's indignation could be heard through the airwaves and she offered a petulant, "Fine," as Shane handed the walkie talkie back to Bernchal with a *go ahead* shrug of her shoulders.

"Jesus, woman, does your hatred know no bounds?"

"No, it does not. What do you want?"

He ignored the open hostility and replied quickly. "Send four girls to meet us between Gaelic Park and the dealership and another one by the old precinct. Have them bring the fireworks we got from the bodega. Tune them all in to this frequency."

The click on the other end of the radio indicated Julie putting an abrupt end to their conversation.

Bernchal looked up at Shane and handed her the radio, asking "Why does she hate me so much?"

"Well, I can't speak for her," she replied as they began to make their way down the ten flights to the lobby. "But if I had to guess, I'd say it's because you're pretty fucking annoying."

"So it has nothing to do with my penis? That's a first…"

"Excuse me?" she asked, surprised.

Bernchal stopped mid-step and looked at Shane, who had turned to stare at him disbelievingly. He cleared his throat and suddenly began to jog down the stairs past her, quickly trying to side-step his verbal flub.

"Shane, let's go. Stop holding up the traffic."

She stared after him and when it was obvious he was on his way down the staircase without her, followed him. At the bottom, he reached the door first and held it open for her and when she didn't so much as offer any word of thanks, decided to nip the awkwardness in the bud.

"Just so you know, Julie's never seen my penis."

Shane stopped midway through the doorway and faced him, perplexed.

"What?"

He back-peddled immediately.

"No one has! Well, of course some people have. Not people. Women, but I mean no one at the college has. Or Julie."

Shane looked at the pained expression on his face and the red rising to his cheeks and held back a smile.

"What?" she repeated, not really sure what he was trying to say but thoroughly enjoying watching him fumble around to say it.

"What I mean is that no woman has seen my penis. Oh God, I mean no woman in the *house*! No woman in the house has seen my penis," he repeated, mortified.

Purposely, Shane brushed him off and patting him in the chest roughly, commenting patronizingly, "I'm sure they would remember if they had."

Bernchal looked up and closed his eyes, praying to the heavens that she would drop the subject. As she passed through the open door and contemplated making a joke at his expense, the walkie talkie crackled and she held it up immediately, silencing it.

Two quick beeps meant the girls were ready and in position. She looked to Bernchal, who was quickly getting over his little slip-up and together they darted across the street from the Leo Building to Gaelic Park.

In the wooded area above the park, they found Sharee, Julie, Carina and Milagros. Julie smiled when she saw Shane emerge from the crowded tree trunks and immediately scowled when Bernchal appeared behind her.

"Violet and Glynis are in position waiting for your command," she said to Bernchal, handing him a walkie talkie from her waistband.

He took it from her and pressing the side button, spoke softly into the radio as the other five women listened closely.

"Okay, so here's what I need from you guys. We're gonna set off an explosion in one of the cars across the street. We need those guys to head back this way and stay away from the institution."

Sharee spoke up, asking the question that lingered on everyone's minds. "Why wouldn't we just attack them where we're strongest? We have an army behind those doors- we're safe there. Why attack out here with only eight of us?"

"Because we don't want them to know that those are our headquarters. You don't bring the enemy to your front door."

Julie looked to Shane, worried. Bernchal locked eyes with each woman and continued.

"We attack down here, away from our home. This way, if one gets away or escapes, they won't bring back a goddamn platoon with them. We disappear. Understood?"

Sharee looked to Julie and then Shane, who offered no objection. Though they were not openly countering his plans, their faces said it all.

"I know you guys got very used to terrorizing these streets and mowing down militia, but I'm pretty sure they are American. Soldiers, probably. So if we can get some cars, some guns and some answers without killing them, I say we try."

His military training was becoming more evident with each word he uttered. Initially, he had offered a suggestion here and there and for the most part allowed Shane to completely ignore him and run the show. For an alpha male used to ordering soldiers around, it did seem like a lot to get used to. But here he was, calling the shots and planning a strategic attack for them to remain safe in and out of the institution.

When no one challenged him, he continued.

"We set off the explosion and when they are headed this direction, Violet and Glynis keep them from turning south. Basically, I want these guys having only one option to travel- north."

Milagros looked to Shane and asked, "What's north?"

She pointed to Bernchal with her chin and he responded.

"The dealership. That's where we want them to go. And that's where we'll be waiting."

Either Violet or Glynis asked Bernchal a question on the radio and as his attention was diverted, Julie used the opportunity to question Shane.

"And why are we trusting him with this?"

Shane looked from Julie's worried eyes to Bernchal as he talked to the other women on the radio. She decided she had fought it long enough and it was time to trust him, to cut him some slack. No, he was not female and he had not been with them from the beginning of their journey. But he had proven his worth more than once and letting him take the reins and run a mission or two had been long overdue.

Shane took a deep breath and looked at Julie again, meeting her concerned eyes.

"He has a good plan. Honestly, he has some good ideas, and the more we can do to avoid wasting resources, the better. He has a way to grab some stuff without killing anybody if we don't have to."

Julie followed her eyes and also looked at Bernchal on the radio, dropping some lame joke on the other end and flirting shamelessly. She shook her head in bewilderment, but only shrugged. She did not agree with giving any power to Bernchal whatsoever. She did not believe him to be capable of betraying them, but she didn't fully trust him either. Anyone could see the way he looked at Shane, the way he followed her around like a little puppy. Julie did not doubt he would not hurt her, but she did not believe he had her best interests at heart, or any of their interests for that matter.

Lacking any real reason to protest the arrangement, she only shrugged and turned back to the other women to discuss strategy.

Five minutes later everyone was in position. Shane, Bernchal and Milagros were inside the dealership, easily gaining access through a display window Bernchal had kicked in one particularly grueling day running from the militia last Fall. They scattered some of the broken glass around the sidewalk in front and waited for their bait.

The men that had ventured inside the Rite Aid drove down Manhattan College Parkway as anticipated. Violet and Glynis sounded a couple of rounds of gunfire that pushed the travelers south and the call indicating their arrival came over the walkie talkie once they shifted in the right direction. Immediately thereafter, Sharee lit the fuse on the end of the M80 Bernchal had excitedly brought back from an abandoned bodega one day and dropped it under the hood of a shiny new Chrysler 200 parked on the sidewalk in front of the dealership.

She made a break for it, sprinting through the broken display windows and into an office on the first floor, where Julie and Carina waited. She ducked behind a desk when the explosion sounded, shattering the remaining windows on the first floor that had remained in tact. A series of smaller pops went off as the fire under the hood of the car spread through the engine block. Finally, the engine succumbed to the heat and exploded, popping the hood right off and straight up in the air. It landed several feet away in the car lot on the windshield of a Hummer, shattering it instantly.

The car sat engulfed in flames for less than sixty seconds before the two jeeps holding the strangers drove up to the dealership. The men exited the vehicles and examined the fiery car and still curious, entered the dealership with their weapons drawn.

Sharee, Julie, Shane and Carina closed the distance between the men and the far side of the dealership where the stairs to the offices and reception area held Shane and the others, waiting. While two of them remained outside and watched the exterior, the other four entered through the spaces left by the shattered glass and drifted behind cars on display. Two were immediately subdued behind a large Jeep Grand Cherokee, shielding them from view outside. The other two made it around a shiny new Buick Enclave and a Jeep Wrangler before they were also taken out.

The two outside called out for their friends and not hearing a response, split up and entered the dealership. One walked right into an elbow in the nose and his weapon immediately confiscated. He was brought down to his knees by a sharp jab to his stomach and on the floor, he came face to face with the barrel of Carina's gun. He looked around the showroom and saw his other men in the same precarious position and reluctantly surrendered, putting his hands behind his head as ordered.

The last one found a staircase around the back of the building that led upstairs. He made his way up and into what looked like an office and as he rounded the corner into the reception area, the butt of Milagros' handgun knocked him out.

The whole thing lasted less than sixty seconds.

Bernchal pulled the semi-conscious man by the shoulders and dragged him down the hall and towards the showroom. At the stairs, he followed Milagros down, making his way as the man's legs roughly bounced off of each step until the bottom, where he dropped him at Shane's feet. There, she nudged him with the toe of her boot as he came to and looked around, surprised to find the rest of his men also on their knees and captured.

Bernchal recognized the red hair he had seen on one of the men from the roof top and stared at him, feeling a slight twinge of déjà vu. He looked at each of the men, their heads hung low, on their knees with their hands on their heads. They were all large guys, muscular and ripped. The tattoos visible on some of them from under their gear indicated military services but the darkness of the showroom and the receding sunlight outside didn't allow for inspection. Bernchal squinted, trying to get a closer look at their faces as an unsettling feeling crawled up his insides.

Shane walked over to the one that looked the least compliant. Instead of looking down he watched her, eyes locked with a smirk on his large face. He had a scar running from above his right eyebrow to the middle of his cheekbone. Bright blue eyes lightened a sun-weathered face and when Shane cocked her weapon and aimed it at him, he lifted his head up to her and smiled.

"Do what you gotta do, sweetheart, but I gotta tell ya- I've seen worse."

Bernchal's ears piqued at the sound of the voice and he walked around Sharee and Julie towards Shane. The man's back to was to him and when he came around Shane, he got a good look and bellowed, loudly.

"Holy shit! Ruderick?"

Ruderick's eyes met Bernchal and an immediate smile of recognition lit up his face. He laughed and shook his head.

"I'd hug you brother, but I'm afraid your little girlfriend here'll shoot me."

Bernchal reached out and touched Shane's arm and after a moment of hesitation wherein she locked eyes on Bernchal and searched his for certainty, she finally lowered her arm and dropped her weapon to her side.

Bernchal reached down and picked the man up under his elbow, helping him to his feet. They embraced as the rest of the women stood watching, confused.

Chapter XXIV

Pleasantries were exchanged awkwardly. Five women hovering over six men, all with their weapons drawn and centered, while the only male in the hostile group held the leader of the strangers in a bear hug. It made for quite the Norman Rockwell painting.

"What the hell are you doing here?" asked Bernchal after he released his friend. He was smiling wider than Shane had ever seen and she watched him, curious, as he embraced the other five men excitedly.

The large man hesitated before putting his hands anywhere other than in view and pointed to Shane with his chin.

"I oughtta ask you the same thing, brother. It looks like you're doing pretty damn well for yourself."

Shane raised an eyebrow and eyed him. She detected a slight Aussie brogue, one faded after years of American dialect.

Bernchal looked to Shane again and this time asked, "Can you ask them to drop their weapons, Shane? For the love of God- we've already determined they're not hostile."

"Have we?" asked Julie, her hazel eyes shining in the quickly fading light. It was past seven in the evening and the sky outside was rapidly darkening. The lack of artificial light in the showroom made their only visibility come from the setting sun, so behind Julie an orange glow lent her angry face an eerier feel.

Bernchal furrowed his brows and looked at Julie, insulted. "Yes, we have. Drop the guns, guys. They're friendlies."

The women looked to Shane for approval, reminding Bernchal once again, lest he forget, that he would never be in charge. She locked eyes with him a moment longer while she considered and finally agreed, nodding her okay.

The other three complied, with Julie being the last to hesitantly drop her gun to her side. She simmered on the side of the showroom, watching the exchange through angry slits.

The men all stood shakily. The redhead rubbed the back of his neck where he'd been blindsided by Sharee just moments ago. The large one looked around at them and at the women, sizing each one up. Finally, he turned to Shane and spoke.

"What exactly was this here- a takedown? Did you intend to do something with us once we were subdued?"

His voice barely masked the anger radiating off of him. It was obvious he was not accustomed to being overpowered by a group of women with guns.

Shane cocked her head to the side and answered flatly, "Ask your buddy. This was his idea."

He continued staring at Shane and smiled, his eyes maintaining hostility despite the expression on his face. Shane stared back, unmoved. Bernchal interjected quickly in an attempt to diffuse an already shaky situation.

"Ruderick, this is Shane. She runs this whole outfit. Shane, Ruderick," he said pointing from one to the other. He did not expect handshakes and was not surprised to see none offered.

"How'd you get to this neighborhood?" he asked in the hopes of creating some good-will among his new and old friends.

"We've been through here a dozen times, following the same slant-eyed scout."

Bernchal and Shane exchanged a troubled glance. As far as they knew, the militia cruised by sporadically, and never in the same vehicle.

"What scout?"

Ruderick entertained their inquiries and replied. "Some jackoff in a sports car. Same guy every second Wednesday of the month. He'd run up and down the West Side Highway from the Heights to Ardsley for a couple of hours and then duck into the park to meet some chick."

"Some chick?" repeated Bernchal, his tone of voice questioning though he had already deduced Ruderick's response. Beside him, Shane kept quiet, her mouth in a thin, tight line, her jaw clenching.

"About yay high," replied Ruderick, motioning below his chin with his hand. "Long, dark hair. Dead eyes."

Julie muttered under her breath, "Fucking bitch..."

He continued, undaunted. He addressed them nonchalantly but his eyes gave away his interest, watching their reactions closely.

"They exchanged information like clockwork. She'd hand him notes; he'd point around, yell some stuff and leave her there, dejected."

"Where?" Julie's urgent request came out stronger than she'd intended and Ruderick couldn't help but smile.

"Everywhere. We followed him around and it was always someolace different: Fort Tryon, that college on the Westchester border. Always a different place, always a 1-2-3 exchange."

He paused for dramatic effect, looked around and made mental notes of their individual reactions. "About four, maybe five months ago, dude suddenly stops coming around. Haven't seen them since."

Shane nodded, silently seething. Mariana's betrayal had been spied on by Ruderick and his men for months it seemed, yet she had remained ignorant. Wordlessly scrambling, she thought back to every run, every single time Mariana would separate from the designated group and instead of chastising her, they would sympathize with her. She cursed herself for never suspecting sabotage within the confines of her own home.

Noticing he'd hit a nerve, Ruderick commented, slyly.

"Looks like I'm referring to someone you may know."

Shane opened her mouth to respond, but Julie cut her off, her voice low and menacing.

"Looks like you should mind your fucking business."

Ruderick bit his lower lip, holding back a laugh, and watched the women closely, his body tense despite the humor on his face. Neither Shane nor Julie relented and they stared right back, essentially challenging him. Realizing the two women had absolutely no qualms with entering into a pissing contest with him, and would likely win, he broke his stare and turned to Bernchal, eager to get some intel.

"So, what's the deal here? You with these scavengers? You know a place we can hole up for the night? We've been pretty much on foot since D.C. and just now got a hold of these two vehicles. Where're you staying?"

Bernchal looked to Shane quickly, hoping for some sort of understanding and maybe a little help. But he knew he would be getting none unless he pled his case to her and begged for Ruderick and his men to stay with them. Instead, he ushered Ruderick over to the side to talk with him and the men, a couple of whom he reacquainted himself with after having been separated upon their return from Africa.

"How the hell did you end up here?" he asked Ruderick after the greetings had been done and the other men were tending to their wounds. The women were off in a corner talking hushed, presumably plotting a way to keep them out of the college.

"After we split, we lost Taylor and Rodriguez," replied Ruderick, his large arms crossed over his barrel chest. He eyed the women as they spoke but he continued addressing Bernchal directly.

"Abernathy disappeared somewhere outside of Maryland."

"Jesus Christ. Anybody else?"

Ruderick shook his head, sadly. His blue eyes were barely visible through the scowl on his face and though he still eyed the women from time to time, he finally made eye contact with Bernchal and answered.

"Williams went back to Jersey, or what's left of it. No one's heard from him since. And Martinez... Martinez found out about his wife and kids..."

"Fuck..."

"Yeah. He fucking lost it. Last we saw him he was headed to D.C. and we were on our way here."

"Damn. How many are you?"

"Six. Derrecks, Torres, Muccio, Hiu, Huvane and me."

Bernchal's voice dropped low, out of earshot. He had yet to discuss the details of his past with Shane to a certain degree and considered it retribution for her secretive nature.

"How the fuck did you get out of the south when we left the camp?"

Ruderick pointed to the redhead with his chin. "Huvane had an in. When we split his people gave us a ride to HQ. You should've seen it. Looked like a scene out of The Walking Dead. We had to lift a chopper and head south to Langley. Militia shot us down over Baltimore. That's how we lost Ryan, and eventually Taylor and Rodriguez. Have you seen anything?"

Bernchal shook his head.

"I headed north. Almost didn't make it a couple of times but these chicks here found me out in the woods. Been with them ever since."

"Just as well," he replied, shrugging his oversized shoulders. Bernchal stood at about 6'4 and steadily built but he was dwarfed next to Ruderick.

"Everything south of here is hopeless. Even worse than this. The land is desolate and the militia's got complete control. We ended up stowing away on some freighter trains for a ride up the east coast and made it up to the upper west side on foot. We commandeered those two jeeps and started driving through the blocks that were once densely populated, looking for shelter. Hoping maybe we could shut down for a bit, take refuge until we reconvene; that is until we encountered these pissed off bitches here."

Bernchal flinched at the insult, knowing jabs like that would not fly back at the institution, that is *if* they were allowed inside.

"I'm sure I can get you fed and recharged; that shouldn't be a problem. But I have to work on a place to stay."

Ruderick raised an eyebrow and smirked. "So you're taking orders from chicks, now? A far cry from the Bernchal *I* knew."

He ignored the sting and walked away, back towards Shane and the other women for a quick pow-wow. Though it had not been in his nature prior to his arrival at the college, Bernchal had learned long ago to play nice. Those women who had saved him, fed and clothed him and brought him back to life were surviving against impossible odds and working their asses off to find their kidnapped kids, so he had not been in a place to demand a position of authority simply because he was male. That was at first. Now that he was part of the inner circle, maybe he could pull some strings for his friends, but he knew if he was to get his way, he'd have to tread lightly.

"Shane," he called out to her as he neared. She looked up from a deep conversation with Julie and Carina and waited.

"Can we talk over here?"

Shane hesitated, no doubt to avoid looking as though she was willingly coming when summoned. Bernchal knew her well by now and she was above all things, fiercely independent. Even appearing to give in to him was going to be a problem for her.

He waited patiently a bit of a way away from the other women talking amongst themselves. Ruderick and his guys were convening by the model cars in the showroom, using the bumpers to prop themselves up. Sharee and Milagros were lingering by the staircase leading up to the offices, attempting to appear disinterested and failing miserably. Their eye bore holes into the skulls of the men and while they whispered to each other, they watched them, suspicion written all over their faces and their hands fingering their weapon expectantly. Bernchal could see that this was going to be harder than even he had imagined.

Carina broke away from Shane and Julie and joined the other two women as he waited close to the broken display window. The flames from the car out front still burned, though significantly less so, and the heat emanating from the explosion reached him as he waited. The pane of the shattered window occasionally released another shard of glass that fell to the concrete floor and surprised them all.

Shane and Julie approached him gingerly, Shane looking blank, as usual, and Julie doing nothing to hide the obvious disdain written all over her face.

He started, watching them both as he spoke to capture their reactions.

"Okay, here's the deal. I served with these men in Africa; all of them. We were part of different units that ended up getting back home together. I know them, and more importantly, I trust them, and I'm asking you to trust *me* and take them in."

Before they could protest, he continued.

"Now you don't have to decide for how long right now, but we do need to go. The explosion more than likely will bring some visitors; if not the fire, then the smoke. We have to leave. I need to bring these guys back with us. They need food, clothes and some shelter, at least for the night."

He turned to Shane, the less hostile of the two, and addressed her directly. "Shane, you know as well as I do that it wouldn't hurt to get some fresh intel on the outside. Our runs lately have been so few and far between, we've squandered our resources everywhere around us. We need new eyes and ears on this."

She ran her tongue absentmindedly against her teeth, under her lips, an act that often indicated serious thought. Her eyes though were trained on his and she considered every word he said carefully. Julie, however, was not moved and she immediately answered, "No."

Shane was just as surprised at Bernchal and they exchanged looks before he questioned, "No?"

She adjusted her stance, crossed her arms over her chest and glared at him.

"You heard me. No. This whole thing is a little too suspicious."

Bernchal stared at her, his hazel eyes glaring in disbelief. "Suspicious? What the fuck is suspicious about asking us to allow six fucking *American soldiers* into the school?"

"It's suspicious because, what? You just happen to know them?" she questioned, her voice rising with each syllable.

"Are you fucking kidding me right now?" he asked aloud to no one in particular, his body tensing in agitation.

"How convenient that out of all the people on this fucking planet, you happen to know the guys we capture; the guys *you* insisted we capture *your* way, might I add?

The men remained oblivious to the exchange but the women were all ears as Bernchal hovered over Julie and fired back.

"Yes, yes, Julie. Out of the all the people on this fucking planet," he repeated. "But did you forget out of all the people on this fucking planet, there are only like fifty men left?! And yes, coincidentally, out of those fifty fucking surviving men, I happen to know six of them. How fucking insane is that, huh? What a goddamn conspiracy!"

He looked at her, shocked and insulted at her accusations. Julie in turn scoffed and glared at him, simmering. Shane started to interject and Julie went off again.

"Its not a fucking coincidence that you show up and infiltrate our camp and all of a sudden, your little friends pop up out of nowhere."

"Out of nowhere?" he yelled, exasperatedly. "Seriously? I've been with you guys for almost two years!"

"And was this your plan the whole time?"

Bernchal looked ready to blow a fuse and he backed up a few steps, seemingly to keep himself from doing something he'd regret. His knuckles were closed tight and his lips drawn in a straight line. The muscle in his jaw flexed as he gritted his teeth and stared at Julie, the anger permeating from him palpable.

Shane put a hand on his arm and looked at Julie with wide eyes, imploring her to back off. Julie complied reluctantly and turned suddenly, sauntering off across the increasingly dark showroom towards the other women.

She turned to him, concerned but still not convinced.

"You understand where she's coming from?" she said to him, more of a statement than a question.

He tried to ignore Julie and instead, plea to Shane's logic.

"You know I'm right. You know we need them."

Shane pondered his proposition. He was right; lately their runs had been worthless. Since Mariana's betrayal, every move they made was anticipated and blocked. Though Shane had intercepted the message and the militia had been unable to find their headquarters, Mariana had nonetheless provided them with enough information to seemingly give them an advantage for the time being. Shane, Bernchal and the women were powerless to go beyond the borders of their neighborhood and any attempt to do so had been swiftly and devastatingly botched.

Still, even knowing this, she was remiss to jump into a new union headfirst. Bernchal knew them, but she did not. She had believed she'd known Mariana and look how well that had turned out.

"Why should we trust them? "

He answered candidly. "You trust *me*."

"Commander, you are asking me go let six guys I don't know from a hole in the wall see all of our secrets and live in here with us like its one big fucking orgy."

Again, he replied honestly and his four words carried immeasurable weight.

"You let me in."

She hesitated, unable to fight him despite her better judgment.

"If somebody comes out pregnant, I'm blaming you."

Bernchal smiled wildly and immediately tried to contain his enthusiasm. Effortlessly switching over to a casual smirk, he pointed his long finger at her and said, "You know something? You gotta get your energy right."

"Excuse me?"

"Your chi. It's off. You gotta get it right."

"Okay," she replied, eyes closed and head shaking.

He walked away from her towards Ruderick, no doubt to deliver the good news.

"You need good juju," he called to her over his shoulder.

Gotcha, she said to herself, wondering if he was actually right.

Chapter XXV

They left to the institution separately, Shane with her women and Bernchal with his men. Shane needed the few minutes alone on foot to ease Julie's reservations and convince the others her decision was actually a good one, through if she were honest with herself, she needed a little convincing, too.

As the two vehicles holding the men drove away, along with some matching car batteries and supplies from the service department of the dealership, Shane and the others started back to the institution on foot. They carefully cut through the old apartment buildings on Tibbett and Orloff Avenues and made their way up the steep hill, adjacent to the city steps connecting the bottom of the hill with Riverdale at the top.

Julie walked alongside Shane doing little to hide her pouting. She shuffled her feet with each step, her small black boots dragging the leaves beneath her and repeating the same crackling sound over and over. After a few minutes of silence wherein she let Julie stew in her own anger, Shane spoke up.

"What was that? Now he really thinks you hate him."

Julie shrugged and spoke through the scowl on her lips.

"I don't hate him. He irritates the shit out of me, but I don't hate him. It was a show; so that those goons don't think we're eager to please."

Shane nodded and pressed forward.

"I know what you're thinking. But we took a chance on Bernchal and we have to take a chance on these guys."

Julie shot her a look of impatience. "But you barely trust him."

"True," she replied, conceding that much. "But he's proven his worth, Julie. You have to admit that."

"Fine, I'll admit that. But honestly Shane, we can't really afford him, so then how can we afford them, too? We are barely surviving as it is. Supplies are dwindling and the runs are yielding nothing. Mariana really fucked us," she added, voice low and sounding lost. Her hazel eyes darkened a little and she looked away from Shane with a forlorn expression on her face, reminding her friend just how much they all felt that loss.

Shane watched her feet as she stepped gingerly along their usual trail towards the college. The leaves crunched beneath her weight and she ignored the sound and focused on Julie and her concerns.

She was right. They were essentially starving. When Bernchal had first arrived, they were doing as well as possible considering the times in which they now lived. A year later, they were just making do, finding enough food and supplies to keep them above water. Now, after another year, a betrayal that had left them vulnerable to attacks on their home front and incapable of refueling themselves further away, they were in trouble.

Food was scarce and they had tapped out all of their resources in the neighborhood. The militia were looking for them now and Shane believed were it not for the remaining rebels who sporadically showed their faces, blew some shit up and distracted their enemies, they'd have been found long ago.

"Everything you're saying is true. But there is no other way, Julie. If there were, I'd have tried it already. We need help. And we have no one we can trust directly. At least these are some guys who… I don't know, *seem* like we can trust. Maybe that's the best we can do right now."

She waited for Julie to process and respond. Her jaw was clenching, unclenching and grinding hard and she tightened her lips in concentration. Shane knew that she pretty much set the rules; it was a position she did not desire but accepted without question. And she knew that if she put her foot down, the others undoubtedly would follow. But she would much rather have them be in agreement than to cause discord that would allow Bernchal's men to muscle their way in and unweave the fabric of their civilization.

Finally, as they neared the top of the hill and turned right through the wooded park towards the school's main entrance, Julie spoke.

"I don't agree that it's the best we can do. But I trust *you*. And if you think this will get us closer to our kids and help us survive until we find them…" Her voice trailed off as she eyed Shane directly, searching for a direct answer.

"I do. I really think we can use them to our benefit."

She paused and decided to ask the question that traveled alongside them, like an elephant forcing his way between them.

"Can I count on you?"

Julie stopped short, taken aback. "That's a hell of a thing for you to ask."

She watched Shane, waiting, who in turn, smiled.

"I know. That's why I asked it."

After a second, Julie broke the stare, rolled her eyes and smiled, too.

"I see some of that fool's comedy is rubbing off on you. Among other things…"

She knew what she had implied, but Shane dismissed her innuendo and pretended, albeit horribly, to act confused.

"What's that supposed to mean?"

Julie smiled mischievously as they walked to the security booth and alerted the women inside to their arrival. A second later, Milagros and Vanessa pushed open the gates and let them in.

"You know exactly what it means," she replied through a smirk. When Shane continued to stare in expectation of a response, she opened her mouth and commented incredulously. "Come on, seriously? It's obvious the guy is infatuated with you. You have to see that," she said, stating the obvious. Shane, speechless, just shrugged her shoulders and continued her pathetic attempt at nonchalance.

"No…" was all she could muster with a straight face.

They approached the main entrance as the gate closed behind them and with a quick and playful nudge, Julie bid her goodnight and disappeared in the darkness. Instead of going her usual route through the cafeteria, Shane shifted and turned past the main building, towards the dormitories.

As she walked alone she digested what Julie had said to her, along with the day's events. A new group of men to not only house, feed and clothe, but to watch as well. Yes, they were with Bernchal, but she was not able to fully trust them yet. Realistically, she was unable to fully trust anyone, Bernchal included, but she had come to not only value his opinion, but to rely on him as well. And with a huff to no one in particular, Shane decided that that behavior would end now. Yes, Bernchal was helpful and intelligent, but she had made a promise long ago, when she doubted she would survive the militia's brutal torture. She had vowed then to never, *ever* rely on any man for anything, whatsoever. And constantly she found herself waiting for Bernchal's opinion, holding off on a decision until she got his input. If she was to lead these women to find their children and avenge them, Shane decided she could not continue down the same dangerous path.

Bernchal was waiting for her outside of her room when she arrived. He was leaning against her closed door, one leg bent and propped up behind him, his long and lean body crouched in a perfectly nonchalant position. With the fit of his jeans and the faded bomber jacket he'd collected from one of the rooms in the new dormitory on Waldo Avenue, he stood out in the empty hallway, like the cool kid on the first day of school. The James Dean-esque quality to his style and disposition always unnerved Shane and her heart did a little jump as she turned the corner and saw him at the end of the corridor.

She immediately shook it off and walked towards him as though he didn't just steal her breath and she hadn't just vowed to stop leaning on him for support.

"Can I help you, Commander?"

Her voice was curt and though she intended for it to be a warning to Bernchal for him to maintain his distance, he ignored it, as he often ignored her many attempts to rebuff his friendship, and smiled at her.

"Hey there. A quick word, if you please."

He put his elevated leg down and shifted to the right, allowing her barely enough room to reach for the doorknob and turn it. She did so and her hand grazed his forearm. He didn't move, so she opened the door and walked through it, pretending not to notice his close proximity.

There'd been a lot of pretending between them lately.

She walked ahead of him and lit the gas lamp on her desk, bathing the room in a dim yellow hue that barely made a difference. But they had become so accustomed to it, their eyes adjusted immediately.

"How's this gonna work?" he began immediately, anxious to deal with the logistics and set his friends up to avoid any altercations between them and the women.

"You mean your little guests?" she asked, an eyebrow raised. Her voice was laced with sarcasm but her eyes told a different story and Bernchal knew she was acting angrier than she felt. He knew it was Julie who had opposed their decision and though Shane had her reservations, she had been able to see the bigger picture.

"Yes, Shane. My 'guests' need some guidelines," he replied, using air quotes.

She walked over to her bed and sat on the edge of it, realizing too late the impropriety of it. He noticed but did not let on.

"I set them up in the same hall as me. I gave Ruderick my room and took the first one in the hall so I can keep an eye on their comings and goings."

Shane looked at him from her position on the bed and joked. "How can you keep an eye on them if you spend all your time on the women's side?"

"You know, you can be very emasculating at times, Shane." His voice was stern but his eyes crinkled in the corners, twinkling.

"And you can be very sexist at times, Steven."

Bernchal broke into a wide grin and lowered his voice, his hazel eyes now fiery and inviting.

"I love it when you say my name."

She gulped, convinced the sound was loud enough for him to hear.

There it was again- that drawl.

Clearing her throat and trying to reset the atmosphere, she stretched out an open palm towards him.

"Do they need anything- clothes? Stuff…"

He shook his head and replied, "I'll find them clothes and give them the basic rundown I got upon my arrival- that super sweet guided tour I received."

She held back a smile and asked, "So what do you want from me? Seems like you got it all covered."

"I just want to make sure we're on the same page," he answered, more serious. He leaned against her desk and turned to face her, eyeing her, and licked his lips considering his next words.

"I know you didn't have to do this, so… thanks. They're good guys. A little rough around the edges, but good. You'll see."

She didn't respond, just nodded and pressed her lips together, a small dimple on the right side of her mouth appearing.

He lingered and she guessed maybe he wasn't ready to leave.

"How do you know them?" she asked.

His expression changed, from pensive to melancholy.

"The war," he replied. His eyes moved from hers to the the gas lamp next to him on her desk. The flickering light moved around and cast shadows around the room. The amber tones in his eyes took possession and dominated the green, and before long she was lost in a sea of yellow.

"After we basically watched the whole of the United States military get massacred in Africa, we ended up in the same squadron. Ruderick and Taylor became our designated leaders. Unofficial command. They got us out of there, back to America; or whatever America had turned into by then.

When we got there, it was originally two battalions, thirty men each, give or take. We got whittled down to forty-six off bat. Somehow we managed to stay safe for the remaining year we were stuck there. Kept our noses clean, avoided the North Koreans like the plague. Learned the genocide was American made. As things got progressively worse here, they got downright morbid over there. We lost twenty more guys to diseases- malaria, exposure. You name it, we went through it. By the time

Ruderick and Taylor got us out of there we were down to fourteen. We jumped a ship headed for Europe and commandeered it back to the US. Got through a port in North Carolina and got captured, sent to a POW camp of sorts. After a couple of months, we managed to escape. That's where we split. I ended up here and he tells me now there's just six of us left. Six. Out of sixty. Unfuckingreal."

He took a deep breath and swallowed, visibly spent.

"With you it makes seven," she contributed softly.

He faced her again and a small smile started at the corner of his mouth.

"If that's your idea of looking at the bright side…"

Shane smiled back, shaking her head. "Not really. I'm not much for optimism. I was just correcting your math."

Bernchal chuckled, despite his solemn speech. More serious, Shane put her head down and stared at her feet.

"I'm sorry you lost your friends."

Bernchal eyed her, grateful. "It seems we know a lot about loss then, you and I. We make quite the team."

She looked up again and made eye contact. Underneath her hard, unyielding exterior and his jubilant, playful one, at the end of the day it seemed they were both immeasurably sad, each having lost so much when the world had changed.

Unable to trust that if he stayed in her room any longer and watched her sitting perched on the edge of her bed for one more second with that somber expression on her lovely face he'd likely never want to leave, Bernchal stood up straight suddenly and cleared his throat.

"Well, I'm off. Gotta make sure these guys don't burn down the place. Talk to you later."

He was gone before she could say anything and she immediately breathed a sigh of relief, reluctantly admitting to herself that she too, might have done something stupid had he stayed.

Chapter XXVI

Outside of Shane's room, Bernchal pulled her door closed and started for the other side of the dorms. He shoved his hands in the pockets of his jacket and walked swiftly, back hunched low and eyes cast downward.

The situation with Shane was becoming complicated, or however complicated it could be considering the world had been overtaken, their government overthrown, her son had been kidnapped and they were on a quest of vengeance and murder to get him back.

He was loyal to these women that had saved his life on more than one occasion, and would do pretty much anything for them. And he was loyal to Shane, for more reasons than that. But his men, his brothers, were back. They had returned from the grave when he thought he had no one but his new all-female family by his side. *What will come next?* he wondered, worried that Ruderick's arrival would inevitably spell trouble for him.

The men were settling in inside the institution, most of them having since stuffed their faces and taken hot showers, much to the dismay of many women, and the delight of a few others. Muccio and Hiu were in the corridor of their side when he arrived. They were using most of the hallway to reload ammunition in their weapons and though they seemed relaxed, he noticed their hands immediately reach for their weapons when he neared.

After exchanging pleasantries and a bit of some good-natured ribbing, he passed them and made it to the end of the hallway towards his old room. He knocked once and opened the door and found Ruderick hunched over the desk, looking over a few maps he'd found on the tabletop.

"Wood," he called, getting his attention. Ruderick looked up at him, acknowledged his presence and went back to the maps.

Ruderick and Shane it seemed, were more alike than either knew, and to Bernchal, that was definitely a recipe for disaster.

"I assume this is the territory surrounding this place," he stated, and without waiting for an answer, continued. "The gates in the front are gonna be a problem if we plan to bring more vehicles up. The slant-eyes we've come across cover everything so they'll have to have seen the fire today. We have to get back to those cars and salvage what we can. If we-"

"Wood," Bernchal interrupted. "Relax. You don't have to plan everything. Just take a load off and rest up. Enjoy the sanctuary."

"There's no rest, Steve. No time to relax. If we are going to develop a plan here, we have to immediately strategize."

"What plan? Jesus, can't you just go to fucking sleep on an actual bed and enjoy it for once?" Bernchal demanded, exasperated. Though more than two years had passed since they'd gone their separate ways during the tumultuous escape from the camp, it was obvious to him nothing had changed. Ruderick was already formulating, already plotting ways to keep fighting.

Ruderick looked up from the map and crossed his hands on the desk. "What's the story with these chicks? How have they survived this long?"

Bernchal looked at him and explained, briefly.

"They've survived because they're smart. And they're fucking terrifying. These women were taken from their homes, separated from their kids and kept in concentration camps, trained to be killers for this new twisted army this whole goddamn disaster was building. I've seen them cut down these fuckers without blinking an eye. We're talking actual military training," he emphasized, hoping Ruderick would see the benefit in working with Shane and the others.

"They've made more progress in searching for their missing kids than we made doing whatever the hell it was they sent us out to do all that time in Africa. This place is a fortress- they got sentries watching the perimeter and scouting the place literally twenty-four hours a day; reinforcements, ammunition. Everything is planned and executed with precision."

Ruderick watched his impassioned speech, expressionless, so he dug deeper.

"Look, Wood, these women saved my life. Another day, hell, another *hour* out there and I would have frozen to death or been eaten by a fucking mountain lion or something. They saved me when they didn't have to; they gave me a place to stay and food to eat when they didn't have to; and they've saved my life countless other times since when we've been out in the field. Don't underestimate them, *any* of them."

When Bernchal was done, Ruderick nodded a couple of times and frowned, creasing his brow and asking him bluntly, "Why are you here with them?"

He was caught off guard but he hid it well. "Excuse me?"

"Why are you here with them?" he repeated.

Bernchal hesitated, unsure of the meaning behind the loaded question.

"I'm not *with* them."

"Then, why are you here?" asked Ruderick, eyes small and questioning. "The pussy can't be that good."

Suddenly annoyed, Bernchal tensed. "Watch your mouth."

With a knowing smirk, Ruderick replied.

"So, there *is* something here."

"There's nothing there. I told you- I was half fucking dead. They literally saved me. I stayed because I had no where else to go," he answered, annoyed. It was true, mostly.

"So it's gratitude?"

Bernchal hesitated. *Is it?* he wondered.

"This is a cause; these women are fighting to get their kids back."

"But it isn't your fight."

Bernchal knew Ruderick was playing Devil's Advocate, something he often did to illustrate a point. And he knew he should present a clear and direct picture of the way things worked at the institution if he wanted harmony between everyone. But he could feel the anger, the frustration bubbling to the surface. Memories of Africa, of the men he had lost and the brutality he had witnessed came rushing back to him and he felt the heat rising to his face as he responded, with measured tone.

"It wasn't our fight in Africa either."

Ruderick squinted his eyes at Bernchal and answered, his voice dropping with authoritative reprimand.

"Yes it was, or did you forget your oath to your country?"

Bernchal snapped and screamed back at him.

"There's no oath left to uphold! That oath got fifty-three of us killed! That fucking oath kept us out there trying to survive when we could have been here with our people, keeping these kids safe and this country safe. What the hell did we come back for if not to help our own people?"

Muccio and Hiu were suddenly at the doorway, leaning against the doorjamb casually as though they weren't eavesdropping. But Bernchal didn't care. He just stared at Ruderick as his chest rose and fell.

Ruderick considered his question before asking "How is staying with a bunch of moms going to help anyone? You should be worried about how we can set things right in Washington, Steve."

The condescending undertone was gone from his voice, replaced with something more patronizing but understanding. Bernchal calmed and rubbed his chin, impatiently. He needed peace between the men and women; he needed synchrony if they were to survive.

"Look, this plan may not restore this country in one shot, but it's a start. These women have intel. The people who took their kids have a direct line to the President, the whole crew responsible for Africa, everything. We get those kids back and we have a place to start from. We walk away now and its lost."

"Steve-"

"Just… just take a look at the operation," he pled, hearing the urgency in his voice but not giving a damn. "It's something else. This isn't some amateur hour, trust me. The militia that tore through here used them. Trained them. Set them up as living, breathing weapons. These chicks wiped them out and took everything, turned it all around and used it to get their kids back. Projections, land surveyance, tracking- they got it all. It's impressive, Wood. And it's definitely worth looking at."

Ruderick considered and relented, throwing his large hands up in front of him and shaking his head. His sharp blue eyes trained on Bernchal and replied.

"Fine, we'll take a look at it. I guess it couldn't hurt. Who's their leader- the mean one with the gun, right?"

Bernchal took a deep breath and replied under his breath.

"Yup. That'd be her."

Chapter XXVII

The first altercation came sooner than Bernchal had hoped, but not as soon as he'd expected. Living for the past two years in a dormitory full of women who had been seemingly captured and enslaved and had had their children taken from them had educated him to their likes, needs and various idiosyncrasies. As such, he had expertly braced himself for their reaction to a new group of unknown men. What he had not taken into account however, was the men's reaction to them.

He arrived to the cafeteria at Shane's behest to an argument already underway. Though he caught the tail end, he immediately recognized the voices of the parties involved and picked up his speed to break it up.

Julie and Huvane were in each other's faces yelling at the top of their lungs as a circle already formed around them. Shane was there, hovering behind Julie, body tense and ready to jump into action. Bernchal rushed to get in the middle and stop it before it escalated or worse yet, Shane got involved.

He immediately elbowed his way through the crowd and stepped right in between Huvane and Julie. Her cheeks were red with anger and she set her lips in a tight line, fuming.

"What's the problem?"

"This fucking neanderthal thinks everyone here is his goddamn slave, that's what the problem is."

At the word 'neanderthal,' Huvane immediately started his counterattack.

His cheeks reddened and hid the freckles all over his face and he reeled back, screaming, "Fuck you, you self-righteous psychopath! It's a fucking bowl of oatmeal-get over it!"

"Whoa! Whoa, whoa, stop! Cut it out!" he yelled, pushing Huvane back by his barrel chest. His dark eyes glared at Julie and then at Bernchal as he directed his anger suddenly at him.

"Taking her side, Bernchal? Seriously?"

Bernchal dropped his arm and got close to his ear, replying quietly, "I'm stopping you from doing something stupid. Walk it off, Huvane. *Now.*"

Behind him, Julie chimed in.

"Yeah, walk it off… *bitch.*"

It set him off and Huvane pushed against Bernchal again, hollering profanities at Julie. Bernchal pushed at him again, shoving him further and further towards the cafeteria exit. Behind Huvane, Ruderick leaned against the brick wall and watched the exchange, disinterested. Bernchal glared at him, pissed. He simply stared back and offered no help so Bernchal pushed Huvane harder until they reached the exit.

"Walk it off, soldier. Walk it off!"

Huvane got his footing and pushed back against Bernchal, shoving him off. He stood still for a moment, breathing hard and contemplating his next move. And though the government was gone and with it the hierarchy of the military, he nonetheless reverted back to his training and decided to follow his superior commander's order. With a sneer directed in the general vicinity of the cafeteria, he turned and walked down the dark corridor alone.

Derrecks and Hiu followed behind him, seemingly undisturbed by the melee. Breathing a sigh of relief, Bernchal watched as Muccio jogged out of the cafeteria and ran after them, throwing over his shoulder, "Don't worry, Commander. We got this."

Bernchal watched them disappear into the dark and when they were out of sight, he leaned back against the wall and took a deep breath. Closing his eyes, he shook his head and reconsidered his misguided quest for camaraderie.

"Things not going according to plan?"

He shot open his eyes and caught Shane angling in the cafeteria entrance, one arm gripping the doorway and balancing her, the other holding a mug. She smiled at him and he was surprised to see it was neither sarcastic nor derisive. Instead, it was sincere, like a comforting smile offered to a friend in need.

He didn't answer; truthfully, couldn't. In the empty hallway, with the rays of sunlight peeking out from the cafeteria and shining behind her, and her long, wild mane of curls cascading down her back with loose tendrils outlining her face, she was breathtaking.

She let go of the doorway and walked to him, the hand holding the cup outstretched and offering.

"This is for you. Figured you could use a cup of hot chocolate. Marshmallows make everything better."

Bernchal accepted the mug and offered a look of defeat.

"Am I so pathetic that you try to cheer me up with a gift meant for a child?"

Shane shrugged her shoulders. "I can take it back…"

He gripped the mug and shook his head stubbornly. "No backsies."

She smiled and kicked at the linoleum, distractedly.

"Making peace isn't as simple as you thought it was, is it?"

He met her eyes and answered honestly. "I didn't think it would be simple, I just… I thought it would be easier than this. It's been a month and no one communicates. The guys are going stir crazy and want to be released and the women-Jesus, the women treat them like they're fucking murderers and psychos."

She gave him a sympathetic look and glanced down the hallway down which Huvane had retreated moments ago.

"We weren't always this well-oiled machine. Before you got here, we went through our own issues. We just saw the bigger picture. That's what helped us get on the same page."

"With all due respect, Cap, there's no way I can get these guys to see the bigger picture. It's enough that they barely take you all seriously. We're dealing with a lot of imbedded sexism. There's no way I can get them to join a mission they don't believe in."

"I'm sure there were plenty of orders you guys had to follow that you didn't exactly believe in."

He considered her words as he eyed her. "I'm not the boss of these men. No one is. I can urge them, even push them to fight for you, but at the end of the day, I can't make them believe in it."

"Sure you can. Do *you* believe in it?"

Bernchal stared back at her but could not reply. The question seemed unanswerable. Did he believe in their mission or was he along for the ride? Did he care about the outcome or did he only care about *her*?

After a contemplative moment of awkward silence, he answered genuinely.

"I do."

"Then you can convince them," she replied with a knowing shrug.

He was annoyed at her certainty, and even more annoyed at his futile attempts thus far.

"That's easier said than done. And it doesn't help that you guys, present company included, behave like schizoid killers."

The lightheartedness was immediately replaced by a different tone in her voice, a defensive tilt in her tongue.

"What would you prefer out there- a schizoid killer or a proper young lady?"

Bernchal detected the change in demeanor and tried to keep it playful for as long as possible, but with Shane, it was often a crapshoot. There was so much he still didn't know about her past and he could never anticipate when the wrong joke or comment would mean the difference between casual banter and a lecture on propriety.

He bargained for the banter and countered. "Can't you be both? A schizoid killer out there and a proper young lady in here?"

She surprised him with her reply.

"I hate to break it to you, but duel personalities aren't what's going to get the job done."

"How do you know?"

She shot him a look, less of anger and more of resignation, as though she had answered the question a million times before and was beginning to accept it would never be understood.

"I know 'cause I've been that. The intelligent, attractive, capable woman in the room that kept every man on their toes. That got the job done back then. That's the woman that showed up and worked in that world, but it doesn't work here in this one. So, if I have to be the schizoid killer with no remorse or compassion, then that's who I'll be if it means getting the job done here. *That's* the woman who'll show up here in this world if need be. That's who we are now."

Detecting the sadness in her voice and the hollow look in her dark eyes, Bernchal pushed further. It was no longer about making him feel better; this had become something more.

"Who were you then?"

Shane scoffed in his direction but didn't really see him. She was gone now, lost in a distant memory of what was.

"Who I was and who I've had to become in order to survive are two completely different people."

Inside the cafeteria, he heard it livening up. The normal chatter inside as the women went about their business was drowned out by their conversation as he dug deeper for information. But he lost his leverage when Elaine and Melody walked through the exit and crossed between them on their way to their posts. Each held a steaming cup of coffee and as they passed, they eyed him but immediately went on their way when Shane, now back from her voyage, shot them a look of authority.

The mood immediately shifted and her face changed seamlessly from disconsolate to amused.

"But that's neither here nor there. The point is we are all here, trying to survive. The question is, how do we do it without ripping each other's heads off?"

Before he could respond, she turned and started down the hallway, away from him.

"I'll leave you to figure that out, then."

Bernchal watched her walk away until he was once again, left alone in the corridor. Having received no help from his only ally and now even more frustrated with her inability to give him any more information than the measly breadcrumbs he'd received for the past two years, he decided to quit while he was ahead. He'd managed to thwart one disaster- why stress over ones that had not yet formed?

He retreated down the same hallway in which he'd been abandoned numerous times in the span of a few minutes and decided to spend the rest of the day sulking in his room, alone. As he walked away, Ruderick emerged from the doorway of the cafeteria and watched him leave, dissecting the verbal exchange between Bernchal and Shane moments before.

Chapter XXVIII

Paola rang the first alarm, a series of small beeps transmitted through the walkie talkies designated to Shane, Julie and a few others, including Bernchal. She set it off when she first caught sight of the military jeep coming up the hill of Manhattan College Parkway and lingering at the intersection of Waldo Avenue. It was too close to them to divert with a distraction somewhere else, so Paola alerted them to its presence so they could brace themselves against a possible attack.

Inside the institution was mayhem, but outside was completely quiet. The gates remained boarded and closed. The cars they used for runs and had since acquired from the dealership thanks to Ruderick and his men were circled back on the grass of the quad, away from sight and hidden in the shadows. Every night, the sentries in the bell tower would distribute various crumbs and goodies on the lawn of the quad to attract birds. Last night it had been Elaine and Melody to set out the remains of a packet of oatmeal, the same packet, coincidentally, Julie and Huvane had fought over. So a dozen or so crows and pigeons pecked at the oatmeal scattered all over the grass, lending the quiet institution an abandoned and deserted look.

Shane stealthily moved through the tunnels under the institution in complete silence. They were not under attack, not *yet*, but she proceeded as though they were. Alone in the stifling darkness, she moved quickly, crossing from the dormitories to the main building in less than a minute.

She quietly slid into the dean's office and closed the tunnel door behind her. Weapon drawn and crouched low to avoid detection from the bay windows surrounding the office, Shane made her way to the office door and opened it, listening for her friends on the other side.

Julie was waiting, gun in one hand and walkie talkie in the other. She had received Paola's transmission and immediately called for Shane, who had been in the shower when the call came in. With her wet hair still dripping down her back, Shane let the office door shut behind her and followed Julie towards the doors of the main entrance.

The lobby appeared empty but Shane knew better. Without seeing them, she knew the women were gathered in the darkest corners, under the staircase, off to the right behind the bronze statue of Socrates and tucked behind the dark shadow of the curtains adorning the stain glass windows.

They all waited with bated breaths, Shane and Julie now ducked low under the largest window on the left side of the lobby whose stained glass was dark enough to peer through and not be noticed. They watched the jeep linger, motor running, right outside their front gates. In position, they all waited.

Bernchal, slightly perturbed to be far from the lobby should the imminent attack commence, gripped the walkie talkie in his hand and waited for a status. Beside him, Ruderick and Derrecks watched, each growing increasingly impatient. They were at the other end of the tunnel, under their dormitory, one foot inside the tunnel and the other holding open the door so they could still receive and transmit a signal.

"So this is what these chicks do?" asked Ruderick, reaching for an unlit cigarette and placing it between his lips, let it dangle annoyingly while he spoke. In the darkness of the tunnel, his bright blue eyes lit up his weathered face with the help of the sunlight peeking through the still-open door.

"They hide and wait to be attacked? What kind of strategy is that?"

Bernchal shook his head, voice low and still listening for a transmission, and answered. "No. They're waiting, seeing what their next move is."

"Why not just blow up the militia's vehicle? Problem solved."

Derrecks waited for a reply, utterly satisfied with himself. Bernchal threw him an exasperated look and shot back, "They don't know where we are, genius. We shoot first and they pinpoint our location."

He shook his head and glanced down the dorm corridor at the rest of the men. They were in full military mode- vests strapped, guns out and loaded, faces grim. Like good little trained soldiers, they awaited their next commands.

The walkie talkie crackled and he heard Julie's voice come out of it, her words curt as usual.

"The car's still idling. No movement so far."

He clicked the button on the side and brought it to his lips. "How many?"

"One vehicle, military grade. Passenger and driver are visible; we do not have eyes on anyone else."

"Okay. Keep me informed."

The walkie clicked twice, indicating Julie's departure from their conversation. She preferred to sign off by double-clicking her indicator button instead of speaking for reasons Bernchal did not know, but guessed to be that she preferred to speak to him as little as possible.

Ruderick spit the unlit cigarette out onto the floor of the black tunnel and poked Bernchal in the chest with the end of his rifle.

"How far do these tunnels go?"

Bernchal stared at him wide-eyed and with his free hand, slowly moved the weapon until it was aimed at the wall and away from him.

"Could you not aim the firearm at my fucking chest?"

Ruderick repeated his request impatiently. "Where do these tunnels lead, Steve?"

He could see the blue eyes twinkling in the darkness, wheels turning upstairs and ideas being mass produced at record speeds.

Skeptically, he replied.

"They filter out and separate. One under the main building, one to the dormitories on the other side of the parkway and one to the woods east of here, close to the park. The entryways are cordoned off to block access from the outside everywhere but the main building." After a slight pause, he asked, "Why?"

It only took one look but he instantly knew Ruderick was about to do something stupid.

"No."

"We're sitting ducks. If we can tunnel out and-"

"No."

"-create a distraction at another point, we can divert their attention."

"No."

"It's simple wartime strategy, soldier. So direct me to proper coordinates and we'll-"

"No!"

The force behind Bernchal's voice surprised him and he stopped mid-sentence.

"You cannot unilaterally take soldiers out and attack that car! What is it that you people don't understand- is it the part where it was specifically explained to you that the location of this institution cannot be discovered, in any way, shape or form? These women, me included, have survived this long because *they do not know where we are*! You go out there and start blasting them away, God knows how many other fuckers they have waiting in the wings to pin us down?"

Behind him, Derrecks spoke up. "It's that chick that turned on them that has him so afraid. Now they think the militia is coming for them."

Without turning to face him, Bernchal took a deep breath. He knew sooner or later Ruderick would catch wind of Mariana's betrayal, though he'd hoped for some time to spin it to his benefit. But here it was, spilled by the idiot behind him eager to go out and get them all killed.

"What's he talking about, soldier?"

Agitated and not in the mood to answer questions from someone who no longer outranked him, Bernchal replied snidely.

"Kill that 'soldier' shit. It's Lieutenant Commander."

Unmoved, Ruderick asked again, much slower this time.

"What is he talking about?"

After a moment's hesitation, he answered begrudgingly.

"We had a situation recently. One of the women was feeding information to the militia in exchange for her kid. We squashed it, but we don't know how much intel she filtered out before we discovered the leak."

Realization hit and his blue eyes sparkled.

"So that was that chick?" he asked, making the connection Bernchal had feared. "The one that used to link up with Corvette?"

Bernchal remained silent.

"Interesting," he added, nodding. "So you had a mole in here and didn't even know it? That's the kind of outfit you got going here? That's what I'm supposed to get in line for? Tell me, did you even know she had turned? That she was getting information to the enemy? When would you have locked it down- after an attack? An inevitable takedown?"

Fired up, he continued, waving a meaty hand up and down the tunnel.

"From what I can surmise, Commander, that woman would link up with Corvette while she was out with the rest of these chicks. Right under their noses, and presumably yours as well. And you want me to just trust that they can keep this place secret and safe? You, my friend, have become so blinded by the pussy here that you've lost your ever-loving mind"

Without waiting for some semblance of a reply, he began laughing sardonically. "This is great. That's fucking stellar. You mean to tell me, we're here following your lead, living by the rules of these fucking broads and out there, the militia could have been setting us up this whole time?"

Bernchal shook his head, arguing.

"No, that's not how they operate. Trust me. I've seen them in action, I've seen their strategies. If they knew our location, they'd have attacked already. There is no structure to them. They're probably outside driving around looking for people to pick up-"

"Then why would you fear more in hiding? If we are so safe, then why not attack that vehicle directly and nip this in the bud?"

"To be smart! We can't just go out there blind and attack them!"

"Well, being smart is being proactive. Maybe you've been out of the game too long, Steve, but waiting to be attacked is not how we fight. I'll take Derrecks and we'll handle this now."

He started to walk down the pathway further into the tunnel and Bernchal called after him.

"You don't have the authority-"

Ruderick swiveled around, hand on his rifle, the red rising to his face. Angry, he spit a wad of phlegm on the tunnel floor and addressed Bernchal tightly.

"Authority? I have the authority of the goddamn United States Government, soldier. Now, I have been cordial since our arrival; I have allowed these girls to go on about their business without a second thought but their lackadaisical approach to war is going to get us all killed!"

"Lackadaisical?" he replied, shocked. Nothing about Shane or the rest of the women was lackadaisical. "Seriously? Holy shit, you're fucking out of your mind."

"That may be so," he said, turning back towards the tunnel and calling Derrecks to follow him with a quick whistle. "Now stand down, Steve. Let us implement a surefire strategy to get rid of this vehicle and ensure the safety of this location."

With no other recourse, Bernchal watched as they slipped further into the tunnel and out of sight. He had not given them the specific directions to exit the institution, but he knew Ruderick's tracking skills were unmatched. He'd be out of the tunnels and creeping up behind the vehicle in less than five minutes.

So when the explosion sounded, he wasn't surprised. It happened almost seven minutes after they had parted ways and about four minutes after Julie's voice had summoned his attention to the walkie talkie, choppily letting him know that the vehicle had turned and proceeded down Waldo Avenue in pursuit of something else.

The boom was not quite as loud as it had been that day the embassy had gone down, but then of course that had been enough explosives to take down a building. This was more than likely one of Derrecks' rudimentary molotov cocktails placed in the gas tank of the militia's jeep. That had been his usual M.O. in Africa and Bernchal was sure nothing had changed.

After receiving the all clear from Paola and Julie, Bernchal alerted the remaining men and left them to make his way down the tunnel towards the main building. As he walked quickly through the dark, he mentally played out the eruption that was likely to occur once Shane got wind of Ruderick's actions.

Chapter XXIX

Bernchal met Shane outside the door to her room the next morning and convinced her to go on a jog with him. Partly, he very much enjoyed spending time with her and getting to know her, however slow and painful the process could be. But mostly, he wanted to keep her from the institution. Ruderick had returned the day before fired up, ready to take over the world. He was spouting orders, commands and lectures and Bernchal had given him the night to ease up and calm down. He hoped that by this morning, Ruderick would have toned down his rampage and started leaving the policy-making to he and Shane.

They went straight for the school track. The temperature was dropping; though still unseasonably warm mid-day, the nip in the early morning air was back and there was a light frost on the grass as they ducked under the fence surrounding the track.

Wet and frozen grass slapped their pants as they walked. Shane, though tall herself, was several inches shorter than Bernchal and the grass was almost to her thigh. She touched it as she passed with gloveless hands, enjoying the chill that traveled up her arm and left her with goosebumps all over.

They jogged in silence on the track for several minutes. It was easy to get lost in the serenity of nature now that the everyday noise had all but disappeared. Bernchal only looked down to avoid the weeds and tufts of grass that reached around the edge of the track and threatened to trip them as they ran. After almost twenty minutes running quietly, he decided to get a few things off his chest.

"You know, Ruderick is the one that got the militia jeep to turn around yesterday. He went out there while we were waiting."

Shane barely acknowledged him and after a few seconds, finally responded.

"I figured that. He doesn't seem the patient type."

"That he is not."

He jogged alongside her, watching as she maneuvered the track and kept at a steady rhythm with his footsteps.

"You know I didn't okay that, right?"

She flashed him a quick look before turning her attention back to the track. Running here was no longer what it had been two years before. It was now more of an obstacle course than a track.

"I know."

"I just don't want you, or Julie, to think that that's why I brought them here, or let them in. To somehow go behind your back and make decisions without you."

She slowed to a stop and bent at the waist, holding herself up with her hands on her knees. He stopped next to her and waited. The wind circled them, sending scattered leaves and dirt in every direction. Shane's hair, loose tendrils that had escaped her tight ponytail, pushed and pulled against her face as he eyed her. Catching her breath, she looked up at him, one eye closed in the glare of the sun.

"I don't."

He considered his next statement for a moment and after some hesitation, came clean.

"He found out about Mariana. About everything."

Shane said nothing, just stood erect, pursed her lips and looked down at the track, at their feet and at nothing in particular.

"There wasn't much to be done by way of keeping it from him. He's like a bloodhound once he's on the trail of something."

He waited for a reaction, but receiving none, continued.

"They went through her room. For answers. Found some communication…"

His voice faded and he looked down at his hands, unsure how to go on. He knew the wound, though months old, was still quite raw, and he didn't want to add salt to it by giving her more to broad about. But Ruderick and his men had uncovered pertinent information and she had to know.

Deciding to rip off the band-aid in one fell swoop, he started again.

"She was feeding them information about all of the runs. From what we can tell, it doesn't look like she ever led them to the school, or to any one person in particular. It looks like they were out looking for stragglers, found her and suckered her into bringing them women to kill. So she would feed them chunks at a time, about where you would all be. And they started laying traps."

"Why?"

She kept her head down and with the wind whipping around them, her voice was so low he barely heard her.

"They promised her her daughter."

Finally, she looked up, squinted at the sunlight and made eye contact. Her face was frozen in a pained expression, as though just talking about Mariana was bring back a host of memories she would rather forget.

"I know why *she* did it. What I mean is, why did they work with her? Why not just kill her? Why not just kill *us*?"

"They don't know who *you* are. It seems they still don't know about this place, so they don't know how many of you there are. They just knew there were some women out there avoiding capture and she was with them, so they got to her."

"Why didn't they just kill her?"

Bernchal shook his head and looked away, momentarily unable to make eye contact while he replied. He didn't want to have to stare into those black eyes while he explained his theory but he faced her again and answered, his tone concilitiory.

"I don't know, Shane. Maybe they saw in her the same thing I saw- someone so lost and so desperate to find her kid that she would do just about anything."

"We're all desperate to find our kids!"

Her face remained stoic despite the agony in her voice.

"But you and every woman in there is doing something about it," he said, pointing back towards the college. "You guys are risking your lives, busting your asses to get those kids back. She wasn't willing to do that. She wanted a quick fix and it cost her everything in the end."

Shane nodded, visibly nonplussed but running on empty for the moment. Bernchal however, had unconsciously riled himself up and he shook his head, suddenly mad.

"It doesn't matter any way. She's fucking dead. And because of her, so are Jolene, Shilan, Megan and Joyce. So let's stop worrying about what she did to us and focus on what we can do to keep the mission moving forward."

He finished, breathing harder than he expected. Surprised, he realized for the first time how angry he was at Mariana's choice. He had not known her well, but he felt just as betrayed and let down as Shane did, partly because she had given up hope and let the very men that took her daughter rope her into serving them; but also because she had indirectly caused the death of four women and had directly put Shane in harm's way on more than one occasion.

Disturbed by his sudden onset of hostility towards a woman who was now dead, Bernchal took a deep breath and looked to Shane, who watched him closely. Resetting the atmosphere, he offered her a hopeful smile and surpringly, she reciprocated with a sweet one of her own.

"Your friend may be nosey as fuck, but at least he answered some of the questions we've had for months."

He nodded in agreement, satisfied. "He knows what he's doing, you know."

"I know."

"I know you guys have survived this long by trusting your gut and making plans. But sometimes, a change is needed."

"Sometimes change isn't all its cracked up to be."

She started walking around the track and he caught up, trying to keep her talking. The more he played up Ruderick's strengths- like military surveillance training, strategy implementation and tactical warfare experience- the likelier she would be to tolerate his weaknesses- like insanity, obsessive behavior and a complete lack of patience or tolerance for civilians.

"True, but you have adapted to everything that's changed. That's why you're alive."

"I'm alive because I'm resourceful."

He eyed her. "And crazy."

"And smart."

"And bat-shit crazy."

Shane smiled and looked away towards the perimeter fence. "And bat-shit crazy."

More silent walking and he watched her out of the corner of his eye, the way her long legs moved under the leggings she wore; the way every hundred or so steps she would flex the fingers on her hand and tighten them again, over and over; the way strands of hair blew around her face whenever the wind picked up around them. She was aware he watched her, but he didn't care.

"What keeps you moving, Shane? Revenge? Hatred? Hope?"

He didn't expect the immediate response he received.

"Grief."

"Grief?" he asked, puzzled.

"Yes."

He hesitated. "But you said-"

"That he's alive?" she asked, a sad smile on her face. Her nose was pink at the end from the chill in the air and she sniffled, wiping her eyes of tears of sadness, or cold, or both.

"Yes. He is alive. But he's been gone for over three years. I've missed so much. I've missed...everything. And I have to grieve that. Grieve for him. And I feel sometimes like if I don't, then I'll forget him. Forget his smile, his face, his smell, his little laugh. The grief and my love for him go hand in hand. Like a marriage."

Bernchal dissected her statement. Shane did not speak as often as he did, but when she did, she usually hit him with some whoppers that left him floored. He could not imagine the torture of being apart from a child, the agony of having your son ripped from your arms and the inability to get him back. He could not even begin to comprehend the regret she felt on a daily basis. But when she allowed him the tiniest of peeks into her inner workings, he felt like he almost understood her pain.

"Is that what keeps you moving?" he asked as she picked up her speed to a brisk walk and he kept up alongside her.

"That, and the fact that I plan to execute everyone involved with taking him."

He smiled as a quick tingle moved through him.

Revenge talk was sexy.

"Ah. So hatred it is."

Shane shrugged and crinkled her nose, noncommittally.

"You call it hatred. I call it... Yeah, no. You're right. It's hatred."

Bernchal laughed and she released a small chuckle.

"You're entitled. If anyone on Earth deserves that hatred, its you, Shane."

Her smile lingered. But she was not one for relaxation, so she immediately picked up her speed and without a word, started jogging. He sprinted and caught up to her a second later, adjusting to run side by side.

"What about after finding him? What then?"

Shane tensed. She hated talk about the future. At one time in her life, she was a planner. A list-maker. Her lists had lists. But since this new world and her son's abduction, she was one-sided. Like a horse with blinders on, her only goal was her son. She did not believe herself to be able to expend the energy to consider anything beyond that.

"I don't know. I don't know that there *will* be a future."

Bernchal slowed and pulled her to a stop with a hand on her arm. He had heard that speech before, that type of language from men fighting alongside him. At some point, most soldiers get to a place where they cannot, or do not want to, envision what life could be like beyond their goal. Bernchal considered it defeatist behavior, and very, *very* dangerous.

"There's always something beyond the goal, Shane. Always something to move towards."

"What?" she asked, sarcastically. "A future in this world?" Her arms raised, she pointed upward, saying "What future does *this* world hold, Commander? What am I supposed to be doing, other than this?"

When he didn't answer, she continued, her voice trembling.

"Why I was put on this earth? For *this*? To have my son taken from me, to live the rest of my life without him, like a fucking cruel joke?"

She was close to tears but she didn't look away. For the first time, she held his gaze. Whether she was no longer embarrassed to display emotion or she had resigned to her feelings didn't matter. Bernchal was content to finally get something authentic out of her that wasn't marred by her sudden need to flee every serious discussion.

"I heard a saying once," he replied, his voice hushed against the raging wind around them. She eyed him curiously and he continued.

'The two most important days of your life are the day you're born, and the day you find out why.' *This* is why you were born, Shane. I've seen you save lives. I've seen you risk yours for women and kids you don't even know. The world went to shit and it needs people like you to get it back. You're the last line of defense between the light and the dark right now. This is why you were born.

And you'll get your son back."

She gulped and he watched her eyes as they burned through his for a moment. Her long black lashes fluttered and she shivered, her lips parting as though she had something to say but couldn't quite form the words. After a second of indecipherable hesitation, she recovered, immediately shaking off any residual sentiment.

"I just want to kill everybody."

He released a loud laugh and felt the air change from heavy to light in almost an instant.

"You'll get your chance."

She turned and started walking again, this time with slow, deliberate steps. He stayed next to her, tucking his hands in the pockets of his pullover. In the quiet, he noticed the sound made by her boots as she purposely stepped in places they had not touched in their previous laps.

She surprised him by speaking, her voice soft and barely above a whisper. "I hate that sound…"

"Why?"

Shane didn't look up from the floor, but she sighed and let out a deep breath. "I don't quite know. It reminds me of…"

She hesitated and finally shook her head and frowned. "I just hate it."

He didn't say anything else and after a while, she looked up at him as though she suddenly remembered she was not alone. Her dark eyes looked haunted, the pupils so dilated they were impossible to tell apart from the brown irises.

"Apparently, I hate a lot of things."

She opened and closed her fist again and suddenly curious, he asked, "Why do you do that with your hand?"

"Huh?" she asked, her eyes locked on his.

"Your hand," he replied, pointing down with his chin.

Without missing a beat, she asked innocently, "What hand?"

He opened his mouth to speak and stopped, watching her. She was avoiding his question, albeit doing a piss-poor job, but avoiding nonetheless.

"*That* hand," he answered, reaching for her left hand and taking it in his. "This one, attached to your arm."

Surprisingly, she didn't pull away, only continued watching him. Her desire to avoid the question couldn't overpower his persistence in getting it answered and she took a deep breath and looked down at her left hand as it lay limply in his.

His larger hand dwarfed hers and he noticed the tips of her fingers were bright red from the cold. He opened his mouth to point it out but she beat him to the punch.

"It gets cold. And it hurts sometimes. It was broken, several times. In several places. I think."

"You think?" he asked, holding her hand more firmly and lifting it to take a closer look.

"I don't really know what was fractured or sprained or whatever," she offered, a solemn expression on her face. She blinked at him with those dark eyes and gave him a quick shrug. "We didn't exactly have any medical attention in the camps."

He glanced at her hand again and noticed now for the first time how her long fingers were slightly bent at the knuckles. Her index and middle fingers angled unnaturally to the right and the ring and pinky fingers were slightly bent in the opposite direction. Her ring finger was swollen and he examined it further, ignoring the residual tan line from her wedding ring.

"You have old bruising in here, Shane."

When she didn't respond he locked eyes with her again and commented, "I'm really surprised you can even use this hand."

She shrugged noncommittally and gave him a sad little smile. "At least it's not my trigger finger, right?"

Bernchal continued to glare, and the self-deprecating look of humor on her face dissipated, easing into one of angst. He wondered if she guessed what he was thinking; if she even wanted to know.

"Do I make you nervous, Shane?"

She made the mistake of drifting back from his eyes to his face and he reeled her in with the expression frozen on it- a mixture between severity and desire. And before she could control herself, the words spilled out.

"Yes! Yes... you unnerve me. I... I have become accustomed to being weary of men," she whispered, her eyes finally leaving his face and landing on the floor between them. He still held her hand and she felt her fingers warming, the sensation traveling up her arm and spreading out like electricity throughout her body.

"All men," she continued. "And I have to- I've been trying to teach myself that not all men are the same. I know you're not like *them*..."

"I'm not," he added, gripping her hand tighter.

"I have to teach myself how to trust again."

He chuckled, attempting to alleviate her obvious uneasiness. "Isn't that something women have been trying to teach themselves for years?"

She smiled and looked at their fingers, curiously.

"I'm working on that."

"We're all works-in-progress, Shane. I know I'm not perfect and I don't think you are."

She looked back up at him and a light flashed in her dark eyes, something between inviting and cautious. He could no more decipher her eyes than he could her facial expressions and he tightened his grip on her hand, stating sincerely, "But you are a very intimidating woman. Do you know that?"

Shane blinked, unsure of his statement and her response, if any. She stared at him unflinchingly and furrowing her eyebrows, replied.

"No one can be intimidated without consent."

He watched her, but she was unmoved and as he stared at her, still holding her hand, he was suddenly stuck with an unusual bout of honesty.

"Then call it a discomfort. One to which *I* am not accustomed."

With nothing left to add, he gently let go of her hand and turned away from her. Convinced there would be no more digging today, he jogged back from the way they came. She continued behind him watching him retreat into the dense trees, dragging her feet and wondering why exactly he affected her the way he did.

Shane felt as though her life was split into two parts- the first was just a memory of a happy life and the second was born after her son's abduction. Her current existence, from the moment she'd known Silas was still alive to this very minute, was spent in a relentless and continuous pursuit of her son. There wasn't room for anything else but the tiniest twinge of hope that hid enveloped in an undeniably palpable fury that propelled her forward. The hope existed, remained like the smallest of embers in a dying candle, holding on to life for as long as possible before its inevitable extinguishing. But it only existed hand in hand with the rage of vengeance, the tireless passion driving her to find her son and destroy everything in her path along the way.

She had no time to expend, no energy left to think of the past or the future. Only the thought of holding him again could consume her, nothing more. So her marriage has disappeared long ago, a lost and forgotten afterthought, like brunch and shopping. Rarely she would have fleeting glimpses of what was, of happiness in the arms of her late husband, passion or love. But those moments were few and far between and there existed now nothing but the empty void that only her son could fill.

As the world had become more and more dangerous for women following her husband's murder, Shane quickly lost all sense of what it once felt like to be safe. It had long become an existence of avoiding any and all contact for fear of rape. Rape at first and then something far, far worse.

So now, with Bernchal and even his men, becoming a staple in her existence, always there and in her face, she had no choice but to make peace with her distrust. She had to accept that the world had indeed changed, as had she, but it did not have to change so much that any humanity was overlooked. Bernchal and his men were good, they were decent men trying to do the right thing. Her inability to interact civilly should not be a hindrance to everything they were trying to achieve. But could she see the bigger picture in all they were attempting to do; could she see past the prize towards an actual future, possibly one that included Bernchal?

Try as she might, Shane felt incapable of thinking about anything other than the search for her son. Frustrated, she brushed off any thoughts otherwise and followed Bernchal's footsteps towards the institution.

Chapter XXX

Bernchal entered the cafeteria first, only steps ahead of Shane. She had caught up to him after leaving the track, but stayed a few yards behind to avoid conversation. He didn't mind; she was a hard shell to crack and he was exhausted from trying.

He came to a screeching halt at the double doors and watched the scene in front of him. He was vaguely aware that Shane was right behind him, about to also walk in and witness what he was processing right now.

The cafeteria was completely rearranged- the tables and chairs that had remained in working order after the college had been abandoned were now lined up against the cement wall, one on top of the other. The only one being utilized was in the northwest corner, just by the cook room. There sat Ruderick, with Huvane and Muccio behind him, and a mile-high pile of paperwork in front of him. Bernchal recognized binders on the table and grunted, disbelievingly. Dossiers on all of the women in the institution, intel Shane and Julie and eventually Bernchal had compiled and painstakingly listed to aid in not only the retrieval of each woman's child, but to track any connections to the militia to avoid another betrayal like Mariana's, were opened and being marked as Ruderick addressed a group of women lined up in front of him. Julie was standing beside Sharee in the opposite corner, arms crossed at her chest, her cheeks red with anger.

He felt her before he heard her. A darkness behind him emerged, as though all of the air in the cafeteria were suddenly sucked out. Shane stepped closer to him until they were shoulder to shoulder standing at the entrance, watching everyone gathered. Against his better judgment, he turned to his left and landed his eyes on her expression, one of mixed horror and absolute fury.

She said nothing to him as her chest rose and fell, only glanced at him briefly before walking towards Ruderick's table. He followed her and as they neared, Muccio tensed, his hand automatically going to the weapon on his waistband. Bernchal shot him a look that immediately convinced him to return his hand to his side.

"What the fuck is this?" Her voice was measured, curt and the words were delivered precisely. If Bernchal were honest with himself, he would have to admit it was actually fascinating to watch.

Ruderick looked up at them and offered a patronizing smirk.

"Ah, Ms. Milian. Glad you could join us. The rest of your ladies don't seem to be much help."

"Help with what? What is this?"

Betzaida, who had been in the cook room watching things unfold and reluctant to get involved without Shane present, walked in and spoke up.

"He wants us to register."

The red rose to Shane's face and she stared at Ruderick as she asked, "What?"

He addressed her directly, his tone authoritative, but friendly.

"Register, ma'am. I don't know what kind of lackadaisical approach-"

"Lackadaisical?" she interrupted. She looked at Bernchal, partially amused. "You can't be serious."

"I am very serious here, ma'am. Now, I know you have a system in place, but it is severely lacking. There's pertinent information missing here on each of the girls-"

"Women," she interjected, increasingly annoyed. "These are *women*, not girls."

Bernchal moved in between them, trying his best to keep Shane back without physically restraining her. Ruderick continued, undisturbed.

"*Women*. And this information is crucial to preventing another incident like such a one that occurred with your little friend. We have a proven system that would prevent such an incident and allow you to monitor each woman's comings and goings."

"There is nothing wrong with our system," she growled as she moved towards him again. Her teeth remained clenched as she spoke and it was obvious she was trying very, very hard to keep from shooting Ruderick in the face.

"You are a guest here, Captain, or need I remind you that we have graciously allowed you and your men to stay here with us in an attempt to exist harmoniously. This is not harmonious."

"Ma'am, harmony will not prevent a crew of slant-eyes from coming in here and shooting us all in our sleep. This will."

Before she could reply, he continued, speaking as though his logic were enough to appease her.

"It's a simple registration to prevent any further sabotage."

She raised an eyebrow and stared at him, the heat coming off of her visible to them all.

"We've done the registration thing, and we're not fucking doing it again. End this shit. *Now.*"

Bernchal took a quick step, again, in between them.

"You couldn't run this by us first? There's nothing wrong with fixing things, but you can't sweep in and start making changes to this place. What the fuck is wrong with you?"

Ruderick looked about to reply with a sarcastic dismissal, but tightened his lips and reconsidered. Finally, he looked at Shane and spoke.

"He's right. My apologies, Ms. Milian. I am used to giving orders, not requesting things."

Shane eyed him, unconvinced. She did not expect his immediate concession and braced herself for further conflict.

"While I have you here, though…"

And there it was.

Bernchal tried to get her attention but she was sucked in. He knew them both, knew that Ruderick loved to pick a fight. Unfortunately, he knew by now that Shane would never walk away from one.

"What exactly do you hope to accomplish here?"

He folded his large hands in front of him on the table and looked up at her, waiting.

It appeared Shane considered ignoring him, for a second. Then she answered, flatly and devoid of any emotion.

"To get my son back."

"And after?"

She shook her head, pissed off to have to answer the same question for the umpteenth time.

"There is no after. There is nothing but that. Don't you get it?"

"What I get is that you're going in there thinking things will change."

She scoffed and smiled patronizingly. "No, I'm not. I don't expect them to give me back my old life. I'm not stupid. What's done is done. But as long as there's a chance of getting my son back, I will not stop."

"Until?"

"Until I have him back. And every last one of them is dead."

"So this is revenge?"

"Call it whatever you want. I'm getting my son back."

He relented and sat back against the folding chair. He looked from her to Julie and back again and asked, "So if you all get your kids back, why not stop there?"

Bernchal sighed, irritated. "Wood, come on. Is this really necessary?"

Julie answered anyway. "Because they'll still be around to do the same thing to someone else."

"How does that affect you?"

"How does war in another country affect an American soldier?"

Ruderick recoiled for a split second but recovered immediately and replied to Julie, in a clipped tone.

"It is my job to maintain peace in my country and follow orders to do the same elsewhere, ma'am. I would think an American citizen that's survived this long would know that better than anyone."

Shane nodded knowingly, and replied.

"We do. We also know that saving some kids will bring us peace, but not make things just. And true peace isn't the absence of conflict. It's implementing and maintaining justice. Always. I would think an American soldier would know *that* better than anyone."

Bernchal smiled and watched the exchange, impressed. He'd seen Ruderick kick ass before, particularly when it came to defending their fight anywhere, but he had never seen someone go up against him and hold their own.

He appeared to be ready to drop it, and once again, changed his mind and asked another question.

"And you don't think we're better off starting over? Starting fresh? Once we reclaim the United States and restore things, we can look back on this time as an advancement."

Bernchal looked from Ruderick to Shane and watched as his eyes twinkled and her jaw dropped open in disbelief.

"Better off'? You can't be serious."

"I am."

Julie and Shane exchanged a look of shock while Ruderick looked on, amused. Bernchal knew he was riling them up, jabbing and jabbing until they would come undone. He also knew there would be no intervention. He could not step in and put an end to the questioning because he knew inevitably, Shane would not allow herself to be saved.

Bernchal stayed back and watched as she took a step towards Ruderick's table. By then, Muccio and Huvane were disinterested and off talking to some of the friendlier women. Shane could have whipped out her hunting knife and slit Ruderick's throat and as fast as he was, he'd have been no match.

Instead, she stepped real close to the table and leaned over, arms crossed and eyes fixated as her voice lowered and she addressed him condescendingly.

"Do you have a death toll?"

"Excuse me?"

"A death toll. A body count. Do you know how many Americans have been murdered since Yenmor took over? No?" she prodded and without waiting for a reply, continued. "I didn't think so. Roughly half of the population of the United States of America. That's about 165 million folks, not counting the genocide he orchestrated in Africa. And that's just the men that were slaughtered when someone was still keeping count. That's not including the thousands of women raped, tortured and murdered simply because they were women, or the children massacred because they didn't serve a purpose. I know you were gone for awhile, but let me fill you in on a few things. There is no government, Captain. And I know on a good day that sounds like the best thing that could have happened to this country, but it's not. Trust me. Along with no government we've got no laws, no protection, no security. Militia police the streets and kill US citizens on sight because of an order by the goddamn president. Its fucking Thunderdome out there. And women are considered persona non grata in this new world. Add to that the fact that there's no medicine and no healthcare and we've basically reverted to the Stone Age. You know that there's absolutely no way to screen for anything? AIDS is rampant and there are no vaccines and no antibiotics. With all of the scientific advances we'd made to all but eradicate the deadliest diseases and now we can't even battle the fucking flu? Forgive me, Captain, if I don't agree when you say we're 'better off'."

He eyed her, at a loss for words over her impassioned speech but unable to drop it. She knew it though, knew that he didn't want the debate to be over, didn't want to give in to her demands.

So she followed it up with a few harsh words, her tone clipped and impatient.

"I should think you would have already figured this out, Captain, but allow me to reiterate it for you," she began, taking a step closer to him. Bernchal took a deep breath and watched, knowing what was coming.

"I have one goal. Whether or not you want to believe it, accept it or join it doesn't make a goddamn difference to me. Just know that I will destroy everything in my path. *Everything.* I will kill and maim and torture and destroy everything and everyone if I have to, because that is the only language that these men speak. So I will speak their language and believe me when I tell you, they will understand every word I say and every move I make."

Her voice, steady and measured, did not tremble, yet the room did. Every wall, every inch of floor, every object in the institution trembled and shook with the power behind her words and her resolve, and Ruderick could only stare at her, speechless.

"I will get my son back. I will get my son back…"

Without waiting for his response, Shane turned on her heel and started for the cafeteria exit. At the doors she looked back and called to Ruderick, loudly.

"And this registration is over. If you need information about anyone here, ask me. Until then, don't ever line my friends up like cattle again, or I'll fucking kill you."

Chapter XXXI

The conflict went on for weeks. The quietest days were the ones when everyone was busy, each side of the fighting line was preoccupied with a task or off to secure supplies or intel, and did not have to run into each other. With a lack of any technology or recreation resembling entertainment, it was odd how twenty-four hours in the day could be filled so easily, yet they were.

The bad days, the days Bernchal wanted to take the shotgun always by Ruderick's side and use it on himself, were random but came on with the ferocity of a flash flood.

He woke up this morning hoping, praying that today would be a good day, but as he neared the lobby and heard the terse words exchanged, he knew his prayers had once again gone unanswered.

He didn't bother figuring out the culprit- it was usually safe to assume the culprit was Ruderick.

"That's ridiculous, lady. Absolutely ridiculous! You act like this is the fucking wild west!"

"And you act like you're one well-organized mission away from fixing everything."

"This is unlawful at best, and sheer madness at worst."

"Unlawful?" she scoffed, humored at the naïve use of a word that had long ago disappeared. "There is no law, Captain. I am not the law."

"No, lady, you are not. You are much, much worse."

Ruderick turned to face him when he walked in, but Shane ignored him, as usual, her attention turned towards her sparring partner.

"This delusion that you can right all of these wrongs overnight, like some sort of vigilante, is ridiculous."

Ruderick turned back to face her and removed the unlit cigarette from his mouth, his blue eyes blazing. The expression on his face lingered somewhere between amazement and agitation.

"You have no problem killing?" he said, more of a statement than a question; as though he knew the answer, but asked it anyway for the benefit of their audience.

Shane shrugged it off with little emotion. "None whatsoever."

"Doesn't that make you just as bad as they are?"

Like a switch being turned on, her eyes lit up.

"We don't kidnap and murder children. We don't rape and enslave women."

He chuckled derisively and rolled his eyes. "But you'll kill them at will because of some vendetta."

Bernchal felt what was coming, he could feel it forming in the room, in the air, in between Shane and Ruderick. The intensity of her stare and his inability to let anything go- Bernchal could see the pot boiling, threatening to explode from the heat.

"Guys…"

Ruderick ignored him but Shane locked eyes with him and gave him a look: *Tell your friend to back off…*

Turning back to Ruderick, she narrowed her eyes into angry slits and fired back, "It's not a vendetta."

"Then what is it?"

"Consider it a public service," she replied with a deadly smirk. "We're ridding the world of evil."

He watched her and realized something. Shane was purposely stirring the pot. He knew her to be confrontational as evidenced by every single verbal dispute with every single human being walking the halls of their institution, not to mention the countless bodies of militia soldiers piled up around the streets of New York City. But he didn't think she would purposely add fuel to the fire when it came to Ruderick and he stood back, eyeing her and wondering what her plan was.

Ruderick responded, exasperated. Another question in the hopes of dissecting her frame of mind, though all he was doing was pissing her off.

"By using their tactics?"

Shane tilted her head, looking at Ruderick as though he were the crazy guy on the corner of 42nd Street holding a sandwich board that said "The End is Near."

"Are we?" she asked intently. "We don't sodomize them before we kill them. We don't torture them, experiment on them, conduct physical tests that would make you cringe. We don't do what they do."

"But you are killing them," he insisted, despite Bernchal's swift elbow to his ribcage. He brushed it off and continued staring at Shane, waiting for an answer.

Shane smiled and answered, "Yes. And enjoying it."

Behind her, Julie smiled too and they looked like two maniacal grinning murderers.

After a pause, she continued.

"We did not ask for this life. *You* signed up as soldiers; *you* volunteered to serve your country, protect it. *We* did not. We were regular people. We did not ask for our kids to be taken from us and to have been held captive, forced into the most degrading, humiliating perversion imaginable all on the whim of some men that hate us simply because they can. We didn't start this. But we learned long ago that the only way to finish it now is by removing whatever concern for their humanity we might still harbor and killing them all. And I have no fucking problem with that. Because if the garbage that started this war, destroyed this country, kidnapped my son and violated me over and over and over again cannot maintain their humanity and mercy in their quest to win this, then neither will I."

The collective breaths being held in the room were released in unison when Shane finished. Her face was calm, her demeanor completely relaxed but Bernchal could see the light glowing brightly behind her eyes. They twinkled, wet from the emotion behind her stirring speech. She watched Ruderick, doing a good job of appearing disinterested despite the very obvious way her entire body trembled when she spoke.

Ruderick waited a moment before asking, "And our flag?"

She shook her head sadly and replied, the regret of an entire people audible in her voice.

"Sorry to break it to you, but that flag that you worship is obsolete."

Ruderick recoiled as though he'd been struck. He could stomach a lot, but he would not, *could not*, entertain talk of treason against his country or disrespect against his flag.

"You know something? That rage you're harboring is destructive. And it's going to get you killed."

Shane snorted and addressed him like one would a small child that just didn't understand.

"This rage is my only compass. Always bringing me back due north. Every time I lose track, every setback- I just think of the reward, which is holding my son again."

She locked eyes with him and menacingly stated, "I will not fail."

Ruderick shook his head and blurted out, "You'll get yourself killed…"

She started to turn away, finally visibly rattled. Julie caught up to her and they both walked towards the main stairs leading up to the classrooms. Angered, Ruderick called out after her, again.

"You'll get everybody killed!"

The lobby was quiet and when he yelled, his deep voice ricocheted off of every nook and cranny, echoing down the hallway and up the stairs. On the first step of the staircase, her body tensed up and her hands curled up into fists at her side. She turned back towards him and locked eyes with him- his dismissive and annoyed, hers wild, lit with an unmistakable fire of pure fury. She screamed suddenly from across the main lobby, a statement so hauntingly powerful, it could not be distinguished if it was meant for Ruderick or for every man behind the abduction of her son.

"I will not fail!"

Her chest heaved and she looked absolutely mad. Ruderick watched her, taken aback by her momentary loss of control while Julie took a step towards her immediately to prevent her from flying back in his direction and wrapping her hands around his throat.

Bernchal could only watch, helpless as she clenched her jaw and her fists over and over, seething. The ever-present tumultuous fire burned behind her eyes and it seemed to him only her skin was keeping her from bursting into flames then and there.

Finally, with Julie tugging at her like an impatient toddler, Shane turned and left the lobby, making her way quickly up the staircase with what seemed like her only ally in tow, an eerie silence left in her wake.

Chapter XXXII

They met Jackson on a particularly warm December evening. The institution had miraculously been without conflict for sixteen straight days since Shane had very publicly made her intentions known, and Bernchal was counting the days off like an imprisoned man waiting for release.

The child wasn't named Jackson yet; he had no recollection of who he was before Yenmor's cleansing had left him a homeless orphan squatting in the BJ's of the Palisades Mall. But once Hiu had lain eyes on that white-blonde hair, those baby blues and that misplaced accent, he immediately renamed him in honor of his favorite television show of day's past, Sons of Anarchy.

Shane and Julie had argued extensively with Ruderick and his men that morning, though they insisted it was merely conversation. Even though she had made her feelings of disdain quite vocal, Ruderick nonetheless enthusiastically offered his unsolicited opinion and the plan was made to make a run into Nyack to replace their dwindling supplies. It was the first real run since Mariana's betrayal and the first official one including Ruderick and his men. Bernchal vouched for them and after much debate, everything was set up.

Begrudgingly, Shane let Bernchal take lead once again. It seemed Ruderick was also adamant about having military personnel run the detail and despite her desire to remind him exactly in whose house he was staying and simultaneously laying him out, Shane let them have their way. A bullet fired from the gun of a man fired the same as that of a woman's.

Bernchal sat next to her in the back seat of Ruderick's Jeep Grand Cherokee and poked fun at her stoic expression until she smiled. Somehow, he could always make her smile lately.

They pulled into the mall parking lot and stopped between two similar looking jeeps. Hiu did the same between two abandoned minivans a few rows down and they all exited the cars, making their way towards the mall entrance. Ruderick pulled lead, with Hiu, Huvane and Julie behind him, followed by Milagros, Shane and then Bernchal. Two carfuls of other women followed and parked alongside them, assigned to sweep the mall and wait in the parking lot to man the perimeter.

The Palisades Mall, at one time, had been a jewel. Shane had been a shopper, way back when, and could always be found at the mall, taking advantage of the selection of stores. After giving birth to Silas she had toned it down some, knowing it was no fun for a little boy to be dragged around store after store for mommy to buy some clothes. So she began go either with girlfriends when her husband had been watching Silas, or as a family with the two of them, also catching a movie at the multiplex on the fourth floor of the sprawling fixture.

They entered through the main entrance next to what used to be Model's, weapons drawn and ready. BJ's stood disconnected from the actual mall, though on the same property, so they would have to cross the parking lot to enter but before they did, they opted to sweep through the mall quickly, eliminating any threats.

They split into two groups: Ruderick took Bernchal and Milagros and sent Hiu and Huvane with Shane and Julie. Bernchal had protested, somewhat unconvincingly but they split anyway and divided the mall in half to shorten the time spent searching. The remaining women would also move through the second and third floors, as well as the east side of the fourth floor.

Ruderick and Bernchal climbed the lifeless escalators to the fourth floor to start their search, with Milagros following behind and holding the rear. At the top, they turned into the west wing and made their way past the old restaurants and multiplex and into what used to be a Target.

"Let me ask you a question, Steve," said Ruderick, breaking the eerie silence occupying the top level of the mall as he lit a cigarette and tossed the match, putting the stick in between his lips and speaking through clenched lips. "How long have you been here?"

Bernchal knew Ruderick well. Time was not something used to measure the relationship between soldiers- it was service. They served together in Africa and barely made it out alive, each saving the other's life more times than they could count.

Bernchal had come to know Ruderick as he would a brother and he knew exactly what he was asking. So naturally, he avoided the question.

"Here? Same as you, my man. We came together. Losing your memory in your old age?" he joked.

Ruderick, in turn, knew Bernchal well and instead of taking the bait, pressed on.

"You know what I mean, smart-ass. How long have you been with these chicks?"

He sighed and turned the corner of the toy aisle, shoving a Monster High doll out of the way with the toe of his boots.

"About two years. Why?"

"And you haven't fucked any of them?"

Bernchal looked back to see if Milagros had overheard. Satisfied she hadn't, he whispered impatiently.

"Them who- these chicks? No, Wood."

"Why not?"

Ruderick led him towards the electronic section and inspected the dust-covered gaming consoles available for use by kids to promote the harassment of their parents purchasing. "I mean, I myself am not one for the whole amazon thing. Especially not while they got guns."

"My man, you wouldn't know what to do with one of these chicks. There's none of that submissive, damsel in distress shit here."

Ruderick agreed, turning into another aisle.

"Exactly. Not my scene. But you? You love that strong, feminism bullshit. How have you lasted two fucking years without nailing one of them?"

Before Bernchal could respond, Ruderick caught a peripheral look of the expression on his face. It was smitten, and he immediately knew for whom.

He scoffed, a smile playing on his lips as the cigarette hung from them.

"Nevermind. I get it…"

Bernchal glanced back at him, annoyed. Though he knew what Ruderick was implying, nevertheless he would adamantly deny it.

"What do you get?"

"You and the evil amazon. But you know what I've been dying to know? What the hell is it that you two got going on?"

Walking ahead of him, Bernchal moved through the grocery aisles with remarkable speed.

"What are you talking about?"

"You and Xena, Warrior Princess. I can't figure out your dynamic."

They both looked as Milagros caught up to them and began to grab some canned food from the shelves and load them into an empty box. Leaving her to her work, they kept going forward into the home decor aisles, silent until they were alone again.

"There is no dynamic," insisted Bernchal, unconvincingly.

They finished their sweep and made their way outside the Target and back to the escalators and waited for Milagros to catch up.

"No?" questioned Ruderick, in that grating tone of voice reserved for moments he was asking a question to which he expected no response and would instead go off on a tangent to prove his point.

"She brings you food. You're next to her every chance you get. You work out together. Talk shit to each other. You're mean to her; she's mean to you. That's not a dynamic?"

There it was.

"Brother," he continued, jazzed up now. "It may have been awhile, but from what I remember, that sure as shit looks like love."

Before Bernchal could counter with misdirection, Shane appeared around the corner with Julie. Hiu and Huvane followed closely behind and confirmed the absence of anyone inside but them. Satisfied, they left the mall and made their way across the parking lot to BJ's.

Though having been abandoned for over four years, BJ's was pretty secure. The doors had been locked from the inside, the outside gate pulled down low enough to cover the entrance but not locked securely. The shelves in each row were pristine but the section housing cereal was almost entirely cleaned out. A couple of large boxes of Fiber One and Total Whole Grain Plus sat collecting dust and spider webs. The snack section was identical: everything but the trail mix and raisins were gone. Same for the beverage section- every aisle they walked down had left only the most undesirable items stocked.

As soon as they entered the giant space, Julie and Shane's guard went up. Bernchal felt something, too but kept his mouth shut. Shane and Julie exchanged looks and motioned to Milagros to look closely.

Surprised that a store of that size had remained un-looted, Huvane made a comment about hitting the jackpot, but Shane hardly heard him. Instead, she focused on the one missing camping tent that was supposed to be on display, and the lanterns not on their designated shelves. Curiously, she looked for the backroom, an employee section or intake area. Julie followed, also suspicious.

It was there, at the swinging door marked "Employees Only" that was hidden behind two barbecue grills stacked one on top of the other, that Shane stood staring at the door. Seeing her, Bernchal walked over and watched her as her head cocked to the side and she walked to door, silently. Wordlessly, he moved the grills and stood back with her, watching. The door was held closed by the inside, with something propped against it to keep it from opening inward.

Ruderick, not one to ask for an invitation, raised his weapon and aimed it at the door. Julie shoved his arm to the left before he could fire and glared at him angrily, whispering, "Are you crazy?" through an angry slit of her lips. Confused, he watched as Shane raised her fist to the door and knocked.

"What the fuck...?"

There was no answer and she knocked again. They waited and he opened his mouth to speak but was silenced by Bernchal's raised brow. Again she knocked, and again nothing. When Ruderick was about to demand they break down the door, they heard it.

It sounded like the shuffling of feet and some whispering. Somewhere behind the door, a familiar click sounded and instantaneously, Ruderick aimed his weapon at the door, with Hiu and Huvane raising and cocking theirs. Julie and Bernchal moved to stop them and with her arms outstretched beside her, Shane stepped closer to the door, putting herself between the door and their guns.

"What the fuck are you doing?" asked Huvane, hushed. "Somebody behind that door cocked their gun- get the fuck out of the way!"

"Wait!" urged Bernchal, stepping between them and Shane. Julie took a step forward as well and waited as Shane knocked again. This time she put her mouth right up to the door and spoke.

"My name is Shane. We're not militia. We're the good guys. Can you open the door?"

Ruderick watched, dumbstruck. *This bitch is fucking crazy.*

More shuffling, more whispering. A voice sounded, one trying hard to sound older than its years through the audible fear and suddenly, he understood.

He realized the cereal, the snacks and the tent were all indications of what the women had already suspected and he shook off the immediate feeling of incompetence.

"I have a gun!"

Shane put her hand to the door. "I know. But you don't need it. We won't hurt you. I promise. Just come out, please."

More shuffling and this time, the sound of items beings moved across the floor inside. All around them the store was silent but for the noise coming from inside the employee's lounge and they waited silently for what would come out of the other side. Huvane and Hiu kept their guns trained on the door, fingers tensed next to the triggers in anticipation of the worst. Shane however, was unarmed and had both hands now against the door, a devastatingly hopeful expression on her face as she looked back at Julie and smiled, waiting.

Bernchal watched her, terrified but knowing that whatever she sensed behind that door would undoubtedly emerge. She was excruciatingly stubborn and short-sighted, but she was never wrong. Ruderick looked to him and shook his head, muttering angrily under his breath, "Everybody's fucking crazy..."

Finally, the door moved. Slightly it budged as the pressure against it eased and allowed it to move inward. It shifted a little into the room and then slowly, began to open outward, in their direction as Shane backed up away from the swing. It was dark inside so it wasn't until the sneakers appeared in the doorway that everyone outside of the room released the breaths they were holding.

A boy emerged, tall and athletically built, his eyes squinting at the flood of light hitting him. He was wearing grey sweatpants with the NIKE check at the hem, a matching black t-shirt and immaculately white sneakers. He was big for his age but his freckled baby face and dark brown eyes gave away his age- he had to be barely fourteen.

Shane reached for him and spoke softly, using a tone neither Bernchal nor Ruderick were aware she could muster.

"What's your name?"

The boy didn't answer, just looked from Shane to the guns aimed at his chest and back to her again. Realizing his hesitation, Shane shot a look to Hiu and Huvane, who re-holstered their guns reluctantly.

Finally, he cleared his throat and answered quietly, "Miguel."

Shane smiled lovingly as his hand unconsciously slipped into hers. "Miguel. Are you alone?"

Miguel had been trained by his aunt before they'd been separated. She'd cared for him when his dad was killed on the street in front of their lower east side apartment and taught him to handle a gun, a knife and to box. She had kept him fed, clothed and warm until she too had been taken from him by the militia and now her words ran through his mind, reminding him to be cautious. And the large men surrounding him were scaring the shit out of him, but this woman in front of him, the tall brunette with the beautiful smile, inexplicably made him feel safe and despite everything his aunt had taught him, Miguel answered honestly.

"Two little kids. We've been hiding for... for months, I think."

"How'd you get here?"

"My aunt found a safe place with a neighbor before she got taken. Gladys. She brought me up this far to some apartments nearby."

Bernchal swallowed hard, ignoring the chills running through him. He took a step towards Miguel who immediately tensed.

"Is she here?"

He shook his head solemnly. "She died. She was too old. For this world."

He paused and watched them for their reactions.

Bernchal pointed back towards the room from which he'd emerged. "Get them. We'll take you somewhere safe."

Though it was not his home to offer, it had gone unspoken that he could offer it nonetheless. A teenage boy and two children: there was no question.

Miguel led Julie and Milagros inside as the rest of them waited, keeping an eye out. He turned on a lantern for light and led them past the missing tent and several boxes of various cereals, canned foods and water bottles towards the door leading to the employee bathroom. There, he fished a key out of his pocket and unlocked the door, pushing it open and calling out into the darkness.

"Buddy? Charley? Come out. Its safe."

More moving about, this time lighter, more tentative footsteps. Two little heads poked out from inside of a stall and quickly shuffled towards Miguel. A caramel-colored little girl, wearing a bright pink sweater and navy leggings, with light-up sneakers illuminating every step she took; and a blonde boy who immediately hid his face behind Miguel's oversized t-shirt.

He led them outside of the break room and introduced them.

"This is Charley. She's seven. My aunt and I found her in Manhattan by herself before we were separated. And this," he added, trying to pull the blonde from his tight grasp, "is Buddy. He says he's four. He didn't remember his name when Charley and I found him crossing the Tappan Zee by himself. She calls him her little buddy so it just stuck. Right, Buddy?" he asked, trying to prod the little guy from behind him. It didn't work and the tiny little hand just gripped his t-shirt tighter and he hid his face further and further behind Miguel's back.

"I'm Shane."

She reached a hand out and with a reassuring smile, motioned for Charley to take it. As intimidating as Shane could be with adults, particularly of the male variety, her rapport with children proved to be the polar opposite and Charley took her hand immediately. She dropped to a squat and pointed to each one of her people.

"That's Julie. She's like my best friend. That lady with the black hair is Milagros. She has a little girl the same age as you. That big guy there with the angry face, is Ruderick; he's not as mean as he looks. He's really a big teddy bear that just loves tickles and hugs."

Ruderick smiled despite himself and quickly shook it off, avoiding the smirk directed at him by Bernchal.

Charley relaxed slightly and Shane pointed towards the men standing behind Julie and Milagros and continued. "That's Huvane, he drives us around and helps us beat the bad guys. And that's Hiu. He plays with way too many toys."

Hiu waved sweetly and Buddy peeked his head out from behind Miguel's shirt at the mention of toys. Hesitantly, he released his grip and walked quickly over to Hiu, surprising him by taking his hand and wrapping his tiny fingers around one large thumb. Hiu shrugged, looked down at the little guy and smiled as though it were the most natural thing in the world.

"And that's Steve," she added, pointing towards Bernchal. Their eyes met and when Charley asked if he was her friend too, Shane nodded.

"Yes, he is."

Bernchal, usually the one to prompt the staring contests, broke this one and cleared his throat. "Let's get these guys out of here, shall we?"

Quickly they filed out of the store, taking with them several boxes of cereal, canned foods and water bottles. For good measure, Huvane backtracked and picked up a large package of toilet paper and they made their way outside.

As they walked to the cars with the supplies and three new guests in tow, they turned the corner of a large dumpster used for deliveries and onto the path of a bear.

He looked to be about seven feet tall, but to Huvane and Ruderick he may as well have been twenty stories tall. He seemed to be casually window shopping but when his large snout wiggled and caught a whiff of human scent, he stopped, the black fur on his back immediately bristling. He dropped low on all fours and released a series of snorts and grunts as Shane and the rest of her group remained frozen to the ground.

"What the fuck...?"

Ruderick let out a whistle and the bear growled, low at first and then louder and louder. Buddy tightened his grip on Hiu's finger and Charley tensed her body and stood a little closer to Shane. Both children, despite their young age, had learned in hiding how to be quiet and perfectly still and their control in the face of a black bear made the fact that they had had to learn how to survive in the first place all the more sad.

Shane, not wanting to fire a shot and give away their location, hesitated for a moment but ultimately, pulled her gun from the holster on her waistband. As discreetly as she could, she cocked it. The bear heard the click and rocked his massive head back and forth, taking a few steps back. It looked like it would retreat and leave them be, and they relaxed slightly.

Instead, it released a roar that seemed to shake the ground and charged them.

The shot fired next to Bernchal's ear and he flinched, startled. The bear faltered and slowed down, his eyes twitching as it tried to understand what had happened. Close to them, close enough to almost make them shit their pants, it finally stopped and with a final shudder running through its massive body, immediately hit the ground, a small puddle of blood instantly forming around his large head.

Charley, seemingly unimpressed, started walking again and passed the dead bear without a second look. The rest of the group exchanged glances but kept moving forward towards the cars. Buddy tightened his grip on Hiu's thumb as his little legs scrambled to keep up their pace.

Miguel released the breath he'd been holding and walking between Bernchal and Ruderick, commented, "Your girlfriend is awesome," in Bernchal's direction. Chuckling, Ruderick unlocked his jeep and motioned for them to get inside while Bernchal avoided his stare.

He rode with Ruderick, despite the ribbing, because he decided to keep his distance from Shane for the time being. If Ruderick and the guys saw something, and even a teenage boy immediately sensed something, he had to switch things up.

Chapter XXXIII

The reunion was surprising. Shane had known the women would welcome the children with open arms. They were all, for the most part, in search of their own missing kids and would not refuse shelter to those belonging to another. What she had not expected was that the children actually belonged to some of the women under her own roof.

Their arrival was marked in the same manner- several of the women waiting for Shane's entrance with questions and hopeful stares. This time, for the first time, she produced something of value.

Charley had walked in first, behind Shane but ahead of the rest of the group. The shout had come from the back of the cafeteria. A cry unlike that of any sound produced in the world. The cry of a mother.

"Charley!"

Sharee half-ran, half-walked in a trance to her daughter and when she realized it was not a dream or illusion, collapsed with her daughter in her arms.

Renewed with hope, the rest of the women pushed and shoved for a look at what else Shane had brought them. Agatha reunited with her nephew, the nephew separated from her when the militia had caught them a year ago.

Hiu walked with Buddy, holding his hand and asking around for any news of his mother. When none was found, he found himself slightly relieved. Buddy was not a toy but he was alone, as was Hiu, and it was then, he casually renamed him Jackson and vowed to keep him safe.

A couple of hours later, after all the new found supplies had been put away and the tears had been wiped, Shane found herself wanting some human contact. It was a rare feat for a reclusive loner like the one she had become, but she craved a conversation, someone with whom to share the good news.

Giddy from the joyful reunions, Shane looked around for Bernchal and not finding him, decided he needed to know.

She ran into Muccio on her way out of the cafeteria and asked him if he'd seen Bernchal.

"He's in his room," he responded, a sleazy grin on his sun-streaked face. Ignoring him, Shane made her way into the dormitories in search of Bernchal.

She knocked once outside of his room and when the wait for a response proved too much, excitedly opened his door and burst inside.

He was standing half-turned, reaching for his clothes on his bed and his lower body covered in only a towel. His torso was wet from the shower and though her eyes lingered much longer than she'd expected or wanted, Shane turned away from him, embarrassed.

"Oh my God, I'm so sorry!"

Bernchal didn't move to cover himself at all and instead, forgave quickly.

"No problem. What's up?"

He knew she was mortified to barge in and catch him almost undressing, and even more so to admit she was mortified. He was completely unbothered by it however, and stood there, still dripping, still half-naked and very interested in what her next move would be. All vows to keep his distance were suddenly forgotten.

With her back still to him, Shane barely whispered, "I'm so sorry, I should have waited for you to open the door..."

"It's fine, relax. What's going on?"

Behind her, Shane could sense not only his amusement, but the fact that Bernchal had yet to cover himself up.

"Are you planning on putting some clothes on?" she asked impatiently.

"Nope. Would you prefer it if I did?"

"Yes."

"Then it's not happening. I'm quite comfortable, despite your shame."

"I'm not ashamed," she lied.

"Then turn around," he taunted.

"Fine," she countered and turned to face him, taking care to maintain eye contact despite his nakedness. He smiled at her, no doubt amused by the red rising to her cheeks. Unable to do anything about her physical reaction to him and his west chest, Shane shook it off and spoke, all business.

"I just wanted to tell you that two of the kids found their moms."

Immediately, the flirtation was replaced by an excited twinkle in his eye.

"Really?" he asked, like a child on Christmas Day after being told Santa had given him a puppy.

Her excitement returned, swiftly replacing the embarrassment of earlier and she smiled. "Yes! The little girl is Sharee's daughter and the teenage boy belongs to Agatha. He's her nephew. Can you believe that?"

Bernchal shook his head in shock. "I can't." He paused, processing the information. "I can't believe it. What are the odds?" he asked rhetorically.

She nodded enthusiastically. "I know. It's pretty amazing, right?"

They stood there, smiling like a couple of idiots, for eternity. Shane bit her lip and her smile got smaller and turned into something else, something mirroring... appreciation, maybe? Like a loving glance at a faithful partner, she watched him intently.

In turn, his gaze became one less about joy and more about longing; not so much lustful with desire but more like a faraway, unrequited stare at one's high school crush. He looked at her and his smile was gone, replaced by an intensity behind his hazel eyes that burned through her.

Suddenly they were both very much aware of the other's presence and instantaneously, Shane was very much aware that he was still undressed.

Normally, Shane would run. She would hightail it out of anywhere the moment things got uncomfortable. Her staying meant she had finally loosened up and Bernchal took this as an indication that he could press forward.

Though neither moved a muscle, he licked his lips and asked her, "Did I ever tell you that I have a talent for letting my imagination run wild?"

Shane shook her head. "No, you haven't."

He drew out his words, the same languid drawl she'd heard him use that day on the track so long ago when she had watched him, mesmerized, as he had lain his long, lean body on the trunk of the fallen tree and talked with her about the normal things they missed from the past. That day she had found it increasingly hard to look away.

"Well, I'm telling you now. I do."

She didn't know what to say other than to respond accordingly. She knew he was playing a seduction game with her. The question was how long she would allow herself to play along with him.

"Do you?"

He smiled, a mischievous Cheshire cat grin.

"Yes, I do. And it's running tonight, Shane."

She gulped despite herself. She knew if she stayed where she was and didn't turn and leave, he would almost certainly breach the distance between them. And for Shane at this moment, the only thing harder than breaking eye contact with Bernchal was tearing herself away and leaving the room. Somehow he made the anger, the fury and the rage always boiling inside of her threatening to topple over, calm and quiet. He simmered the inferno within her that drove her forward and though recently she had questioned herself for allowing him that power, she now found herself wondering if him possessing that power was really such a bad thing.

A knock behind her did the hard work for her and instantly, Shane broke the stare and backed up a few steps, turning to face Ruderick in the doorway, an unlit cigarette dangling from his lips, his eyes twinkling.

"Interrupting?" he asked, amused.

"No," she practically shouted. "No."

Behind her, Bernchal moved to his bed and picked up his jeans, holding them nonchalantly in front of him to cover his suddenly vulnerable state. Ten seconds ago, he had no problem with nudity when it was just Shane in his room. Shane *and* Ruderick in his room however, proved to be a problem.

Ruderick noticed the move and to him, the air in the room reeked of sexual tension. Cutting him some slack, he faced Shane and commented.

"That was a pretty sick shot with the bear. You're quite the marksman."

"Markswoman," she corrected. "Thank you. But I just happened to be the one to take the shot. No big deal."

"Well, in any case, you're pretty fucking ballsy."

"Me?" she asked, surprised at the compliment. She and Ruderick had not exactly gotten along since his arrival and this was possibly the first real conversation they had had.

"Yeah. You're a badass."

Shane looked to Bernchal, who watched their exchange, interested.

"Nah," she brushed it off. "I just get the job done. There's time for fear when the job is done."

Ruderick nodded, impressed.

"And that's what makes you so badass."

"If you say so," she offered.

Ruderick removed the cigarette from his mouth and turned to face Bernchal.

"Is it wrong that I'm aroused right now?"

"Okay!" interjected Bernchal, immediately stepping awkwardly between Shane and Ruderick. He clenched the jeans in his hand and kept his back to Shane purposely.

"Let's try to stay on topic…"

Shane put her head down to hide the smile spreading across her face as she slinked past Bernchal and made her way out of the room.

"I'll leave you to your little game, boys."

When she left, Bernchal looked to Ruderick, his hazel eyes wide with shock and annoyance.

"Seriously?"

Ruderick ignored him and made his way to the only chair in the room, the same one on which Shane had sat that first morning after the women of the institution had fished Bernchal out of the snow and brought him inside.

Plopping his huge frame down, the chair squeaked under his weight in protest and he leaned back, plopping both feet on top of his desk, he returned the unlit cigarette to his lips and glared.

"Holy shit, Steve. The sexual tension between you two is like a goddamn soap opera. Why don't you just fuck already…"

Chapter XXXIV

"Shane?"

Julie's hushed voice in the darkness of the tunnels brought Shane out of her daydream and she snapped to attention.

"Yeah?"

They shuffled along the interior of the tunnels, one in front of the other, gas lamp leading their way as they scanned the ground for anything suspicious during their monthly check on their way to the dorms. Julie cleared her throat and head down, tossed an inquiry back over her shoulder in a quiet, mousy voice.

"Being around these guys, all these soldiers… it doesn't make you think about… men?"

Shane shrugged to herself and frowned. "What about men?" she asked, oblivious.

The humor in Julie's voice could be detected in the darkness and she joked, "Okay, I know you're a robot and all-"

"-Fuck you-"

"-but could you at least for one second think like a normal woman?"

Shane offered an honest but thinly veiled response. "We are not normal women, Julie."

"Okay, not normal. Then just a woman. A red-blooded woman with eyes."

Shane knew where the questions were leading and couldn't help but comment, "Please do not tell me one of those goons caught your attention."

Insulted, Julie scoffed loudly and it echoed down the tunnel. She kicked at a rock beneath her foot and moved forward again with Shane close behind, her voice less timid than moments before.

"No! Not *these* guys."

Shane chuckled and she pressed forward. "But… but I can't help but think sometimes…if these guys are alive and here, *with* us, then, it makes you wonder, doesn't it? How many more of them are there? Soldiers. Regular men. Good guys that see us as more than just… just what the rest of them see us as."

Though she scarcely believed it, she nodded in agreement and offered Julie a small and hopeful smile in the dark.

"I didn't used to think so. But now… I'm thinking they're out there. Trying to survive, just like us, I guess."

"Yeah, I guess…"

Julie sounded disappointed and even though she could barely stomach the thought of salacious gossip at this point in her life, Shane relented and replied.

"You sound like Steve. All he ever wants to talk about lately is the future."

Julie turned to face Shane suddenly, her eyes wide like a teenage girl about to interrogate her best friend about a cute boy. She held up the gas lamp up between them so that it shone in her eyes.

"And I wonder why that is, genius."

Ignoring her, Shane shook her head and walked around her towards the door to the dean's office.

"Don't make it into something. He just… He's a planner. He's thinking ahead. Besides, he respects me… like a soldier," she added, unconvincingly.

"Yes, yes he does. You're 100% right. He respects you as a soldier. As a leader, as a mother." After a mocking pause, she continued, a sparkle in her hazel eyes visible as they neared the doorway.

"And as a woman. He respects the hell out of you as a woman. I'm sure he'd love to just respect you all…night…long. Over and over and over…"

Her voice trailed off and Shane refused to acknowledge her. In spite of her exterior, she blushed, the heat rising to her cheeks and she was suddenly very grateful for the darkness.

She climbed the three uneven steps and reached for the doorknob as Julie followed quickly, poking her in the back with her free hand.

"You can't run from the inevitable, Shane. He is not going anywhere."

"Get your head out of the gutter," she growled. Though it went unseen, Shane rolled her eyes and turned the doorknob, pushing the door open and calling over her shoulder, "That man doesn't want me and I don't want-"

She was cut off when the door flew open and Bernchal stood on the other end, smiling. Momentarily shocked, Shane hovered outside of the office, one foot on the step below her, and stared at him, her voice caught in her throat. Behind her, Julie could barely contain a laugh and leaned against her, her face buried in Shane's mane of long hair as her body twitched in a fit of giggles.

Unable to conjure anything intelligible, Shane clamored inside the office and pushed past Bernchal, making her way quickly out of the dean's office and into the main lobby. Confused, Bernchal looked to Julie who offered her condolences with a pat on his shoulder as she entered the office and followed behind Shane.

In the lobby, Shane walked past Ruderick as she continued in a huff towards the women's dormitory and gave him a hostile glare. He returned the favor and by the time Bernchal joined them, the air was immediately more tense than it had been before Shane's arrival.

Her and Ruderick's inability to coexist was well-known and very obvious throughout the institution, but Bernchal still struggled with bringing peace among his old family and his new one. And though he admitted to himself he could never make them friends, he hoped to possibly make things peaceful, or rather more peaceful that they had been since Ruderick's arrival.

In turn, Ruderick did not trust Shane. He knew she was dead-set on retrieving her son and all of the missing children, but he could not trust her. Or any woman in his presence for that matter. His mission was clear, had always been clear- to restore the United States of America, by any means necessary. And he would not allow some woman and her rag-tag group of rebels to disrupt his mission or interfere with the restoration of his flag in any way, shape or form.

While the women enjoyed the small victory after finding those kids, Ruderick devised a plan to hijack Bernchal's attention. Yes, it was rudimentary and juvenile, but he needed the shelter without the hassle that came with it, and if he could keep his man from consorting with Shane long enough, Ruderick knew he could get him to see things his way.

He volunteered Bernchal to assist him with a run to the dealership where they had reunited for some spare parts under the guise of building a generator. He was barely handy with a hammer but Derrecks could build anything, so Bernchal bought it and they left through the tunnels under the college along with Julie, who insisted on tagging along.

Her disdain for Bernchal was obvious and Ruderick welcomed her along, hoping that she could help maneuver him out of their favor.

The militia had been pretty silent lately and the dealership was untouched for the most part since they had left it. The sidewalk in front of the broken glass windows no longer had any ash from the fire but the charred concrete was visible through the light snow that had started falling overnight. A light dusting covered much of the area and their boots left wet footprints on the worn carpet beneath them inside of the showroom.

Bernchal stayed inside the showroom, foraging for any pertinent supplies, and together, Julie and Ruderick made their way to the lot where the newer cars had been stored and began to pop open the hoods, searching for functioning batteries and spark plugs.

Ruderick watched Julie as she worked, her blonde hair pulled back in a tight ponytail, her cheeks red from the cold air. She expertly untangled the wires and loosened the bolts, freeing the battery from under the hood of a Jeep Wrangler.

Feeling his eyes on her, Julie shot up a question through the silence.

"How well do you know Bernchal?"

He was caught off guard but played it off. "Steve? Hell, me and that pretty boy go back years. Served in Africa together before making our way back into this hellhole."

"What was in Africa?"

He looked up and smiled with his steady eyes, a mischevious expression written all over his face. "Your supreme leader keeping details from you, blondie?"

She rolled her eyes and he continued, amused by her ignorance. "Okay, okay. I'll divulge. Africa was a holy mess of bureaucratic bullshit, sweetheart. A goddamn shitshow. We got shipped out to help a small nation being slaughtered by some natives working with those motherfucking slanteyes and because this joke just keeps better and better, it all turned out to be part of the same grand scheme that flipped this place upside down. We barely made it out, along with the rest of these guys."

"Why'd you go in the first place?" she asked, thoroughly intrigued. "Why would you care about villagers on another continent?"

"I'd venture a guess that despite this outfit here, you have absolutely no military service, huh?"

Without waiting for a response, he continued.

"You go where you're sent, blondie. Wherever you're shipped to. If there's conflict in the North Pole and Santa Claus is murdering his innocent elves, you hitch up that sleigh and take your ass to Christmastown."

Bernchal finished up inside the showroom and noisily made his way into the lot, dragging a crate of junk with him. He made eye contact with Ruderick, shot him a reprimanding look and proceeded towards a row of brand new Chryslers against the back wall.

Ruderick continued to watch Julie as they worked and a few minutes of awkward silence later, she looked looked up from what she was doing and met his blue eyes, annoyed.

"What?"

He brushed it off and looked back down at the engine shaft of the car under which he worked and replied, nonchalantly.

"Nothing. Just wondering what your duties are as the Vice President of this place."

Behind him, Bernchal called out from the back of a Chrysler 300 as he searched for materials in the car's trunk.

"Seriously, Wood? Again with this shit? Can we have one fucking day of peace without all of the goddamn questions?"

Ignoring him, Julie replied.

"I'm not the Vice President of anything."

"Then why do you follow her around all the time?"

Unbothered, she barely looked up and replied curtly. "I don't follow anyone around. I do however, interject those times you piss her off so that she doesn't slit your throat. So you should be thanking me instead of bothering me."

Bernchal chuckled behind them and Ruderick brushed him off quickly.

"But you are Milian's right-hand man. Or woman."

Julie took a deep breath and reminded herself that his goal was to get under her skin, so she could not let him succeed.

"Something like that."

She pulled the rest of the battery out and put it on the floor beside her. Shutting the hood, she walked over to a Chrysler Town & Country and fiddled under the dashboard for the button to pop that hood.

"Why do you ask?"

Ruderick smiled with his back to her and called out over his shoulder, "Just wondering why you are second in command and she's the alpha dog."

Julie shut the door of the minivan harder than she'd meant to and tried to downplay her frustration.

"There are no ranks in our home, Captain. This isn't the military."

"But you admit that she is in charge."

Julie bristled with annoyance, but answered flatly. "Yes, she is."

She yanked the battery out of the Town & Country and almost dropped it on the windshield of the Camaro behind her. Regaining her composure, she shut the hood of the minivan and reached for the Wrangler's heavy battery. With a grunt she lifted them both and started for their Cherokee, parked inside the showroom in between two gleaming new cars.

"Need help?" Ruderick offered, popping up behind her suddenly. She brushed him off and walked to the showroom as Bernchal struggled to listen when he saw Ruderick following her in.

"I'm just saying, Julie- Julie is it?- I'm just saying, why aren't *you* running things?"

Julie dropped the batteries on the linoleum floor by the Cherokee and turned to face Ruderick.

"I know what you're trying to do here. No, I don't want to be in charge, and no, I'm not going to stage some sort of coup to be in charge just because you're trying, however pathetically, to drop a few hints. If you have a problem with Shane, you take it up with her. Obviously that hasn't worked for you so far so I can't imagine you'll be particularly successful, but that's the way it is. I suggest that if you want to keep taking advantage of our hospitality, you figure out a way to get along with her because she is the one in charge and she can very easily put a stop to that at any moment, got it?"

Without a response, she opened the door of the Cherokee and lugged the batteries inside, dropping them on the backseat as Ruderick watched, admonished.

Bernchal appeared at the entrance to the showroom and bellowed loudly. Ignoring him, Ruderick asked her, "Fine then! But just answer me this- why *her*?"

Julie shut the car door and turned to face him, hands on her hips. "You have no idea what happened to her, what happened to all of us. You come in here with your fucking military strategies and your sexist bullshit and you look at us like a bunch of bitter chicks that just shoot guns for fun. You have no clue what we've all been through, what she went through to get here."

Taking advantage of an open door, he pressed on.

"Then tell me. Because she sure as shit doesn't talk other than to tell me how much she fucking hates me."

Bernchal watched from the doorway as they spoke, his eyes on Julie as she considered answering Ruderick's questions. They waited silently until finally, she spoke.

With a deep breath, she glanced between them both and answered.

"In the beginning she couldn't function. She couldn't... She'll kill me if she knows I'm telling you this... But you should know. You ought to know the resolve that lies underneath that hard exterior.

In the beginning she couldn't function. Walk, talk. The simplest things. She shut down when they took him. She fought them, tooth and nail. But they ripped him from her arms and she lost it. Complete meltdown. Everybody thought their kids were dead... It wasn't until she found out they were alive, found out Silas and the rest of them were alive, still stood a chance, that she finally woke up.

And that was it. They tried to beat her into submission, within an inch of her damn life. They beat her 'till there was almost nothing left to beat. She still wouldn't budge."

Julie's hazel eyes became hauntingly clear as she spoke, her voice raising with the turn of each sordid corner, her body tensing at the recollection of the horror they had all endured.

"The experiments, the tests. Most of us found out the hard way it was easier to not fight. It was easier to just... Just put your head down and do what you needed to do to survive. Not her. She would not give in. She just...couldn't. She's not built to give in.

She waited long enough for the training, long enough for the planning and the opportunity, and then she set it up. But by that time they'd moved the kids and destroyed any paper trail. She interrogated anybody left behind and whoever had a hand in separating anyone of us from our kids, she made them pay.

We've been preparing ever since. Hunting them down, getting one step closer to getting our kids back. And we will. And you can roll your eyes and shake your head and believe us all to be martyrs. That's okay. We'd all gladly die for our children. For the chance to see them again, to hold them, to free them, to know that we can end this and keep another mother from having her child ripped from her arms? We'd all gladly be martyrs. And she'll lead us there."

Intrigued at this woman's power over her loyal subjects, Ruderick took a step towards Julie and again demanded, "Why her?"

"I don't know!" she shot back. "Maybe its because she's so detached. Maybe its because she's so goddamn robotic. She's doesn't flinch when it comes to killing one of them. Maybe that's why."

Bernchal nodded knowingly to himself, agreeing. Her description was dead-on, whether he had known Shane for two or twenty years, he knew her well enough now to believe every word Julie was saying.

Julie looked solely at Bernchal then and continued, locking her eyes on his and addressing him without hostility or impatience for the first time since they'd met.

"Or maybe its because she eats, sleeps and breathes revenge. I don't know the reason, and honestly, I don't give a shit. I'm not sure exactly why she's the one. But I know she is."

With nothing further to add, she turned away from them and left the showroom, indicating her intent to depart. Absent a reason to object, Bernchal and Ruderick wordlessly finished up and followed her.

Chapter XXXV

Back at the institution, Bernchal walked to the cafeteria from his room to check on Derrecks' progress with the manmade generator. Ruderick's sorry attempt at intervention had fizzled immediately, but the plus side of their adventure was their retrieval of enough supplies to actually make use of them.

He noticed Shane seated by herself at one of the tables, which had since been returned to their former positions in the cafeteria. Mug of hot chocolate in one hand and a steaming cup of coffee in the other, he made his way to her with Julie's revelations still fresh on his mind and without waiting for an invitation, dropped the cups on the table. Pulling up a chair beside her, he straddled it and spoke.

"My illustrious leader, can I ask you a question?"

She reached for the mug of hot chocolate without making eye contact and when her hand gripped it and pulled it towards her, Bernchal held fast. She looked up from the list of inventory she'd been working on and annoyed, sucked her teeth.

He held on to the mug and leveled her with his eyes. "A serious question."

Indicating her approval with an eye roll, he released the mug and she placed it in front of her.

"I'm serious, Shane. I want to ask you something. Something… personal."

Shane took a deep breath and put down the pencil. Crossing her hands over the paper on the table, she looked up at him and offered a defeated sigh.

"What is it?"

"I want to ask you something," he began awkwardly. "In a non-judgmental way. I'm just curious."

Now intrigued, Shane ushered him along with an expectant smile. "Go ahead."

"If what *they* wanted was your… compliance, and you would have gotten your son back… why didn't you just do what they wanted?"

She blinked, unsure of the significance of his inquiry. Noticing her hesitation, he added, "I've been thinking about our situation. About our search for the kids and ways we can outsmart them. What if we lure them in, like promise to deliver a group of women that escaped in exchange for some kids, specific kids? A bait and switch," he continued, his eyes bright with excitement.

She eyed him, somewhat thrown off by his questions, but at the same time, grateful that he was coming up with ideas to get her son back.

Smiling politely, she shook her head.

"I tried that already, I really did. I know, I don't exactly seem the type to comply-"

"That's an understatement..." he interrupted.

"But I tried," she continued, ignoring him. "And it didn't work. They don't care about those of us that escaped other than using us as target practice. It's not about disobedience. It's not even about control. It's just a means to an end."

Bernchal nodded understandingly, albeit visibly disappointed.

"Besides," she continued, "if I do what they want me to do in order to get my son back, then I'd have to do what they want me to do in order to keep my son. And it'll never end. They'll keep doing the same thing, over and over, to other women. And that's not fair..."

Agreeing, he shook his head slowly. "No, it's not."

After a moment of silent pondering, she looked at him again, her dark eyes suddenly disillusioned.

"You think I should just comply to get him back?"

"No," he replied, adamantly, his head shaking back and forth. "No. I was just... I was hoping I had found the golden ticket, that's all." He smiled sheepishly and she looked away.

"For the record," he added suddenly, "I don't think you are capable of complying with *any* orders."

She knew he was complimenting her, so she smiled.

"I'd like to think I'd be brave enough to have done the same thing, Shane. You women are... something else."

Unable to think of a response, she cleared her throat to shake off the awkwardness. He opened his mouth to speak but she beat him to the punch, immediately back to business.

"Speaking of which, Commander, keep your guys away from my girls."

"Excuse me?"

"Your men. Get a leash on them. All morning I've heard stories about how your guys keep creeping into our side of the dormitory."

She waited expectantly for a response and he stared at her, bewildered.

"And?"

"And nothing. Keep them restrained."

Bernchal chuckled and shook his head. "Hate to break it to you, Shane, but those are grown ass men and women. All consenting adults who by the sound of it, are also satisfied customers. All of those women have both the right and ability to say no if they want to, and I'm guessing they don't."

Shane started to say something and stopped herself.

He continued. "Besides, ever thought that maybe they're lonely? There's nothing wrong with wanting some companionship. Don't you?"

"Don't I what?" she asked, immediately and visibly uncomfortable.

"Don't you think about that? Companionship? Finding someone? After you get your kid back, that is."

She cleared her throat and looked towards the cook room at nothing in particular.

"I have too much on my mind to think about that."

He looked at her skeptically. "Keeping your eyes on the prize doesn't mean you can't deviate from your plan."

With a sly smirk, she replied quietly.

"That's kind of exactly what it means."

"Not deviate then. Alter your plans. Make room for something…

unexpected."

He let the question hang between them and she purposely brushed it off.

"Everything in this world is unexpected."

Bernchal leveled her with his eyes until she met them and finally gave in.

"I haven't… I haven't really thought that far ahead."

"You should."

She glared at him, annoyed. "Why are you so optimistic, given how stellar things have gone in our lives?"

He picked up the cup of coffee and took a sip, pointing to himself with his thumb.

"Sanguine."

"Excuse me?"

"Sanguine. I'm sanguine. It means-"

"I know what it means," she interjected impatiently.

"Okay then. That's why. I'm naturally upbeat. You're the dark one that pulls me into your black abyss of despair. But this will be over soon. And you have to think further ahead that just the next truck you're gonna hijack. You have to plan for the future we're creating here."

Shane shook her head and took a deep and troubling breath.

"Why? To focus on what I had and lost? What I'll probably never find again?"

"Why wouldn't you?" he asked, his voice full of optimism. "Not everybody out there is a North Korean murderer and not everybody in here wants to kill you."

She eyed him and he reconsidered, his eyes twinkling in amusement.

"Well, maybe they all do, but they care about you, too. I…do. I care about you."

She watched him, waiting for the inevitable joke. When he continued solemnly, he surprised her.

"You are certainly cold. Vicious, even. But... you have a fire inside of you that most people, myself included, have never had the privilege of seeing. You are one tough cookie, Shane. But you are loved."

He paused, not so much for dramatic effect but more to gather his thoughts and pick his next words and as per usual, he went with humor to alleviate the building tension.

"I for one plan on surviving this shit storm and living life like its a goddamn carnival. Think about it- no taxes. No bills. No 9 to 5 job. It'll be Utopia."

She released the breath she had been holding and smiled, suddenly and completely disarmed. He gave her a quick wink and pressed forward.

"You can have a life again when you get the kids back and all of this is over."

She offered him a sad smile and whispered, "Doubtful," as she got up to leave, the ignored mug of hot chocolate remaining untouched. She took a few steps and as an after thought, turned back and leaned over the table, meeting his curious eyes.

"By the way, Commander. Maybe you and your men were never briefed on what went on while you were gone, and that's okay. But you should know that no woman in here had the right or the ability to say no to any man for a very long time. Not one."

Chapter XXXVI

He thought about her departing statement for several minutes after she had walked away. As he swirled the coffee in the small cup back and forth, he contemplated everything Julie had told them, and now Shane's cryptic words. Remembering all of the jokes he had made to Shane, in front of her, about the women of the institution; the playful ribbing, flirtatious banter- all of it- and he asked himself, how many times had he been out of line? How many comments had he made that had gotten under her skin, but she had never let on? No matter how innocent his intentions may have been, he could not stomach the thought of having had offended Shane, or worse yet, scared her.

Like a lovesick teenager, he went after her. In his past, Bernchal had been carefree, a loner with a devil-may-care attitude. Since meeting Shane, that easygoing nature had transformed into… something else. He felt a pull of sorts, a desire to protect her, not as though she needed his protecting, but because he wanted to take care of her, wanted to be the sort of man on which she could lean. And though having trouble adjusting to that new sensation inside of him, he was strangely comforted by it.

So he went after her without a second thought as though it were the most natural thing in the world, and found her lingering in the math lab, standing over a desk and tinkering with one of the old computers. He didn't know her to be particularly inventive but every so often he would find her taking something apart and using the smallest of items to solve a puzzle somewhere else, like completely unhinging an old microscope to use the tiny screw inside to fix Miriam's glasses.

"Shane," he called out, startling her.

She dropped the computer tower on the desk and jumped, staring at him in annoyance.

"What the fuck, Steve? You scared the shit out of me."

He walked into the classroom and made his way past the rows of desks to her.

"Spoken like a true lady."

He pulled up a chair and sat behind her as she set to work again, watching her bite her lip and try to unscrew the back panel of the tower.

"Gotta tell you, if you'd have sat in front of me in high school like this, I'd have flunked out."

Without looking up, she shot back. "Flunked out in 1892? That would have been hard."

Loudly, he began to laugh appreciably and elicited a wide smile from her as she pulled out the screw she was fighting for and placed it gingerly on the corner of the desk

Ruderick sauntered in before he could come up with a smart response and she immediately tensed. He noticed her body stiffen and her brows furrow as she put the panel back on the tower and screwed it on, hard.

"Milian. Just the person I was looking for. I got a couple of questions."

Bernchal tried to intercede. "What now, Wood?"

She shot him a look of reproach and looked up towards Ruderick, who made his way down the aisle and sat across from them in an empty chair. He dropped a small notepad on the desk in front of him and fished a pencil from behind his ear. With the same chewed-up, unlit cigarette dangling between his lips, he eyed her and, much to Bernchal's dismay, began.

"It's just the one kid?"

The words came out slowly and precisely. "Excuse me?

He looked from her to Bernchal who stared, nostrils flaring. Undeterred, he repeated his question. "Your son; one kid, right?"

Shane closed her eyes and replied, trying to retain her composure.

"Yes."

"How's your health?"

Her eyes shot open. "Why is this relevant?" she asked, obviously miffed.

Ruderick looked at her as though the answer should have been obvious.

"You're leading this huge 'army' of warriors," he replied, his tone serious despite his sarcastic use of air quotes. "Your credentials need to be verified."

"Verified, really?" Her tone was dangerously tight. "That's rich."

From behind her, Bernchal laid his head in his hands and asked, "Is this really fucking necessary, Wood?"

"Yes," he replied, focused. "Who wants to follow a leader that's about to keel over from some disease?"

She scoffed, smiling in derision. "Disease?"

Then, almost immediately, her eyes darkened and she shot back at him, "Okay. No problem."

She dropped the screwdriver on her desk and stood, her chair coming back with enough force to startle Bernchal. He looked up from his defeated position and watched as she crossed her arms and squared off with Ruderick. Lips set in a tight sneer, body coiled and ready to strike, she began.

"So my health? Alright, what exactly do you want to know? I was healthy my whole life. Under-active thyroid in my twenties. College educated, law school graduated, married and one kid by the age of twenty-eight. Pretty normal but enjoyable life on the professional fast track until a fucking sociopath decided to come along and take ownership of my vagina. After that? It gets a little muddy."

Her voice shook and Bernchal could barely hear it above the thunderous sound of his heart beating inside his chest.

"You see, I can tell you I've had one child, but as to how many pregnancies? You have to ask the countless men who held me hostage and conducted multiple experiments on me, including in-vitro fertilization and dozens of terminations, all without anesthesia, by the way. Good times. What else? I can tell you how many consensual sexual partners I've had, but I can't seem to recall how many men have used my body as a fucking testing ground. The number of times I was violated by guards, doctors, so-called scientists, militia and random passersby who knew they had complete and utter autonomy over every female body on the planet; for some reason that number eludes me. As for my overall health, well, I'll be damned, but I'm a little stumped on that one. Because between beatings, sexual assaults, being bed-ridden with concussions, broken bones, dislocated shoulders, Oh! And once a broken jaw after I made the mistake of trying to stop a fifteen-year old girl from being gang-raped in the middle of the street- that was fun, by the way. Sorry, but it's a little hard to narrow down exactly how many body parts have been broken, sprained, fractured, dislocated or injured in any way, shape or form. My bad."

With a final attempt at sarcastic nonchalance, she dropped her hands to her side and addressed Ruderick,

"Other than that, I'd say I'm in excellent health. Does that answer your question?"

When she received no reply, she walked away quickly, leaving them in silence. As she left she bumped her desk and the screw she'd so painstakingly retrieved from the computer tower rolled down the slanted top and landed on the rug without a sound.

Bernchal finally released the breath he'd been holding and began to feel his pulse returning to normal. Every word, every single word she had uttered had been torture to hear; he could not begin to comprehend what it had been like to live it.

Enraged, he turned to a shocked Ruderick and slammed his fist on his own desk.

"Goddamit, Wood!"

Feigning innocence, Ruderick shrugged his shoulder and asked, "What?"

"What the fuck is your problem?" he asked, hissing through his clenched teeth. Rising, he leaned over his desk and pointed at the doorway after Shane. "Can't you just accept that she is who she is? Why do you have to do this *every single fucking time* you're in a room with her?" he demanded, enunciating every syllable forcefully.

Ruderick pursed his lips and answered honestly.

"Because she's cagey."

Bernchal shook his head and scoffed. "Ever thought maybe she's just trying real fucking hard to forget the past?"

He began to make his way towards the door and stopped when the screw on the floor caught his attention. Bending at the waist, he picked it up and dropped it in the pocket of his cargo pants, turning to look at Ruderick, his face riddled with disappointment.

"With everything we saw in Africa, I would think you of all people would understand that."

He moved quickly down the hallway of the classrooms, towards the staircase. He bounded down at record speed and made it to the main entrance. Shane's silhouette on the grass in the quad caught his attention through the stained glass window and he watched her for a moment with one hand on the handle of the large wooden door.

He could see puffs of her breath floating in front of her as she sat on the freezing grass, knees to chest. Taking a deep breath, he pulled open the door and walked through the doorway of the college's main entrance towards her.

Wordlessly, he plopped down on the grass next to her and retrieved the small screw she'd worked to release from his pocket, handing it to her.

"You left this behind."

She offered a little smile and plucked it from his hand, careful to not make contact with her fingers.

"Thanks."

"What do you plan to do with that?" he asked, interested.

She squinted as the fading horizon lit up their seats with the last orange glows of the evening. Though only four in the afternoon, winter in New York was notoriously dark and as the sun began its decent for the night, the fast approaching darkness was still no match for the rays of light hanging on for dear life.

"Charley, Sharee's daughter, she wanted to play with one of the model planes in the old physics room, but the battery cover keeps falling off. I figured I'd give it a try with this," she replied, holding up the tiny screw in front of her. She examined it by the light of the sunset and drifted away again into her own world.

Bernchal sat next to her, stretching his body out and leaning back against the grass. He folded his arms behind his head and propped his neck up as he watched her from the corner of his eye. The grass was freezing- the cold was biting his ass cheeks and making them numb. But he ignored it to keep her company.

"I used to think there was too much noise sometimes. That it was too loud. Now I'd kill for some of that noise in my head."

"You said that once."

He perked up. "Keeping tabs on my topics of conversation? You *do* care, Shane."

She put the screw in her pocket and continued to avoid eye contact.

"Can you remember the last time you saw a firefly?"

Shane turned toward him this time, still without meeting his eyes. She stared at the grass beneath his feet and asked, "You mean lightening bugs?"

"That's what they call them in the Bronx? We Brooklyn kids refer to them as fireflies."

She nodded and he continued.

"I can't remember the last time I saw a firefly. Or lightening bug. I'm pretty sure they don't care what they're called, even though I would surmise that being called a bug is bad enough, though is being called a fly really any better?"

She sighed as he rambled on.

"I think the last time I saw one was when I landed back in the States after that stint in Africa. The harbor in North Carolina was full of them, all buzzing around, dancing around, disinterested in us. Do you think they think of us as predators, or they just go on about their business unaware that we even exist?"

"Maybe we are to them what house flies are to us- annoying and in the way."

He nudged her with his knee and brought a smile to her face.

"Good point."

He could tell she wanted to talk, wanted some sort of connection to vent, but getting Shane to open up was a delicate game of cat and mouse which he had not yet perfected, but at which he liked to believe he excelled.

"Can I ask you a personal question?"

"Okay."

"You told me about Jolene. And about some of the others. But what about you?"

She hesitated. "What about me?"

He dove straight for the nitty gritty, trying not to pry, but pressing hard enough for results.

"What did they do to you? When they had you captive, I mean. What happened?"

Shane scoffed and expertly misdirected his inquiry.

"You mean what could they have done to make me so mean and heartless?"

Bernchal raised an eyebrow and continued watching her.

"Not what I was asking."

She shrugged and eyed his boots, silently counting the holes for the laces over and over again to distract herself from the flood of memories that were lingering in her subconscious.

"It's cool. I know that's the general consensus. I know I can be a little cold."

"A little?" he asked dramatically.

"I don't have much of a choice," she commented, resignation in her voice. "I'm responsible for everyone here."

He licked his lips and took a shot.

"Mariana's… situation shouldn't make you question everything you've done. That was a rough choice to make."

"Spare me the criticism," she replied quietly, her voice devoid of all levity.

"I'm not criticizing. I don't know if I could have made that choice. It was a tough call."

Shane finally turned to look at him and eyed him, barely hiding her surprise. Her dark eyes peered into his, full of question and torment.

"But was it the right choice?"

He tried to ease the immense amount of second-guessing he imagined she did on a daily basis.

"I doubt you'll ever get the answer to that. You're doing what you have to do."

Turning away again, she hugged her knees closer to her chest and whispered, "At what cost?"

He watched her, unable to conjure any reassuring words.

She looked past the perimeter fence, towards the sun that was now almost completely set just over the trees surrounding the college, her eyes dark and a forlorn expression on her beautiful face.

"I don't like who I am right now. Who I've had to become."

He almost didn't hear her. Honestly, he replied, "This world changed us all."

"But are we supposed to let it change us?"

He sat up and wiggled next to her, shoulder to shoulder. With a gentle nudge, he leaned close to her ear and said, "There's nothing wrong with you."

She glanced at him and he added, playfully.

"Nothing a good lay wouldn't fix."

Before she could respond, he laughed it off and repeated himself, softer this time.

"There's nothing wrong with you."

Shane shook off the intimacy of their exchange immediately and joked, "No less than you, I guess."

Bernchal leaned back on his elbows. The grass beneath him was cold and wet and he could feel the moisture seeping through his pullover. After a pause, he tried again.

"You still haven't answered my question."

He saw her shoulders rise and fall with a heavy sigh and after a moment of hesitation, she started.

"My little speech back there got you curious, I see. Well, there's not much to tell. When they took Silas I tried to fight and got myself thrown in solitary for weeks. Like I told you before, they convinced us our kids were dead so we'd be less combative while they tested us."

He heard the difference in her voice when she said that one word, and asked, "Tested?"

She replied flatly, her delivery quick and crisp and devoid of all emotion.

"Experimented. Sexual...attacks. Sodomy. Torture. Psychological mind games. They… they would tie us up and do whatever they wanted and act as though they were studying us. Like fucking guinea pigs. And those of us that hadn't been rounded up like cattle and were actually still free- it was no better. Men roamed the street- militia, Americans- doing whatever they wanted and there was nothing we could do about it. You could fight, sure," she added, with a dry chuckle. "But how can you possibly fight five, six, sometimes groups of men? The streets were no safer than the camps. So it was a lot of… a lot of stuff I'd rather not revisit."

Bernchal swallowed hard and cleared his throat. "This happened to you?"

"Yes. Not that long ago but enough time where I can pretend like it's a thing of the past. A long forgotten past. Buried deep along with my once outstanding shoe collection."

"Holy shit…"

She glanced back at him, but his eyes were trained upward toward the dark sky, struggling to take everything in. She looked back at the trees and continued.

"Anyway, we found out our kids were still alive, held somewhere. And we basically revolted. Killed all those sadistic shit-heads in the process. They'd moved the kids by then, but we got our revenge on the ones we could find."

They remained silent for several minutes, he absorbing everything she had said and fighting for her to let it all out; she absorbing everything she had been through and fighting to keep it all in in. Above them, the sky suddenly appeared black, as though the power had gone out instantaneously. Gone were the amber rays of sunlight still fighting for exposure, replaced by blinding darkness and the sounds of the nocturnal animals coming out to play.

She glanced at him, catching a peek through her peripheral vision of his face in the darkness. His jaw clenched, his mouth set in a tight, straight line. His face was frozen somewhere between anger and understanding. She sniffled and looked back down at his boots, counting the lace loops again. Any view was easier to stomach than the look on his face at that moment.

Bernchal tried his best to appear calm but the inside of his chest felt scorching. He caught her nervous glance in his direction and did not want to show her the emotion he was feeling so he attempted to keep his expression as neutral as possible, but her story, her *unloading* of it, had been excruciating to witness. Hearing it from Julie and even being in the room as she scolded Ruderick minutes beforehand were nothing compared to listening to each word out of her own mouth. The thought of her being beaten, subjected to that level of brutality, or overwhelmingly enough- *raped*- was enough to make the bile in his throat rise and threaten to spill. It hurt to hear and worse yet, it hurt to picture. But he resisted the urge to go off into the dark and use a tree trunk as a punching bag so that he could stay there next to her.

He swallowed hard and tried to get his breathing back under control. At least he understood now. He had felt for some time that he knew her well; but he had not, not really. Not until this moment. Not until he knew what had happened while he and the other members of their military had been gone and had left them unprotected. Not until he knew about what had been done to her, what she had gone through; and even then he believed he might never know the sordid details further than what she had reluctantly provided.

But he felt that now, he finally got it. It was more than the quest for her son that moved her. It was an undertaking of both revenge and redemption; revenge against those that had kidnapped her son, and redemption for what had been done to her. Now he could actually say that he fully understood her thirst for righting the wrongs that had been committed against her and every other woman alongside her.

After a drawn out moment of reflection, Bernchal summoned the energy to keep going.

"I've noticed you're pretty big on revenge."

She smiled to herself and looked down at the grass beneath her feet.

"It seems that way, doesn't it? Really, I just believe in handing out the comeuppance that people deserve. I gave them their chance to do the right thing. I warned those bastards that if they took my kid, I'd make them pay. They took my kid, so I made them pay. Just making good on a promise."

"I can respect that."

She shot her head back and eyed him with a look of equal parts detachment and appreciation. He didn't understand how one person could possibly conjure so many facial expressions in one sitting but Shane appeared to be an expert at the indecipherable look. So he watched her and wondered what she was thinking, as he often did, as she stared back at him.

"It feels weird," she whispered, her voice not much more than a flighty echo in the quiet night. "Talking to someone else about this... someone *not* female."

He didn't respond, just kept his eyes trained on hers as she processed.

She hesitated, no doubt embarrassed to be so forthcoming, and continued. "It's been a really long time since I've talked about anything other than planning and surviving to someone I'm close to."

He nodded his head slowly and acknowledged her words, his next ones formed and out of his mouth before he could second-guess himself.

"So... we're close?"

If he had not been staring at her, he wouldn't have noticed the ever-so-slight way her chest stopped moving when she'd heard his question, its undertones wrapped deceivingly in innocence. Her face remained frozen but her eyes suddenly glowed in the darkness, the color of her pupils as black as everything around them. Unable to break the stare and admit the affect his words always had on her, Shane continued watching him, her gaze penetrating past the innocence of his question and right on to the deceiving undertones.

Clearing her throat, she tried to mask the red that rose to her cheeks with flippancy. "Why are you so interested in this anyway? Since when do you need details?"

He frowned and blew it off. "I don't need details. But if I'm spending the rest of my days strapped to your side, I should know some background, don't you think? I've told you everything there is to tell about me."

"That wasn't much, Commander. You're like an open book."

"And talking to you is like pulling teeth. But we're getting somewhere."

She broke the stare finally and looked away, into the empty night completely devoid of any light. A night where not even so much as a star was visible in the sky. Bernchal wondered if maybe the universe knew how immediately their lives had been turned around and in response, had removed the stars from their galaxy as punishment.

After a second of silence, she turned back to face him, a peaceful look on her lovely face. With the sky behind her exaggerating the darkness of her eyes, Shane replied, so quietly he hardly heard her.

"And where's that?"

He didn't know if that was an invitation or a dismissal and he dared not ask. After two and a half years by her side, in her home and immersed in her world, Bernchal knew he loved her. He loved Julie and some of the other women, too; cared for them like family. But it was different with Shane. He was *in love* with her and despite his best efforts, he had become completely invested in her future. So if he had to act as though their exchanges were innocent flirting and he didn't in fact want to rip her clothes off and ravage her there on the grass in the center of the quad, he would do it. If he had to act as though he would fight to the death beside her because her cause was noble rather than the fact that it had become *his* cause, he would do it. If it meant he would continue to fight alongside her until he could be more to her than just another soldier, he would do it.

So he laid down on the freezing grass and put his hands behind his head again, propping himself up to stare at the pitch black sky. He nudged her with one bent knee and replied.

"I'll let you know when we get there."

Shane turned back to stare at nothing, this time smiling to herself as she whispered, "Okay."

Inside the institution, Ruderick took a puff from his cigarette and squinted as the smoke blew back in his face when it ricocheted off the stained-glass window in the main lobby through which he watched Bernchal and Shane, his mind turning.

Despite his repeated warnings, Bernchal seemed hell bent on being with this woman. And though he knew her mission and her reasons for fighting were honorable, she was nonetheless a liability.

While he considered his next move, the small black radio in his back pocket that was undetectable to everyone else vibrated, and he pulled it out and clicked the receiver.

"Ruderick."

The other end crackled through the static until another voice could be heard clearly.

"Williams here. We found Martinez. When do we arrange an extraction?"

Ruderick lowered the volume and looked around and when he was satisfied he was still alone, he brought his eyes back to the quad on the other side of the stained-glass window and spoke, a smile spreading on his weather-beaten face.

"Not yet, Williams. Just wait a little bit longer…"

Chapter XXXVII

It had taken some time to get used to having Bernchal around; not just for

Shane, but for all of the women in the institution. They had been on their own,

essentially anti-male, for so long, it was quite the shock to have a man suddenly

around, *all the time.* Most of the women were agreeable, if not accepting, of his

presence. But for Shane, it hadn't been easy.

After over two years of seeing his face every single day, of his hanging

around and bothering like an annoying younger sibling, Shane had finally gotten used

to having him around; more used to the idea than she cared to admit. But now, with six

more men around, constantly in the way, she was ready to explode.

Tired of turning and finding a man lingering in every corner of the institution,

Shane retreated into the locker room adjacent to the gymnasium more and more

frequently in the two months after the arrival of Bernchal's friends. The room was

barely utilized by the rest of the women, though the men's room on the other side of the

gymnasium had recently been getting its fair share of use lately.

She kept a small box of belongings that she'd gathered before and after

they'd made the college home inside one of the lockers and tried her best to keep away

so as not to dwell over the darker points in her history. But on days like the one in

which she was currently existing, when everyone and everything around her had gotten

her to the point of almost boiling over from the frustration and impotence of not finding

her son, Shane would go the locker room and look through her things.

After hitting the track particularly hard that morning and avoiding any human

contact all afternoon, Shane made her way into the locker room alone. She used her key

to unlock the master lock and placing her gas lamp on the bench in between two long

rows of lockers, she stood in front of number 421 and stared at the unopened door.

April 21st.

The day she had met Dixon after bumping into her tall, distracted first love

on line in Dunkin' Donuts. He'd been reading his emails on his blackberry, holding a

stack of papers he planned on grading under one arm and his briefcase under the other, all while strategically balancing a steaming cup of coffee that managed to shoot up into the air and all over the front of his polo shirt when they had made contact.

He had asked her to dinner on the spot and the rest, as they say, had been history.

She took a deep breath and reached for the handle, pulling at the rusty latch until she heard the click she expected and opened the small door.

Inside, she rifled through a handful of maps of the former United States that she had kept after their first raid of the college, and lingered absentmindedly with her hands inside the locker. In the back of her mind, she knew what she was avoiding, but she lied to herself over and over and tried to keep her hands busy thumbing through old maps until the lies became no match for that voice.

As though they operated with a mind of their own, her hands obliged the masochistic voice inside her that seemed to thrive off the pain eating her up day in and day out, and she reached deep into the locker, past the textbooks and maps and other fossils of old life, and emerged with a beat-up leather wallet.

After Dixon's murder that day in the school in which he had taught for fourteen years, Shane had kept his wallet. He'd forgotten it that morning. After rushing out to hit the gym before school, he'd left it on the nightstand next to their bed. He had called her as he waited for the school bus to pick him and his kids up for the class trip they had planned to see a new reptile exhibit at the Bronx Zoo in preparation for their winter projects on animal species. He had called her to ask her to bring the wallet to him because he could not get on the bus without it, and she'd heard the kids in the background, excited and chattering; tiny fourth graders climbing the walls waiting for their bus. She had told him she could not leave her office at that moment because she'd been expecting a call from a judge but that she would fax a copy of his driver's license should he need it. And they had said goodbye normally, as they always did when they knew they would see each other again.

She had said goodbye to him then not knowing that that would be the last time she would ever hear his voice again.

And like a glutton for punishment, Shane had kept that wallet. She had kept it throughout the escape from the home they had shared, after her son had been taken and she's been imprisoned and tortured and finally freed. She had kept it all that time, smuggling it from place to place so that she could retain something, anything, that once belonged to her dead husband, something he had touched and had held.

She flipped open the flap of the wallet, feeling the softened brown leather give a little after so much time in a locker without being opened. She took a deep breath and inhaled the smell- worn calfskin and man.

Despite her better judgment, she reached for the tiny picture tucked into the enveloped pocket and gingerly pulled it out.

That toothless grin. The tossed brown hair, one curl, like Superman's cowlick, hanging over his forehead. Those bright brown eyes, always laughing, always smiling, always so warm and full of love.

Her eyes watered and blurred until she struggled to see Silas' face through the tears that immediately spilled over and down her cheeks. She wiped them with the other hand roughly and stared at the picture, wrinkled and fading at the corners.

Behind her, the door opened and she heard Bernchal's voice booming into the empty room, bouncing off the metal lockers and echoing all around her.

"So this is the only room in the whole damn place to find some peace and quiet? I swear Shane, I didn't see the big deal about mixing your group with mine at first, but now I'm realizing the mistake. How could you let me talk you into it? Big fail on your part…"

He stopped when she didn't face him and instead, wiped her eyes and struggled to shove the picture back inside the wallet and return it to the locker.

"You okay?"

"I'm fine," she replied brusquely. The corner of the tiny picture caught on the fold of the wallet pocket and when she shoved it further inside, the picture bent in the middle, a crease appearing along Silas' smiling face. She struggled to keep it together as she fumbled with the picture, trying to simultaneously straighten it out and put it back inside.

"Shane?"

Her hands tripped over themselves and the tears blinded her. Her fingers felt like dumbbells carelessly stumbling over each other, no finesse at all, and she dropped the picture and watched helplessly as it floated down, down, to the linoleum floor beneath her and right under the row of lockers.

"Fuck!"

Bernchal walked over to her as she dropped the wallet onto the bench behind her and started to get on her knees to search for the picture.

"Whoa, whoa. Relax. Let me help you."

"I got it," she replied through clenched teeth. The tears fells from her face and landed at her feet in tiny, silent droplets. Her composure threatened to fall apart.

"Let me get it, Shane. Chill."

He held her off with one hand to her shoulder. She relented and he dropped to his haunches and tugged at the tiny corner still peeking out from under the locker. Carefully, he pulled at it with his index finger until it came back out and he retrieved it from the floor. Standing up, Bernchal brushed the dust off against his jeans and turned it for a look, his eyes landing on the minuscule smiling face of Shane's son.

She reached for it and snatched it out of his hand. The last semblance of control she had over her demeanor gave way and her eyes burned again, the tears filling them up immediately.

"I'm fine," she whispered, in response to his unasked question, while the tears started falling again. She tried to wipe them away.

Bernchal reached for her hand and she pulled away suddenly.

"I'm fine. Just..."

He reached again and she reacted, pushing against him and slamming the locker door shut. It bounced defiantly against the hinge and popped back open.

"Leave me alone!"

He grabbed both of her hands suddenly and held them down against her sides. She wiggled, struggling against his grip.

"Let go…"

He held her and bent at the waist to make eye contact, speaking to her with a calm, soothing voice.

"Listen to me. You need to hit something, hit me. You wanna break something, I'll find you something to break. You're allowed to feel more than just anger all the time. You are human, and crying doesn't make you weak."

Like a sage old guide, he somehow knew exactly what to say to destroy the thin sliver of control she gripped so defiantly, refusing to let go. He broke through her grasp and the control slid away, almost mercifully, as the floodgates began to part.

She stilled and stopped fighting against him. Refusing to make eye contact, she listened as he lowered his mouth to her ear and whispered.

"He's your son. It's okay to cry for him."

The remaining hold she had over her emotions disintegrated like ash in a strong wind. Her face crumbled and with no ability left to maintain control, she broke down.

Her knees gave way and Bernchal caught her effortlessly and held her as she sobbed, her body trembling against his.

The flashes here and there, the vulnerable moments wherein she'd slipped up and allowed him a view to which few were privy into her inner workings; those times she'd been so emblazoned with rage that he had seen firsthand the passion and fire that drove her- all of that culminated into this moment of clarity. She was grieving for her son and allowing him to witness it. To Bernchal, it was both tragic and beautiful.

She sniffled and sobbed into his chest, moistening his t-shirt with her tears. He hugged her to him, stroking her hair and allowing her to let it out.

Her voice came out gargled and muffled against the fabric of his shirt. She inhaled sharply and spoke to him, the words spilling out in sporadic gulps of air.

"I see it played out over and over again, the same way. Him being ripped away, the terror in his eyes, the terror in his voice. And I'm tired of remembering it that way. I'm tired..."

He kissed the top of her head sweetly until the tears began to subside. Still holding her, he whispered, "You're not alone."

She shook her head against his hard chest, her curls tickling his chin.

"Having warm bodies around you doesn't mean you're not alone. It's different."

"It *is* different," he agreed. "But you found everybody else for a reason. And I found you..."

After a moment, he whispered to her through the wisps of curls between them.

"I think maybe tortured souls, lost and sad people, have a way of finding each other. Like spotting each other out of a crowd. Somehow make their grief or whatever it is that's eating them more tolerable. Maybe knowing there's another person out there feeling the same way you do, even just an iota of your pain, I think that makes a person feel somewhat whole."

His grip tightened and for the first time, she was not afraid. She was not weary of his touch or anxious of what it meant. Strangely, she became calmed, inside and out. The fire that burned indefinitely was suddenly controlled. It had not been extinguished- only the return of her son could do that, she knew. But she felt a sudden tranquility inside of her, as though the stormy black clouds that had been growing steadily, day by day, were now outside of the institution instead of hanging directly over her, and she felt the peace of knowing for the first time in a long time what it felt like to be protected.

She continued to cry though the sobs became fewer and more far between. He rubbed her hair and kissed her head softly as the last of the emotion left her. Her body finally stilled and she pulled away a little, her cheeks streaked with fallen tears.

Their eyes met, and he reached for her face, moving loose strands of curly hair away and tucking them behind her ear.

Bernchal noticed that her eyes were no longer veiled with the darkness of fear lurking behind them. She did not flinch at his touch. Instead, she held his gaze and he realized he no longer felt like a stranger in her eyes; he had not felt like a stranger in a very long time.

This time, for the first time, Bernchal's close proximity did not bother her. Up until this moment any time he was too close to her or reached out with an innocent touch, Shane felt nothing but terror inside of her; a quickened heartbeat and suddenly sweaty palms made her hyper-aware of the tension in her body.

This time, her heartbeat quickened for a different reason; her body tensed, not in fear of what had been in the past but instead in anticipation of what could be. And though it was not the first time he'd made her feel simultaneously deaf, dumb and mute, it was the first time she was not resisting.

His thumb grazed her cheek and the warmth transferred from his skin to hers. She shuddered and he moved it across her jawline, watching her. Wiping the tears from her face, her eyes closed involuntarily and he moved closer to her, his lips mere centimeters from hers.

The door flew open and Bernchal's head turned to their uninvited guest as his voice shattered the stillness of the locker room.

"Am I interrupting something?"

The switched flipped, the moment lost. She became instantly aware of Ruderick's presence and her own precarious position still entwined in Bernchal's arms.

Shane replied sharply, "No," and pulled away from Bernchal much rougher than intended. She turned away from him, ignoring the disappointment in his eyes, and bent at the waist to retrieve her late husband's leather wallet, which still sat on the bench in the middle of the locker room.

With a dry chuckle and that insipid grin, Ruderick raised an eyebrow and muttered under his breath, "Doesn't seem that way to me…"

Shane threw the wallet into the locker and slammed her hand inside, foraging for maps, annoyed.

"Why don't you worry less about the way things *seem* and more about your men constantly trying to catch the rest of the women showering? It's unseemly. It's perverted and I'm fucking tired of hearing these women screaming all afternoon."

"Touché," he replied, still smiling. He glanced at Bernchal who could only glare at him. Brushing it off, he cleared his throat and spoke loudly.

"We got info on Martinez."

Bernchal, watching Shane as she kept herself occupied, realized what Ruderick mentioned and turned to him, suddenly.

"What?"

Ruderick repeated himself, exhibiting all the patience in the world.

"Martinez. He put the word out. He made it to D.C."

"Are you serious?"

Ruderick nodded and Bernchal let out a surprised laugh. "Holy shit."

Shane slammed the door of her locker shut and turned around, her arms full of textbooks. Eyeing her suspiciously, Ruderick clammed up and stared, waiting for her to leave. Oblivious, Bernchal prodded him for more.

"And?"

Lacking any basic tact or subtlety, Ruderick looked to Bernchal, then Shane, then back again, waiting. She noticed the pause and eyed them both, scoffing in their general direction.

"Captain, you're *my* guest; not the other way around. You'd do well to remember that the next time you want to get my secrets and not return the favor."

Pushing past Bernchal, she started to make her way out of the locker room. He tried to stop her with a hand on her arm, calling, "Shane-" before she she cut him off.

"It's fine," she replied, coolly. "You boys talk shop."

Ruderick pushed open the door leading out of the locker room and held it for her as she passed. Once she was through, he pulled it shut and turned to face Bernchal, who stood waiting, the anger permeating from his pores.

"Was that necessary?"

Like one would a small child, Ruderick addressed him with a patronizing smile.

"Commander, they're civilians. As honorable as their mission may be, these women do not have the same agenda we do. Our mission is to restore the United States of America, not babysit."

He shook his head and released a deep breath. "It's not babysitting. Jesus Christ, Wood, when are you going to accept that their whole operation, no matter how un-American it may seem to you, is legitimate? Why are you constantly undermining them, particularly her?"

Ruderick recoiled, as though he could not believe the words coming from Bernchal's mouth. After a moment his expression changed to one of puzzlement and he chortled, barely containing a sarcastic laugh as he responded.

"I don't have to accept a goddamn thing, Commander. These women don't mean shit to me. I have made that very clear."

"Yes, you have," he muttered exasperatedly under his breath. Ruderick continued with his speech despite Bernchal's obvious lack of attention.

"And I have no plans to modify a single decision based on their little 'operation', despite your obvious attachment to them and their so-called leader."

"Wood-"

"I'm serious, Steve. Look," he started, changing his tone from condescending to understanding in one fluid motion. "I know you feel you owe them and I get it. I do. Soldiers- we form attachments during battle and we carry that sense of gratitude with us, turn it into a debt we're determined to repay. I get it. But you work for the United States of America. That flag, that ideal, should be your number one priority. Not some chick and her kid."

Bernchal shook his head and stared at him in disbelief.

"It's not a sense of gratitude, you ass. This is a cause, just as much of a cause as any we've ever fought. Afghanistan, Africa- those were orders. Those were obligations. This is different. We're talking about children. Living, breathing *American* children! Kidnapped and held hostage by the same people that stepped all over your precious flag and shit all over your precious ideal."

He took a step towards Ruderick, his eyes pleading for a little leeway. "This is a chance to get those kids back, return them to their moms. Their goddamn mothers who have been suffering and dying inside without their kids."

Unmoved, Ruderick replied, "I don't trust her."

He exploded. "She knows that! I know it, she knows it- everybody knows it! But you know what? She doesn't give a fuck! She couldn't give two goddamn rat's asses whether you trust her or not. She's going on with or without your help, Wood. And that's probably what burns you up the most, isn't it? The fact that she is fully functional and self-sufficient without any of our help. She doesn't need any of us."

Nonchalantly, Ruderick locked eyes with him and asked, "Then why do *you* stick around?"

Bernchal was unable to conjure any type of adequate response and as he suddenly averted his eyes and stalled, Ruderick's expression changed. He scoffed and pointed at Bernchal, accusingly.

"Wait a minute. You... You're actually in love with this chick," he stated, incredulously. "I thought you just wanted to fuck her but, holy shit...You love her."

Bernchal was suddenly, annoyingly and embarrassingly tongue-tied. So he shook his head and attempted the best look of arrogant impatience he could muster. He pushed past him and made his way to the door, exiting as Ruderick called after him as the door closed.

"Watch your six, Steve."

Chapter XXXVIII

Like a seasoned football team trying a new play, the militia grew bolder.

As the weather changed and the ground started freezing, their visits to the top of the hill increased. Drive-bys at first, which were carefully monitored by the sentries on the tower and roofs. Then they started circling, up from the dealership all the way through the old Henry Hudson Parkway.

They had yet to breach the perimeter, but they were getting more daring with each visit. Like a curious child poking at the glass of a fish tank, the militia crept closer and closer, seemingly intrigued about what lay inside the doors of the institution, but not curious enough to venture inside.

Shane, Bernchal, Ruderick and Julie had discussed this new development at length. Ruderick pushed for a complete blitz, convinced they knew everything about their institution and were preparing for an attack. Julie countered his argument, logically explaining that if the militia knew they were inside and based at the college they would have attacked a long time ago. Shane sided with Julie and Bernchal, who had begun to feel as though he were showing up merely to play the part of being involved, offered no avenue of compromise whatsoever.

The distrust floating between them was increasing, with each meeting, each discussion about policy and procedure, the cards were laid out on the table and they never changed. Ruderick was firmly planted dead against anything Shane and the other women had already implemented. Julie sided with Shane on all matters and Bernchal remained pit up against each party, feeling like a traitor to Ruderick and an asshole to Shane.

In late December, Ruderick advised Bernchal that he had some intel on the whereabouts of some higher-ups, a few scientists that were just below the President on the totem pole of Shane's wrath, but he refused to name his source. Within minutes of his revelation, hell had been unleashed upon them in the form of several angry women, namely one in particular.

To Shane, Ruderick's refusal to not only provide her with pertinent information about the people connected to the abduction of her son, but also reveal his source of said information, was as treacherous as Mariana's turn against them. However, despite the considerable amount of threats she lay against him, of which there were many, Ruderick refused to budge and Shane was left with a seething hatred for the man who was supposed to be on her side and who had just graduated to public enemy #1.

Days after Ruderick singlehandedly turned every woman in the institution against anything with a penis, Bernchal was approached by Muccio and Hiu, who summoned him to the chapel for a powwow. He followed them, noting on his way down the darkened corridor of his dormitory how silent the rest of the institution seemed lately. Since planting more security outside their walls and scattered all over the immediate vicinity of the college, the inside had seemed much less alive with activity. And since Ruderick's news, he had not seen or spoken to Shane in over three days and he deduced that he too, had joined the growing list of persona non grata.

Ruderick was waiting for him in the administration office, two doors down from the old chapel. Manhattan College had been a Catholic school, Jesuit to be exact, with a chapel attached to the outskirts of the property for worship and use by the student body. Before the militia had begun sneaking around, the women would often cross the quad in daylight to reach the chapel, which was located on the west end of the property, just above the woods leading to the track field. With the soldiers now lurking around every corner and more eyes on the lookout on the rooftops nearby, the women now utilized the subterranean tunnels created after the school had been taken over by them. The tunnel that Shane kept closed off that Ruderick had reopened a few weeks back was now the designated route under the quad towards the chapel. He walked the tunnel now, following Muccio and Hiu and led by the glow of their flashlights.

They opened the doors for him and he walked into the office, looking around. Ruderick had not yet tried to redecorate as he had attempted in the cafeteria so the large mahogany desk sat where it had when the college was bustling with coed life, in the east corner, under the windows and away from the sunlight. Tonight, with a sky lit only by the moonlight, Ruderick's silhouette was half-hidden in the shadows and the scowl on his face appeared deeper than usual

"Why the secrecy?" asked Bernchal immediately upon entering the room. Ruderick lifted a large hand and pointed out of the door past Bernchal and towards the direction of the chapel.

"Because *they're* keeping secrets."

Bernchal looked behind him and saw Muccio leaning against the doorway, disinterested. Beyond him, Hiu watched the hallway for guests.

"What the fuck is going on?"

"I'll tell you what's going on. These bitches are up to something. They've been congregating all day, in and out, in and out, coming and going with boxes they keep hidden when they pass one of us. Has your little girlfriend said anything to you about what they're plotting?"

Rolling his eyes upward, Bernchal released a breath, muttered *Holy shit*, and replied impatiently.

"She's not my girlfriend. And no. And you're fucking paranoid, Wood. Nobody's plotting anything."

Ruderick rose and pointed again at the chapel, his voice low and secretive.

"You know homegirl was not happy with my news and even more pissed off I won't give her any intel. She's plotting something, Steve. I can feel it. She's just the type to sabotage our operation because she doesn't get her way."

"Let me fill you in on how Shane operates, okay? She is not going to plot some shit behind your back. She's not the type to do anything underhanded. What she would do is wake you up with a gun to your face and let you know that she's going to do something, and then force you to sit there and watch her do it. *That's* the type of person she is."

Ruderick took a couple of steps and approached Bernchal, his eyes dancing with conspiratorial ideas. "I'm telling you, they're up to something. It smells shady. It looks shady. It sounds shady."

"You're losing your mind, Wood."

Before Ruderick could react, Bernchal shook his head and tried a different approach.

"Listen, I'm sure whatever you're seeing has a rational explanation. Shane and most of the women here- they're creatures of habit. They don't suddenly start doing weird shit unless there's a reason for it."

Nonplussed, he looked about to reply when Hiu rapped on the wall outside the room. Bernchal turned to follow Ruderick's eyes and caught sight of Jisel passing them on her way to the chapel. Though it was just a fleeting glimpse, he did pick up on a small box in her hands.

They continued staring as the double doors of the chapel creaked opened. Slight chatter could be heard as it traveled down the corridor towards them until Jisel let the doors close behind her and everything was silent again.

Ruderick stared at Bernchal when he turned back to face him. "You see?"

"See what? She was holding a box. Big deal."

Ruderick pushed past him and walked to the doorway, hands up as though he could not comprehend how he was the only person sensing a conspiracy in the air.

"Take a look, Steve! Take a look at them. They're up to something. I know it!"

Realizing that he was getting nowhere fast, Bernchal reluctantly followed him out of the door of the administration room and towards the chapel, with Muccio and Hiu close behind.

The chapel doors were heavy and wooden and swung open inward. With no window into which to peek, Muccio propped his hand up against both doors and gave them a slight nudge, holding them open just enough for their eyes to peer inside.

Feeling like a peeping tom, Bernchal questioned his sanity seconds before arching his neck and squinting through the small opening allowed by Muccio's hands and looked at the women inside.

They were sitting in the pews, occupying the first several rows, all shoulder to shoulder. Their heads were down for the most part, some of them whispering to the neighbor on the left or right, some of them hunched over and apparently sobbing. Candles at the alter were lit, and a small shrine of sorts was haphazardly set up at the steps leading up it. Boxes of all sizes leaned up against the steps and at the top was a larger candle, lit and glowing.

It was fairly quiet, with the occasional sniffle or whisper carrying across the room and making its way back to him. Bernchal stared, confused, until a realization hit him when Jisel stood from her seat on one of the pews and made her way to the alter, placing the box she had been carrying on the steps.

He snapped his head back and looked to Ruderick, his eyes glowing brightly with anger in the dark hallway. Muccio let the doors close and watched as Bernchal shook his head and addressed them tightly.

"What day is it?"

They shrugged between them and Hiu offered, "Tuesday, I think."

"Date," he corrected himself. "What *date* is it?"

Ruderick replied, "The 25th," and Bernchal's heart sunk.

"Holy fucking shit…"

"What?" asked Hiu, intrigued.

"It's Christmas."

"What?"

"Christmas!" he yelled, exploding with anger. Immediately, he lowered his voice and looked back at the doors of the chapel, hoping no one inside heard him. "It's Christmas day. The 25th of December. It's Christmas, you fucking morons. You know, Santa? Reindeer? Carols?"

Hiu turned pale, as though he were suddenly ill, and Muccio muttered, "Jesus Christ," disbelievingly.

"Yeah, him too..."

Ruderick remained unconvinced, his bright blue eyes becoming small and accusatory as he asked, "So this is what they've been doing all day? Planning Christmas?"

Bernchal shook his head, willing himself to keep from giving Ruderick one good, solid punch in the jaw.

"They're exchanging gifts on behalf..." He stopped, obviously upset. Taking a deep breath, he laughed derisively and pinched the bridge of his nose, finally continuing. "On behalf of their missing kids, you heartless pricks. They do this every year. Probably because its so goddamn painful to be without them today of all days."

He shook his head, unable to conjure up a reason to stay there with them. Backing up down the hallway, he pushed past Hiu and reached Ruderick, getting close to his face. He dropped his voice to a dangerous level and laced with sarcasm, demanded one answer.

"How's that for conspiracy? Huh, Wood? Shady enough for you?"

Ruderick stared back at him unmoved, but did not respond. With disbelief written all over his disappointed face, Bernchal shoved him out of his way and made his way down the hallway. Ruderick cupped his hands around his mouth and called after him, "You're not gonna make me feel like an asshole on this, Steve."

He stopped in his tracks and swiveled towards them, his face stretched into a derisive smirk.

"You know something? That's the funny thing, Wood. A normal person would automatically feel like an asshole right now."

With a hint of defense in his tone, Ruderick replied dryly. "And a normal person would not be so gung-ho about killing everybody in her path."

Bernchal knew the tit-for-tat was counterproductive, but he couldn't help himself, and he walked back towards Ruderick, his hazel eyes glowing in the dimly-lit corridor as he growled.

"You're right. You're 100% right, Wood. A normal woman wouldn't be out here right now and that's the whole point of this goddamn crusade. A normal woman would be home, safe and sound, *with her son.*"

Without missing a beat, Ruderick fired back.

"And with you?"

He licked his lips and smiled, shaking his head back and forth as if to say, *You get one of those, and that was it.*

He pointed a finger at Ruderick, whispered, "Fuck you," and disappeared down the hallway back towards the male dormitory.

After a long walk through the dark tunnels alone wherein he childishly kicked around mounds of rocks and dirt to let off some steam, Bernchal went back to his room.

Holy shit! How in the hell could he possibly maintain order or even, daresay, form an actual union among everyone if Shane hated Ruderick and Ruderick refused to trust Shane? The bigger question he had though, in further reflecting on how he had found himself in that predicament, was how he had unknowingly gravitated towards two people who seemed to be exactly the same.

He paced his room, stomping his feet like a spoiled toddler, mulling over everything. He was plagued by indecision, loyalty and heartache. Torn between two rational but completely different points-of-view, he gripped the side of his head as he felt a headache coming on.

Knowing there would be no answers to his problems tonight, he straightened his shoulders and shook it off. There was nothing he could do about Ruderick right now, so he opted instead to focus on what he *could* do.

Retrieving something he'd picked up some time ago during one of their runs when things at the institution had been a lot more peaceful, Bernchal made his way back to the chapel, grateful to have avoided the rest of the guys upon his arrival. He found a comfortable position against the wall outside the double doors and waited.

Inside, Shane could only take so much of the somber mood and after the obligatory pep talk, she said her goodbyes to everyone and sniffling, headed to her room alone.

When she exited the chapel, she was surprised to find Bernchal right outside leaning against the wall, perched in his usual casual stance with one leg propped behind him. The gas lamp resting on a folding chair next to him flickered pathetically, barely lighting the darkened corridor.

She wiped her eyes and looked back to the swinging chapel door behind her, hoping he didn't catch sight of the tears before she had wiped them away.

"What's up?"

He peeled his long body off the wall and took a step closer to her, simultaneously revealing a rectangular item in his hand. Without speaking, he extended his hand and offered it to her. She met his eyes and confused, asked "What's this?"

Wordlessly, he pushed it towards her and she took it, turning it over to discover a picture frame. With a shy smile, she inspected it further and heard his voice, suddenly far away.

"It's a Christmas present..."

It was small and rectangular shaped, white at the border with a faded and chipped red apple in the lower right hand corner. Above the picture were the words 'World's Best Teacher' engraved, but the word 'Teacher' was crossed off and 'Mother' was handwritten with a red marker.

"...found it in one of the old hobby stores. I know it's cheap, but..."

In the frame was the picture of Silas that she'd shoved back into her locker two weeks ago.

She held it up, fingering it gently, tears in her eyes. Letting out a little sigh, Shane closed her eyes and clutched the frame close to her with one hand, wiping the waterworks with the other.

Bernchal bent at the waist, trying to meet her eyes, asking, "You like it?"

She nodded her head and tried to put herself back together again. Touching the frame again, she stared at her son's face and whispered, "I do."

"Good."

After a pause, she looked up at him, worry written all over her face.

"Why'd you do this?"

He cleared his throat, visibly uncomfortable but trying his best to disguise it.

"I just figured…" he started, hands scratching at the back of his neck and his eyes suddenly avoiding hers. "Christmas without your kids must really suck. So I figured at least this way you can look at him."

She choked back the flood of tears that threatened to spill and nodded, glancing down at the frame again.

He hesitated for a second, and then blurted out.

"I don't like to make promises, Shane. Ever. But… I… if I can help it, this is the last Christmas you'll spend without your son."

Her face crumbled into her hands and the tears flowed freely. The breakdown was brief and she composed herself quickly.

Finally nodding in his general direction, she said nothing. After a second or two of emotional silence between them, she laughed aloud and pointed to her face, joking between the tears, "See? This is why I don't cry in front of people."

Bernchal chuckled, glad for the mood change.

She walked to him suddenly, her eyes wet from tears and lighting up the black hallway. Approaching him, she put her free hand on the left side of his chest, just above the hammering of his heartbeat and rising on her tip-toes, kissed him gently on the cheek.

"Thank you."

Shane walked down the dark hallway silently, overcome with emotion and leaving him there, unsure of his own.

She started back towards her room, clutching the picture frame to her chest.

At this moment she was surprised by her own feelings, shocked that she not only allowed Bernchal to see her that way- *again* -but also had grown so comfortable with him that touching him seemed second nature. A peck on the cheek; that emotional embrace two weeks prior- she felt like a teenager falling in love. And that was a problem.

She had made her sentiments known. Bernchal knew her one mission, her only mission, was the retrieval of her son, and the return of those missing kids to their grieving mothers. He knew the deal. He had known it when he had made their little college home two years prior, and he knew it now. Nothing had changed.

So why then did she feel like every time he neared, those thoughts went out the window and all she could think of was pulling him into her room and locking the door?

She shook her head and rolled her eyes at herself for behaving like a child. It was a gift, a sweet gesture from a thoughtful friend- nothing more. So Shane brushed off any overt feelings of love and lust and walking faster, jogged down the tunnel until she made her way through the dean's office and into the main lobby.

As she turned the corner of the hallway, she ran right into Ruderick, who scoffed when he realized who she was. She, in turn and not one to ever be outdone, loudly sucked her teeth when she bounced off of him, rolled her eyes and without an apology, continued down the hall towards her room.

His voice, loud and aggravated at the other end, stopped her in her tracks.

"What's your fucking problem with me?"

Shane turned and walked back towards him purposefully, and with her voice low and threatening, stood close to his face and countered, "What's *your* fucking problem with *me*?"

His bright blue eyes twinkled and gave away his amusement, despite his attempt to appear angrier than he felt. He considered for a moment and then spoke up, significantly less hostile than a second before.

"You're always…on. Don't you ever stop?"

She met his gaze with one of indifference and replied.

"You're always here. Don't you ever leave?

He smiled, amused.

"Touché."

Shane shook her head impatiently and turned to walk away again.

Ruderick cupped his mouth with his hands and shouted down the hall after her.

"I think this means we're becoming friends, you and I."

Chapter XXXIX

The initial blast happened at 7:13am, about two hundred yards from Shane and Julie. Bernchal, Ruderick and Derrecks were a few feet ahead of them, closer to the institution and right in the center of the explosion.

For several seconds following the burst of fire, Shane couldn't hear anything. She'd gone up in the air and hit the ground with tremendous force. Reluctantly sitting up, she took a breath for the first time and immediately began to cough.

She heard nothing.

The dust had not yet dissipated, the smoke surrounding them was impenetrable. She felt herself call out to Julie and Bernchal, but she heard her own voice come out muffled and distant, as though she were under water.

All around her the silence was deafening. She felt leaves and dirt falling on top of her like raindrops and could see the billowing smoke begin to dissolve, but she still couldn't hear a thing.

Withdrawing her weapon, she pushed herself backwards with her legs and shoved herself up against the trunk of a large tree whose top half was missing, waiting.

The ringing came first. A high-pitched squeal, like the toot of a dog whistle. It started low at first, and then higher and higher until she felt like her head was going to crack open. She shut her eyes tight and dropping the gun on the ground, gripped the sides of her head with both hands, desperately trying to stop the sound.

Then came the back noise. A call in the distance, words being shouted. A cacophony of sounds and names all blurred together, invading her senses all at once. She kept her eyes shut tight, her hands to her ears, and letting out a small cry, squeezed.

Eventually, the ringing in her head calmed, but remained. She peeled her eyes open and took another deep breath, releasing her ears as the noises started to take form and normalize.

Peering from behind the tree truck, she spotted feet walking in her direction. She found the gun, cocked the safety back and waited, until finally she saw Julie emerge through the smoke.

Shane returned the gun to her holster and rose to run to Julie. They met in a newly made clearance in the woods behind their home.

"What happened?" she managed as another bout of coughing hit her and she almost doubled over.

"I think it was an IED. Everything's leveled- all the trees from here down a mile are fucking gone."

Shane shook off the coughs as Julie patted her hard on the back. Standing and trying to regulate her breathing, she rubbed the dirt and ash from her eyes.

"Where are the guys?"

They locked eyes and Julie shook her head, an alarmed expression overtaking her face. "They were right on the blast, Shane."

Her heartbeat quickened and immediately she felt a panic rise up inside of her. But she willed herself to be calm and search for their friends. Her friend.

Turning, she started back towards the direction they were headed before the blast. The five of them had set out that morning to follow militia that had been seen shortly after dawn roaming the woods behind the institution.

Julie called their names and Shane struggled to hear her through the ringing. She followed her towards their original path, searching the ground for them, for anything- a weapon, a boot, a body.

Julie stopped short and pointed to something on the ground, flat against the white snow fifty feet ahead of them.

A foot, boot-clad, peeked out from under a shrub. It was still.

Shane gulped and started to walk towards it. She saw denim jeans attached to the body and broke into a jog, reaching it immediately.

She half fell, half threw herself, landed on her knees and sliding into the shrub, grabbed at the body laying face-down in the snow. A portion of its skull was gone, the dark brown hair matted with brain matter. There was blood everywhere. She grabbed at the torso, yanking and trying to flip it on its back so she could see if it was Bernchal.

"Steve!" A yell rose out of her, but she hardly realized. Her hands awkwardly pulled until she used all of her weight to yank the body over and flip it. She fell back on her bottom and it landed on her thighs, Derrecks' dark brown eyes peering up at her, lifelessly.

Her heart hammered mercilessly in her chest, the pounding louder than the ringing in her ears. She released a breath and heard in it an unmistakable sigh of relief. She looked up at Julie who watched, scared. Determined to resume her search, Shane pushed Derrecks' body off her legs and rose from the ground, shaking her head as she addressed Julie.

"It's not him."

Her voice sounded detached, as though it were coming from someone else. The hammering in her chest would not relent and she tried desperately to control her breathing. *Why do I feel like this?* she asked herself.

They heard her name called from behind them, back from where they had emerged. A yell in the distance, muffled by the smoke and trees and ringing in her ears and the incessant beating of her heart.

Ignoring the obvious danger around her, Shane took off towards the sound, pushing past the brushes that still stood and the trees that had been knocked down, threatening to trip her as she ran. Julie followed closely behind and finally they cleared a mangled set of branches that were still smoking and on fire and stopped, chests heaving. Shane cupped her hands over her mouth and called his name, strangely aware of the terror in her voice.

"*Steve!*"

She franticly searched the trees that still stood for any sign of life. Finally, she saw him limping towards them, through the smoke. His face was covered with dark ash, and he was holding his right shoulder, blood on his hands and running down his arm.

She closed the distance between them at record speed and surprised herself by instinctively reaching for him before she knew what she was doing. Clumsily falling into him, she wrapped her arms around him and squeezed, crying out when they touched and she confirmed he was in fact, alive. He returned the gesture and despite the throbbing in his wounded shoulder, immediately enveloped her in a hug that lifted her off the ground, holding her tightly against his chest and burying his face in her hair as he breathlessly whispered her name. Inhaling the scent of her shampoo, he closed his eyes, feeling an instant rush of relief, gratitude and fear.

With her face smooshed up against him, Shane closed her own eyes and inhaled sharply, utterly bewildered by her reaction.

He released her and reached for her face, roughly yanking on her chin as he examined her for wounds and pushed her hair behind her ears. Satisfied she was unharmed, he wordlessly took her hand, pulling her behind him. Motioning for Julie to follow, they ducked down low, behind some remaining brush and tried to find Ruderick.

They retraced their steps to Derrecks' body, moving quickly and silently through the forest. A wind tunnel funneled through the trees that were still standing, picking up and dropping the refuge from the blast. Leaves, dirt and ash surrounded them, twirling in and out of their faces, picked up and amplified by the bitter cold already in the air. Bernchal gripped Shane's hand tighter, pulled her closer to him, and she followed willingly, acutely aware of their increasingly complicated scenario.

The rustling of leaves alerted them to activity and they immediately took cover behind the large trunk of a seemingly unaffected tree. The three of them bunched together behind the trunk listening, Julie next to Shane and Shane awkwardly pressed up against Bernchal.

Julie saw movement first. Her weapon was out in a flash and before either Shane or Bernchal could react, she popped off three shots, the sound surprising Shane and making her jump reflexively.

To her right, three militia soldiers dropped to the ground one by one as the head shots landed perfectly. Shane exhaled and looked to Julie, who winked in her direction and peeled herself off the tree's trunk, carefully continuing back on track. Bernchal let out an impressed whistle and followed behind her, pulling Shane with him.

"Steve.."

A voice called out and they ran towards it, finding Ruderick slumped over, tucked in between one of the trees that had been blown back by the explosion and some neighboring brushes. His right leg was extended in front of him, a nasty gash on his shin peeking through the ripped fabric of his cargo pants.

Immediately they tended to him, Bernchal taking off his parka and using it to tie Ruderick's leg at the knee while Shane checked him for more injuries. Finding none, they helped him to his feet, all two hundred and eighty-eight pounds of him. With an arm extended over both Bernchal and Shane, Ruderick hobbled with them as Julie led the way out of the clearing and into the denser part of the forest that had remained unaffected by the blast.

Behind them, the few small flames that remained in the shrubbery began to subside in the cold, wet air, the crackling drifting away as the embers reached the snow beneath them like the wick of a dying candle. The air settled and became much more quiet as everything that had been lifted and twirled around them was now fallen on the snow at their feet. Now, all they heard was the crunch of the frozen floor beneath them as they made their way to safety.

Chapter XL

Close to the institution, about fifty or so feet from the separation between the woods and the perimeter of their property, the second blast went off. This was much further, not quite on top of them as the last one had been, so the four of them were just knocked to the ground rather than having been thrown several feet in the air.

Bernchal pulled Shane to him immediately upon impact and tucked her underneath the safety of his body, so they rolled a few feet away and stopped against the fence surrounding the college. He pushed her deeper into the ground and held her underneath him, looking around and searching for answers as she coughed again; the snow, dirt and dust from the explosion once again filling her lungs and choking her.

That grating sound, which had not fully left her, came back stronger this time, the ringing in her ears overpowering the outside noises around her, exacerbated by the pressure of Bernchal's body on top of hers. She nudged him but he would not relent and held her below him, and she squeezed her eyes shut again, peeling her arms out from under him and pressing her hands hard against her ears.

Julie was up in seconds and she picked up Ruderick under his arms and pulled him towards Bernchal and Shane. He was conscious, but stunned, so she was pulling dead weight. Scrambling, her small feet stumbling and sliding on the snow, she heaved as she dragged his massive frame.

"It was a mine," she said breathlessly as she and Ruderick reached them.

Bernchal nodded in agreement and satisfied that they were still alone, rose from the ground and crouched low, pulled Shane up to her feet. She tried to muffle the coughs in the crook of her elbow and Bernchal gently patted and massaged her back until they subsided. She hocked up a wad of phlegm and spit it out much to Julie's disgust.

"This was a set-up," she managed hoarsely. "They saw us approaching the fence."

Bernchal looked at her and then at Julie, his eyes small and concerned. "Our location's been compromised."

He pulled a walkie talkie out of his pocket and clicked it a few times, alerting the institution with their standard emergency protocol. When a series of beeps sounded in response, he clicked the mic and spoke low, his voice hurried and unusually tense.

"Toggle to beta. Alpha channel is not secure. I repeat- Alpha is an insecure channel."

A few seconds later, he turned the knob at the top of the walkie and waited until finally, confirmation came through that the channel for communication had shifted to their secondary line and the transmission had been received.

Motioning for Shane to help him with Ruderick, Bernchal coaxed him into standing position and with his large arms draped over he and Shane for support, hobbled along the fence in the opposite direction. Julie followed them, weapon drawn and watching their backs as they proceeded cautiously along, mindful of the ground beneath them for more traps.

Ruderick trodded along with them, trying his best to remain conscious and apply most of his weight on Bernchal. He shifted his balance, mistook his footing and went down when his knees gave out from under him, pulling Shane with him. They landed with a hard thud on the snow and suddenly, Julie put a hand out to silence them, her other arm outstretched before her. The darkness of her handgun stood out in contrast to the white blanket of snow surrounding them.

Bernchal dropped his hold on Ruderick and retrieved his weapon as well, staring at the large trunks of the trees unaffected by the first blast, looking for any type of movement.

A flash appeared from the far right, just a few yards from their original exit point. It crossed a few trees and disappeared again. Julie trained her eyes and waited and a second later, a figure emerged in the clearing of the trees that were blown away and started to run west. Julie whipped her gun in that direction and aimed, just as Bernchal whispered loudly, "We need him alive!" Adjusting her line of sight, she dropped her weapon a quarter of a centimeter and took the shot. The running man reacted at the same time the gunshot sounded throughout the wooded forest and he dropped to his stomach, arching his back and grabbing wildly at the wound in his calf.

They waited ten seconds before starting to move, just in case he wasn't alone. Before running towards the wounded militia soldier, Bernchal looked back to Shane and ordered her to stay with Ruderick. She complied and reluctantly admitted to herself that the fact that she'd barely heard what he'd said was enough to keep her away for the moment, so she jerked and pushed Ruderick into a sitting position, propping him up against the fence, and obediently, albeit begrudgingly, waited for them to return.

Julie hunched low to the ground and sprinted for the man with Bernchal close behind her. Weapons drawn, they closed the distance and reached him just as he realized they were near and flipped on to his back, attempting to retrieve his gun. Foiling his back-up plan, Julie stomped at his blood-soaked hand and kicked the gun away.

The man grunted in pain and began issuing a series of threats in his native tongue. Ignoring him, Bernchal flipped him back over onto his stomach and used flex cuffs he'd found in the old security booth of the school to isolate him. He started to pat him down and immediately pulled a hunting knife out of a holster around his ankle and unfastened a machine gun strapped to his back.

"Where are your buddies? Huh? You alone, asshole?"

The man spat at the ground and replied in Korean.

"You gonna stick with that?" he growled, grabbing the man's checks between his thumb and index finger and squeezing hard. "You here to blow up me and my friends?"

Undeterred, the man avoided Bernchal's eyes and snapped his mouth shut, grimacing when Bernchal let go and shoved his face into the snow beneath him.

"There're probably more on the way," he said to Julie, standing back up and peering around the woods. "We have to move."

Julie pointed to Ruderick with her chin. "He's not fit to walk, much less run. And we have to interrogate this one," she added, stabbing at the man with the toe of her boot. He tried to wiggle away from her and Bernchal nudged him back in place.

"I'll call for a ride. At the very least, we can get out of here and question him in a more secure location."

Agreeing, Julie kept her weapon drawn and gave Bernchal her back as she scanned their surroundings. He bent at the waist and forced the man to his feet, shoving him towards Shane and Ruderick at their place on the fence.

There, he threw the soldier against the chain-link fence and it rattled when he made contact. Slumping to his knees, he kept his eyes trained on Ruderick, who stared back unimpressed. Shane rose and took a step closer to Bernchal to speak without detection.

"What'd he say?" she asked abruptly. Bernchal could tell immediately her wheels were turning and she was envisioning rescuing her son with whatever information they could force out of this guy.

"Nothing. At least not in English. We gotta move out of here and question him with a translator."

"And where the fuck are you digging one up?" inquired Julie, her voice laced with sarcasm. "The U.N.?"

Ruderick kept his eyes on the man, but replied nonchalantly. "We got all sorts of surprises, sweetie pie. One of which is an honest-to-God Korean-American with a knack for his mother tongue."

Shane met Bernchal's eyes, hers wide in surprise. "Hiu?"

Bernchal nodded and quickly continued, hoping to get out of their precarious position before more of the man's friends showed up.

"We have to move now. Hiu'll bring the jeep and pick us up, take us somewhere safe for now. We can warn the institution to implement a lockdown and be on the lookout, just in case they make their way there."

She shook her head, unconvinced. "A car over here? They'll see it."

"Then we'll have to outrun any tails."

Julie piped in, her eyes still scanning the woods for intruders. She had her back to them and her gun still drawn and spoke to them over her shoulder.

"They've been stalking us for days and now they actually set up an attack on land that, as far as we know, has only been used by us for months. If we load up into a moving vehicle, they'll see it and follow us. Or worse. Who knows if they have any fucking rocket launchers laying around."

Bernchal pointed back towards the college and replied, his tone clipped and impatient. "At this point, we don't have much choice. We can't go back to the institution this way and we can't stay here. We'll be sitting ducks." He pulled a walkie talkie out of his pants pocket and lifted it to his mouth and with his finger hovering over the call button, eyed Shane and Julie for any objections.

Shane shook her head as if to indicate he had her approval so he flicked the button and called it in. Alerting Betzaida on the other end of what might be coming their way, he asked for Hiu and Muccio to pick them up across Gaelic Park immediately.

Helping Ruderick to his feet, they started towards the park running alongside the perimeter of the fence until they reached the far west side where it jutted out and turned back towards the institution. With Shane shoving the militia soldier along and Julie keeping an eye out behind them, they crossed into the open space of the park and moved quickly along the tall weeds encircling the track.

Seven minutes later they cautiously stepped out from the cover of the trees and plants into open space and ducked behind the garage of the dealership. Listening for an idling engine, they caught sight of Hiu and Muccio tucked inside the service entrance, the tail end of the jeep sticking out of the driveway. Pulling Ruderick, who was now more useful save for a slight limp that slowed him down, Bernchal made a beeline for the jeep with the women following closely behind.

Hiu immediately took Broadway north and kept to the side streets of Yonkers, turning right at Caryl Avenue and following it down and around the residential neighborhood towards McLean. Ruderick sat up front with him while Muccio and Julie babysat the perp in the middle row of the vehicle. Bernchal and Shane sat in far back seat and watched as Hiu guided them away from their usual stomping grounds and further into Westchester County.

When he sat back against his seat and rubbed some of the residue dirt and ash from his eyes, Shane reached over and jabbed at the open wound on Bernchal's shoulder with her fingertip. He groaned in pain and pulled away, but she grabbed his elbow and pulled him back towards her so she could examine the wound. Retrieving a small, square paper napkin from her back pocket, she dabbed at it, cleaning the blood around it.

"Why didn't you tell me you had a translator?" she asked quietly, eyes on the gash.

He grimaced as the napkin poked and prodded his sore shoulder and watched her work.

"I figured you knew that."

She didn't respond, only cleaned some more and satisfied that was the best medical treatment he would be receiving until they were back at the college, she rolled the napkin into a ball, released his arm and sat back against the seat. Bernchal ignored his wound and questioned, "If you had no one to speak the language, how the hell did you interrogate the others?"

She looked up at him with a dark smile and raised one eyebrow before replying.

"You'd be surprised how much English they can speak when they really have to."

He held her gaze for a moment longer, marveling at how someone with so much passion and fire for good could also harbor that much hatred for the enemy.

"Hiu said Torres and Huvane were locking down with Sharee when he left. They tripled the watch and have eyes on every post. The institution should be good."

She nodded and looked away, obviously worried for her friends, or more likely, her home.

Noticing that Hiu was passing the highways and coming up on Tibbetts Brook Park, Bernchal pulled himself forward and ignoring the shooting pain in his right shoulder, called out to the front row.

"Pull in here, Hiu. The park has a visitor station. We can patch up Wood's leg."

Wordlessly, Hiu complied and swung a quick left up the hill and headed towards the park. In the front seat, Ruderick grimaced when his weight shifted on the left-hand turn and his leg pounded in pain. Behind him, the prisoner swung to the right, leaning on Julie, who shoved him back to the left, disgusted.

Tibbetts Brook Park used to be a 161-acre woodland with a large swimming pool surrounded by a lake on the outskirts of the Cross County Parkway. Before Yenmor's presidency, the park closed for a few seasons and reopened with a state-of-the-art aquatic center and lazy river and new, revamped grounds. After Yenmor destroyed any chance of summer fun, it remained an abandoned area, inhabited mainly by random animals hiding out in the woods and a straggler or two using the property to hide from militia. Whether Yenmor's soldiers were scared of wild animals or rebels laying in wait didn't make much difference- they stayed out of the parks for the most part.

Hiu followed the driveway down the large hill, past the empty security booths, until the concrete that used to be a path for cars gradually dissolved into broken cement blocks and jagged edges overrun with ivy and moss. Weeds jutted out from beneath the snow and under the ground and manipulated the plates of asphalt until they were all scattered and lifted from the ground. Combined with the ice, it created an obstacle course for potential visitors.

He maneuvered the large vehicle over the open crevices like an expert, handling the road easily as the massive tires rolled over the floor like a tank. They followed the edge of the grass forward, past the open park where visitors used to barbecue and picnic, and settled about a quarter mile in. The visitor's station was just past the public restrooms, on the left of the driveway. A hundred small bushes, that had once been planted and maintained for aesthetics, were overgrown and completely covered the center and the small parking area behind it. Once parked, they were undetectable from the outside and behind them, the woods allowed no visibility in any direction.

After Muccio did a quick sweep inside, they climbed out, one after the other, and Bernchal helped Ruderick hobble out of the car and into the station. Inside, they gravitated towards the center of the small space, away from the windows, despite the darkness of the shaded forest around them.

"There a back room in here?" inquired Hiu as he looked around. "Something private?"

Shane pointed to the tiny hallway just past the water cooler and the map of Westchester County on the wall above it. "There's a room in the back. Not big, but walled off."

"How's the sound?" he asked, and she immediately knew what he meant.

"Quiet. The walls are reinforced and that room is centered between this and the back storage space. It's silent."

Nodding, Hiu motioned to Muccio and together they picked the militia soldier up by his underarms and dragged him to the back room. He struggled fruitlessly as his feet barely touched the ground and his hands remained tied behind his back. He called out to the rest of them desperately and they watched as he disappeared into the darkness.

Chapter XLI

Shane immediately began to search for a first aid kit as Bernchal helped Ruderick to a small love seat in the corner and sat him down. As the banging of drawers and cabinet doors reverberated throughout the small wooden station, the screams from the backroom began, slow at first and then increasing in intensity.

His wails became muffled by the fabric Hiu and Muccio shoved into his mouth and the dense woods around them. Of the six of them, Bernchal seemed to be the only one not at ease with their decision to torture the information out of him. He'd seen battles, fought bravely and had had to kill on more than one occasion before and after the shit-storm that had hit his homeland, but this was different, and he cringed with each agonizing screech. And though he was bothered, he decided not to let on considering his prior commanding officer, two women and two men below his rank all seemed fine with the torture of another man. Apparently, this was how how things were done now.

Shane slammed shut a cabinet door above the desk in the center of the office and turned around with a small white tin box in her hands. Without saying a word, she moved over to where Ruderick sat on the love seat, his injured leg outstretched before him, and she dropped to a squat and started nursing his wound. He watched her curiously, as she unwrapped bandages and removed disinfecting cream from the box to tend to him. Though every touch was excruciating, he never flinched and only eyed her as she worked. The screams behind them were overlapped by the incessant chatter between Bernchal and Julie just to fill up the sound.

When Shane was done and stood up to admire her work, Julie leaned in close and whispered something in her ear. Shane nodded and replied quietly, "Yeah, exactly," as Julie turned from her to walk away. As she passed the love seat, Ruderick reached a hand out and grazed her, asking, "Help me up, Blondie." She eyed him, irritated, and he reiterated his request.

"Help me up, *please.*"

Obliging, Julie reached her hand out and took his giant one, pulling him to standing position. He wavered a bit but put his injured foot on the floor and tested it. Satisfied it would hold his weight, he followed her outside, and called over his shoulder as he walked out of the front door.

"We'll stand watch outside."

Shane watched them retreat and close the door behind them. She turned to Bernchal and holding the tin box in her arms, walked to where he sat on a folding chair next to the desk and said "Okay, all I have left is what that one over there didn't hog up, so let's see what we can do."

She pushed a large outdated desk calendar out of the way and set on the edge of the desk, facing him, and put the tin box next to her, opening it. She retrieved some of the same disinfectant cream she'd used on Ruderick and a large packet of gauze. Without making eye contact, she ordered, "Take off your shirt."

Bernchal complied and started to shrug out of his parka and then his thermal shirt, jokingly replying, "If you wanted me undressed, Shane, all you had to do was say so."

She ignored him and kept her eyes on the tin box to her side until he was done. She would not glance at his broad shoulders, or the way his arms tightened and flexed as he eased out of his clothing. She would not peer at his strong back or at the muscles that ebbed and flowed as he moved in the chair. She would not look at his taut stomach, down by the waist of his pants, where his tan from outdoor summertime workouts was all but gone. And she certainly would not stare at the v-shaped arrow at the edge of his hips, below his abs, flashing like a neon sign in her face.

She would not look.

So she unwrapped a package of gauze and laid it on her thigh, and searched in the tin box for medicated wipes with which to clean his wound.

When he was done, he waited patiently, watching her, as he often did, as she concentrated on tending to him. He did not mind the reversal of fortune- the turn of events from a year ago when she'd sat on her bed with bruised ribs and he had been the one to nurse her back to health.

She started to pat the area around the gash lightly with a wipe, applying gentle strokes to clean the dried blood and prevent infection. Not wanting to hurt him further, Shane put her left hand on his chest to counter the pressure given by her right. She felt his muscles tighten and though flustered by the contact, she pressed on.

"How long have you known Julie?"

Shane blinked, surprised by the question. Usually Bernchal would throw a comment out, some sexual innuendo or sleazy remark to rattle her, but he normally saved their heart-to-hearts for their runs on the track. Shrugging it off, she continued to clean his cut, undaunted.

"I've known her since grammar school," she answered, her head down and close to his face as she worked. He could smell her shampoo again, a tropical scent mixed with the residue of the explosion.

"Really? That's why you guys are so tight?"

"Actually, we went to different high schools. Lost touch."

"I guess it's kind of hard to keep your social circle intact when the world's gone to shit," he joked.

She offered a crooked smile and continued. "So we went on with our lives, separately. She lived out in Queens, in Astoria. As you know, I was out here. Then, after everything happened and Silas was taken, I got moved a bit between one camp and the next. We found each other in the last one. She'd gotten there before I had, knew the ropes. I wasn't much for following commands at first."

"When have you ever been?" he interrupted.

She flashed him a quick smirk and continued applying the disinfectant cream to his wound. Her hands moved over him gently and though it burned like hell, he was grateful for the attention.

"Anyway," she continued, exaggeratedly. "She's the one that basically brought me back to life. Got the intel on the kids that were alive and helped me figure out a plan."

"So, Julie's the mastermind behind the great escape, huh? Wow. I knew she was crafty but I didn't know it was that serious."

"Oh yeah. Julie's damn near a genius." She met his eyes and hers lit up in recollection. Animatedly, she went on about her closest friend. "I didn't know a damn thing about strategy, warfare, reconnaissance. You know she used to be an actress?"

Bernchal eyed her, disbelievingly. She nodded and reached for the gauze and placed it on his gash carefully, patting it into place. Finally, she grabbed an ace bandage and unwrapped it, placing one side under his arm and holding it in place with her hand, began to wrap it around his bicep with the other.

"She was on her way up. Small parts in TV shows, she even had her own comedy troupe. She got cast for a blockbuster film but then... well, you know what happened."

"Seriously?"

"Yup. A very serious actress, too. Did all her research for roles, really knew her stuff. So when the time came, she was able to use that information to help us."

She tightened the bandage as it neared its end and rummaging through the tin box, pulled out two fasteners and placed them on one end, adjusting them to hold the gauze in place. Bernchal considered his next question carefully and knew the type of memories he was likely to drudge up, but Shane was being uncharacteristically forthcoming, so he decided to take advantage.

"She's never mentioned her kids... Are her kids alive?"

Shane met his eyes with a look of curiosity in hers. Softly, she replied.

"Julie doesn't have kids."

He looked at her confused and she offered a small smile. "I get why you would think she does, but she doesn't."

She sat back up on the desk and eyed her work.

"And just so you know, Commander, not every woman that fights with us has kids. Some of them fight because they get it."

He nodded and continued to watch her. If he made her uneasy, she no longer showed it.

"If Julie's the brains, then you're the brawn?"

She smiled to herself. "Some might say."

"Why isn't Julie in charge?"

"No one's in charge," she corrected him, softly.

"Shane," he replied, his tone direct. "It's me. Come on."

She flashed him a quick look and relented. "When we first ran, first escaped and we set out on our own, we made the decision to go at it together. All of us. To become a unit, and to find a place and make it a home, or as much of a home as it could be. We made that decision together and every decision since."

"But *you* have the final say."

She shrugged. "I guess I'm just bossier."

He chuckled and ignoring him, she continued as her hands worked against his bare skin.

"It's easier for me, anyway. Julie never wanted the responsibility. She's after justice; nothing more, nothing less. Everything else is just fluff to her. I guess at the end of the day, I like the organizing; the planning. It keeps my mind occupied so I don't feel sorry for myself. I'd have to say, that's probably what it comes down to."

"So basically, she doesn't have that killer instinct; that psycho, go-for-the-jugular-"

"Oh stop," she joked, the smile on her face spreading. "You're making me blush."

He smiled and watched her, not believing for one second that Shane led because she liked to plan. That was bullshit. He'd learned enough about her by now to know that Shane led because she was the best woman for the job. And maybe she was too polite to step on the toes of her closest friend and say it out loud, but he knew that there was no one else who could lead as mercilessly, ruthlessly and passionately as she could.

Examining his shoulder, she decided her wrapping job was not perfectly even and furrowing her eyebrows, she leaned in close to him again, one hand reaching under his bicep to readjust the bandage. Her ponytail fell over her shoulder and grazed his arm. Casually, he picked up the curls and swung them back over her shoulder.

Too many things between them were crossing back and forth over the ever-changing line of casualness lately.

"Do you ever cut your hair, Shane?"

She smiled and shook her head without meeting his eyes.

"My hairdresser's been busy lately."

She leaned in a little closer, examining her handy work. The wound was clean and covered. But she didn't want to pull away just yet and the thought alone was making her antsy. Combined with the terror that had almost crippled her when she thought Bernchal had been killed, and her instinctual reaction to wrap her arms around him when she discovered he hadn't, Shane was internally reeling with no foreseeable outlet. So she lingered over his shoulder for an unnecessary amount of time, dissecting the sudden rush of feelings she had, until now, managed to keep at bay for so long.

Bernchal considered her close proximity and took the opportunity to talk candidly.

"So touching is okay now?"

She swallowed but continued prodding at his wound. "Touching to mend wounds is always okay."

He watched her, amused.

"And ignoring the obvious? What's that then? Do you even want to talk about that back there?"

"What?" she asked, still enthralled by his shoulder. Her long fingers moved the bandage around, up and down by mere centimeters, giving the illusion of adjustment to mask her discomfort.

"That moment. That thing back there where you actually treated me like a human being."

A flash in her eyes gave away her true feelings about his line of questioning, but she continued indifferently. "As opposed to…?"

The screams coming from the back room had long since faded and were drowned out by their conversation. Shane eyed his shoulder, poking and over adjusting to keep herself occupied and he continued watching her, amused by her attempt at nonchalance.

"The shit you wipe off the bottom of your boots before coming back after a long, wet day of searching for supplies, Shane. The way you usually treat me."

Rolling her eyes, she shot back, "You're so exaggerated."

"I am not and you know it. Now, tell the truth- what was that?"

Under her breath, Shane replied, "If I would have known that a simple hug would turn this into an inquisition, I would have just waved."

He chuckled and stared at her, very aware of her obvious avoidance.

"You can joke all you want, my friend. But that was more than just a hug. You showed me your cards."

Finally looking up, she met his eyes and questioned, "What?"

"Your cards. You see, I've always suspected, but now I have *actual* confirmation."

Shane bit the inside of her cheek and hesitated, then taking the bait, finally asked, "Confirmation of what, you raving lunatic?"

"Of the fact that you love me. You always have."

She scoffed, blowing him off with the flick of her wrist.

"Okay, buddy."

His face remained close to hers and he lowered his voice enough so that it began to feel as though only the two of them were there.

"Laugh all you want. But I know you do. You couldn't bear the thought of life without me, could you? You were so overtaken with emotion, that you just had to touch me, didn't you?

She stared back at him with one raised eyebrow, seemingly unimpressed. Rolling her eyes again, she took a deep breath and smirked. He ignored her and continued, leaning closer to her as he spoke.

"It's alright. I know you're having a hard time reconciling those feelings there, champ. So I'll let you take your time. This is an apocalypse, after all. But it seems I have to fill you in on something…"

Her face was dirty, smudged from rolling around in the ash and snow after the explosions so he reached out with his thumb and gently wiped her cheek. His finger purposely grazed her lip as he stopped moving and made sure her eyes, which had absentmindedly traveled to his generous mouth and were watching, enthralled, as he spoke, made their way back up and met his before he whispered, "I'm not going anywhere."

The mood shifted and the light in his eyes changed, from a twinkle to a flame. Shane gulped, her body immediately tensing. Her hands, still wrapped around his strong bicep, were unconsciously frozen in place. He leaned in again and stopped centimeters from her, lowering his voice until she had to strain to hear his seductive growl.

"I'm right here."

Unable to speak, she watched him and waited. When her heart did beat again, it was irregular- stumbling and erratic punches against her chest wall that were clumsy and out of rhythm. He mercilessly let her sit there, speechless and dumbfounded, while he fanned the flames inside of her like an expert arsonist and after a moment, he smiled and started to back up.

"I'm gonna look for something to eat. You know I get ornery when I'm not fed."

Shane peeled her hands off of his arm and did her best to brush him off. Wordlessly, she leaned all the way back on the desk, rising and giving him her back as she moved the items inside the tin box around to appear preoccupied. That fascinating tin box that right now was the only thing keeping her from releasing the breath she'd been holding since, it seemed, she'd touched him.

Bernchal got up and made his way to the same cabinets she had foraged only minutes beforehand. With his one good arm, he started banging doors and searching for canned foods. The room suddenly exploded in sound and a gunshot coming from the back room startled them.

The front door flew open and Julie ran in followed by Ruderick, both of them with their guns drawn. Bernchal immediately took a few steps to his left and somehow managed to put himself between Shane and hallway leading to the back room as he fumbled for his weapon with his left hand.

Their eyes on the darkened corridor, Muccio emerged, wiping his hands with what looked like a blood-soaked t-shirt. Hiu followed and looked surprised when he glanced up to find the four of them staring, waiting for answers.

"What the fuck was that?"

Muccio offered a scowl in Julie's direction and pushed against a small door to his left, peering inside the bathroom when it opened. Reaching in the tiny space, tiny enough that he could touch the sink and still keep both feet outside the door, he turned the faucet and the sound of struggling pipes flooded the station.

"He is no longer useful."

A few drops fell out of the faucet and Muccio cursed under his breath, taking what he could and trying to clean the blood off of his hands.

Shane tried to peek around Bernchal, but he nudged her back behind him and stepped closer to Hiu, questioningly.

"What'd you get?"

Hiu looked up at him and smiled.

"An address."

Chapter XLII

Bernchal felt Shane tense up behind him, her entire body becoming rigid, like an electrical wire giving off an explosive amount of energy. He felt her breath against his bare back, noticing the quickness of it. As though the sound in the room had been muted, he could almost hear her heartbeat behind him and he knew Hiu's words were exactly what she'd been waiting all this time to hear.

Trying not to overstep his boundaries, he tentatively reached out a hand behind him to keep her back and addressed Hiu directly. The longer he could keep the situation contained, the better.

"What address?"

"A safehouse. In Philly."

"Philly?" Ruderick asked, surprised. Hiu and Muccio nodded their heads and pushed past the rest of them to peer out of the dirt-covered window.

"He held out a lot longer than I expected."

Ruderick agreed with Muccio and pointed out, "Those slant-eyed fuckers can be pretty tough."

Without looking back at Ruderick, Hiu tersely called over his shoulder, "Watch your mouth."

"What safe house?" pushed Julie. She glanced back at Shane who stood behind Bernchal, body tight and eyes sharp, watching the exchange. "What exactly did he say?"

Hiu looked back at Julie and replied, impatiently. "Well, we didn't exactly get a fucking novel out of it. The guy did resist some."

"But what did he say? What kind of safe house is it? Who's there?"

Muccio, the least understanding of the two, shoved Hiu out of the way and took a step towards Julie, temper flaring.

"Look, we don't know where your fucking kids are. Okay, lady? This is what we got and if you think you can do a better job, you should have been in that room doing what we did instead of out here with your thumb up your ass while we did all the dirty work."

"Okay, okay. Take a fucking break," Ruderick intervened. With one large bear hand on Muccio's chest, and the other hovering in front of Julie, he put himself in the middle and ordered a truce.

"We got intel. That's good. No need to spoil the mood. You two," he continued, pointing to Muccio and Hiu. "Why don't you take a walk? Go secure the perimeter so we can get the fuck out of here."

With a final hostile glare at Julie, Muccio turned and followed Hiu out of the front door, both drawing their guns before letting the light wooden door shut behind them. Inside, Ruderick turned to Julie and asked her for some tolerance.

"Just give them a minute to come down. It's not easy to do what they just did and shut it right off. It takes some time."

Julie eyed Ruderick but eventually relented and turned abruptly towards the bathroom. She shut the door behind her and sat on the toilet lid, head between her knees, and let her wheels turn in private.

Ruderick looked at Bernchal and with the slightest humor detectable in his gruff voice, said "Put your shirt back on, Don Juan." Without a smile, he left him to do just that and followed Muccio and Hiu outside, hobbling out the door.

Bernchal released his breath and turned to look at Shane, who was still frozen behind him. She met his eyes and he could see the dormant volcano come roaring back to life.

"What's in Philly?" she asked him, jaw clenching.

"Hell if I know. We need more information."

"We have an address."

He retrieved his thermal shirt and eased into it, the wound on his right shoulder burning as he moved.

"An address to what? How the fuck do we know what's there? How do we know it's not a trap? Like I said, chief, we need more information."

She opened her mouth to say something else but shut it tight when the front door opened and Hiu stuck his head in, calling them.

"All clear. Let's head back."

Bernchal palmed his parka and looked at Shane again, the tightness of his mouth indicating he was done discussing the subject for the time being.

"We'll figure this out at the school. Get Julie and let's go."

She wanted to remind him that he was neither her father nor her commanding officer and would not be ordering her around ever again, but decided against it. *Silence is golden*, she reminded herself, and she moved to the bathroom, tapping on the door for Julie to open.

Outside, Muccio stood watch over them as they piled into the jeep to make their way back to the Bronx.

Upon their arrival at the institution, the wrought iron gates opened for them and Betzaida was waiting on the other side, eager to speak to Shane. She climbed out of the jeep leaving the men behind, she and Julie immediately joined Betzaida in a quick run-down over the day's events. Sharee was waiting for them in the main lobby and together they headed towards the cafeteria for a powwow.

Bernchal jumped out of the jeep and helped Ruderick out and into the school property. Jackson was waiting for Hiu when they arrived in the lobby and ran to him as soon as the doors closed behind them. Hiu picked him up in a bear hug and walked with him towards the dormitories. Muccio grunted his goodbyes and followed, likely on his way to deliver the news of Derrecks' death to the others.

Before they separated in the lobby to go clean off the day's muck and mess, Ruderick whistled to Bernchal, who turned and met his eyes. Pointing with his chin, he led him to the dean's office for a quick meeting.

"We have to decide what to do about that safe house," he began as soon as the door shut behind Bernchal. His steel-blue eyes sharp and bright in the sunlight pouring in through the large windows, he lifted a meaty hand and pointed a finger back towards the door. "There's no way these crazy bitches can head out there without some inspection first."

Bernchal shrugged noncommittally.

"I agree. But you try telling them that."

"The mean one listens to you. Just tell her to hold off."

Bernchal scoffed and shook his head, rubbing his chin absentmindedly.

"I see you have yet to learn how things work around here, Wood. She does not listen to me. None of them do. She may consider my advice- my professional, expert advice- *sometimes*. But she does not listen to anyone. If she wants to go to Philly, she'll go to Philly. And there's not a damn thing any of us can do about it."

Ruderick raised an eyebrow and responded frankly. "Then she'll get herself killed."

Bernchal only stared back, unable to reply. Ruderick took a deep breath and advised Bernchal to talk some sense into Shane while he got more information on the safe house and they agreed to reconvene later that evening.

Bernchal made his way through the tunnels and towards his dormitory to shower. Under the water, which was just south of lukewarm because there was no water heater to normalize temperature and instead they relied on a water system improvised by college kids, he analyzed the situation.

He had no concrete information to dissuade Shane from traveling to Philadelphia in search of her son. *Yet.* He had no intel on what waited on that end or whether or not it was a set-up orchestrated by the militia, who incidentally had been a little too close for comfort lately. He had no way of knowing if the information that soldier had given to Hiu and Muccio under duress was accurate or nonsense spouted during torture.

Basically, he knew nothing.

He let the water, with surprisingly strong pressure, slam against his shoulder and though painful, it began to feel better. It wasn't warm enough to generate any steam, and he felt the chill from the draft under the bathroom door, but he could not complain. It was a far cry from a hot shower but in this day and age, one could not afford to be picky.

With no clear cut plan to proceed, Bernchal finished his shower and dressed, ultimately deciding to just wing it. He would speak to Shane, lay out the consequences of crazy missions without proper information, and hope for the best.

Fifteen minutes later, he went in search of her. Inquiries to Sharee and Julie, who was still filthy from her roll in the snow earlier that morning, indicated Shane had gone off to shower. Bernchal went in pursuit of her, fully admitting to himself that he hoped to catch her before she was done.

No such luck. Shane was in her room, back to the door and long, brown curls soaked wet and cascading down her back. Tiny droplet of water fell on the bed where she sat, concentrated on investigating something on her arm.

He cleared his throat in her doorway and she looked up, surprise on her face. He'd noticed, despite her many attempts to disguise it, that lately she had exhibited significantly less hostility towards him. It only took two years but he was beginning to feel as though he was getting somewhere.

"Talks. You busy?" he asked as he walked into her room without invitation, as he often did, and made his way to her.

She looked down again, fiddling with her elbow and as he neared, he noticed she was eyeing a large, deep scratch across her left elbow.

"What the hell is that?" he asked, surprised. He had not noticed blood or any indicating injuries on her after the blast.

"A scratch. I think it happened with the first explosion," she replied quietly as she stretched her arm in front of her and attempted to turn it to get a better view.

He reached for her to investigate. "Let me see."

"I got it…" she mumbled as she strained to turn her shoulder and see the wound.

"Its physically impossible for you to turn that way, Shane. Let me see."

With a dramatic sigh, she relented and lifted her head back up, avoiding eye contact.

"Fine."

He reached for her arm and simultaneously, sat on the edge of her bed next to her. The springs of the mattress creaked under his weight and though she tried to hide it, he could tell she was a little nervous to have him in that position.

Holding her left arm, he turned her elbow over slightly and looked at the gash. It was long and rather ugly, reaching from the middle of her tricep, over the curve of her elbow and down to her forearm, just above of wrist. She'd cleaned it well in the shower, but it shone, wet with tiny drops of blood appearing inside the open wound.

If it hurt, she didn't let on.

"When did you notice this?" he asked, reaching for the disinfectant cream on her bed that she'd used on his earlier.

She braced herself for the sting coming and closed her eyes tightly.

"In the shower. It didn't hurt before."

"It was probably the adrenaline. Julie told me you were thrown pretty far back. It had to have been a broken branch or something."

She nodded and pried open one eye, watching him work. He'd applied the cream as he spoke and she hardly noticed. He cut open a piece of gauze with his teeth and ripping it in half, laid each piece over the gash. Finally, following the same pattern she'd used only a few hours beforehand, he used an ace bandage to hold the gauze in place and secured it with a few fasteners up and down her arm.

When he was done, she tried to bend her elbow and grimaced at the stinging pain.

"Don't bend it. Not yet. At least sleep with it straight, let the wound start healing and closing. It's gonna burn when you finally bend it but you don't want to make it bleed again by doing it too soon. It's gonna leave one hell of a scar but there's nothing we can do about that."

She tightened her lips and continued fussing with her arm.

"How's your shoulder?"

He brushed off the question, shrugging casually.

"I'll live."

She finally looked up at him and eyeing him for a moment, hesitated. Pursing her lips, she considered her next words and finally turned her eyes to the other end of her room, towards the door, and addressed him.

"I know why you're here. To convince us not to go to Philly."

He continued watching her and nodded.

"Yeah. But I'll use any excuse to come up to your room. You know that."

Her cheeks reddened and he smiled at her discomfort.

In the beginning, her inability to joke around with him, the way she would tense whenever he came near or the way she would flinch or rear back when he tried to touch her, whether innocently or not- it was disheartening. Bernchal often felt less like a guest and more like an intruder in her life and the lives of the women in the institution. The repulsion or all around hostility he received from everyone around him was a lot to take at times and were in not for the fact that he neither knew what they had been through nor had any other place to go, he would have fled long ago. But if he were honest with himself, he would have to admit that from day one, he had wanted to stay, and he had stayed not only because he had nowhere to go, but also because he had come to care for everyone, particularly Shane. Otherwise, he reminded himself, why else would he have gone to such lengths to make her comfortable with him? And as he watched her disguise the red rising to her cheeks, he took great joy in making her uncomfortable for different reasons.

She blew off his comment and turned to look at him, that same boiling cauldron of passion dancing in her eyes.

"We *have* to go."

Bernchal licked his lips and replied softly, careful to not drive her over the edge.

"We don't have anything yet. Let us at least get some more information."

"There's no time," she replied, desperately.

"How do you even know anything he said is legitimate?"

"How do I know its not?" she replied, a hopeful smile on her face. "This, *this* is the first lead, the first real lead we've had in forever. How can I ignore it?" she asked, the frenzied pleading in her voice pulling him over the fence towards her line of thinking.

"What if it's a trap?" he asked, his own voice now obscured with the same desperation but for an entirely different reason.

"Then it's a trap," she offered, low and quiet. They were alone in the room with the door wide open and though there was no sound coming from the hallway, they whispered as though discovery was just around the corner.

"I don't know what to tell you. We know what we're getting into. We knew it long before you came around."

Exasperatedly, he wiped his mouth and shook his head. "Jesus Christ, this is insane. Let us investigate, please. Let's wait until-"

"I can't," she interjected. Shaking her own head, she pleaded with her eyes. "I have to do this. I have to."

He got up abruptly, the mattress groaning in protest. Pacing the small room, he walked hard from one end of her bed to the other, head down and lost in thought. She stayed seated on the edge, watching him, feeling like she owed him an explanation to a question she did not understand.

"This is suicide! You know that, right?" he asked her suddenly. Without waiting for a response, he continued. "You should be terrified."

She cocked her head to the side and eyed him, questioningly. "And you think I'm not? You think I envision some walk in the park? I know what's waiting out there. You may think you do, but trust me, *I* know what's out there. I've been part of what's out there for years, Commander. I know what to fear."

"Then why don't you?" he pleaded, dropping to a squat in front of her. Without thinking, he placed both hands on her knees and searched her eyes from some rationality, the act devoid of promiscuity and sensuality. Casting aside his pride, he begged her to listen to reason.

"Why aren't you scared enough to not do this?"

Shane staved off the tidal wave of feelings that hit her in the chest and blinked several times. Her eyes locked on his and she replied rigidly, determination lifting her voice from the timidity of earlier.

"Because I don't have time for it. Fear is nothing but your brain inventing an outcome that hasn't happened yet. I don't have the luxury of feeling fear! I have a job to do. And that's the only thing that matters right now. So I have a choice- I either let this happen to me because I'm too scared to react, or I get the job done. That's it."

He shot to his feet, surprising her, and pointed to his chest.

"Fine then. *I'm* scared for you. You happy?" he asked rhetorically, the anger in his voice barely masking the fear enveloping him. "I'm fucking terrified that you'll go out there and instead of finding your kids, it'll be a set-up. And you'll get killed… Or worse."

She offered him a sad smile and timidly asked, "Commander, where's that famous ego of yours?"

He scoffed and turning from her, replied. "My ego went out the door when I knelt in front of a group of women and begged to not be killed. My ego, Shane, became a thing of the past the day I met you."

She licked her lips and replied, "You know, you *know*, that I can't not do this."

Incensed all over again, he swerved back towards her and fired back.

"Yes, you can. You can do the smart thing and let my guys go in there *first*."

She started to shake her head in protest and he asked, "And what would your husband think about this suicide mission?"

When the words were out, he instantly regretted them. But she did not react as he had expected. Instead of recoiling, she smiled sweetly and nodded, as though she understood why he'd asked that question.

"I'm sorry. That was-"

He stopped when her hand reached for his. Their fingers touched and he squatted in front of her again, this time listening to her reasoning instead of begging her to agree with his.

"It's fine," she whispered. She held his hand and locked eyes with him, once and for all confirming his fear that there was no talking her out of going.

"He would be doing the same thing, Steve. Maybe not in the same manner that I've done them, but he would go to Philly, too. He would do whatever it took to find his son."

Bernchal turned away from her and tried to disguise the look on his face. Mixed with the doubt and anger about her marching headfirst into God knew what, he felt a twinge of jealousy. He tried to shake it off but after a second, he accepted it. Why wouldn't he be jealous of this faceless man? The man that had been lucky enough to meet her when the world had still been whole; had dated her, courted her? The man that had made love to her, proposed to her and promised her the world? The man that had built a home with her and had given her a son? This faceless man had done what he wanted nothing more than to do- he had loved this force of nature; had loved this tumultuous and terrifying force that had him turned inside out.

Damn right he was jealous of him, corpse or not.

He looked back at her and tried one last time to appeal to her heart.

"Please, Shane."

She took a deep breath and managed, barely, to conjure the same words again.

"I have to go."

With nothing left to say, Bernchal rose and nodded, defeated, and walked away from her.

He knew if he stayed near her for another second, he'd do something reckless.

In the hallways of her dorm, he picked up his pace and made his way back into the tunnels towards his own dormitory in search of Ruderick.

Tearing open Ruderick's door, he barged in and barked commands.

"They're going, so we need as much information as possible. *Now!*"

Ruderick, who was laying on his bed with his injured leg propped up on a pillow, glanced up at the intrusion ever so nonchalantly and replied, dryly.

"Couldn't get her to do what you wanted, could you?"

"Fucking stubborn ass psychopath…" Bernchal muttered under his breath as he made his way further into Ruderick's room, slamming the door shut behind him. He paced there as well, stomping on the hardwood floor and grinding his teeth as he made his way from one end of the small room to the other.

Ruderick held back a laugh and though he was enjoying the moment, came clean.

"I talked with Hiu. The info's legit."

Bernchal froze in place and demanded, "How do you know?"

"Connects from the outside. Martinez is in D.C. closing in on the program leaders. There's no indication that those kids she's looking for are in Philly, but there's definitely something at that safe house. It's guarded, but lightly. Couple of commandos. It's not impossible."

He released the breath he'd been holding and immediately began to plan.

"What else? Guards? Artillery? Scouts? And what about dude from this morning- could he be an indicator of further activity in this area? What if they're giving us this information to draw us out and then-"

"Steve!" Ruderick yelled to stop the one-sided inquisition. "Jesus H. Christ, son. Slow the fuck down."

He took a breath and attempted a different approach.

"I need to know everything you know."

Ruderick scratched his temple and watched Bernchal, all love-sick and turned inside out.

"I just sent Hiu over to her with the address and details. I don't know why you're getting yourself all bent out of shape- you know you're going with her."

Bernchal bit his tongue and exhaled sharply, turning again to pace the room once more.

"She drives me crazy."

"Obviously."

He glanced back at him and added, "Like clinically insane, rifle on a bell tower *fucking* crazy."

Ruderick smirked knowingly and responded. "I'm sure your loins are going wild."

"My loins?" he asked, incensed. Holding his hands out in front of him, he added, "It's my hands that wanna choke the shit out of her."

With a sly smile Ruderick pushed further. "You want to fuck her, too. Admit it."

"Wood-"

"My man," he interrupted, his voice taking on that grating, patronizing know-it-all tone. "She aggravates you because you want her."

He scoffed but answered honestly. "Wanting her doesn't change how fucking frustrating she is."

"Ah! But you *do* want to fuck her? You finally admit it?"

Bernchal threw his hands up in the air, maddened with frustration.

"Of course I do! And I hate her at the same goddamn time."

Ruderick leaned back against the wall behind his bed and crossed his arms over his burly chest, closing his eyes and wittingly nodded.

"That's love."

Chapter XLIII

Despite the hatred the women in the institution seemed to have for Ruderick and his men, things came together surprisingly smoothly after Hiu gave Shane the information on the safe house. Within minutes, a meeting for every able body had been called and organized and they all piled into the cafeteria, waiting for instructions.

Shane, Bernchal, Ruderick and Julie sat on tables in front of the cook room while everyone else sat in available chairs or stood, waiting. They chatted restlessly, the women occupying most of the large space while Muccio, Hiu, Huvane and Torres lingered to the left of the cook room.

The air was charged; the tension in the room palpable. The men were eager to be off and part of a mission for the first time in months. The women on the other hand, were waiting for information, resting on the slightest twinge of hope that their struggle was nearing an end and they would soon be reunited with their kidnapped children.

Julie slapped the table on which she sat a few times, calling everyone's attention. Next to her, Shane raised a hand and the women in the cafeteria suddenly quieted. Bernchal, propped up against the table where Ruderick sat behind him watched, impressed that one person could command that much loyalty.

"Okay, so here's what we got," she began, voice loud and assertive. "As most of you know, a couple of mines and IED's were set off this morning. One of the men, Derrecks, unfortunately didn't make it back."

She paused for dramatic effect, letting the death of one of the men sink in.

"We also were able to catch one of the militia soldiers staking us out. We took him with us to interrogate him further. What these guys got," she concluded, pointing to Hiu and Muccio, "was information on a safe house."

The room erupted in questions. Women shot up from their folding chairs and demanded answers, some of them edging dangerously close to Shane's table. Bernchal rose from his position and did his best to calm everyone down while Shane climbed the table and stood on it, and putting both hands up in the air, addressed them.

"Wait! Wait. Listen to me. I know you have questions; so do we. Let us give you everything we know first before you start asking anything."

The women calmed, some taking their seats again, others wiping their noses and sniffling away the tears that had already begun.

More gently, Shane spoke to them again. "We do not know if the kids are there. We do not know if the kids are even okay. We only have a location of a safe house and we plan on going there, tonight, and investigating further. Obviously, it goes without saying," she added, eyeing Milagros, who had her mouth open to speak and shut it quickly, "that our number one goal is our kids. We will turn every stone to find them; this is just one of those stones."

She glanced back at the men, indicating that they now had the floor. Ruderick cleared his throat and began, his voice devoid of the condescending tone he usually used to address the women and replaced with the military timbre of a seasoned soldier addressing his troops.

"The safe house is in a row of abandoned townhouses in downtown Philly. We got it down to the block, but have to search for the exact spot."

A voice called out from the women hanging on every word. "What's in this safe house?"

"Like Ms. Milian said, that we don't know. But here's what we do know: it's largely deserted. Militia is scattered around Pennsylvania but for the most part, out of the immediate area. Intel puts it in a two story and the room we're looking for is underneath, in a storm bunker of sorts. That's all we got."

"Who's going?"

Bernchal chimed in, not caring in the least if he was stepping on Shane's toes. She may be going against his wishes and heading to Philly to investigate, but he damn sure was going with her.

"A team of twenty. Six men, fourteen women. Four vehicles. Whatever we find, we will reconvene here to map out the next steps."

Betzaida stood up from her seat and stepped over to Shane's table. "I want to go."

Taking cue, one by one, women jumped up and volunteered for the mission. Shane and Julie exchanged looks and counted out the best women for the job and silenced everyone else with their hands. Some of them clamored over the others, eager to offer themselves up for the good of their kids. Authoritatively, Shane turned them away and when she had her twelve, nodded to Ruderick for him to wrap things up.

"In addition to your fourteen," he continued, "we need another four in a vehicle posted at the city limits. Whoever's pulling that duty, come talk to me."

With a curt nod in his audience's direction, the meeting ended. Ruderick climbed down from his table and limped over to Shane and Julie.

"You and whoever you picked be ready to go at 0400 hours."

She nodded. "Got it."

With a final look back at Bernchal, he hobbled off to join the rest of the men to the side of the cook room.

Bernchal eased closer to Shane and Julie and motioned over to the men with his chin.

"They're antsy."

Julie raised an eyebrow and glanced back at them gathered around Ruderick, listening intently at whatever orders he barked. Like obedient soldiers, they complied with his demands and split up, each going their own way to follow through with their boss's directions.

"Anxious to kill some bad guys?"

"Anxious to feel useful," he corrected her. Solemnly, he continued. "They may come off as brain-dead meatheads, but they only want to serve. First their country, and now whatever's left of it. They just want to get out there and help you guys."

Julie dropped her eyes, slightly embarrassed to receive a lecture. Shane however, was unmoved and as Ruderick limped closer to them after directing his men to their jobs, she addressed Bernchal tightly.

"The best way for them to help us is to do what they're told."

Behind Bernchal, Ruderick chimed in, his tone dismissive.

"So my men are just supposed to do what they're told, huh? Like a couple of faithful dogs? Why don't you quit *playing* soldiers and let the real ones handle this?"

Shane's face spread into a wry smile, but her eyes remained cold and dark and she glared at Ruderick for a second too long before replying.

"We tried that already. It was called America. Hundreds of years of old white men ruling this country and look at where it's gotten us. So this time, why don't you just step aside and let women do what should have been done in the first place? Maybe this way we'll all come home alive."

She held the stare a moment longer and satisfied she'd had the last word, pushed past him and Bernchal and made for the exit of the cafeteria with Julie close behind.

He took a step forward behind her as though he were making a move to reach for her, but Bernchal held him back with one arm on his burly chest. Still fired up, his fists opening and closing in anger, he yelled at her.

"Hey!" he called out, his tone tight and measured, giving every indication that he was advising her to tread lightly. "I lost a man out there today."

She turned back to face him and gave him a surprisingly understanding smile.

"I'm sorry for your friend. Really, I am. He seemed like a very good person. But we've lost forty-two women since we've been here," she responded stoically. "Maybe now you understand what *we've* been going through."

Bernchal's hand on Ruderick's chest rose and fell with each breath while he watched her, frozen to the ground. As she turned around to walk away once more, he realized he was still being held back and he shoved Bermchal's hand away, angry. Not easily offended, Bernchal just tossed him a knowing look and stood his ground, making sure no chairs would be thrown. After a few seconds of stewing in his own rage, Ruderick simmered down and retreated, mumbling under his breath as he lumbered away.

Behind him, Bernchal shook his head impatiently and went off in the opposite direction in search of Shane.

He caught up to her in the main lobby about to enter the dean's office and head through the tunnels to the dormitories. He didn't have to address her; she instinctively knew he was behind her and simply held the door open for him to follow her through it.

In the tunnel, she moved quietly along with no light. He followed her, stepping gingerly to avoid tripping on the uneven dirt floor beneath them. A small sliver of light from the door to the office that had closed behind them lent the only visibility for a few feet and then once past it, it was gone and they continued forward in the dark.

"Why do you have to antagonize him; antagonize everybody? You riled him up for no reason," he said to her, his voice strangely loud and deep in the dark path.

Only a couple of feet from him, she replied, her own voice light and relaxed.

"Not *no* reason, Commander. I may be a hothead, but nothing I do comes without a purpose."

"And what's your purpose for pissing him off and making him hate every woman here?"

"What's the last thing a pissed off sexist wants to do?" she asked rhetorically and without waiting for his reply, he heard her answer her own question.

"To lose to a woman. He hates me, so now he wants to beat me."

Considering her statement, Bernchal prodded along behind her and finished the thought.

"And now you lit a fire under his ass."

Even in the dark, he could tell she was quite proud of herself. Having long since vowed to keep her ego in check, Bernchal called out to her.

"You are astonishingly evil."

She did not reply, but he knew she was smiling, so he commented, "That was not a compliment."

"Well, I'm taking it as one," she muttered as they neared the other end of the tunnel.

The streams of daylight coming through the large bay windows in the main entrance of the dormitory traveled under the large wooden door to the tunnel and as they got closer, he was finally able to see Shane's silhouette walking through the dark. Her curly brown hair appeared in the shadowy light and he saw her, head turned and neck craned in his direction. He saw her looking back as if to make sure he was still behind her before she reached the door; making sure he was still with her.

That infuriating game of Frogger they remained playing, that back and forth- there it was again. A push/pull between them that had him feeling, in the back of his mind, like he constantly took ten steps forward and a frustrating nine and a half steps back.

And right now in the man-made tunnel beneath the hallways of the university above them, in the musty darkness surrounding them, he almost asked himself why he kept pushing forward if she was always pulling back.

But the second he saw her silhouette, turned back behind her like a mama bear glancing casually over her shoulder to ensure her cub babies were following in her footsteps, the simple act confirming what he already knew deep inside, he felt that final push that propelled him over the nine and a half step finish line towards salvation.

So as she walked up the makeshift steps to open the door, he came up close behind her, reaching out to put his hand on the doorknob as well. Her hand was already there and his landed on hers and he waited, watching her.

She'd been looking back into the darkness so her eyes were still adjusted to the blackness of the tunnel. She could make out his outline, standing close enough to touch her on the top step; a top step which was barely big enough for one person and now held them both.

His jaw clenched; she could see the muscle moving. She could feel his closeness but could not make out the details of his eyes and whether or not he was looking at her. She did not know if he waited to be sure they were alone, or to make sure there was nothing happening on the other side of the door. Or for something else.

Shane watched him in silence, waiting until her eyes could properly adjust to the small sliver of light available under the door behind them so she could see his face. And like an optical illusion, they did adjust and his face began to appear in the darkness: the generous mouth and lips, unsmiling and serious; his chiseled jawline and strong cheekbones; and finally his hazel eyes, trained on her and also waiting.

So close she could feel his breath on her face, he whispered, "You waited for me."

She didn't know to what he referred so she remained silent.

"Why are you waiting for me, Shane?"

She sighed, a faint sound from deep within released in it and filling the empty tunnel. She knew a part of him was taunting her, daring her to make a move since he had long ago made his feelings very clear. But it was the other part of him, the darker less transparent part that gave her pause; and every time she came close to just reaching out and touching him, landing her hands on his skin in one selfish moment, she would catch a glimpse of that part of him and wonder why exactly she should forgo all of her plans to just give into him.

"Steve…" she started, her tone torn and slightly tortured. After a moment's hesitation, she finally asked, "What do you want?"

"Isn't it obvious?" he replied, quietly.

Her face contorted into one of pure sadness. She looked as though she didn't just misunderstand his feelings, she could not comprehend why he felt them in the first place.

"Why?"

He offered a quick shake of his head and eyed her in the darkness, the expression on his handsome face a mixture of anger and impatience.

"I don't know why! For fuck's sake, Shane- you really think I know that?" he asked sarcastically. Holding back a derisive laugh, he inched closer to her and continued. "You drive me crazy, woman! You're rude, you're snarky. You make me feel like a burden half the time and like an idiot the other half. But I'm in," he continued, softer this time, his features serious again.

"I live and breath for this place now. For you. I'm in…"

She froze.

Shane had thought of nothing, *nothing* else but her son for the past four years. Nothing but the idea, the hope of holding him again. Nothing but finding him okay despite the very real possibility that he was not. Nothing but the thought of being reunited with the son that had been taken from her. And intermittently she would envision the death and destruction she would deliver upon those who took her son, but mainly she only thought of her son and getting him back.

And now Bernchal… with his hazel eyes and languid walk; with his wry humor and ability to see through her down to the very core of who she was; with his incessant need to tag along and just be there, all the time; with the way he made her feel, for the first time in in an excruciatingly long time, safe and protected and sane… Bernchal with his hands firmly gripped around her heart and intent on squeezing her life's marrow out until there was nothing left…

Unable to accurately explain in words why exactly she would not, could not treat him as though this were another time and life were normal and she were just another woman and he were just another man, Shane did the only thing she could bring herself to do.

She pulled out the hand that was still gripping the doorknob and along with the other cupped his face and standing on her tip-toes, kissed him.

Her lips landed on his and she sighed. Despite the protest coming from her brain, reminding her that her priority was her son, not this man, everything inside of her body and heart screamed for contact, begged and pleaded for some normalcy, and Shane allowed herself that one tiny, miniscule moment of self-gratification before walking out into the unknown. And though it was electric and breathtaking and amazing all at the same time, it was also sad. Soft and incredibly sad instead of the sultry and passionate exchange that either had so often imagined; him vividly, her secretly.

He reached for her, pulling her closer to him, and tightened his arms around her waist. He started falling, immediately, into the embrace but she pulled away suddenly. When she released him and stood back, opening her eyes and with the increasing light meeting his, the agonizing look in hers said everything that she could not. A tempestuous storm raged behind them and further solidified Bernchal's belief that she was even more conflicted than she let on.

He was taken aback by the intensity of that kiss and her abrupt ending of it, and when she turned from him to open the tunnel door and walk through it, Shane left him behind in the darkness, breathless.

Chapter XLIV

They piled into four cars to make the trip, the fifth car with the women manning the city limits already ahead and scanning the nearby area for residue militia. Shane interrupted the usual flow of their procedures and opted to ride with Ruderick and Julie instead of Bernchal. She did so childishly, without explanation, and only hopped into the other vehicle at the last minute to avoid his eyes or anyone's questions.

If Ruderick had a snide remark or smart-ass thing to say, he mercifully kept it to himself during the ride.

She felt like a ridiculous teenager, but she could not help it. There were a plethora of feelings and emotionally-charged thoughts running through her head and she could not bring herself to ride for two hours in a vehicle with a man who would either question her about them or entice her into conversation or more.

Shane could not allow herself to be dragged into an unfocused situation. She had to concentrate on the plan at hand- keep her eyes on the prize. With Bernchal around, now so *available*, she would be worried about him, concerned about his safety, concerned about his nearness to her. He had always been able to unnerve her these past two years with his hazel eyes and overwhelming presence; but now it was different.

They had embraced; touched.

They had kissed.

How could she do what she had to do it there were another person on her mind besides her son? How could she get the job done if she were not 100% focused on finding her son?

Bernchal, with his lovely eyes and disarming manner, was becoming a distraction; one which she could not afford.

So she risked alienating herself if it meant she could remain completely focused on the task in front of her.

They rode in silence the whole way, Julie up front with Ruderick assisting in navigation, keeping an eye out for the three others cars following them; and Shane in the backseat, pensive. She utilized the quiet time to sort out her emotions, something she detested but found absolutely necessary given the current situation, and when they finally arrived, she was convinced that she was right- too much was at stake to be acting like a lovesick teenage girl.

They piled out of the cars in separate corners covering a two block radius; their jeep on the northeast corner and the others posted on each side. Following the same plan implemented so long ago when Bernchal had first arrived, they each shut off the ignition and rolled into the boulevard silently, each vehicle to its predetermined destination.

The night was overcast and crowded, with so many clouds in the sky that not a single star was visible. The moon hid behind the clutter and peeked out every so often, lending the broken asphalt beneath them an ethereal quality.

The townhouse was situated on Race Street, just west of the Liberty Bell in downtown Philadelphia. Immediately perpendicular to their point of meeting was N. Marvine Street, where Bernchal's vehicle occupied the southeast corner. Betzaida was to man the corner of Summer and N. Carmac and Hiu was to have eyes on the southwest point of N. Carmac and Race. They waited in silence, cars quiet and lights off for the indication that Torres had set up a vantage point on the middle of N. 12th Street. Once there he was to get to the top of the Four Points Sheraton across the street from the destination and alert all parties to his visibility. He did so three minutes later and they were off.

Shane and Julie exited the vehicle, weapons drawn, eyes out. Right on time, they rendezvoused with Bernchal, Sharee, Carina and Huvane and with Ruderick, they made their way closer to the address. All communication was done through the walkies on a necessary basis. Otherwise, they were synchronized to the second and had a go plan for every alternate scenario.

Before calling the meeting of every resident at the institution, Shane demanded they cover every possible outcome, from best to worst. Painstakingly, she and Bernchal had gone through all potential sequence of events so that they could keep radio chatter to a minimum and avoid alerting any random militia to their arrival.

With eyes on Torres at the roof of the hotel, Muccio whistled to them from his spot at N. Carmac and Race. With a series of hand signals, he relayed Torres' update- no visibility into the destination.

"Just as we figured," whispered Bernchal, not disturbed in the least. He dropped the binoculars to his side and turned to face the rest of them, all business.

"Okay, we got no eyes on the inside. But we planned for this. The good news is there're no bodies on the exterior. All rooftops are clear from here to 13th."

They glanced at their watches and matched them up.

"We got three minutes to get in, seven minutes to sweep. No exceptions. We all know what that means, right?"

Shane nodded but kept her eyes trained on her watch and Bernchal continued.

"LZ is this point right here. If Torres doesn't have eyes on one of us in exactly ten, two teams are coming in. So, let's keep this a private party, shall we?"

With those words, they synchronized their watches and split.

Shane and Ruderick made their way directly into the townhouse, with Bernchal and Julie close behind. Her hand gun at the ready, Shane took lead and guided them up the front steps and inside the vestibule. Carina, Huvane and Sharee waited for their mark just below the staircase leading into the premises, while Milagros and Deirdre took watch on each corner of the property line to spot anyone running out of the building after their arrival.

Their intel had directed them to the two-story structure, indicating that there may be a sub-basement or bunker underneath. The front door was locked but took Bernchal a total of twenty seconds to pick and open, letting them inside. The entrance was empty, as was the staircase leading up. It was deathly quiet and they listened intently for several seconds before moving forward.

With her weapon trained, Julie started up the staircase, knees bent and body crouched low. Lit by the few rays of early rising sunlight creeping through the windows of the vestibule, her hazel eyes scanned the landing above her as she climbed, with Bernchal behind her. She rounded the angled staircase and neared the top, slowing down to scan the dark hallway above her head. One large door was shut to her left and another on her right separated by a narrow corridor.

With a nod to Bernchal, they finished the climb and crept up to the door on the left. Julie put one hand on the door and waited, listening and feeling for any movement on the other side. With her eyes on Bernchal's, he gave her the signal to proceed and she backed up from the door.

With a step back, Bernchal swung his right leg back and kicked at the doorjamb with the ball of his foot and the wooden door cracked immediately. The lock gave way and the door swung open, flying back and banging into the wall behind it.

Light spilled in from the uncovered bay windows facing Race. The room was empty save for a steel table in the center of the room with a laptop on it. An open doorway in the back right of the room led to an empty bathroom which by the looks of it, had not been cleaned in months. After investigating the table for wires or plugs, Julie gave a quick loud whistle, two short high-pitched bursts to alert their friends downstairs that they were clearing room #1 with 7:24 remaining. Bernchal closed the laptop lid and picked it up, dropping it under his parka, between his chest and his bulletproof vest.

As they moved out of the room and down the hall to investigate the second room, Shane and Ruderick swept through the downstairs, clearing the kitchen and a second bathroom. As with upstairs, the restroom looked abandoned and unkempt, the only indication that the empty house had been used at all. There was a brown ring around the water in the toilet and the small porcelain pedestal sink had a faint green stain where the leaky faucet's drip landed continuously. The film surrounding the interior of the shower stall shone and Shane leaned inside to touch the ceramic tile, glancing at the residue on her fingers.

"This soap scum is soft," she whispered to Ruderick, who watched her, curious. "Somebody's been here as recently as last night."

He furrowed his brow and backed up out of the small room to let her out. Another whistle from upstairs indicated the second floor was clean.

They moved back into the kitchen and looked around more. Bernchal and Julie joined them and the four of them scanned every corner of the kitchen for some indication that there was more to the townhouse than met the eye.

With the click of his tongue, Bernchal wordlessly called to them and they neared an alcove just outside of the kitchen area, next to the outdated refrigerator.

The tiny room was the size of a telephone booth and had nothing but an empty shelf on the right wall closest to the fridge, and a small rug on the scuffed wooden floor. It was the rug that interested Bernchal and he poked at it with the toe of his black boots, lifting it by the corner.

It was small and rectangular, with fringed edges and a hideous pattern of stripes which seemed, in some misguided attempt, to be specifically chosen to brighten up the small space.

Shane got close to Bernchal to see what he was pointing at with he edge of his boot and as Julie and Ruderick also tried to crowd into the tiny space to see, they pressed her closer to him. She tried not to meet his eyes but from her peripheral view she saw his face spread into a sly smile, indicating that he knew she was trying to avoid him and he found it annoyingly humorous.

"Trap door?" asked Ruderick, his large burly frame hovering in the doorway and blocking all the oxygen in the 4x4 room.

Bernchal shrugged and locked eyes with him. "Only one way to tell."

Ruderick wasn't much for apologizing for his brute strength or the way he threw it around, so barely batting an eyelash, he grabbed Julie by the biceps and effortlessly lifted her two feet in the air. Before she could even protest, he turned around and deposited her on the linoleum floor of the kitchen behind him. Looking back to Shane, he raised his eyebrows and she quickly shot him down, stepping past him into the kitchen to avoid sharing the same fate.

He inched past her and dropped on his haunches to investigate the floor. Palming it, he fingered the rug and softly pushed it to side, revealing the crack in the floor to which Bernchal was referring. The linoleum was even with that of the kitchen, though slightly more faded, but the patch of floor where Bernchal and Ruderick poked around was off-kilter. The grout around the square of flooring was grayer than the rest of it even though it was covered by the rug and should have been more pristine. A corner edge was not lined up with a neighboring tile and were they not looking for an access point, they might not have seen it. Ruderick felt around and found a small groove in the tile big enough for him to shove his large fingers under and get a good grip.

Grunting and signaling with sounds coming from deep in their throats, Bernchal and Ruderick discussed their discovery and called for Shane and Julie to join them. Using his hand, Bernchal motioned their intention: pry open the trap door and go in, two by two, sweeping through whatever they encountered.

Shane glanced at her watch- 4:04 remaining.

She held up four fingers to Bernchal and he nodded, counting off to Ruderick before they suddenly palmed the floor and pulled the tile up, revealing a door less than three feet wide leading to a ladder. The door snapped back and landed on the floor with a thud that was almost completely muffled by the rug. Silently, they watched as Ruderick got low to the ground and waved his flashlight around the interior in an attempt to fish out a shooter. With no movement arising, Shane counted off three minutes with her fingers and they started down the ladder one after the other.

They were greeted by a stifling concrete tunnel, barely high enough for Ruderick to stand upright, leading to a steel door just beyond the reach of their sightline above. In formation, they reached the door and were surprised to find it unlocked, the doorknob turning in Bernchal's hand easily. Opening it, a flood of light and sound came pouring into the minuscule hallway.

President Yenmor had only been seen on one occasion since declaring war on the United States, and that was an obscure sighting in Washington D.C. in October of 2021. Since then, he had all but disappeared into the annals of D.C.'s political underground or anywhere else he had dreamed up before destroying his country.

Bernchal did not remember him to be so tall, so lanky.

Neither did Ruderick or even Julie, truth be told.

But Shane did.

She remembered every groove of his face, from the strong, squared chin to the deepest blue eyes that twinkled behind the tortoise-shell reading glasses he always balanced on the tip of his nose; from the way his broad shoulders wore the suit jackets as though they weren't just tailor-made for him, they were expressly sewn together by their designers with his body in mind to the trusting, almost patriarchal smile he gave the American public when he ran, won and was re-elected. That same smile he had plastered all over the television sets before the world went to shit and that same smile that lingered on scattered posters and signs around New York City when she had been on the run with her son.

She remembered every single detail about the man that singlehandedly destroyed her world.

So when they opened the door and came face to face with President Yenmor, she recognized him immediately.

The two commandos on either side of him at the end of the large medicinal room looked surprised, but he did not. He looked almost amused, with a wry smile on the edge of his attractive mouth as he watched what unfolded.

Their weapons were drawn, the commandos' were not, so the shots fired came quickly and precisely. Two in each chest, *Pop, Pop!* and they dropped immediately. One was down and out for the count but the other had some life left, and Julie shot off two rounds that finished the job.

Yenmor barely flinched.

He was behind a large steel table, a replica of the one holding the laptop upstairs, and was holding a file in his hands, opened and under review upon their entrance. Behind him, a printer connected to a surge protector that was plugged into a generator hummed and buzzed, spitting out sheet after sheet. A laptop was hooked up to the end of it and the screen was open to a shot of the North Korean flag, something which any American alive to that point had become all too familiar with.

Behind that was a large erase board, with strategic outlines and military jargon written in marker. One of the dead militia soldiers held the eraser for it in his lifeless hand.

Shane walked quickly past the dead bodies and up to Yenmor, her handgun trained on his forehead.

"Whoa! Whoa!" Ruderick called to her when recognition set it.

He rushed over to her. "Do you know who it is you have a gun pointed at right now?"

Shane answered, her dark eyes locked on Yenmor's icy blue ones. "Yes. That's why I have a gun pointed at him."

Immediately disregarding Ruderick standing a foot away from her, Shane stepped closer to Yenmor, jabbing the tip of her gun into his skin. His stoic expression cracked under the pain of her pressure and he winced slightly.

"Where is my son?" she asked, low enough that Julie and Bernchal, who were still back towards the door, strained to hear her. They stepped closer to them, watching.

Yenmor offered a politician's smile.

"I don't know to whom you are-"

"Where is my son?" she screeched, her voice bouncing off the crisp, white walls and slamming back and forth in echoes. She gripped the gun so tightly the whites of her knuckles were visible and Bernchal eyed her, seeing a vein in her forehead pulsing. She pressed harder and forced him back against the white wall.

Though slightly more concerned, Yenmor only offered a dismissive shrug. "I don't know who your son is."

Ruderick eyed the dry erase board and tried to decipher the writing. Random numbers jumped across the board, jumbling around each other with no clear or decipherable interpretation. 389118770751 written over and over again. He shook his head, clearing his mind and trying to figure out what they meant.

Attempting a different approach, Shane licked her lips and addressed Yenmor again. "Where are the children, the kids stolen from their mothers and imprisoned by you?"

His eyes danced, as though just hearing the words spoken by another person reminded him how proud he was of his actions.

"Oh, the program children? They are long gone from here. You'll never find them."

Julie tried to step closer to him but was held back by Ruderick's large arm against her waist. "Why did you take them? Why did you run that program?"

Yenmor looked at Julie and offered a smile, holding it steady as his eyes scanned them all and moved slowly, deliberately back to Shane.

She looked about to ask him for the whereabouts of the children again, but instead cocked her head to one side and frowned. Releasing a defeated little sigh, she shook her head slowly.

"You won't tell us, will you?"

His smile widened, as though they had finally figured out the answer to his riddle.

"Never."

She nodded once and then pulled the trigger.

Involuntarily, Julie screamed and reached a hand out desperately as though she could have stopped the bullet if she were closer.

Yenmor's head ricocheted with the impact and slammed against the wall behind him, leaving half of it there as he slinked down to the ground and gathered at Shane's feet. His blue eyes remained open, though the area above his right eyebrow was completely gone.

Julie's wails reverberated around the open room.

"You killed him! Jesus Christ, Shane! How are we gonna find them now?" Her voice came out in choked spurts, the sobs quickly taking over her body. Ruderick put a large hand on her shoulder, trying to keep her steady.

Shane looked at her, silent. With no answer to offer, she could only wipe off Yenmor's blood that had splattered on her own face and stare back.

Footsteps behind them caught their attention and Huvane, Carina and Sharee appeared at the door, eyes viewing the carnage around the room. It took them several seconds to place the body laying by the wall with its head half blown off as the former President of the United States.

"That's Yenmor?" asked Carina, in a half scream that dripped of panic.

Huvane looked from the body, to Shane and back again, trying to piece things together. Sharee only offered a dry chuckle and turned around, giving them her back so they would not see the tears that threatened to spill.

Julie's eyes brimmed over and her own tears began to fall uncontrollably. "We'll never find them," she managed before the sobs racked her body and she allowed Ruderick to comfort her in an awkward embrace.

Shane dropped the gun to her side and continued staring at his lifeless body as the blood poured out and pooled underneath his head. Fragments of brain matter that blew off and landed on the wall behind him began to unstick and fall to the floor, creating a disgusting squish in the eerie silence. Spent, Shane leaned against the wall and taking a deep breath, slumped down.

Her knees bent and she dropped to the floor, body and soul depleted. Hanging her head, she put her face in her hands and breathed, praying for an answer. Wordlessly, Sharee, Carina and Huvane filed out of the room. Ruderick led Julie behind them and with a final desperate glance back at her friend, she followed him. On her way she ripped the laptop on the table from the plug and yanked it to her chest, hugging it close to her as she walked away.

Bernchal stepped to Shane, dropping to a squat beside her, and placed one hand softly on the nape of her neck. She neither flinched nor pulled away, so he stroked the tiny hairs on the back of her neck, offering her a reassuring touch whether or not she would admit she needed one.

She looked up at him then, her eyes larger than usual and wet with tears and exhaustion.

"Did you see him?" she asked, her voice haunted. "Did you look at him? He was never going to tell. He was never going to give us anything."

She sniffled and stared at him, the pleading in her face and words begging for consolation.

Bernchal believed that *she* believed she had to kill Yenmor. He did not look into his eyes as she had. But Shane had and what she had seen was a man without remorse or fear; a man who had had no problem wiping away half the country's population; and she had known then that he would not be swayed into giving them the one thing they were after, the very thing he took.

No. Bernchal knew there had been no other choice but to take Yenmor down.

So he nodded his head, agreeing with her in an attempt to assuage some of the responsibility she was likely shouldering. She closed her eyes again and tucked her head into the crook of her folded arms, between her knees.

He felt her goosebumps rise and ignoring them, massaged her along her neck. He placed his other hand on her other shoulder and let it rest there and finally, she reached up and put her own hand on his as if to provide the gratitude she could not vocalize.

He waited for her to collect herself and after a few seconds of stillness, she did. Taking one final deep breath, she opened her eyes and lifted her head, meeting his gaze. She gave his hand a small squeeze and rose from the floor. With one last look at the man that orchestrated everything that led to the destruction of her life, Shane stepped over his still body and walked down the corridor towards the others.

Bernchal rose from the ground and looked at Yenmor's corpse on the floor beneath him, the rage he had had under control now bubbling up inside of him. Reminding himself one more time that he was on a mission, he gritted his teeth and forced himself to turn away and follow Shane before he emptied his clip into what was left of the dead man's skull.

He fell into place behind Shane at the ladder leading back up into the kitchen and together they emerged from the townhouse. The sun was close to rising and had begun its peek over the skyscrapers in downtown Philly, casting rays and shadows along the boulevard and directly over the trees lined up on Race Street.

Shane asked for Julie but Ruderick reassured her she was taking a moment to herself inside the townhouse. She was about to head back inside for her when she heard the call.

"Shane!"

She looked back at the front door, confused.

Another yell, this one much more earnest and urgent than before.

"*Shane!*"

She tossed a look of alarm to Bernchal and took off running. In seconds, she was back inside the townhouse, up the front stairs and into the foyer, calling Julie's name.

"In here!"

She followed the sound of Julie's voice and as she turned the corner that separated the dining room and the kitchen area, she felt Bernchal behind her, also running.

Julie stood in the center of the kitchen, the laptop hanging open in her hand. Her cheeks were pink, her eyes watery and glistening in the dim light spilling in from the window behind her. She sniffled and locked eyes with Shane, her voice coming out in one breathless line.

"I found them…"

PART THREE

Chapter XLV

The institution was alive; the vibrations running through its hallways and hidden tunnels were tremendously powerful and within a short time after their return from Philadelphia, the energy within its walls had taken on a life of their own.

The women were formulating a plan and getting ready to follow through, while the men were uncharacteristically quiet, watching it all unfold.

Julie had discovered encrypted files on that laptop and they led to Arlington, Virginia. They could decipher no further than that and as such, the location of the children was hotly debated on the ride back to New York and when it was established that a team would head out immediately in search of them, Ruderick was the only voice of dissent.

As Shane and the rest of the women reconvened and began to prepare for their departure, Ruderick summoned Bernchal and guided him back to the same insipid administration office near the Chapel for a private meeting.

"What time are you heading out?" Ruderick inquired quietly as they made their way into the office and he shut the door behind them. Inside, he walked straight to the large desk with no trace of a limp remaining, and turned to sit on the edge of it, facing Bernchal with his burly arms crossed.

"They want to leave as soon as possible but I talked them back to 1500 hours."

Ruderick nodded but said nothing, so Bernchal continued.

"It's a straight shot to Arlington. We should be there by 2100 and able to use the darkness to lay cover. Shane swears the animals have stayed out of the capital and the surrounding areas, so we just have to draw out the guards and find a way in."

He paused, waiting for a response. Ruderick only eyed him curiously and after a moment of silence, he continued.

"This won't be your average snatch and grab, so we cannot proceed with extraction until we have the enemy pinned. We got no intel so our only route is to eliminate them from jump. Thank God R.O.E.'s went out the window the minute the shit hit the fan," he added with a wry laugh. Ruderick only stared at him stone-faced and Bernchal immediately began to feel uneasy.

"What the fuck is going on, Wood?"

"We found the kids."

Furrowing his brow, Bernchal smirked. "Where the fuck you been? I was there when we got the location."

Shaking his head, Ruderick replied, choosing his words carefully.

"No. We found the kids… and they're not in Arlington."

His heart sank when the words hit him and all of a sudden he felt off-kilter, as though the inertia of climbing the stairs to the office were now kicking in and making him move. A chill ran through him, his breath caught in his throat and he blinked several times, finally getting a grip and asking the inevitable question.

"Are they dead?"

"What?" asked Ruderick, surprised. "No. They're alive. At least I think they still are. But what I'm saying is that they're not in Arlington."

Barely taking a second to acknowledge the overwhelming wave of relief coursing through him, Bernchal cocked his head to the side and with his eyes suspiciously small, he asked, "How the fuck do you-"

"Williams," he interjected. "He's alive and he has ears to the ground."

Unable to enjoy the news that one of his friends was not in fact dead, as he had been originally told, but alive and out there helping them, Bernchal started to slowly shake his head back and forth when realization kicked in.

"Tell me I'm wrong, Wood. Tell me I'm wrong and that you haven't known Williams was alive this whole time, out there in the fucking streets and didn't say anything about it. Tell me you haven't been communicating with him and going behind Shane's back, *my back*, and trying to set shit up on the low. Please," he pled, his tone an even mix of disbelief and rage.

Ruderick licked his lips and stared at him, expressionless.

"Williams is alive," he repeated, trying to re-control the conversation. "He knows where the children are and they are not in Arlington. He has gotten us-"

"Are you fucking shitting me?" Bernchal exploded. "Are you fucking serious, Wood?"

Ignoring him, he continued with his speech while Bernchal watched, incredulously.

"He has gotten us the intel and we leave at 1200. We will extract the children and tie up the loose ends of the program."

After a moment wherein he could only stare, open-mouthed and silent, Bernchal asked, "And what about them?" as he angled a thumb in the direction of the other school building and crossed his arms. Legs apart and chest out, he took a combative stance and asked again, "What about them, Wood? You don't plan on bringing along the mothers of the very kids you're rescuing?"

Ruderick took a deep breath and frowned, slowly shaking his lead left and right. "No."

"So they're going off to Virginia to what, find emptiness? A fucking empty warehouse or something? Or worse yet- an ambush?"

"I cannot speculate as to what they will find in Virginia but I can guarantee you it is empty. There are neither children nor program leaders of any sort. Arlington is effectively abandoned and has been so since the President moved out of the White House to-"

"The President was killed, remember? Four goddamn hours ago. By *Shane*, Wood- the very person you are trying to keep in the dark about the location of her fucking son."

Ruderick closed his lips tight at the interruption and continued watching Bernchal silently.

"You have to tell them what you know."

"Absolutely not."

"Wood, they are going out there. We have to come clean-"

"No!" he yelled suddenly. Despite the sunlight blazing outside, the corner of their building faced west and was still hidden in the shadows of mid-morning, allowing his blue eyes to sparkle in the dark room. "I will not compromise the lives of my men or the lives of dozens of kids- potentially more- because they cannot follow orders."

Bernchal chuckled dryly. "The sheer fact that they cannot follow orders should be enough to convince you that they need this information. Look," he started, his tone considerably calmer. "I guarantee you, I personally vouch for the fact that if you tell them, if you tell Shane what you know, she'll let you take lead."

Scoffing, Ruderick jerked his head back, "No, she won't. She'll try to control the situation."

Bernchal could feel the reasoning slipping away and he tried desperately to grasp it before there was nothing left.

"There *is* no way to control the situation. Control is an illusion. We thought we ran our own lives before everything went to hell, but look how easily it was taken. That's because we never had it in the first place. Don't you get it? We don't even have enough details to know what they're walking into. At least this way we can keep the casualties to a minimum if you-"

"She shot the goddamn President of the United States! Right in front of us! Didn't wait for information, didn't let any of us question him," he added, his hands counting off his statements one by one as if to illustrate his point. "She decided, unilaterally, to kill the one person, the *one* person Steve, that could have led her to her son. If you think that's the type of person that I'd trust to lead any mission, you're just as bat-shit crazy as she is."

He rose abruptly and approached Bernchal, catching him off guard. His eyes bright with authority, he lowered his voice and addressed him once more.

"I absolutely will not, under any circumstances, allow a group of civilian women to accompany us on this mission. I absolutely will not, under any circumstances, allow a group of civilian women to undermine this mission and I absolutely will not, under any circumstances, allow them to destroy the little hold we have on this situation with their hysteria and untrained approach."

Bernchal watched him as they both stood their ground, squared off, chests heaving. His clenched his jaw and though he was not willing to come to blows with his friend and once commanding officer, he could feel himself beginning to lose what little composure he had left.

Ruderick sensed it too and took a step back in an attempt to diffuse the situation.

"There should be nothing of harm in Arlington. Trust me. Let them go, let them look around and they'll find nothing. Then they'll come back. We will be a quarter day's journey ahead of them anyway. We will extract the children and bring them home."

"Trust you?" he asked, scoffing. Bernchal closed his eyes and shook his head, disbelievingly. "And if you're wrong? If they encounter militia and cannot protect themselves- what then? Or what if we can't find the kids, or those kids are already dead? Do you have any idea what that will do to them? We owe them that much, Wood. Fuck the President, fuck the politicians and the fucking militia. We- you and I," he stated, his index finger motioning between them back and forth. "*We* owe them their kids, whether they are dead or alive. We owe them that much. And you are robbing them of that. You are keeping them from that joy or that pain, whichever it may be."

Angered, Ruderick responded defiantly.

"I don't owe anyone a goddamn thing."

Bernchal leaned forward, ignited.

"You don't owe them?" he repeated rhetorically. "You and I don't owe them? These women, these *American citizens*- we don't owe them anything? Not our protection? Our help? We don't owe them the safety they should have gotten from us? Instead of being here, at home, protecting our own people, we were off on another continent fighting a psycho's war, trying to stay alive and smuggling our asses back to this damn place to find it destitute and fucking destroyed. To find all the men dead, the women fucking robots and the goddamn kids stolen! That's not something we should have been here to handle, Wood? That flag, that ideal that means so much to you- does it not represent the very people in this building? The ones trying to find and save their kids? Goddamnit, Wood…"

But there was no compassion meeting him when he paused, suddenly unable to continue.

He took a step back and eyed Ruderick, his tongue folded on his lower lip, feeling close to tears. Ruderick's resolve was stronger than ever and one look into those steel blue eyes, he knew he would not budge.

"You're wrong. And you fucking know it."

Turning, he walked to the door and threw it open. As he stepped through, Ruderick's words stopped him in his tracks.

"This is classified information, Commander. You keep your mouth shut about this mission."

He walked through the doorway and turned left to head back to the dormitory and he heard Ruderick's call behind him in the hallway, the gravity in his voice bouncing off the walls and still following him long after his exit.

"That's an order, soldier."

Chapter XLVI

Bernchal made it to the cafeteria as Shane was addressing the rest of the women. None of the men were to be found and he stood as the solitary male figure, once again, among the group of women. Only this time, they regarded him as an equal, a brother, a friend.

"I'm not gonna make a fancy speech, or give some grand pep talk," she said, her voice flat and calm. She stood up in front of the table where they had sat less than twenty-four hours beforehand and looked out at all of the faces before her. Her tone was direct, no nonsense.

"I'm just going to fill you in on some basics. I have a son. He's seven years old now and there is nothing on this planet more important to me than him. That means I will do whatever I have to do to get him back. That thing other people feel, a tug at their conscience or pangs of guilt- I don't have that," she stated, her hand on her own chest. With a finger pointed in the general vicinity of their destination, she continued. "So whoever or whatever is in my way will be removed. It's that simple. I will not hesitate. I will not think twice. I will stop at nothing.

If you can't commit to that, if your ethics and morality are so that you cannot take a life to get the job done, stay out of my way. If you cannot see yourself pulling the trigger while looking into the eyes on the person at the other end of the barrel, stay out of my way. And if you don't want this enough to put your own life on the line and sacrifice yourself for this cause, stay out of my way."

Most of the women just sat in the folding chairs around the cafeteria and watched her speak. She was not wild with passion, burning with rage, or emotional. She was none of those things. Instead, she spoke to them as though she were giving them the specials on this evening's menu. Her voice was clear and her eyes bright but with expectation rather than the usual incense that flamed behind them.

Bernchal looked around the room and glanced at each woman, all with their eyes drawn and targeted on only her, their heads nodding in unison and in agreement.

He realized she was so much more than their leader, their reluctant president. She was their way to their kids; and they would follow her to their deaths if they had to.

"If however, she continued, "you want your own kids back as badly as I want my son, you're welcome to follow. But know this- I will not turn back for anyone and I will not slow down for anyone. So keep up."

She swiveled and gave the crowd her back, indicating the end of the meeting. Most of the women lingered, but some shot up from their chairs and made a beeline for the cafeteria doors, eager to get to their rooms and get ready to follow Shane into action.

He avoided the women exiting by him to make his way to her, some of them patting him on the back, each tap another turn of the blade he was about to shove into Shane's back.

"For someone who isn't big on speeches, that was pretty inspiring."

She looked up from the table where she and Julie huddled over a map and smiled politely. Julie, in rare form, offered him a small smile before scooping up the map and as she rolled it, reached out to tap Shane on the forearm with it, indicating her departure.

He waited until Julie was out of earshot and turned back to face Shane, who began to load a few supplies into a backpack.

"If your goal is to inspire fear, I'd say job well done. It seems everybody has a death wish now."

Shane looked up from the backpack, hand midair.

"I'm surprised at you. Genuinely," she said softly, her brows furrowed and face angled towards him with a look of reproach. "You think so little of us to imagine that we'd be turned away by the threat of violence, death? That we would leave our kids out there because someone said some harsh words?"

Bernchal swallowed, suddenly feeling like a chastised child. She paused for his answer and when he could offer none, continued.

"When you're in, you're all in. You underestimate the lengths a mother would go to for her child, Commander. You underestimate women."

Her dark eyes searched his for something and all of a sudden he felt small, like a traitor. He looked away from her, finding it increasingly hard to stay strong under the scrutiny of that intense stare. When she would break eye contact in the past, he would have been able to gaze at her for hours, mentally willing her to submit. But now that she was no longer running away from him and he was harboring such a huge secret, he found himself the one unable to stare back.

She tugged at the strap of the backpack she was absentmindedly filling and Shane could feel the nervous energy catapulting off of him. It was foreign, rare for someone like him to seem preoccupied, but she felt the uneasiness just the same.

Turning her attention back to the backpack, she tried to mask the fear in her voice as she jokingly asked, "A little early in the morning to try and talk me out of this, isn't it?"

When he did not respond, she sighed quietly to herself, already knowing the answer.

"And that's not what this is," she stated matter-of-factly, as she kept her eyes down and packed her ammunition into the backpack.

He wanted to tell her the truth. He wanted to shake the determination out of her and convince her to drop the mission and let him and Ruderick handle things. He wanted to take her in his arms and forget everyone and everything as he lost himself inside of her.

But he could not. He dared not.

So he took a deep breath.

"Look," he began choppily. "I'm heading out. With my squad. In a different direction."

"I figured as much."

She continued to look down, keeping her hands occupied. Everything on the table in front of her, from the loose maps of the East Coast to a random can of Carnation Milk- she was packing everything but the kitchen sink.

He noticed the shift in her body language and tried to explain.

"We have a mission to complete."

"And what mission would that be?" Her voice dripped with sarcasm.

"Don't be an asshole."

"Me?" she asked, incredulously. With a derisive smile on her face, she finally made eye contact. "Typical. Classic move- deflect all responsibility."

"Responsibility for what?" he demanded, suddenly. He eyed her with a newly found reservoir of anger building up inside of him and his hazel eyes bared down on her before he added, "None of those kids are mine."

Shane nodded, the smile gone and replaced by a knowing glare. "I know that. Trust me."

Unsatisfied, Bernchal kept going, trying harder to convince himself than her.

"My responsibility is to my country, my men and my mission."

She shook her head and bit her lip. Their history floated between them, the undeniable sexual tension, their embrace… that kiss. It was circling the air, from him to her and back again, assaulting them both. Eying him, she let go of the backpack and took a step closer to him.

"That's pretty funny coming from you. 'Cause when I found you, Commander, half frozen and starved, you didn't give two fucks about your country or your flag."

"Well I do. It can exist again. And I'm of better service restoring it than-"

She waved him off with the flick of her wrist and turned back to continue distractedly packing.

"Than trying to save some kids that don't even belong to you. Got it."

He hesitated, but finally blurted out, "I can't."

She kept her eyes on the bag to avoid his. "I said I got it," she replied.

"Don't try to guilt me," he added, his voice low.

"I'm not."

"Shane…this isn't my fight."

She put a palm on the table in an attempt to keep herself clam. She could feel him pulling away, feel his heart no longer involved, and more than anything- above the fear of going out there alone after becoming so dependent on his assistance and more importantly, his presence- she hated herself for ever becoming dependent on him in the first place.

"You've made that very clear."

"This isn't my fight," he repeated, and she could feel the carefully woven fabric of her composure quickly unraveling.

"Then what is?" she asked, turning again to face him. She kept her hands glued to the table, back hunched over as though she were being held captive, so that she did not say what she really wanted to say, that if he had to leave her he should have done so in the beginning so that she would not have come to care for him this way, and instead asked, "Huh, Commander? What will you fight for?"

Insulted, he recoiled. "Get off your high horse. You're no better. Don't act for one second like you actually give a fuck for anything or anyone other than your son."

The true reality, that they were both too frightened to admit to one another, ricocheted back and forth within the hurtful words they fired at each other.

"Just because I have my eyes on the prize doesn't mean I don't acknowledge everyone fighting alongside me. Every woman, every mother and every lost child. I just mourn differently."

He said it before he could stop himself.

"By ignoring the dead?"

Shane took her hands off the table and stood up straight, her eyes burning through his.

"Fuck you."

"Fuck me?" he asked, surprised.

"Yes, fuck you. I don't have to explain shit to you."

Fired up, he took a step closer to her.

"What about Jolene? Huh? What about them?" he asked, pointing behind them, indicating the remaining women of the institution. "Scared women that are willing to blindly follow you into this glorious battlefield? Most of whom won't come back at all. Don't you owe them an explanation? Don't you owe them a reason?"

"You want a reason?" she asked, rushing up to his face and stopping inches from him.

"Yes!" he shouted.

She paused for a second, and then unleashed a holy reign of hell on him.

"Marcus Negron. Terry-Ann Miller. George Mullins. Tomas Velez. Eric Crosby. William Lim. Orville Smith. Devon Underwood. Antonia Rodriguez. John Matthews. Luis and Daniella Gonzalez. Ricardo Contreras. Gregory Pimental. Miguel-Angel Martinez. Lisa Lloyd. Arturo Zerega. Cristina Damon. Jullianna Vazquez. Victor Abatte. Andrew Caputo. Samantha Garcia. Emily Fleurimond. Vincent Mitchell. Ritchie and Timothy Woodson. Michael Boley. William Boutte. Eddie Castillo. Daniel Liu. Thomas and Jonathan Rowe. Charly Alexis Sinkler. Robert Harris. David Texeira. Stacey Wallach," she said, her voice shaking from anger and torment, as she checked each name off one by one.

And with the last one, she enunciated it slowly, pronouncing each syllable like another slap across his face.

"And Silas Hayden Milian…"

He did not respond, only looked away from her despite their close proximity. She stood her ground and spoke again, the emotion in her voice audible through the rage.

"You don't even have one good reason for not fighting. I have thirty-seven reasons why I am."

He continued to avoid her stare and just as she was about to turn back to her table, he reached out and grabbed her by the forearm, his fingers quickly digging into her skin. She turned back to face him and did not pull away, feeling through that one touch the desperation in this, his final act of redemption.

"I shouldn't care," he whispered to her, his mouth close to hers despite the few remaining stragglers that lingered in the cafeteria. She felt his breath against her face, heard the agony in his voice and with those three words, understood that he was leaving her for good.

She locked eyes with him finally and shot back.

"Then don't."

"I shouldn't care," he repeated, even softer this time.

His eyes pled for an understanding that she could not provide.

"Then don't!" she yelled, surprising them both.

Incapable of forming a response, Bernchal finally let her go. Shaking his head, he turned his back to her, leaving the cafeteria and Shane, as she stood watching him walk away, her hands shaking.

On the way down the corridor towards Ruderick's room, he passed Torres, who eyed him but intuitively said nothing. Still seething, Bernchal slammed open the swinging door leading out of the hallway and walked through it as Torres continuing forward, unbothered.

Reaching Julie, who was walking in the opposite direction from the other end of the hallway, Torres handed her the keys to one of the vehicles they had commandeered from the dealership. Ruderick's parting gift to the women was an extra set of wheels.

She grabbed the keys from Torres and nodded her thanks, continuing past him and towards the cafeteria doors. The darkness of the hallway in the tombs of the institution barely masked the anxiety permeating through its halls and Torres felt it.

He called after her, the patronizing tilt of his voice obvious.

"You have no idea what you're getting into."

She stopped and turned back to face him and smiled sardonically.

"I know. But obviously that's what we have you guys for, right?"

He shook his head, irritated. "I know you're being a sarcastic ass right now. But you're right. You *are* lucky to have us."

"No," she countered, and walking towards him, she raised her hand and pointed a finger in his face. "I'm not lucky. I am realistic. The ones in over their heads are you and your men. This is not a military operation, soldier. It's a fucking suicide mission. And I know what I'm willing to die for. Do *you*?"

He could offer no answer, though she waited for none. As quickly as she had rushed at him, she dropped her hand, offered an indecipherable smirk and turned away from him, making her way into the cafeteria.

Stunned, Torres shook it off and made his way back towards the male dormitory to pick up further instructions. On the way, he passed the open doors of the cafeteria and caught wind of the women reciting a saying, all of them speaking in unison. He peeked in and saw them, some cleaning weapons, some packing bags, others tying boots or getting ready in some fashion or another.

All of their voices melted into one as they spoke in waves, each woman echoing the other's last words until the sound turned into a symphony that filled the empty space and cascaded down towards the end of the hallway, threatening to spill through the front doors of the institution and on to the streets of New York City.

I will reach my field of battle by any means at my disposal.
And when I get there, I will arrive violently.
I will rip the heart from my enemy and leave it bleeding on the ground,
because he cannot stop me.

Chapter XLVII

Williams had traced Martinez and the children to Washington D.C., but only had enough intel to get Bernchal and his men as close as the city before losing his visual. His last communication with Ruderick came approximately two hours before they departed, one hour before Bernchal and Shane had had it out, and six hours before the women were set to leave the institution towards Arlington.

When they left, they did so quietly. Feeling like a thief in the night, Bernchal slinked off with the rest of the men without speaking to Shane after their blowup. They piled into their vehicles and as they drove away, he looked back at the institution, hoping for a miracle.

He believed in their mission but he knew Ruderick was right- Shane and the women were nothing short of a ticking time bomb. This close to a resolution, this close to finding their kids made for a volatile situation wherein someone like Shane, who already disregarded outside opinions, would go against any advice offered and walk right into a potentially catastrophic scenario. He trusted her, but he did not trust her decision-making at this point. Regularly, yes; he trusted her with his life. But at this stage, Bernchal feared she would give in to her impetuous side. He knew she would not stop until she found her son and what scared him was that she would endanger the lives of all those around her to do it. And that was something he preferred to avoid if he could.

So they set out at 1300 hours, a quarter day's journey ahead of Shane, in the hopes that they could locate the children, neutralize the threat that remained and bring them home.

Silently, Bernchal wished for that miracle. Not in finding the kids- of that he trusted William's abilities completely and believed that he would undoubtedly locate them. Instead, he prayed that the damage that had been done between he and Shane was not indefinite. He hoped that in bringing her son home to her, he could undo the destruction to their relationship, or whatever it was, and get her to see that once her son was home and in her arms again, the future was not yet drawn out and they could make of it whatever they pleased.

They drove less than two hours before he could already see the northeast district of Capitol Hill coming into focus from the highway. They had taken some back-channel roads and steered clear of the turnpikes to avoid detection and it had been a pretty quiet ride. For the most part, on runs like this, Bernchal always had the same sneaky suspicion- that the worst of what had been done was close to over and soon a new era would begin wherein they could rebuild all that had been taken from them.

They passed a checkpoint within the city limits and surprising them, a large Jeep, military grade, drove out from the shoulder hidden behind some fallen trees onto the Whitehurst Freeway, its tires squealing. Ruderick and Bernchal, in the lead car, were suddenly blocked and directly on path to collide with the Jeep. Slamming on the brakes, Ruderick pulled the steering wheel sharply to the left, narrowly avoiding the front bumper of the large vehicle as his own came to rest a few inches away while it's passengers were tossed around inside.

Both vehicles idled for several seconds, sizing each other up. The Jeep's windows were tinted; Ruderick's were not, and he balked at the exposure as he retrieved his weapon and waited.

"What the hell is this?"

Finally, the passenger window of the Jeep dropped, revealing a tattered cloth unfolding from the window and waving in the afternoon breeze. Vaguely, Ruderick could make out a crudely drawn bird fading on the torn fabric.

"What the fuck does that mean?" he growled, his finger on the trigger of his trusty shotgun.

Bernchal released the breath he'd been holding and threw himself forward, reaching for the glove compartment, opening it and rummaging through its contents roughly. Franticly searching, his hands finally emerged holding an identical piece of fabric. He lowered his own window and much to Ruderick's surprise, waved it.

The Jeep moved forward all of a sudden, shifting to the left and waiting next to their vehicle. Ruderick stared at Bernchal, confused.

"What the hell is that, Steve?"

Bernchal urged him forward and Ruderick reciprocated, reversing until both drivers were face to face as he responded.

"Peace symbols. The only way to communicate your intent."

The Jeep's window lowered and Ruderick balanced his finger above the control button, turning to address Bernchal.

"You sure about this?"

"Open the fucking window, Wood."

Complying, he shrugged and lowered the window.

Gray eyes stared back at them. A man, not a day over twenty-five, sat in the driver's seat and though young, his face had the weathered look of a soldier who had had just about enough fighting to last a lifetime. Dressed in army fatigues and a hat perched high on his bald head, the soldier nodded at them both and leaned back in his seat so they could peer further inside his vehicle, revealing three other passengers, all dressed in army colors.

Ruderick cocked his head to the side, questioning, "Service?"

The soldier nodded, motioning to the insignia on his chest, his nameplate glistening in the sun.

"Private First Class Worthington. Got PVC Marshall, Melendez and Simmons," he added, pointing to the other men in the car with him.

Ruderick nodded and responded, his tone slightly friendlier than that to which Bernchal was accustomed.

"Good to meet you, son. Captain Woodrow Ruderick, Army Ranger. This here's Lieutenant Commander Bernchal, Navy."

The soldiers, acknowledging rank, stiffened and suddenly raised their hands to their temples, saluting Ruderick and Bernchal. Stunned for a second, Bernchal shook it off and returned the salute, inexplicably touched by the gesture.

"What is your business in DC, Captain?"

"We got word that a group of kids are being held in the city. Any information on that?"

Worthington shook his head, his eyes penetrating theirs.

"There's a medical facility at Georgetown, constant foot traffic. The outskirts are closed up but we can't clear the schools without giving ourselves away."

They nodded and Bernchal pointed past the highway, towards the nation's capital beyond the horizon.

"We're going in hot, just down Whitehurst. Got one other car with us," he added, hooking his thumb and pointing towards Huvane, Muccio, Torres and Hiu in the car behind them. "It's a search and rescue... we hope."

"Do you need cover?" Worthington offered, though he looked worried. "We can block this road for a couple of miles but we don't have the manpower for-"

"It's alright, son," interjected Ruderick, calmly. "If you can just control the flow of activity here to give us an escape route, we can handle the rest."

"Consider it done, sir. Good luck out there, Captain. Commander," he added with a nod of his head. He led off another round of salutes and his men followed his lead, once again formally acknowledging Ruderick and Bernchal.

Bernchal replied, "Likewise," and they parted ways, their cars filing further into the city as the Privates turned back into the shoulder to await another visitor.

A few mintes later, Ruderick's truck glided slowly around Dupont Circle and ran alongside the Anacostia River towards the H Street corridor. Williams' last contact led them to a potential lockhouse in Georgetown University and they needed to secure the perimeter before heading in.

They eased up onto Virginia Avenue and parked the vehicle they were in. The plan was simple: Huvane and Hiu were to secure a larger vehicle, a school or GUTS city bus with which to transport the children; Torres and Muccio were to rendezvous with Williams at a designated location while Bernchal and Ruderick would continue onward into Georgetown University.

Williams had laid it all out for them before they lost contact and had directed them to members of the President's cabinet who were rumored to be alive and centrally located in historic Healy Hall of Georgetown. They believed it was there that the children were being held.

The duos set off in their respective directions, Huvane and Hiu towards the main campus metro station, Torres and Muccio up Virginia Avenue and Bernchal and Ruderick along Pennsylvania Avenue towards the university.

Weapons out and eyes on all visual points around them, Bernchal and Ruderick walked quickly on the avenue as it shifted left and right through the residential neighborhoods of the nation's former capital. The streets were eerily silent; every few seconds the squawk of a bird or the call of some wild animal could be heard above the sound of their footsteps lightly trotting on the freezing asphalt beneath them. The townhouses and buildings were abandoned, boarded up and deserted. In New York, the occasional raccoon or skunk would pop out of nowhere if only to remind humans that animals now ran most of the show, whereas in Washington D.C., it seemed everyone and everything was all but gone.

Keeping in time with the rest of the men, Bernchal and Ruderick arrived at Healy Hall fifty minutes later. The main campus was a grand layout of architectural beauty that stood out and within the silence of its surroundings, seemed every bit authentic of its medieval architecture.

Ruderick called his location into the tiny mic attached to the shoulder of his vest and five seconds later a faint rumble of static sounded as Muccio and Huvane checked in as well.

They entered through the double doors of Riggs Library, walking slowly through the darkened halls towards Healy. They passed under large ornamental paintings of Jesuit brothers and Georgetown's coat of arms as they made their way past Gaston Hall before they heard the voices.

It started faintly at first, like the distant sound of a television set when first arriving at the home of a host. It increased as they walked, faster and lower to the ground, as they reached the vast hallways of the school and when they made it into the gray slab of concrete east of the quad, it was clear as day.

Two voices resounded, one overlapping the other and controlling the conversation. Bernchal eyed Ruderick and indicating his intentions, pushed through the glass door marked "Department of Biochemistry and Molecular & Cellular Biology" and walked into the school's science lab.

A chalkboard off to the side had numbers on it, the numbers also written on the dry erase board at the president's safe house- 38.9118° N, 77.0751° W. All around the room, countertops filled with beakers and jars of liquids lined the four walls and in the center was a sink with a large faucet and a blood-soaked towel hanging on the edge. Bernchal followed the tiny droplets of blood falling from the towel down to the linoleum floor and around to a gurney in the center of the room, above which two men stood over the body of a small girl strapped to it. Her thick brown hair had been chopped to the ears and lay underneath her in uneven strands that stuck out from behind her neck. Her mouth was taped closed and around the edge of the tape it was red and raw. Her eyes, large as saucers, were a bright blue and shone with undried tears. Her tiny wrists and ankles were strapped in and she was completely naked.

Both men wore lab coats; one was taller, wiry, holding tortoise shell glasses between the index finger and thumb of his right hand as he reached for a handkerchief with his left to clean them; the other slightly shorter but with an athlete's build. His crystal blue eyes shot to the door as soon as they walked in.

"Who are-"

The question was overshadowed by the heartbreaking shriek released from the small girl on the gurney. Her body was raised from the blanket beneath her, the vein in her forehead bulging as she let out a blood-curdling scream that was barely masked by the tape over her mouth. The man with the piercing blue eyes did not flinch, only calmly took one hand and covered her taped mouth with it as he continued staring at Bernchal and Ruderick.

If he had not believed Shane and Julie, if he had not really and truly been convinced of the atrocities they had endured at the hands of an administration which had effectively donated their bodies to science, Bernchal would not have accepted that what he had just walked into was actually real.

Moving quickly, he took several long steps towards the gurney with his weapon raised and aimed it at the one with the glasses, who cowered back and bumped his bony hip on the gurney.

"Untie her," he growled, and the tall one could only look from the barrel of Bernchal's gun to the other man and back again.

Ruderick closed the distance from the door and brought his weapon up to the temple of the blue-eyed man, who stood watching them, cool and collected.

Bernchal spoke again, this time his words slower and more pronounced.

"I'm not going to tell you again."

The tall one gave one final desperate look to the other man and relented, reaching quickly for the straps of the gurney. As he fumbled to untie them, the little girl whimpered, her sobs the only sound in the large room.

Ruderick shoved the blue-eyed man and forced him over to the other side of the gurney, next to his floundering friend. Motioning to the nameplates on the pocket of their lab coats, he addressed the blue-eyed man.

"Dr. Walter Robideaux. Are you behind this scientific shit show?"

Robideaux's handsome face was clean-shaven and sun kissed and he stared back at Ruderick, unmoved by the gun aimed at his head.

"I am the acting scientist in this facility."

"Scientist," repeated Bernchal, scoffing to himself. He poked at the other man with his gun to get him to untie the little girl's straps faster and addressed Robideaux.

"Where are the children?"

The tall one finished and stood straight and Bernchal caught a glimpse of his name tag.

Dr. Preston Allwood

Both of them ignored the question and Ruderick repeated the words while Bernchal picked the little girl off the table and using the blanket to wrap her up, set her down on top of a steel table behind them. He turned his attention back to the two doctors.

The tone in Ruderick's voice was indicative of his quickly losing patience. Robideaux kept his cool, but Allwood fidgeted and Bernchal found his in. With the barrel of his gun still aimed at Allwood's chest, he walked up to him, eye to eye until their noses were almost touching.

"Where are the fucking kids?"

Allwood gulped and tried to glance at Robideaux but Bernchal blocked his view. He started to shake his head back and forth, stuttering.

"This is a government program-"

Ruderick kept his weapon on Robideaux's temple, both of their blue eyes locked in a sort of pissing contest, as he addressed Allwood.

"Who implemented the program?"

With a sneer, Robideaux answered him, the inflections in his baritone voice giving away his complete and utter arrogance.

"That's classified information."

Bernchal shook his head. "Look around, guy. There's no government to answer to."

"It's still classified."

With a hard nudge, Ruderick pushed his head back and growled, "So un-classify it."

Robideaux held his ground and tightened his lips, but Allwood looked to be seconds from vomiting. With a final push into his chest, Bernchal cocked the safety of his gun and felt him jump when it clicked.

"It's a government program!" he blurted out. With no desire to be shot over something he clearly never orchestrated in the first place, Allwood opened his mouth and the words spilled out.

"It was implemented by the paramilitary organization working with the President."

"Who's the leader?"

"No one knows him. Yenmor teamed up with some well-known fugitive, a sort of terrorist that was wanted for crimes against the North Korean state. He was the only one crazy enough to work within the United States government to get the ball rolling."

His narrow chest heaved, up and down, as though the very act of speaking had drained all of him. Eyes wide, he waited as Bernchal watched him, his curiosity piqued.

"Why would our President do this?"

"Why not?" chimed in Robideaux. Much more relaxed than his partner, he barely glanced at Ruderick's weapon trained on him and instead, shifted his strong body to face Bernchal and answer him directly.

"He is the Commander in Chief, leader of the free world. He can do whatever he pleases."

Ruderick scoffed and muttered, "*Was*," under his breath. "So what they said is true? You guys really did do this?"

Neither replied and Bernchal shook his head, a short derisive laugh coming out.

"What the fuck... Some kind of sick, government science project?"

"Project?" repeated Robideaux, seemingly insulted. He furrowed his brows at them, looking from each one to the other as though they were new to the game and couldn't possibly understand.

"This wasn't a project, gentlemen. This was a new way of life for this country."

"What was wrong with the old way of life?"

"It was imperfect. There were too many flaws. Democracy in and of itself is a flawed system. This was a way to cleanse the population, start anew."

Ruderick poked him hard with his gun bringing his attention back towards him. "And the people that died?"

Robideaux offered a dismissive shrug. "The greater good will always outweigh the needs of a few."

Ruderick smiled and his blue eyes flashed with amusement. "In this case, doc, the few are fighting back."

"An unforeseeable sidetrack."

Bernchal laughed, completely disbelieving what he was hearing.

"An unforeseeable sidetrack?" he repeated. "Seriously? You didn't see that coming? You didn't in any way, shape or form anticipate a bunch of pissed off women wanting their kids back?"

Robideaux looked to Allwood for assistance, but the timid man offered none. So with a smug smirk on his handsome face, he continued staring at Ruderick.

Still somewhat in shock, Ruderick asked, "So then what was the point?"

Robideaux replied hurriedly, as though they should have known the answer.

"A new world order. Females policing this great country. Women who have been... broken in, if you will. Trained to do what must be done without the pull of the heartstrings."

"And male soldiers weren't good enough to pull this off?" asked Bernchal, what little was left of his patience wearing very thin.

"Think about it. Wrap your brain around it. What on this earth is stronger, more resilient, than a mother who has lost her child? What on this planet could possibly be tougher?" Without waiting for their response, he answered dramatically, "Nothing, gentlemen, that's what. We needed a new breed of soldiers. One that is willing to live or die for their orders, willing to kill on command without a second thought as to ethics and propriety. Sure, if you're lucky in a bunch you find the occasional sociopath willing to do anything for a thrill, but that's too volatile. They are self-serving. What we needed was a different take on the way things have been done, a new spin. And we found it. Beat them down, break them down, and the ones that are built tough, the ones that can survive, will. And they will emerge gloriously, like a phoenix out of the ashes ready to do the bidding of he whom commands her."

Bernchal pushed Allwood back with the barrel of his gun and stepped closer to Robideaux.

"Well, those little weapons you created, they are on their way, doctors. Here. And believe me when I tell you, they will destroy everything you have done. Just tell us where the kids are and we can give them back and avoid a massacre."

Robideaux snapped and pushed Ruderick's gun away from him, throwing himself in front of Allwood and getting in Bernchal's face defiantly.

"No! Do you know how hard we've worked to set this up? Absolutely not. We will deal with whatever comes this way. Whoever it is."

Ruderick chuckled. "My friend, I've seen this woman in action. You do not want to go toe-to-toe with her."

"One woman? That's all?"

"No, that's not all. It's a fucking troop. She's just the one running it."

"So give us the information on her."

Bernchal chimed in. "There is none. We never saw her." He shut his lips tight and didn't need to glance at Ruderick to know he would do the same. He had no problem keeping this psychopath talking for some intel, but there was no way in hell he'd give them anything on Shane or the institution.

"You never saw her?" he asked dubiously.

"Nope."

"And the rest of them?"

"Some. We were isolated."

"What did they get from you?"

"Nothing," he replied, increasingly angered. "We were fed, kept warm and left alone. We didn't speak."

"Did they reveal anything about their operation?"

Ruderick replied, returning the gun to Robideaux's chest, this time pushing him back towards the gurney and away from Bernchal and Allwood.

"Nothing. Just that they plan on coming here and taking back their kids."

"How do you know that?"

"I'm trained to know that."

"What else do you know?"

"That your best bet is to return those kids and get the hell outta dodge."

Robideaux and Allwood exchanged a strange look that Ruderick missed, but Bernchal caught. He cocked his head to the side, stared at Robideaux and asked, "Tell me, what did you hope to accomplish with this program? What could you possibly stand to benefit from kidnapping kids?"

"It wasn't kidnapping. This program serves a purpose."

"Which one is that? You want soldiers, then you recruit soldiers. Draft them. What's the point of stealing kids from their fucking moms?"

"Thank you for the tip, soldier," he responded quietly and turned his attention to Allwood to speak.

Bernchal continued, interjecting before Robideaux could talk.

"This whole asinine operation has got to be the biggest mistake in the history of this country."

"Thank you, soldier."

"I mean seriously, pack your shit up, all these fucking computers and stat books and fucking reports and make a run for it before they get here."

"Thank you!" he yelled, a crack in his steel exterior finally appearing.

Bernchal tried again to reason with them.

"They'll be here in a matter of hours."

Allwood looked to Robideaux and asked, "Is that enough time?"

"We wont be able to properly dispose of the bodies, but we can-"

Bernchal's heartbeat quickened and he asked, "What bodies?"

"-burn and shred the records-"

"What bodies?"

"-and leave before anyone gets here."

"What bodies!"

Robideaux looked up from his concentrated conversation and replied coolly. "We're tying up loose ends."

His own shell suddenly coming undone, Bernchal pushed his weapon into Allwood's face and yelled at Robideaux, asking "The kids? The fucking kids? You're going to kill the kids?"

"Sir-"

"They are children!"

"They are liabilities. They are a strategic move, a means to an end."

The coldness in his voice was terrifying and Ruderick responded, "What end? Slaughter?"

"Officers, you've overstayed your welcome-"

"It's Commander," he corrected. "Leave the kids. Leave them and just go."

"No!" he screamed at them, spittle flying from his mouth as he looked back and forth between Bernchal and Ruderick and shook his head like a petulant child. "I will not compromise this program for anyone! Least of all a group of angry women on a mission." Behind him, the little girl scurried down from the steel table and crawled under it.

Bernchal chuckled and shook his head. "You are so fucking clueless. You have no idea what's in store for you."

"What do we have to be afraid of?"

"Her. Are you really that naive?"

"All we've done-"

"No," he interrupted, putting his free hand up to silence Robideaux. "Let me tell you what you've done, doctor. You took a woman with absolutely no fear and no regard for caution and you gave her purpose. You gift-wrapped a set of mercenary skills and handed them to her on a silver platter. And if that wasn't enough, you then took away the one thing that mattered and dangled it in front of her, basically daring her to get it back. What you did was create a fucking machine and now you have the audacity to stand back and wonder how to stop her? Give her back her son and you stand a fighting chance of survival. But if you kill this kid, those kids, she's coming for you. I guaran-godamn-tee it."

"With what army?"

Ruderick bellowed loudly and asked mockingly, "And what army do you have? Huh? Teenage boys toting guns they can't even lift? Don't let the tits fool you. This chick's got bigger balls than I've seen on any man I ever served with and she's not gonna stop till she has yours in her fucking grip. If I were you I'd reevaluate my position. Yesterday."

"I'll take that under advisement, sir."

"You do that."

Robideaux turned to face Allwood and with a hint of willful and deliberate disobedience, calmly stated, "Kill them."

Bernchal turned the gun to Robideaux's face and pulled the trigger. Robideaux's head snapped back and with the force of the shot, he slammed against the gurney, bouncing off of it as his body slumped to the floor.

Allwood started shaking and stared at the lifeless corpse with his mouth frozen in an "O" of surprise. Bernchal returned the gun to his head and re-clicked the safety for dramatic effect.

"Where are they?"

Allwood froze and Bernchal asked again. "Tell me where the fucking kids are."

He began to stutter and Bernchal took a step closer to him.

"Does it look like I'm playing around? Ruderick, ask his friend here if I'm playing around."

Ruderick dropped to one knee and put his ear up to the dead doctor's lips. After a second of pretending to listen intently, he lifted his head and replied, "The good doctor has confirmed that you are, in fact, not playing around."

Bernchal cocked his head and stared at Allwood until he finally relented and came clean.

"They're in the medical school. All of them."

Bernchal reached out at grabbed Allwood by the lapels of his labcoat.

"You're coming with us."

Chapter XLVIII

Bernchal pulled Allwood to him and swiveled to leave the lab. Behind him, the little girl cowered under a large steel table and watched them, large eyes following their every move. He had forgotten she was even in the room and instantly regretted shooting Robideaux in front of her.

Whistling to Ruderick, he pointed to the girl and Ruderick followed his eyes until he saw her there. Walking gingerly to her, he squatted in front of the table and whispered to her.

"Hey, sweetie. You okay?"

She nodded hesitantly and peered around, leerily.

"Okay. Do you know where the other children are?"

She shook her head and held back more tears.

"Okay. Me and my buddy are going to go find them. Can you stay here until we come back for you? We won't let anyone else hurt you."

She was obviously scared to be left alone and pulled her knees close to her chest, hugging them tightly. Bravely, she nodded her head again anyway.

"Okay," he said, smiling widely. For an intimidating man, he was certainly a teddybear with a child. "We will come back for you. I promise." He reached out and gave her a small squeeze on her forearm. "I promise."

Rising, he indicated for Bernchal to follow him and with Allwood firmly in his grip, he did so.

They made their way out of the lab and back in the direction from which they entered, Bernchal holding his Argentina .38 special and Ruderick with his AR15. As they walked, Ruderick's earpiece came to life, Torres' voice coming through and filling the empty and expansive hallway.

"You've got visitors…"

Ruderick eyed Bernchal and responded low into his mic.

"Redirect, soldier. Where am I headed?"

In the distance, Bernchal heard the faint crackle of gunfire.

"Leavey Student Center, one click west. Martinez and his men have a stronghold on the radio station."

Bernchal breathed a sigh of relief. *Music to my ears*, he thought, grateful to have some more manpower waiting for them.

Ruderick shifted in a wide fork in the main building, heading west under Torres' advisement. Low to the ground, they crouched along the expensive tile flooring, their boots hardly making a sound, while Allwood's shuffling was almost as loud as his wheezing. The gunshots outside grew in volume and intensity and Ruderick brought his mic close to his mouth, ordering "When it clears, send Muccio in to extract a little girl in the Science Lab," before signing off.

Silently they pushed forward a little less than three-quarters of a mile before arriving in a large, modern facility. The wide room opened up and outward so that each level above was visible from below like the courtyard of a hotel. On the bottom level where they stood, large circular couches were spread out, all surrounding a large projection television built into the center wall that was now covered in dust and spider webs. Small tables were haphazardly strewn throughout the expansive room and several textbooks and laptops were still propped up on upright tables, indicating that when the school evacuated, it did so without warning.

Huvane and Hiu indicated their arrival and the four of them stepped gingerly further into the center. Before they split and were reassessing their ammunition, they had taken five minutes to set explosive throughout the university's main campus. Though a shame to destroy such an architectural marvel, they were all in agreement that any location contributing to child torture had to go. So they ran throughout the building, from the lab to the student center, and using the property survey, set the timers. Drilling holes in the walls and planting a small wire to a portable battery, Huvane rigged it to explode approximately thirty seconds after detonation.

Bernchal caught the sight of movement in his peripheral vision and immediately trained his weapon to the left of the student center entrance, towards an enclosed alcove to the left. Under a large sign indicating "Student Radio Station," Martinez walked through an open doorway and faced him and Ruderick.

His dark eyes scanned each of them flippantly and without a word, he turned his back to them and walked back inside the separated alcove. Bernchal and Ruderick glanced at each other, confused.

According to Ruderick, Martinez had flipped out when he had discovered the death of his wife and children upon his stateside return. Going rogue, he had left the team when they had escaped the prisoner camp and headed for D.C. in the hopes of getting to the bottom of the coupe that had flipped their nation upside down. Their last indication that he was alive had come two months prior when Williams had given Ruderick his whereabouts and even then, Martinez had known nothing of his men. He had not known if they were alive or how many of them were left and now seeing them, he made no indication that he even cared.

Though Bernchal did not expect a tearful reception or ticker-tape parade, he did believe that a fucking handshake would have sufficed.

Ruderick shrugged and followed Martinez. Behind him, Allwood said nothing and obediently complied when Bernchal gave him in a shove towards the station. At the entrance door, Ruderick leaned back and whispered over his shoulder to Bernchal, "Is it just me, or does this motherfucker have a screw loose?"

Without waiting for his confirmation, Ruderick stepped through the doorway and into what appeared to be a command center. Various control panels and electric gages adorned the interior of the room, with microphones and speakers propped in each corner. Martinez hovered over one workstation with an exorbitant amount of buttons as another man sat in a swiveling desk chair beside him, fiddling with the controls. A third man quietly lingered in another corner, watching them as they entered. He was not military, but was dressed in camouflage and holding an AK-47 in his hands.

Bernchal shoved Allwood inside and fingered his own weapon cautiously. Ruderick looked around and addressed Martinez, who continued to ignore their presence.

"Hey, Martinez- what the fuck are you doing in here?"

He did not look up from the control panel and spoke to him from the side of his mouth, as though he were addressing Ruderick in secret. His brown eyes continued to stare at the other man's hands while he worked, pressing buttons and turning knobs. He was enthralled and his voice came out as though mentally, he were a million miles away.

"We're radioing instructions."

Behind them, Hiu and Huvane appeared, their weapons drawn but not aimed. They nodded to Ruderick and Bernchal and stood in the background, squaring off against the solitary man in the corner.

"That shit don't work," Hiu commented, laughing.

Quietly, Martinez replied, "Everything works if you know how to use it. "

He had an uneasy calm to him, an almost eerie serenity in his gait. He was avoiding eye contact and speaking much softer than the usual manner they had grown accustomed to in Africa. Back then, he had been loud, boisterous and confident, the polar opposite of what stood before them.

Martinez continued to disregard all of them and pointed to a screen that suddenly lit up with a point that flickered in the center. Huvane clamored for a closer look and asked, "How the fuck is this lit up? There hasn't been any goddamn electricity in ages."

Martinez ignored him and addressed the man in the seat. "That's the drop off."

Bernchal strained to stare at the screen and noticed the numbers highlighted in the quadrant to which Martinez had pointed. He leaned over and whispered to Allwood, "What are the coordinates of the university's medical school?"

"How the hell should I-"

He was cut off by jab to his ribs by the butt of Huvane's M16 assault rifle. He doubled over in pain and groaned as he hit the ground.

"You want another one?"

Allwood straightened and reluctantly replied, "38.9118° North, 77.0751° West."

Bernchal stiffened.

The numbers matched. The safe house. The lab. They all lined up.

He looked to Ruderick who immediately took notice.

"Martinez, what are those coordinates for?"

"A strike."

Allwood chortled, despite his moaning. "It's pointless. The place is streaming with our soldiers."

Huvane offered another hit to his ribcage, this time sending him to the ground heaving. He bent over at the waist and hissed into his ear.

"Those pieces of shit on your payroll aren't soldiers, you dick."

Bernchal moved close to Martinez, his eyes on the man in the corner still gripping his rifle.

Ruderick continued to stare at Martinez, questioning him.

"What kind of strike, brother?"

Martinez remained silent and continued to stare at the screen.

Bernchal interjected, impatiently. "We found the kids that were kidnapped by the President. Let's just go get them."

Ruderick silenced him with a glare.

"Martinez, I asked you what kind of strike you got planned."

Finally, he made eye contact. A dead, soulless stare met Ruderick evenly and answered with measured detachment.

"We're blowing it up."

Calmly, Ruderick replied. "There are survivors there. Kids. "

"They're dead."

Bernchal's heart dropped and he swiftly wondered, for a fleeting second, if this what was Shane felt each and every time she was given different and contradicting news about her son. It had to be the same, but certainly much, much worse.

He grabbed Allwood by the collar of his shirt and picked him up roughly.

"Is it true?" he demanded.

Martinez watched, silent.

"Is it true!?"

Allwood shook when Bernchal's voice boomed through the small studio.

"No!" he yelled frantically, shaking his head back and forth. "No, it's not true. They're still alive. Walter never gave the order. They're still alive…"

When Bernchal released him and he tried to fix his shirt, Hiu kicked him hard in the back and silenced him again.

Ruderick turned again to Martinez and tried to reason with him.

"You heard him. They're alive."

"How do you know that's true?" he asked, and like a light switch being turned on, his eyes were suddenly wild.

"Because we know. We can save them."

"Why?" he screamed uncontrollably. His fists clenched at his sides and he pounded on his thighs with each syllable. "Who saved my kids? Huh? Who saved them?"

Ruderick put his hands up and took a step closer to him.

"Lee, I'm sorry about your kids. I am. But we have a chance here to save dozens of others. They're just kids, man. This is supposed to be a war amongst men; they shouldn't have to suffer. We can save them. Wouldn't you have wanted us to do the same for your kids?"

"But no one did!" he shouted. Allwood remained frozen to the ground and the rest of them just watched the agony in his eyes helplessly. His voice was full of torment. Tears rushed out of him and spittle flew from his mouth as he screamed.

"No one saved them! They're dead!"

"Martinez-"

He moved abruptly to the radio, suddenly calm. His voice was controlled and purposeful again.

"I'm making the call…"

Bernchal suddenly picked up his firearm and cocked it, aiming at Martinez from less than five feet away.

"I can't let you do that."

Martinez' men, who up to that point were fiddling with the radio or watching the exchange disinterestedly, suddenly came to life and quickly held up their own weapons, both aimed at Bernchal. Huvane and Hiu responded accordingly and trained their own weapons on each of Martinez's men.

Ruderick, the only soldier unarmed, pointed out the obvious.

"This isn't what we should be doing, but I gotta tell you- you pulled the losing hand in this scenario, Lee. Now, I'm not trying to lose a man here, any of them. So get your boys to drop it."

Martinez locked eyes with Bernchal and studied his reserve. After a drawn out staring contest, he motioned for his two guys to drop their guns, which they did. Hiu and Huvane remained at the ready and Bernchal's gun never moved from its target.

Martinez turned to Ruderick and calm again, said, "We need to take that militia out."

"And we will. After we get the kids out."

"I got a whole crew in place ready to blow that place sky high," he added, his eyes dancing maniacally. He took a quick step towards the radio receiver and put his hand over the walkie talkie on the desk. Bernchal responded by taking a step closer to him.

Ruderick put a hand on Bernchal's chest, stopping him.

"I know you do, brother. But give us a chance to get those kids out."

Martinez locked eyes with Ruderick and a darkness spread across his face.

"For what?"

Ruderick blinked and nonchalantly brought his hand to his own holster, fingering his gun. His voice measured, he looked at Martinez and hoped there was still something left to reach inside of him.

"You kill those kids and you're just as bad as the men that killed yours."

Martinez lingered over the walkie talkie, seemingly considering Ruderick's words with his back now to everyone. They all waited with bated breath until finally, he spoke, his voice devoid of all humanity.

"Then I guess I'll be meeting them in hell."

He picked up the walkie talkie, clicked it on and started to shout his commands when a shot fired. The deafening boom filled the room and Martinez's men flinched. Allwood shrieked when the blood from Martinez' forehead splattered all over the window facing the student center.

Bernchal lowered his gun just as Martinez' lifeless body slumped forward onto the radio transmitter. His hand let go of the walkie talkie and it crashed on the floor.

Ruderick released the breath he'd been holding and looked from Martinez' corpse to Bernchal, who remained stoic as he re-holstered his weapon.

Chapter XLIX

It turned out Martinez' men weren't as loyal as they seemed. Upon his untimely death, they split, leaving the rest of them to clean up the mess and continue onward to find the children. A few minutes later, the gunfire happening outside the school breached its walls and their sanctuary was no more.

Stepping over Martinez' corpse, Ruderick called Bernchal, Hiu and Huvane to attention as he communicated with Torres using the school's radio system. Ruderick wiped some of Martinez' blood off the mic and brought it to his lips.

"What's your ten?"

Crackling could be heard above the shots fired in the background, and Torres' choppy voice came through the speaker system in the room.

"Get outta there! We got militia coming in from the west and several unidentified vehicles in front. They're all convening at-"

The transmission was cut off and Ruderick called out into the mic, hoping to get it back. After several seconds, the speakers roared alive again and Torres' shaky voice came through.

"We have lost visual, I repeat- we have lost visual! We are under heavy fire-"

Ruderick locked eyes with Bernchal who gave him a nod indicating his consent.

"Abandon post. Do you copy, soldier? That is an order- abandon your post!"

After receiving no reply and only listening to a static transmission after several seconds, he dropped the mic to his side and addressed the rest of the men.

"We're on our own, boys. We got no eyes so we're going in hot."

Hiu nodded his agreement and Huvane let out a loud yell.

"That's why they say the only easy day was yesterday, right, Cap?"

Weapons locked and loaded, they proceeded to exit the radio station, Ruderick first in line, followed by Hiu, with Allwood between him and Bernchal and Huvane holding up the rear.

The gunfire erupted immediately, with several shots landing in the wall right behind them as the control panels inside the station were decimated with bullets and set off a series of tiny explosions. Allwood screamed and tried to hide behind Bernchal, gripping his biceps and using him as a human shield. Shoving him off, Bernchal aimed at the entrance to the student center where it appeared the shots were coming from, and opened fire.

The other men followed suit and two militia soldiers ran right into their bullets, their bodies immediately riddled. They dropped to the floor and the shots at them ceased.

"We're sitting ducks," whispered Hiu, breathlessly. "We have to find cover."

More gunfire sounded from the same entrance to the student center. With nowhere to go but the radio station, Bernchal and the men hunkered down and opted to use the overturned tables and couches inside the large room as cover. They each scrambled and planted themselves behind the first object they could find to conceal themselves. Though they were severely outnumbered, if they could at least control the room, they stood a chance.

Bernchal dragged Allwood with him, determined to keep him alive until the kids were located. There was no way he would lose the one connection he had to those kids. He hauled him by the collar of his labcoat to a large metallic coffee table and with one hand, lifted it off of one set of legs and turned it over, squatting behind it. He pulled Allwood down with him and silenced his sobbing with a hard nudge. For a man capable of torturing women and children, he seemed comically adverse to warfare.

The sound of gunfire started again, this time significantly closer to the entrance of the student center and the men steered themselves against their positions and waited, weapons ready. A militia soldier appeared around the corner of the entrance but stopped before he was fully inside and pivoted to look behind him. Gunshots popped off in quick succession- *pop, pop-* and the soldier's body bounced as they hit his chest. He dropped to the floor a second later.

Behind him, two more militia soldiers ran in and in his peripheral, Bernchal caught sight of Ruderick behind a large leather couch, holding his hand out to him and the other men, indicating for them to wait it out. The militia stopped just in front of the loveseat behind which Huvane hid and looked around, their weapons out. One of the men searched franticly for a place to hide and resigning, swiveled to face their assailant who entered as his arm rose to fire.

"What the fuck..."

Hiu whispered under his breath and the rest of the men hiding followed his eyes to the large doorway of the student center just as Shane entered the room, her arm outstretched and her weapon ready. The militia soldier took too long to react before realizing that the woman who had arrived was the one killing all of his friends. He lifted his gun to shoot but what he didn't anticipate was that Shane would be quicker than him and before he could aim his weapon, hers was already firing, making two neat holes in his chest. He slumped over and she rushed to catch him, using him as a shield as she pushed forward towards the other shooter behind him.

Caught off guard by his buddy's demise, the second shooter collected himself and fired every round he had, but they all landed in his partner's back, absorbing the impact as Shane closed the distance between them. At point blank range, she shot him once in the face and undaunted, pushed the body off of her and looked around.

The shooter's body dropped to the floor, his head lolling over and facing Huvane's direction. The dead man's eyes stared straight ahead and Huvane broke contact to look up at Shane, his own face frozen in an expression of shock.

Behind Shane, Julie, Sharee and Milagros entered the student center and looked around. Ruderick began to rise from his position, as did Bernchal and Hiu and the women all faced them, amused. It seemed that as the men set out alone and in secret in order to protect the women, it was the women who had shown up and saved the men.

Bernchal pulled Allwood to his feet and brushed himself off. He smiled tentatively at Shane and she pointed her chin in his direction.

"What are you doing here?"

He responded slowly, scratching his chin. "I'm here to rescue you."

She released a short laugh and eyed him, amused. "And how's that going for you?"

He replied, embarrassed, "Not too well, actually."

Shane nodded, hiding her smile, and looked around the room.

If he had suspected that their relationship, or whatever it was, had been damaged because of their earlier exchange, the relief in her eyes upon finding him alive and well was enough of an indicator that it had not been. Shane rarely displayed any affection for him and despite their previous moments of intensity including that morning's kiss, she normally played it close to the vest when it came to her feelings. But when their eyes met and they saw each other again, he knew she was happy to see him and all was forgiven.

They would eventually talk about the words they had spoken earlier, but not right now.

She looked back towards him after assessing the damage around the room and addressed them all.

"We saw Torres and Muccio outside. They've moved to the back to clear our way out. You guys ready to go?"

Because he did not like the idea of being rescued, and because he could think of nothing better than to piss off the very woman that had rescued him, Ruderick scoffed. Loudly. Shane snapped her neck to the left to get a good look and he shook his head, a patronizing expression on his face. She glared at him, her eyes immediately freezing into dark pools of pure hostility the moment they met his stoic blue ones.

"You need more time hiding?"

Ruderick took a step forward, his mouth agape to respond and noticing it, Bernchal interjected.

"Ruderick found the kids. They're here, Shane."

Slowly, she turned her head back to face him. As the information registered, her eyes darted back and forth between them, her face contorting in an expression of both shock and optimism. She locked on Bernchal's and beseeched him for the truth, her voice pained and wary.

"Really?"

He nodded, dumbstruck. He'd seen her make a million faces; most mad, some kind, a few- and by far his favorite- loving. But this was a look he had not yet seen.

It was hope.

"You were right. They're here. He's been tracking them this whole time," he said excitedly, motioning to Ruderick with the hook of his thumb.

She looked at Ruderick, who only stared back at her, expressionless.

Bernchal continued, plowing forward in the hopes of creating some good will between them. "He didn't want to tell everyone. He... We were afraid of sabotage. "

Ruderick kept his eyes on Shane and interrupted Bernchal.

"I was concerned about your women. I didn't trust them. So I didn't tell you. And I didn't tell him, either. It was my call."

Shane nodded and replied tightly, "You know where my son is?"

He nodded his head. "How the hell did you get here? What happened to Arlington?"

She replied, her tone even and unfeeling, but the twinkle in her eye gave away her amusement.

"I told you before, Captain. You are a guest in *my* house. No secrets..."

Ruderick licked his lips and nodded slowly, trying to hide the smile forming on his lips.

"Touché," he answered back and broke eye contact, slightly admonished.

All business again, Shane turned to Bernchal and asked, "Where is my son?"

"He's in the Medical School building."

"Where?"

Ruderick chimed in, his tone authoritative once again.

"It's not that precise, sweetheart. I got us the location. Now we just have to kill everybody here and get the kids."

Bernchal asked, "Where's everybody?"

"Yeah," threw in Huvane, his voice doing little to disguise the sarcasm written all over his face. "Where's the rest of your army?"

Deadpan, Shane replied, "Killing everybody here."

With a final glare, she turned and walked back in the direction of the entrance, with Julie, Sharee and Milagros following. Bernchal shot Ruderick a look and immediately made a break for the doorway, pulling Allwood with him to catch up. Hiu started after them and Huvane reluctantly did the same. Ruderick shook his head and finally smiling, fell into line behind them.

They turned the corner and finally catching up to Shane, Bernchal and Ruderick walked alongside her and fired their questions. Julie, Milagros and Sharee walked a few yards ahead of them, weapons out.

"What's it look like outside?"

"They were on their way in when we got here," she replied as they moved forward. With the perimeter secure, they stood upright and walked confidently down the hallway. "Muccio and Torres were pinned but they got out and reloaded with us. They repositioned themselves and gave us cover to come in and clear the inside."

"And don't worry, we got the little girl you saved in the lab."

Trying and failing to conceal the smile playing on his lips, Ruderick looked away from her and nodded his head.

She stopped walking and turned to face Ruderick, who stopped short when she suddenly appeared in his face. Taking advantage, she questioned him.

"Why didn't you tell me?"

He hesitated for a moment, as though he considered lying about his reasons. Deciding, he quickly brushed it off and answered candidly.

"So you crazy bitches could have followed? Hell no. We needed to get in here and evaluate before we had some emotional chicks getting their hopes up."

Not offended, she only stared at him, eyes boring into his as she processed his words.

"So you've been looking for the kids this whole time?"

Ruderick looked taken aback by the question. "What do you think I am, a monster? I was raised by a single mom. First moment I met you, warrior princess, I knew you were no joke. I knew you'd never stop 'till that kid was found. You gotta respect that."

It was Shane's turn to hide the smile on her face and she raised her eyebrows, surprised by his candor. She turned away from him and started walking again, mocking him over her shoulder, "So rough, tough Ruderick has a soft spot…"

Hiu and Huvane let out a laugh and Ruderick silenced them immediately with an icy glare. He turned back towards Shane and called after her, still searching for an answer to their arrival.

"It was that laptop, wasn't it? It had the coordinates," he guessed, irrationally agitated that he had not been able to figure it out without Williams' help from the outside.

Shane smirked and raised one eyebrow but continued facing forward, responding as she walked.

"Arlington was a decoy. We were always headed to D.C. The minute Julie figured it out, we were always headed here. We just needed to be sure nothing would get in the way."

He nodded, realizing, quite embarrassingly, that he was the 'nothing' that had been in the way.

Though satisfied with the answer, he found himself simultaneously irritated that she was right. Instead of joining their crusade like Bernchal had, he and his men had tried to take over the mission from the beginning and she had resisted every step of the way. They could all see the bigger picture, but he had been too stubborn and egotistical to see it and though he had thought himself a true hero for searching at all, to do it he had stepped on the very people that needed the search in the first place.

Ironically, after all of the conflicts and secrecy, they had all ended up in the same place anyway.

As they neared the corner of the corridor, Shane turned to Bernchal on her left and asked, "So, where are we headed?"

Bernchal poked an elbow at Allwood, who until that moment was following them blindly. He objected loudly and shrunk away towards Hiu, who only shoved him back towards Bernchal. Getting the point, he answered meekly, "The building is less than a mile from here, on Reservoir Road."

"Who's this?" asked Shane, pointing to him with her chin.

Huvane nudged the doctor forward with the tip of his rifle and called out, "This is one of the geniuses who orchestrated this whole thing."

Shane stopped suddenly at the corner and turned to face them. Her entire demeanor changed. In a split second, she went from a woman on a mission to a woman out to kill.

Pouncing like a cat, she immediately went for his throat, lifting him off the ground and slamming him against the wall of the hallway in one movement. His body thrashed against the concrete wall and he cried out, landing on the hard, linoleum floor with a hard thud. Without a word, she unleashed on him, kicking him in the ribs repeatedly. Julie rushed over to the altercation as the rest of the men had unconsciously already formed a circle around her, watching helplessly. Bernchal finally realized what was happening and reached for her, dragging her away as she continued to stomp at Allwood, at one point narrowly missing his head.

Ruderick reached down and picked Allwood up, tossing him roughly back against the wall and holding him there with one large, beefy hand as he coughed and gathered himself.

"What the fuck, Shane?" asked Bernchal, still holding her as she struggled against him.

Before she could respond, a crash at the other end of the hallway pulled their attention away.

One of the militia soldiers blindly entered the corridor, his gun drawn and aimed at the first face he saw, which happened to be Ruderick's. Shane, closest to the corner and currently fired up and ready to rip off anyone's head, jabbed at the soldier's wrist and he dropped his weapon just as the shot fired, the bullet whizzing down the hall inches from Ruderick's head.

Ruderick aimed his gun to fire, but Shane stepped into his line of sight. She caught the soldier on the chin with a right hook that sent him crashing into the concrete wall and when he ricocheted back towards her, delivered an upper cut that brought him off his feet. Another soldier appeared behind his buddy and she turned, giving him her back and jutting her bent arm forward, catching him in the nose with her elbow. He dropped to the ground holding his nose, the blood gushing between his fingers. Once he landed, Shane withdrew her weapon from her waistline and fired two shots, one at each man. Their bodies jumped when the bullets hit and satisfied, she turned back towards Bernchal and Ruderick as she put the gun back in the waistband of her pants casually.

"Holy shit, Steve," whispered Ruderick, dumbfounded. "No wonder you're in love. This chick is sexy as hell."

Addressing her directly, he asked, "Did they teach you karate in these fucking camps, too?"

Shane ignored him and made her way to Allwood, who was hunched over next to Ruderick and holding his aching side. She grabbed him by the collar of his shirt and lifted him to his feet as he stuttered in protest.

"Where are the kids?" she growled at him, shoving him against the concrete wall again.

"I don't know what you're-"

Bernchal poked him hard in the chest with the end of his gun and advised, "Think long and hard about your answer. You saw what she did to your two goons there."

Allwood swallowed and looked to Shane, who was standing a few inches from him, her body rigid and ready to attack.

"Those kids are an integral part of this operation," he answered her, unconvincingly.

"Those kids were not yours to take," she replied through gritted teeth, her voice dangerously low.

"You cannot understand the importance of this operation. You cannot begin to fathom-"

"You destroyed this fucking country," she said incredulously, interrupting his speech and staring at him as though he were insane. "You destroyed the world for us, for me. You took my son and countless other kids, and for what? To prove a point? To flip the script, change things up? What the fuck was the purpose; what were you hoping to achieve?"

"We tried to fix this world!" he hissed at her, suddenly animated. Moments before, with a gun against his head, he looked ready to denounce their project and abandon ship; and now berated by a woman in search of her child, he seemed to come to life with a renewed sense of confidence in his work.

"We did the hard part! Who would have done the unthinkable to get the job done? You, Commander?" he asked, pointing to Bernchal. He turned his attention back to Shane. "You- a woman?" he spat at her, his eyes wild with self-importance. "No, *we* did it. We designed a world where everyone could be equal."

"No one is equal!" screamed Shane. "Women are enslaved and tortured, men are killed and children are kidnapped. How is that equal?"

Allwood backed up at her outburst. Indignant, he cleared his throat and answered, "The plan is not without its faults. But it is designed to weed out the inferior so that the surviving population can make this country a super power again. This is just the beginning; this program is only the beginning. There is so much more to come..."

Bernchal eyed him. When it had been he and Ruderick threatening him, Allwood had been a mess, a puddle of blubbering nonsense. But with a woman leading the interrogation, it looked like Allwood had suddenly found his balls and it only further confirmed that the men behind the current fiasco had not one ounce of respect for a single woman.

"You're fucking sick," she replied, shaking her head. Slowly, she removed her gun from her waistband and fingered the trigger.

"We saved this world!" He trained his eyes on Shane a took a step towards her, his voice patronizing. "You seem to have forgotten one very important detail- you are alive because I *made* you. *I* trained you and *I* taught you how to survive. You wouldn't be here without someone like me to have done the groundwork. And now you turn on us, question the very hand that feeds you?" he asked, his finger pointed uncomfortably close to Shane's face. "You will pay for each and every wanton act of anarchy-"

Bernchal placed a large hand on Allwood's narrow chest and shoved him back against the wall, hard.

"Watch yourself..." he warned, his voice dangerously low.

Shane stepped close to Allwood, ignoring Bernchal and gripping her handgun so tight, the whites of her knuckles were visible.

"Is my son alive?"

"When all is said and done, I will be known as a pioneer-"

"Is my son alive?"

"Your son is a pivotal part of this revolution and-"

"Is...my...son...alive?"

He might have finally noticed the tone of her voice or seen the blackness in her eyes. He might have finally paid attention to the tension in her body or the grip she had on her gun. In any case, Allwood shut his lips tight and suddenly went pale. Shane brought her face so close to his that their noses almost touched. His cowardly blue eyes were transfixed on hers and he gulped, loudly, anticipating her next move.

"Is my son alive?" she repeated as she brought the gun up and leveled it at Allwood's temple, pressing it against his skin as he shuddered.

"It's too dangerous-"

"The most dangerous place in the world for you, at this moment, is between me and my son."

"Listen to reason-"

Shane took a step back and with the barrel of her gun still pressed against the side of Allwood's head, wordlessly pulled the trigger.

She barely waited to see his body drop. Silently, she stepped over him and turned the corner, continuing down the corridor towards the back exit of the school's main campus, wiping the splatter of Allwood's blood off her as she walked.

Ruderick looked to Bernchal, who only offered a small shake of his head before following Shane and the other women out of the room. After exchanging glances, Ruderick whistled and looked down at Allwood's body one last time before motioning for Hiu and Huvane to follow him down the corridor.

"Holy shit… that chick is crazy as hell."

Chapter L

It took less than thirteen minutes to reach the medical school and they walked it in silence. The entrance of the three-story facility was nothing more than two sliding glass doors which no longer operated on electricity, so Hiu pried them open and forced the doors to slide on the track to let them in. There was no alarm system or militia policing the perimeter or the entrance, and they waltzed right in. Muccio and Torres were still holding down the exterior and the remaining women from the institution were providing cover for them, so the militia that had attempted to protect the school's main building had not yet moved towards the medical facility. They hoped this allowed them enough time to find the kids and get everyone out.

The lobby was pristine, as could be expected from a medical facility. Various rooms, all with their doors wide open, ran alongside the walls around them, leading to a large staircase above a set of elevators. A smaller door, to the left of the elevator bank, indicated a separate stairwell and they split up to investigate.

Huvane, Hiu, Julie, Betzaida and Sharee went up the large staircase slowly, weapons drawn, followed by Carina and four of the women, who would split to search the third level. Shane, Bernchal and Ruderick turned to the second stairwell and made their way down.

They moved in absolute silence, only their footsteps and breathing heard in the darkness. Gone were the pops of gunfire in the distance and the sounds of movement within the city limits of the former nation's capital. It was chillingly quiet as they maneuvered through the halls of the Georgetown University School of Medicine.

For the women marching in the pack, it was a moment of truth, the time to ante up. Now was the time that they would prove their worth, to their children and themselves.

For Shane, it was nerve wracking. She tried to maintain her composure as they had walked, spread out in military V formation across Reservoir Road, but she was having a hard time. Though she had been certain, absolutely, unequivocally, without a doubt certain that her son was alive, the panic inside of her was quickly rising up and if she did not release it soon, she felt as though she would burst, from the tension, the fear and the horror of what could possibly lay ahead.

Bernchal looked at Shane as they walked slowly down the staircase. Her face was pale, all color drained as she walked gingerly next to him, her eyes darting back and forth among the shadows. She held a gun with her arms outstretched in front of her, not her usual revolver, but instead a Glock 19.

Her hands were shaking.

Above them, muffled by the concert separating floors, gunfire sounded. Ruderick's earpiece crackled, Hiu's voice coming through.

"We got militia on top two floors. Some broke through and are headed down. Watch your six."

They wordlessly scrambled down the stairwell until there was no further path and ran into a door leading into a basement of sorts. As they walked through the doorway, the little brightness remaining from the sunlight peeking through crevices and door cracks upstairs suddenly disappeared and left them in complete darkness.

Gunshots sounded from the end of what seemed like a hallway and the three of them dropped to the ground suddenly. Shane felt Bernchal push against her, covering her with his body and shoving her into a corner. Beneath her, she felt a soft lump and tried to find its source.

Lights popped at the end of the hall and the gunshots continued. She felt pressure against her right hand and realized Bernchal was holding it down, keeping her from firing her weapon in the direction of the lights. Because guns emit a spark when fired, their shooters were visible in the darkness each time they took a shot, and so would they be if they fired as well.

So they had to wait.

Shane's free hand stumbled along the floor, feeling the softness next to her feet. There was a smell in the air, within the mustiness of underground and the smoke and residue from the gunshots. It was heavy, dense and overpowered everything around her. She recognized it, remembered it from a tucked away corner of her memory bank and the tiny hairs on the back of her neck stood. Her left hand stopped trying when it felt string and she followed it until the combination of scent and stimulation made sense.

A forehead, nose. A mouth.

Tiny, so tiny.

Her hands moved over them and started shaking, shaking more than they already had been. She wanted to reach for her flashlight and shine it on the floor but she could not reveal their location. She wanted to jump up and run down the hall, screaming her son's name; but she could not.

So she sat very still and waited until the gunfire slowed and finally, feeling Bernchal push her a little harder against the corner, he lifted his hand off of her weapon.

She had eight bullets; Bernchal only had four and no extra magazines to reload. But Ruderick had his trusty MP5K and he opened fire, sweeping back and forth across the floor as the bullets rained down on the other end of the hallway. He stopped to listen and heard the tell-tale sound of bodies dropping to the floor. *Thud. Thud. Thud.*

Ruderick and Bernchal communicated via morse code on their hands and set up a final shot. Crouching low, they moved three feet over, pulling Shane with them, who was all too happy to escape the corpse that she had been up against since their arrival. In the other corner of the hallway, Bernchal aimed his flashlight and counting off, shined it towards the other end as Ruderick aimed his weapon and with his finger light against the trigger, waited. They peered down the hall using the light and made out three bodies slumped on the ground in the shadows.

Satisfied they were now alone, Bernchal pocketed the flashlight and returned them to darkness. He reached for Shane and pulled her to a standing position and turned to make his way down the hallway. She stood still, stopping him in his tracks and tugging at his hand to return to the corner.

"What is it?" he whispered, his tone much more paternal and patient than usual. Shane knew he was handling her with kid gloves because they were so close to finding the children, or something altogether different, and normally she would have called him out on it. But at that moment, she was more concerned with her find than with his behavior.

"Come here," she insisted as she pulled on his hand and lowered herself to a squat until he too, was hunched over beside her. He hovered over her right shoulder, close to her skin, and she felt his breath against her face.

She was aware, but did not mind. She was uncharacteristically grateful for the closeness.

"Touch," she directed, as she led his hand to the figure on the floor and guided him. When realization hit him, Bernchal snatched his hand away, his breath caught in his throat.

He fumbled for the flashlight and taking a deep breath, snapped it on, shining the light on the ground at their feet.

The body was about 3 feet long, still a baby by most standards. Emaciated, frail and dirty, his eyes were closed, his face at peace. Stringy, blonde hair was matted to his head and hung in long wisps up to his neck. He was undressed save for little dingy, white socks on his tiny feet.

Bernchal did not know Silas, but he remembered the picture Shane had clutched that day in the locker room, the same picture she now treasured in the silly frame he had given her. This little boy with the stringy blonde hair, bless his soul, was not Silas and for that, he was regrettably thankful.

Shane's eyes were wide and haunted in the glare of the flashlight, and Bernchal turned the light away from the little boy and pulled her to stand. She complied, stood and fell into line behind them as he and Ruderick started for the other end of the hallway.

She tried not to look back as the light from Bernchal's flashlight guided them forward and drifted away from the little boy, but after a few steps, she couldn't help it, and she turned her head as Bernchal led her. The little light that remained shone down the hallway and away from the body of the little boy, somebody's little boy; and Shane wiped away a small tear that fell as she faced forward again and followed Bernchal and Ruderick.

They reached the end of the corridor and stepped over the bodies of the soldiers. Blood oozed onto the cement beneath their feet and for the most part, was soaked up in the cracks and nooks of the floor. But where it pooled, they avoided and walked over the bodies to turn the corner.

Streams of light poured out from under one of the doors that was closed and barely illuminated the next corridor into which they stepped. It was a sickly yellow glare highlighting the floor up and down the hallway and when their eyes adjusted to the combination of light and dark, they could make out small piles across the floor in front of them.

Small piles, just like the little pile from which they had turned away.

Suddenly, Shane took off running down the hallway. Ruderick, knowing what was in store ahead, tried to reach for her to pull her back but she broke free and, stumbling around in the dark, searched frantically. Feeling around, her hands working clumsily, she touched the bodies of small children and flipping them over, searched their faces for recognition.

She knew her son's face, knew the face of every child for which she had been searching for the past four years. She knew every single detail, down to the very last freckle, the very last missing tooth, the very last smile. She knew those children inside out, and more importantly, she remembered everything about her own son. The way he smiled, the way he wrinkled his nose when he was upset, everything she had held on to desperately for four years.

So as she searched the bodies of children laid out on the concrete floor, thrown like garbage, tossed aside as though their little lives had not been relevant, significant or crucial to the people that at one point in time had loved them with everything they had, she searched for her son.

The walls were piled with their bodies. Around them, debris filled the empty space and they tripped and crawled, looking. Bernchal tried to keep up with Shane as she haphazardly turned over the bodies of some children, with each one that was not her son, releasing a short breath of relief and immediately, refueling the panic inside of her to find him.

Ruderick radioed Hiu, demanding, "Can you spare somebody? Anybody? We need help to search!"

The children, the dead children no longer deemed useful by the sick fanatics that had ripped them from the arms of their mothers, were tossed out like yesterday's garbage, and left to rot in the stench of a dungeon.

All around them the ground was littered with tiny, broken bodies. Bernchal held back the bile that threatened to escape and forced himself to be strong for Shane should one of the bodies beneath them turn out to be her son.

Franticly searching and still unsuccessful, Shane looked back at Ruderick who was lingering over a small brown-haired boy. She lunged towards him, falling and pushing off of Bernchal, who tried to hold her back. Screaming, "Let me see!" she fought against him until he released her before she could pull them both to the ground. Crawling over bits of broken wood and loose paper, she turned over the body at Ruderick's feet and cried out, "It's not him!" Bernchal reached for her, lifting her to her feet and holding her as she began to sob.

Forcing the moment to pass, she controlled herself again and pushed off of him, moving forward and still gripping his hand. Behind them, Ruderick bent over and gently closed the eyes of one of the kids as they passed. He looked up at Shane, shell-shocked. He had never seen her so wild with emotion, so raw. She had always maintained her composure in front of them; even moments of anger and rage had been carefully kept in check. This was something else entirely; something so natural, it was nothing short of heart-wrenchingly pure.

They climbed over debris and began to shout Silas' name and the names of the other kids that had been taken. Finally, they made it to a door with a tiny sliver of light peeking out from the bottom. Most of the door was completely covered with either bodies of children or garbage strewn about. Shane stopped in front of the door and called quietly, "Silas?" her voice small and losing its power.

Ruderick and Bernchal began to dig the door out so it could open, using their hands and bloodying themselves moving wood, dirt and bodies.

They cleared a path to pry open the door and when the knob would not turn in his hand, Bernchal kicked at it with his boot-clad feet over and over again until it broke and snapped off. Reaching into the hole left behind, he finagled his fingers in and pulled at the door, prying it open.

The light was coming from a small gas lamp in the corner of the room. There was nothing around it, nothing to sit or sleep on. Nothing but more dirt and garbage on the floor. The stench was unbelievable. Their eyes watered immediately from the rank odor that immediately escaped once the door had been opened. They looked inside, their eyes searching, wandering around the room, until they saw it.

In the center, a small group of children were gathered together. Shoulder to shoulder they sat, obediently waiting for instruction, completely silent. Though their ages ranged from toddlers to teenagers, there was not sound among them. Bernchal and Ruderick searched their faces, looking for any sign of movement.

Shane, the last one in the room, pushed Bernchal and Ruderick out of the way when she entered and gasped.

She saw him immediately. He was a little older, no longer baby-faced but still so much a baby. His brown eyes were no longer wide in wonder and excitement, but instead were small and weary, darting around suspiciously. He was not smiling, as she had always tried so hard to remember him, and he blended into the crowd of other undressed children, sitting cross-legged on the dirty floor.

Shane cried out, said his name in a tortured wail that rose from somewhere deep within her throat and sounded like it came from another person. She cried out for him and he immediately turned to face her.

He remembered his name.

He remembered what his name was and when he heard it, he turned to her and when he saw her face, he remembered his mother; her touch, her feel, her scent, her face.

She could not move from where she stood, and she began to cry. The tears did not wait to be released; they flooded over her eyes and poured down her cheeks as she watched him. He rose from the ground and without breaking eye contact, moved to her. He was small for his age, lack of nutrition and unbelievably horrible circumstances had kept him small and he was still the size of a four-year old boy. But he was strong, and he walked assuredly to her, stepping over the other children who could only watch in amazement.

Shane kept standing, stayed on her feet, until the moment he stepped into her embrace. Then her knees buckled and she fell to the ground, pulling him with her. For the first time in over four years, she felt his touch and she could not breath.

She didn't think he'd really recognize her, or want her. She'd feared he had forgotten every inch of her. The way she would rock him when he sat on her lap. Her voice when she'd sing to him at night, or the soft kisses she would leave on his face. She'd feared he had forgotten every inch of her. But when he lifted his head and met her eyes, when realization and hope had collided and the mother he had cried for every night was finally, mercifully standing in front of him and he'd risen and walked into her extended arms, every doubt erased.

She pulled him to her and snuggled her face into his hair, kissing him through tears that burned as they fell. Sobbing, she squeezed so hard she thought she might hurt him, but she wouldn't, couldn't let go.

Bernchal could only watch the exchange mesmerized. He wiped his eyes before the tears could fall and began to follow Ruderick's command as he moved past him and addressed the remaining kids, ushering them to stand and follow them out, while Shane and her son sat on the floor, embracing.

Chapter LI

It took a bit of gentle coaxing to mobilize the children. The older ones recognized that they were being helped and immediately complied with Ruderick's instructions. But the younger ones, those who had only known this environment and had become indoctrinated with their captors' mindset, were afraid to move. They believed, as one little girl was brave enough to voice, that they would be punished if they tried to leave.

After some sweet-talking, a little hand-holding and a lot of bribing, they were able to motivate the smaller children to follow in the footsteps of the older kids and do as they were told.

All in all, Ruderick and Bernchal stepped out of the feces and urine infested room with twenty-seven children, of all ages, sizes and races. Shane stepped out carrying her son, cradling him in her arms and determined, at least for some time, to never let go. She recognized in the group several faces belonging to kids for whom she had searched far and wide and she was both excited and nervous to begin the trek back home and reunite them with their loved ones.

They tried to keep the younger kids from peeking as they balanced and maneuvered down the hallway littered with bodies of children just like them. Most of the older ones snuck a glance and were not the least bit perturbed; something which saddened Shane and terrified Bernchal. To imagine what those kids had seen, witnessed and endured during their time held captive was something which he was not prepared to examine.

They got all of the children past the bodies of the soldiers and to the end of the corridor from whence they came and Ruderick radioed upstairs again, requesting clearance to hit the staircase and bring them all out of the building. After several minutes of radio silence, finally a crackle of noise followed by static, and the clear and concise words of "Did you find them?"

Ruderick brought the mic to his mouth to speak and was interrupted by pops coming from above them. The radio screeched and picked up on the sounds upstairs- gunfire and panic.

Ruderick looked to Bernchal and licked his lips in concentration. They were stuck downstairs in a basement with thirty kids and dozens of dead bodies festering in the dark. They had about ten or so bullets between them and nowhere to hide should they encounter militia.

Patting a dark-haired girl on the head, Bernchal nudged her to the corner of the hallway and stepped around her to talk with Ruderick out of earshot.

"We're pinned here. No info, no eyes. No ammo."

Bernchal nodded, well aware of the dire situation.

"And that's not even the bad news…"

"Wood," he commented, his eyes on the kids around them.

"We gotta get out of here, Steve. We got twenty-something kids to get home."

Bernchal looked to Shane, leaning against the wall behind her, still cradling her son. She watched their exchange with interest, her dark eyes visible under the glow of Bernchal's flashlight. He quickly broke eye contact and dropped his gaze to the floor, not wanting her to read the anxiety in his stare.

Careful to keep his lips tights and unable to be read, he mumbled, "We have to get to higher ground. Can the guys clear a path?"

Ruderick tried the radio again to no avail. It was dead silence both on the other end of the line and in the hallway. The children waited obediently, all squished together in the black corridor as they tried to contact their people upstairs for some assistance.

The gunshots started again, this time closer to them. Bernchal shut off his flashlight and they immediately looked to the stairwell and listened, waiting for indication the militia had arrived. They steeled themselves in front of the children, trying to bunch them together and push them back towards the soldier's bodies on the other end as they waited, their own weapons ready.

The door to the stairwell burst open and Julie poked her head inside the hallway, illuminated by the sunlight streaking in from upstairs.

"Shane?"

Bernchal did one better than just calling out to her. He snapped on his flashlight, shining it on the children that stood behind he and Ruderick waiting. Julie's eyes landed on each kid and immediately welled up as she nodded her head, approvingly. She saw Shane holding her son and a few tears brimmed over and ran down her cheek, highlighting the large smile on her pretty face.

Regaining her composure, she whispered, "Let's get out of here."

Bernchal ushered the kids forward, his hand landing on the small of Shane's back as he nudged everyone towards Julie. Ruderick held up the rear, gun still drawn. With a final glance down the dark hallway at the bodies of the soldiers, they got the last of them through the stairwell door and proceeded up the stairs to the exit.

The rest of their people waiting upstairs parted like the Red Sea when they walked through the stairwell door- Sharee and Hiu to one side, Huvane and Cecilia, one of the women from the institution, to the other side. They stared at the children with eyes as wide as saucers until Ruderick shot them a reproachful look. None of the children belonged to any of them, so there were no tears or sobs. They simply watched them come out of the stairwell, one by one, their tiny feet and filthy bodies following the child in front of them, doing as they were instructed to do. It was both beautiful and haunting.

Bernchal guided the children forward and spotted the chaos outside first; he was facing east, towards the front entrance and its sliding glass doors, and he saw the crossfire being exchanged. He saw the vehicle that drove up to the entrance and right through the glass, shattering it into a million pieces and scaring the children. He saw the two soldiers leaning out of the truck windows, their rifles pointed at them and their fingers positioned over their respective triggers. And he saw Betzaida and Milagros, their arms extended as they fired off round after round at the truck that just kept coming.

Ruderick and Bernchal immediately tried to shield the kids and scatter them. Bernchal took a bullet to his shoulder, the very same shoulder that had not yet healed. Wounded, he dropped to the floor behind the couch in the lobby. Sharee dove behind the information desk and safe under the protection of the metal block, started firing at the soldiers, shooting through the windshield and immediately killing the driver, who slumped over on top of the steering wheel.

The jeep stopped half way through the entrance, its back wheels lifted slightly above the trackline of the sliding doors and still spinning uselessly while the front burned rubber on the linoleum floor, but did not move. The two remaining soldiers inside immediately vacated the vehicle and took cover behinds its large doors and continued to fire at them.

One child caught a bullet in his neck and went down, his eyes still open as he fell. Shane ran behind one of the pillars holding up the winding staircase leading to the second story and shielded Silas and another small girl with her body. The older kids dropped to the floor, pulling as many younger ones down with them as they could. Huvane got several children back behind the cover of the staircase before he was hit in the back several times. He dropped to one knee and continued pushing kids behind the stairs as they pulled at his hands, trying to drag him to safety. He took three more bullets in his torso before finally succumbing at the feet of the kids he saved.

Ruderick watched the melee as he popped off four shots from his assault rifle, none of which made any real dent. The soldiers were still alive, still behind the doors of their vehicle, sweeping the floor of the facility with their bullets and mowing down all of his people. And worst yet. he had only two bullets left and knew Bernchal only had about three remaining in his chamber. With no other recourse, he took a deep breath and psyched himself up to run forward to draw their fire so that Bernchal could get a shot in. The maneuver did not need to be discussed beforehand; he had fought alongside Bernchal in Africa and the States when they had returned, and he knew exactly how his mind worked. Bernchal would take the kill shots the second they released their hold.

Clutching his rifle, he pushed off the back of the couch behind which he had taken cover and darted for the bay windows on the left of the lobby overlooking the reception area. Just as he had anticipated, he drew their fire and as soon as they set their sights on him, Bernchal took aim and fired two rounds, one at each soldier. Though they were behind the front doors of the jeep, his accuracy was dead-on. Both soldiers died instantly, dropping their weapons and sliding to the floor, neat holes in their foreheads spilling blood that pooled beneath them and spread across the linoleum under the jeep's tires.

Ruderick ran into the bay window and stopped just short of breaking through it, the force of the run having had propelled him forward. He felt the stabs at his side, three short and quick taps along his ribcage. Shaking it off, he stood and surveyed the damage. Through the bay windows he could see scattered bodies outside on the grassy knolls of the facility grounds; mainly militia, though he recognized a few as women from the institution.

He groaned as he lifted his arm, waving for Bernchal to take the children out. Shane peeled herself off the wall and pulled her son by his hand, grabbing another little boy and running towards the vehicle blocking the entrance. Bernchal passed him as he pushed several kids forward, no longer gentle nudges but instead frantic shoves to get them through the doors and onto the bus waiting outside.

Ruderick limped as the last of the children filed out and when he was alone inside, he put his hand against his left side and looked down, the blood immediately covering his fingers. Suddenly physically spent, he felt the final bit of strength he had left seep out of him as his knees buckled. Trying to stay upright, he wavered a bit, hobbled on one foot and finally gave up, dropping to the linoleum.

He closed his eyes for a moment and felt a sudden and unfamiliar rush of peace, but was quickly interrupted by Bernchal, who came back inside searching for him. When he spotted him on the floor, he called to him.

"Let's go."

Ruderick took a deep breath, as painful as it was, and shook his head.

"Can't."

Bernchal prodded impatiently. "Stop being a pussy," he urged, though he knew deep down something was not right. Unprepared to deal with it, he pushed. "Get up."

"I can't."

"What do you mean you can't?"

"Steve... I'm done."

He eyed him and in denial, shook his head.

"Let's go."

"I'm dying," he said, dead-pan. He closed his eyes and grimaced.

Bernchal scoffed, asking, "How the fuck would you know that?"

"I just saw my mom."

"So?"

"She's been dead for fifteen years." He peeled open his eyes and after searching, landed them Bernchal, the color quickly draining from his face. "I'm dying, brother."

Shaking his head, Bernchal shrugged his shoulders dismissively, wincing at the pain from his wound. "What the fuck am I supposed to do with that?"

"Leave," he ordered, barely conjuring enough strength to lift his right hand and point towards the exit. "Save the kids. Save the chick. Get the fuck out of here."

"And you?"

"Me?"

He laughed and it quickly turned into a wet and strained cough, blood leaking with each exhale and splattering on his chest as he looked down. Ignoring it, he said, "I'm gonna sit right here and wait for these slant-eyed fuckers. I got a nice little grenade ready for them."

Bernchal hesitated, his stare locked on Ruderick and the way his blue eyes were dimming rapidly.

Shane appeared at the doorway behind them, her hand clutching her son's as he waited on the other side of the glass trackline, out of sight. Bernchal did not notice her presence, but Ruderick could see her out of his peripheral view, and he spoke up, despite the energy involved in doing so.

Addressing them both, he asked, "You know what's funny?"

Bernchal did not respond and he continued, undeterred. "I laughed at this scheme. You know that? Thought them all crazy fucking bitches, nut cases, for doing all of this. For trying to get these kids back. Fucked up shit is, my momma would've done the exact same thing for me. I should've known better... we all should've known better."

Nodding, Bernchal offered, "You do now."

"Yeah... Listen to me. Take these and get out," he insisted, pushing his rifle and two grenades he dug out of his pocket towards Bernchal and groaning in pain in the process.

"Get these kids outta here. Muccio and Torres are watching the perimeter; they got the bus, they'll get you out, get you somewhere safe. Let this place fill out with those bastards. Let them all pour in. I'll take it from there."

Bernchal reluctantly picked up Ruderick's trusty MP5K and fingered the grenades cautiously.

"I don't wanna leave you here."

Ruderick answered dryly, "You don't have a choice."

"Wood-"

"It's a fucking order, Commander. Get out of here..."

Bernchal took a step back but hesitated. Shane stepped into the lobby and reached for him, putting a hand on his forearm. He barely noticed her there and she eyed Ruderick, a look of questioning on her face.

More solemn, Ruderick addressed her and answered her unasked question.

"I'm good..."

"You sound like me," she said, offering a sympathetic smile.

Ruderick turned to Bernchal again and in his usual authoritative voice, said, "We got a plan. Stick to it. "

Bernchal clenched his jaw, hardly aware that Shane's hand still lingered on his left forearm, gently tugging at his sleeve and pulling him out. He did not feel the droplets of blood that spilled down his arm from the gunshot in his shoulder.

Ruderick used the last bit of strength inside of him to wave Bernchal off and loudly commanded, "Go! Now!"

Shane pulled Bernchal towards the doorway and he struggled a little. But Ruderick screamed again, waving his hand in the air.

"Go!"

Finally, Bernchal turned and followed Shane and Silas through the trackline enclosing the doorway and didn't look behind him.

With them gone, Ruderick checked around him, making sure he was still alone. With his right hand, he dragged himself over a few feet behind the large couch and towards the stairwell, where Huvane's body lay. He reached for the backpack he'd been carrying and grimaced as he placed it on the floor and opened it. Carefully, he removed a handful of explosives and the wire connection to the detonator, opening the handle and gripping it. He tried to extend his other hand and quizzically, noticed that he could not even lift it.

He crawled backwards and leaned back against the staircase and coughed again, blood spurting on his pants. He wiped his mouth and looked up, noticing from his vantage point that the could see clear through the bay windows. With a smile growing on his weathered face, he witnessed Bernchal and Shane leading the kids out, down the grass in front of the facility.

He allowed himself to lean back and close his eyes and he could feel, quite astonishingly, the life leaving him. He thought of all he had done in his life, his thirty odd years of service to his country, the friendships he had formed and brotherhoods he had fostered. He thought of the wife he had never married and the children he had never had; the relationships he had destroyed and the people he had killed in combat; the father he never knew and the mother he would now see again.

He smiled softly to himself and opened his eyes, his mother's face blurring in and out of focus, dancing in the fading sunlight in front of him.

"Now," he said aloud, addressing her. "Down to business, momma. I'll be seeing you in a second or two. Just do me a favor and check with the Big Guy for me; make sure its cool. 'Cause I'm about to tear the shit off some North Koreans…"

He fingered the detonator and waited.

Outside, the children ran down the grass of the facility's property line and towards the city bus idling on Reservoir Road. They ran despite the absence of shoes on their feet and followed the waving hands of the women edging them on.

Some of the women, ignoring the urgency of the speedy exit they were trying to make, spotted kids of their own, or ones they recognized in the bunch and broke through the crowd, picking up young kids, or grabbing at a teenager and pulling them into an embrace. Winded, stunned and still very much in fear, the children looked like a herd of zombies, their eyes wide in shock and their bodies simply following the directions being barked at them from all sides.

Bernchal, Shane, Silas and Julie held up the rear of the group, with about two dozen or so women in front of them helping the kids towards the bus. Shane looked in front of her, her hand gripping her son's with no intention of letting go, and realized humbly that though they were successful in retrieving many children, they had lost a large number of friends, including Huvane and Ruderick; and as she ran towards their way out, she realized that finding the children was only the beginning and they would now have to figure out a way past the substantial hit they had now taken against them.

The gunshots started out of nowhere and no one had their weapons ready. Bernchal ducked a bullet that missed him by inches and stumbled, catching himself quickly and with renewed energy, pushed harder, urging everyone to run faster. He pulled a walkie out of his pocket and shouted into it as he ran, "Fire at will! Fire at will! Fire at will!"

Another bullet whizzed by Shane, inches from her face, and hit the ground in front of her, exploding a chunk of dirt and grass from the floor. She lost her footing and went down, tumbling into an avalanche of grass and feet with a teenage boy running in front of her. She let go of Silas' hand immediately to keep from bringing him down, too, and tried to stop the fall, but the hilly grounds gave them momentum and they rolled down and to the right of their intended path. Finally stopping, Shane shot up and tried to help the teenage boy to his feet. He wobbled a bit and she grabbed at him under his arms, trying to get him up and running again.

To her left, Bernchal looked to make sure she was okay and groaning in pain, picked up Silas, taking off for the bus. She waved him forward, signaling for him to go on with her son and she lifted the teenager up, holding him until he could focus. With the clarity returning to his eyes as he shook the fall off, she started again for the bus, pulling him with her.

As they cleared the bottom of the hill, Shane saw tufts of grass all around them exploding. She looked up to see militia bearing down on them from the opposite direction, about six or seven soldiers shooting at them.

She was behind everyone, still dragging the teenage boy with her, and was several yards from the bus. But Bernchal was almost to it and she watched, hopeful, as he cleared the property line of the facility and hit the sidewalk, running full speed with Silas in his arms.

Twenty feet from their escape vehicle, a militia soldier stepped out from behind the bus and took aim at Bernchal and Silas, turning his weapon towards them. Unable to retrieve his own firearm as he held on to the little boy, Bernchal came to a stop, immediately shifting his weight and turning around. He dropped to one knee, held Silas in his arms and completely shielding him with his body, closed his eyes and steered himself against the onslaught of bullets that was coming.

Shane watched as she ran full speed towards them, horrified. Her gun was drawn but she was not yet close enough to take the shot. She ran, her shins feeling like they would split open, her feet pounding the grass as she left the teenage boy behind her and forced her body forward as fast as she could. Finger on the trigger, she neared the soldier and aimed.

Suddenly more shots sounded and the soldier with his gun aimed at Bernchal and her son dropped to the ground, his body shaking with each bullet that landed. She looked up and followed the source of gunfire and could vaguely make out the images of

Torres and Muccio perched on top of a fire truck at the end of Reservoir Road, several yards away.

As she closed the distance between them, Bernchal opened his eyes and looked around, surprised to still be alive. He turned his head and saw the soldier on the ground and watched as more of them were taken out, the bullets flying faster now. As he gathered Silas back in his arms and stood, the last of the militia fell and the remaining children ran to the bus and piled in.

He turned back just as Shane ran up, reaching for her son and taking Silas from him. Her eyes met his and she stared for a second before turning and following the rest of the crowd, tears streaming down her face.

Bernchal watched her climb into the bus and then signaled towards Muccio and Torres, motioning for them to abandon their posts just as a militia truck climbed the property grounds towards the facility. It bounced up and down over the hills and came to stop just in front of the entrance, several soldiers climbing out and with their weapons drawn, pouring into the school.

He climbed into the bus and whistled for Hiu to peel out, sending them to the fire truck to pick up Torres and Muccio. They climbed in and he stayed standing and held on to the pole behind the driver's seat as the door to the bus slid shut and it began to move east.

Still too stunned to speak, Bernchal looked back at the facility through the large, dingy windows of the bus as they cleared Reservoir Road. When the bus made a sharp left turn and began to make its way down towards Capitol Hill, the once imposing edifice suddenly exploded.

Chapter LII

The wrought iron gates opened and the bus drove onto the grounds of the institution almost four hours later. Private First Class Worthington and his men had done as promised and kept their escape route clear, leading them home without incident, but they had had to draw out their travel, despite the urgency to get home, to avoid tails. By the time they arrived and the gates shut behind them, the remaining women at the school were waiting and immediately encircled the bus, eager to see who was stepping off.

It was a bittersweet homecoming. While Silas and twenty-six other kids had made it back, the loss they had encountered was immeasurable. Between Huvane, Ruderick, and the nineteen women that had died back in the facility, it was devastating.

The kids disembarked the bus slowly, prodded on by the women who had pulled them to safety and guided towards their loved ones. It quickly became a madhouse and Shane had to force several women into the main building's lobby to reunite them with their kids, or deliver the painful news that their child had not yet been found.

In a scene reminiscent of families searching for their lost loved ones after 9/11, Shane held her son and walked through the room, trying her best to match up child with mother, or motherless child with childless woman. The wails were unbearable as some women saw the children brought home and scanned their faces, looking for their own until realization set in and the hope to be reunited with their own baby was snatched away.

Some of the kids with no family wandered aimlessly, most still too traumatized to even speak. The older kids that found their mothers remembered them immediately, but the smaller children could not be swayed and they cried against the stranger holding them, unaware it was the very mother they had prayed to every night since separation.

Bernchal watched the chaos, taking it all in, his heart broken. Among all of that, his friend, his mentor had been lost and he could not bring himself to help the mothers that screamed, falling on their knees and sobbing uncontrollably for their dead or still missing children. Some of them grabbed at the surviving children, shaking them by the shoulders and begging for information about their kids.

It was absolutely heartwrenching.

He snuck away, head down and his left hand clutching the wound in his shoulder, making his way towards the dean's office. At the door, a little girl, about nine or ten, tugged at his jacket and he looked down, recognizing her as one of the only kids who had spoken to them upon their arrival in the basement.

She smiled up at him, her dirt-covered cheeks resembling a filthy cherub. Bernchal smiled back at her, his eyes misting up as she held his gaze. Behind her, Julie walked over to them and put her hands on the little girl's shoulders, addressing him.

"This is Layla. She's Mariana's daughter."

Bernchal's eyes locked with Julie's and he felt like he'd been punched in the chest. Mariana's daughter had made it home, but her mother would not be here to greet her.

Wordlessly, Layla slipped her hand into his and grabbed it tightly, and Bernchal, surprised, squeezed back as best he could, even though the gesture shot a surge of pain down his right arm. Julie took Layla's other hand and together, they moved away from the dean's office and towards the large staircase leading up to the women's dormitory.

Shane watched them walk away and she held Silas to her, the tearful reunions unfolding all around her. After several minutes, she tore herself away and carrying her son, made her way up the stairs towards her own dorm room.

All around her women clutched children, theirs or not, and cried. Sharee, who had found her own child after they had cleared the mall several months ago, tried to bring order to the school and Shane gratefully left her to it, wanting to revel in finally reuniting with her son.

Upstairs, she walked into her room and leaving the door wide open, disregarding the cries of joy or despair filling the walls of the institution, she sat on the edge of her bed with her son on her lap and stared at him.

She rocked him, gently, and caressed his stringy brown curls. She brought her face to his head and even through the stench of sweat, filth, dirt and excrement, even through the years of neglect and torture surrounding him, she breathed in and smelled him; that distinctive scent that she had first smelled when he had been handed to her at the hospital upon his birth, and she had smelled every night for the first four and half years of his life. That specific 'Silas' smell that she had dreamt of, that she had cried for, that she had fought and bled and stayed alive for over the past four years.

She sat there, humming to him, feeling his hands tighten around her, feeling his body loosen and relax against her, and the tears streaming down her cheeks as she accepted that she had finally found her son.

Bernchal left Julie and Layla in the women's dormitory, down the hall from Shane, and turned to leave. As an afterthought, he walked to her room and snuck a peek at her as she put Silas to bed.

She lay him down and he protested a little so she quieted him, lovingly caressing his hair until he calmed and immediately drifted off to sleep. She sat on the edge of the bed and watched him, one hand on his tiny, scrawny back.

Bernchal watched her as she stared at her sleeping son, her head down and the tears falling like tiny droplets on the bed beneath her. Suddenly, as though she could feel his presence looming behind her, Shane looked up and saw him watching at the door. Awkwardly, he offered a crooked smile and turned away quickly, immediately making his way down the hall.

He was almost at the end of the corridor when he felt Shane grab his arm. With the commotion in the institution, he hadn't heard her approaching and when he turned, he met her tear-stained face.

He watched her silently and with no warning, she threw her arms around him in a tight grasp, her hands gripping his back as quiet sobs moved through her. His eyes watered and he returned the embrace, holding her tighter against him despite the increasing burning sensation in his shoulder.

They remained entwined for over a minute, each desperate to cling to the other for a longer time, until she finally let go and turned to walk back to her room, holding his hand as she walked away and reluctantly, letting go.

Chapter LIV

Bernchal did not see Shane for eighteen days.

Eighteen excruciating, torturous days.

He missed her. He yearned to be around her, to joke and banter. He wanted to see her smile, that mane of uncontrollably long, chestnut colored curls; those black lashes and even blacker eyes. He wanted to talk to her about what had happened, about the people they had lost and what was to come. He wanted to see Silas, talk to him, get to know him. He wanted so much to just be around them.

He missed his friend.

He kept to himself and to occupy his time, nursed his wound and worked around the institution. There was still so much to do, so many children still missing. And though Shane had had her happy reunion, so many women were still praying, hoping for theirs, and Bernchal could not leave them to fend for themselves. So he implemented stricter guidelines for coming and going, set up more condensed runs so that they did not require as many and redesigned the security scheme with Julie so that the women and newly-found children inside could feel more secure.

On the nineteenth day, Shane came to see him.

She left Silas in the cafeteria with Sharee, Betzaida and some of the other women and children, and walked casually across the quad when she had been told he was outside helping Hiu and Muccio put up some barbwire atop their perimeter fence.

Silas was able to be apart from her in increments now. On the first night, there had been no sleep for either of them. The nightmares were brutal; he would sit suddenly straight up in bed, his eyes wide with terror, and let out a blood-curdling scream until he could be calmed within her tight embrace. Up and down the hallways of the institution, the walls bounced around the same sound, from room to room in the dormitory with rescued children reliving their recent past every time they closed their eyes. But now, he was trusting more, recognized Julie and Sharee and some of the other women. So she took the opportunity, as he played with some of the other kids, to find Bernchal once more.

He was up on a ladder, holding the end of the razor sharp wire so Muccio could arrange it over and around the metal spikes at the top of their wrought iron gate, when he saw her walking towards him. In the fading sunlight, with her hair casually loose and cascading over her shoulders, she was a stunning sight, and he froze.

When she neared, she looked up at him, one eye squinted to keep out the sun, and smiled.

"Hey."

"Hey," he replied, climbing down and leaving the wire hanging for Muccio to finish alone. At the bottom rung, he winced when his shoulder brushed up against the ladder.

"How're are you healing?" she asked, concerned and motioning to his wound with her chin.

"This?" he feigned, pointing to his bandage. "I'm good. Nothing on it."

She nodded and looked up and down the fence, watching Muccio work a few yards away. "I haven't had a chance to talk to you after…"

"Well," he interrupted politely. "You've had your hands full. How are the kids?"

"Okay. Or at least getting there."

"Silas?"

She looked back to him and held his gaze. "He's…he's okay," she answered unconvincingly. "Adjusting, I guess."

He cocked his head to the side and watched her, knowing instinctively she wanted to say more. "You guess?"

Surprisingly candid, she responded.

"I don't know. He hasn't spoken. At all."

"Well, give him some time. I mean, look at what he went through. I'm sure he's just processing. Guys are like that. We internalize and compartmentalize. It's how we cope."

She listened, her dark eyes wide. With a reassuring smile, he added, "He just needs a little bit of time to just break it all down. I'm sure he'll come around."

She shrugged and looked away again. "I don't know."

"You're concerned?"

She opened her mouth to speak, hesitated, and then shrugged again.

"You're probably right. But… he was kidnapped. Alone for four years. All that time, he's gotta be asking why I didn't come for him. Right?"

She glanced back at him after her question and searched his eyes for an answer.

He read the panic in her face, the absolute uncertainty and doubt.

"Shane, you organized a rebellion, took down a tyrant's army and basically Ramboed the shit out of the bad guys. All to save your son. To save all of those kids. Nobody thinks there was anything more you could have done. Nobody but you."

She relaxed a little and offered a shy smile.

"Look, kids are resilient as hell. Definitely more than you or I could ever be. He'll be okay. Trust me."

She held his stare again and the smile disappeared.

"I'm so sorry about your friends. About Ruderick."

He nodded, his turn to break eye contact and stare at the ground. "Thanks. But he went out a hero. They all did."

"All of you," she added. "What you sacrificed to help us…" She swallowed back her tears and continued, softly. "We can never repay you."

"I don't want-"

"I know," she interrupted. "But, I'm… I'm trying to say thank you. For getting my son back. For everything…"

"Oh…"

He cleared his throat stiffly, proving once and for all that all of his arrogance and conceit had always been a mask for a humble interior.

"No thanks are necessary."

An awkward silence passed between them, something cavernous and wide and which had never occurred before. She was uncomfortable, though that was nothing new; but this time, so was he.

"I want you to know that I was always on the mission with you."

She eyed him, confused and he finally conjured the strength to elaborate.

"Your son. The kids. Even though I left with Ruderick, I was always on your mission and-"

"I know that."

"-and I just need you to know that."

"I know that," she repeated, her voice barely a whisper.

He nodded, averting her eyes. "When we left that day…"

His voice trailed off and he was unable to continue as too many memories and emotions and regrets immediately resurfaced. It was suddenly too real for him and Bernchal struggled to express himself.

Shane lingered for a moment and then as though she had summoned up some courage, took a step towards him and reached for his hand. The gesture surprised him considering their track record in the physicality department. He allowed his hand to be held and he watched her curiously.

She took another step, this one bringing her close enough to embrace him, and elevating herself onto to her tip-toes, brought her face close to his. She placed a gentle kiss on his left cheek, her soft skin brushing against his. With her lips on his face, she whispered, "Thank you," and released him, turning at once and walking back in the direction from which she'd come.

Bernchal remained standing against the ladder, watching her retreat and the way she moved until Muccio whistled loudly. Brushing it off, he turned towards the ladder and climbed back up, grunting in pain as he lifted the wire and tried his best to keep his mind on the task at hand.

Shane went back to the cafeteria to retrieve Silas and spent the next few hours wrapped in her son's arms. They lay on the bed and embraced as she talked to him softly, regaling him with stories of him when he was little and the world had once been normal and whole. He still did not speak, but every so often his brown eyes would light up over something she mentioned, or his face would spread into a wide smile, revealing his missing and spoiled teeth.

He drifted off to sleep in the early evening and leaving him under Sharee's care, she took the opportunity to check in with Julie. Time back with her son had restricted her from keeping up with her duties around the institution and though grateful for the help, she was somewhat disappointed to find that things had been running smoothly in her absence. Bernchal had kept things going with Julie's help and she mentally checked off yet another item on the list of things she owed him.

After an hour chatting, Shane left Julie's room and walked back to her own. As she reached the doorway, she overheard talking but didn't catch Sharee's voice in the exchange. When she neared, Bernchal's booming voice could be heard mid-conversation in what seemed to be a very animated story.

... So there we were, stuck behind the wall, looking for you kids, and we find you. You guys were super smart to stay in there. Avoid the ruckus outside. I for one hate noises like that. A long time ago, before you were born, soldiers like me had to travel to this other country to fight. It was hot and full of sand, so you ain't missed much. Anyway, at first every single night there was fighting. All those noises every single night. Then it got quiet and calm for a while, almost normal. We relaxed. But the worst part was when it got comfortable, felt like regular life. And then the noises would happen all of a sudden. Some of us would be pretty scared. Was it like that here?

After a pause he continued. *Were you scared?*

She waited and then suddenly, very faintly, heard the beautiful, unmistakable sound of her son's voice. A sound she hadn't heard in over four years. A sound that moved right through her, instantly reaching her heart and stopping her breathing. She wiped the tears that had suddenly sprung forth and closed her eyes, taking it in.

Were you scared?

Bernchal brushed it off.

Well, I am not embarrassed to admit this, but yeah, I was scared. Sometimes I was. It's okay to be scared. Even manly men get scared. But you were pretty brave back there. You know who else is brave?

Smiling, Shane waited for another Captain America reference as she sniffled and was surprised to hear him finish.

Your mom. She was... so brave. She never stopped, even when everything happened and everyone else thought we would never find you, she never stopped. Because all she ever dreamt about was finding you. And I know this because she wouldn't shut up about it either. I know everything about you, my man. I know you like wrestling. You know how? Your mom. She told me. And that you love soccer. And Lionel Messi was your favorite soccer player. I know a lot because your mom talked about you all the time. Even when she missed you a lot, which was every single minute of every single hour of every single day. She would talk about you all the time. Tell me how she used to play soccer with you, and you guys would go swimming and do everything together. And while you were gone, she talked about you, even those times it was really, really hard for her to talk about you because she missed you so much and it made her super sad. She would still talk about you, and pray for you and thought about you every moment. And she never stopped looking for you. Not once. So yeah buddy, she's pretty brave, too. Just like you...

Shane realized, quite embarrassingly, that she was hugging herself and she quickly dropped her arms and looked around the hallway, wiping her eyes. Most of the women were scattered around, enjoying their reunions or planning to find their children, relishing in the pertinent duties of the institution being handled by the remaining men. She was alone in the dormitory and she smiled to herself.

Pushing off of the doorway, Shane took a deep breath and wrapped on the door, pretending to just arrive. Sharee was nowhere to be found and Shane figured she'd asked for Bernchal to cover so she could attend to something inside the institution. He looked up from his position on the floor sitting cross-legged across from Silas, and smiled.

"Capitán. What's up?"

Shane bit her lip to keep from blubbering all over him and instead, smiled back. Unable to conjure up any type of coherent response, she took another deep breath, her shoulders raised as she searched his eyes for some slack.

But he just stared back at her, confused by her behavior. She had often been uncomfortable around him but this was just odd.

Shane quickly gave up the rouse to look composed and walked to them on the tile floor. Reaching for Silas, she held out her hand for him to take it and he did. She yanked him up and said to Bernchal, "We're going for a walk," before pulling Silas behind her and walking through the door, leaving him staring after her, dumbfounded.

As they walked down the corridor towards the staircase leading to the main building, Silas' small voice asked, "Where we going?"

Shane stopped for a second, her heart immediately swan diving into her stomach. There it was again, that sound; that lovely, melodic sound she had missed for so long.

She reached for him, picked him up and held him in her arms, leaving soft kisses all over his face. Though already eight years old, he did not protest and instead, put his head on her shoulder and let her carry him wherever she wanted.

She spotted Sharee in the lobby of the main building and called to her.

"Hey. Thanks for watching Silas before."

Sharee offered a sincere smile and waved off the gratitude. "No problem. I would have stayed but Bernchal forced his way in, as usual."

Shane furrowed her brow and looked at Sharee, unable to conceal the quizzical expression on her face.

"You didn't ask him to fill in for you?"

Sharee shook her head and replied as she made her way up the stairs towards her own waiting child.

"No, it was his idea. He came in to check on you guys, started playing with Silas like the overgrown man-child he is and shooed me away."

Shane nodded but said nothing and watched her walk away, her heart doing a set of ridiculously juvenile somersaults in her stomach. Trying desperately to ignore her own insides, she made her way to the quad.

Silas fell asleep sitting on the cold grass, propped up against her legs as she sat behind him and stared at the stars. Unlike that night she had sat outside with Bernchal and stared at a starless sky, tonight the moon up above lit up everything around her and every star was visible in the sapphire distance. Above the trees waving in the wind, the lights took turns twinkling, each outdoing the last, until it looked like a synchronized light show above her.

In the silence of the night, without the mourning mothers and searching women and distraught children, without the fear of death and danger lurking behind every corner, and without the hopeful, anxious stare of the man that had saved her son and very obviously wanted more from her, Shane contemplated everything that had happened in the past four years. She dissected her marriage and her happy home and accepted that her husband would have wanted her taken care of and with someone who would give their life for her son.

Check.

She pondered a life beyond the walls of the institution, past the runs and scavengering, after the threat of the militia would inevitably subside, and realized that all she really wanted in life, now that she had her son back, was to live her days out beside someone who made her feel truly alive.

Check. Check.

As the animals and insects of the city awoke and began their nightly song, so too did Shane's consciousness as she finally accepted reality. Sharee had unknowingly deciphered the nagging questions weighing on her shoulders, the ones to which she had already known the answers but had been too scared to admit; or too stubborn, or too much of both.

Men like Bernchal were one in a million; they had been before the world went to shit and that generalization was pretty much fact now. And there existed no real reason, whether actual or made up by a fearful heart, as to why she should continue pining away secretly for a man that clearly loved her as she loved him. He owed her nothing and yet had given her everything and more importantly, was still there, hands outstretched, arms waiting.

Chapter LV

Feeling for the first time a contentment in her heart and a fullness swelling within her, Shane scooped her son up and brought him back to their room, placing him in the small bed they were sharing. With a sweet kiss to his head, she shut off the light and leaving the door slightly open, tip-toed down the corridor towards Julie's room.

She knocked twice and barged in without an invitation. Julie looked up from her bed, her strawberry blonde hair falling over her shoulder as she cradled Layla, who was fast asleep in her arms.

Shane mimed her apologies and walked over to Julie's desk, pulling out the chair and sitting in it, eyeing her expectantly. She leaned towards the still open door and keeping an ear out in case Silas stirred, turned to look at Julie with a pitiful expression on her face.

With the roll of her hazel eyes and a patient smile, Julie quietly asked, "What's the problem?"

Shane shook her head and shrugged. "I don't know!" she whispered, exasperated. "I have no idea what the problem is. I feel like I'm... I'm suffocating, but at the same time, I am... overwhelmed with-with happiness. *I have my son back.* Shouldn't this be enough?"

Her eyes watered and she watched Julie, desperate for some clarity. Julie offered a sympathetic smile and replied.

"You cannot base your happiness on whether or not everyone else finds their kids. Just because there's still work to be done doesn't mean you can't live until it's done, Shane. Don't feel guilty for what you have. *You got your son back,*" she added, her voice hopeful and up-lifting.

Wiping the tears, Shane nodded and Julie continued.

"You have to find a way to move on without knowing what the future will bring. Not everything is meant to be planned."

After making sure she had Shane's ear, she dove in.

"How is Steve?"

Shane froze and averted her eyes. She could not reply and simply shrugged her shoulders, failing miserably in her attempt to appear casual.

"Why are you avoiding him?"

"I am not," she replied, petulantly.

"You are. He stands outside with those damn puppy dog eyes watching you walk by without even a smile and he looks devastated. What the hell is going on?"

She hesitated and seeing the level of frankness in Julie's stare, finally came clean as the words spilled out of her.

"He saved Silas."

"I know," replied Julie, confused. "He saved all of us."

"No," she insisted. "I mean he *saved* him. He was holding him and came under fire before he got on the bus. He protected him. Used his body as a shield to protect him."

"*Holy shit...*"

"Exactly!" she exclaimed, then immediately shut her lips tight when Layla stirred. Lowering her voice, she asked, "What the fuck am I supposed to do with that?"

"Thank him."

She glanced at her, annoyed, and Julie continued, firing back against her icy stare.

"Shane, what are you doing here?"

Shane looked taken aback. "What?"

"What are you doing *here*?" she repeated. "Do you even know? Because it seems to me you're waiting for some sort of confirmation. Or not even," she said, head tilting observingly. She pointed at Shane's face and asked, "You want me to talk you out of it, don't you?"

"I have no idea what you're talking about," she replied, her eyes circling the room and avoiding contact.

"Yes, you do. That man is in love with you. Are you in love with him?"

Wringing her hands, she looked down at them and replied in a whisper. "I don't know."

"Don't give me that bullshit."

Shane met her eyes and countered. "It's been years, Julie. Years since any of us had any semblance of a normal life. I don't even remember what that shit feels like. All of that is another life, another time. I don't mind having it, but… I'm not gonna go crazy chasing it."

Julie opened her mouth to reply and Shane cut her off, continuing.

"And I don't really know him. I mean, I do, but I don't *really* know anything about him. What's his history, who his parents are…" Her voice trailed off when her argument ran out of steam.

Julie rolled her eyes again, irritated by Shane's inability to concede. "That's a cop-out and you fucking know it. When you think of your husband, what do you remember? His death? The camps? The running?"

She shook her head slowly. "No."

"It's him, isn't it?" she asked. "The good times and the sex and the laughs and the memories?"

Shane said nothing and Julie continued.

"You remember *exactly* what love feels like. Just because we now have this shitty past doesn't mean you don't get to deserve something good. And all that garbage about not really knowing him? Come on," she whispered, her expression a mix of affectionate cynicism and loving impatience. "You've known him long enough. All of this is just an excuse to avoid the obvious."

Julie glanced down at Layla's peaceful face and tapped a quick kiss on her forehead before laying her gingerly down on the mattress next to her, letting Shane mull over her words. When she was done making the small girl comfortable, she rose from the bed and walked around the small frame, sitting on the edge and facing Shane, knees to knees. Julie met her eyes and Shane began to bite the inside of her cheek, troubled. Julie, knowing all she needed was a swift kick to the ass, shook her head and spoke to her matter-of-factly.

"You are in love with him. I know this because believe me, Shane, you'd be certain if you weren't. So then *what are you doing here?*" she asked exasperatedly, her hands in front of her, palms up, begging Shane to listen to her logic. "I'll stay with Silas."

Shane's features tightened in concentration and she looked towards the door, her body rigid on the chair as though she were trying to keep herself from sprinting to Bernchal's room. Knowing her well, Julie raised an eyebrow and whispered, "What is it?"

Candidly, Shane replied, her hushed voice doing nothing to mask the sound of self-doubt.

"You know what went on in those camps. Outside the camps. I've been… I've been broken, Julie. What if… What if I can't be… whatever the hell it is that I'm supposed to be for him?"

Julie smiled sympathetically. "You are."

"But-"

"It's like riding a bike, girl."

Shane closed her eyes, partially mortified, but mostly grateful. She took a deep breath and peeled them open slowly, knowing Julie was watching her expectantly.

She was.

"Go," she urged, pointing towards the door with her chin and a twinkle in her eye. "He's waiting for you."

Shane pursed her lips and considered Julie's words. She shot her a sweet look of nervousness and with the slightest twinge of hope in her voice, asked, "You think so?"

Julie brushed her off. "Girl, please. That man's been waiting for you since he got here."

Shane said her goodbye and feeling like a giddy teenager, tip-toed back to her room. Silas was fast asleep and she walked over to the bed and snuck a quick peck on his soft cheeks. After almost two weeks back in her arms and at the institution, he was looking better. His cheeks had started to fill out again, thanks to Agnes' constant plowing of soup and vegetables, and the color was back in his face, eliminating the gauntness with which he had returned. Even the night terrors had slowed down both in frequency and intensity.

She started for the hallway before she could talk herself out of it and paused at the door to her room, glancing back at her son and considering her next move. She knew and accepted that deep within her, past the adoration for her son, the love of her late husband and the strength of will it had taken to survive these past five years, she had naively maintained a fleeting hope for a normal life, one that involved the love of someone by her side. What she did not know was if that someone was Bernchal, or if she was simply overwhelmed with a sense of obligation because of all he had done for her. He had saved her son, saved countless of women and children, and had inevitably saved her, realistically and figuratively. But was there more?

Finally accepting and admitting to herself that she had to at least find out, she quietly made her way through the tunnels and into the men's dormitory. At his door, she momentarily had second thoughts when she looked down at herself and realized she was in nothing more than an oversized t-shirt and flip-flops. But she shook it off, muttering to herself, *Go big or go home*. Taking a deep breath, Shane threw caution to the wind and stepped out of the sandals, tapping softly on the door to his room.

Chapter LVI

The knocking startled him and he called out, "Come in."

She gulped and turned the doorknob, opening the door and slipping in silently.

He was standing next to his bed, naked but for jeans that hung against his taut stomach. He looked up at her when she walked in and hardly blinked. The bullet hole in his shoulder was bandaged and the angry bruise on the right side of his face when he had thrown himself against the door to reach the children was all but gone.

The door clicked shut behind her and Shane jumped, spooked. Wordlessly, she stared at him and waited, her back to the door, her bare feet freezing against the icy linoleum.

Bernchal watched her and she could see the surprise on his face. His eyes moved from hers to her body, traveling up and down slowly, lingering on the hem of the shirt that hovered at the apex of her thighs. Her long, brown hair fell wildly around her face, the curls in the front landing against her breasts, hiding them from view through the barely-there fabric.

"Where's Silas?" he asked, his hazel eyes bright against the backdrop of his fading gas lamp and meeting hers again.

"With Julie."

She took a deep breath, pushed off the door and walked towards him. He tensed and watched, unmoving, his eyes following her as she crossed the room.

At his side, Shane hesitated for a second and then reached out, fingering the bandage on his shoulder though her eyes never left his. Her hand traced the square fabric softly and moved across his chest, gently over the tuft of hair in the center, trailing the goosebumps that appeared and moving upward towards his face. She stroked her thumb back and forth against the stubble on his chin.

She'd often wondered what it would be like to feel his skin beneath hers. Not the way they had touched in the past- under medical necessity or during impromptu embraces in times of crisis- but like lovers who would explore every inch of each other without the worry of darkness, death and destruction constantly hovering over them. His skin did not disappoint, and she could feel the heat coming from him, contrasting with the cold floor beneath her.

She shuddered from the chill that spread through her and he reached for her hand and gripped it, hard, moving it from his face. Breaking the silence, his voice carrying with it a haunting deepness she hadn't heard before, he asked gruffly, "Is this gratitude?"

His eyes searched hers and it seemed to Shane that he was looking for more than just a night of passion, confirming what she already knew, had known all along.

Gently, she pulled her hand away and kept her eyes locked on his. Tired of it all, she answered truthfully.

"Maybe a little part. You saved my son," she said, her voice fading into a whisper. "But, more than that, this is me... grabbing a little bit of happiness wherever I can find it. Whether it's real or not-"

"It's been real for me since day one..."

"-even if it's temporary..."

Her voice trailed off as his response overpowered her uncertainty and she froze, waiting and watching his eyes glow in the darkness. Finally, he pulled at her hand again, this time holding it tightly against his bare chest as she slowly advanced towards him, a small smirk growing on his generous mouth.

"Why would it be temporary- you going somewhere?"

Shane smiled and allowed herself to be pulled into his arms. He released her hand and cupped both sides of her face gently with his. Brushing the mess of loose curls from her face, he tucked them behind her ears and caressed her jawline with his thumb. Their eyes locked and the smile on her lips faded as she watched him, all fire and intensity and passion exploding from the yellow in his irises.

Suddenly, the smirk was gone and he moved forward, pushing her back towards the wall until she hit it, hard. Her hands flew up and gripped his biceps as she sucked in a mouthful of air and watched his eyes, waiting.

He pressed his body against hers and stalled long enough to stop her heart from beating. Centimeters away, merely centimeters from her mouth, he lingered seductively, a flame in his eye beckoning to her as she waited, her body charged and wired. Instinctively, her mouth parted for a breath and he pounced, his lips landing on hers incredibly fast.

And as she let him ravish her and greedily returned the favor, she realized that in him she had found what she had not known she needed. It was as though the two years they had spent denying their attraction and building a friendship was simply a foundation for this. It went beyond passion and lust and the affection she had for him; Bernchal awoke in her feelings that she thought long gone and for the first time in a very long time, Shane gave in and allowed herself to be swept away.

~

She was sitting outside on the quad, her bare feet sinking into the cool grass as Silas played a few feet away with Layla. They rolled a rubber ball back and forth between them and every so often he would look back at her to make sure she'd seen him expertly catch it.

The flowers in the trees surrounding the institution were already blooming and the sun was shining brightly on the grounds. Shane tossed her head back and balancing herself up by her arms, closed her eyes and let the warmth wash over her as she wiggled her toes and buried them deeper in the grass. All around her, the birds chirped and tiny crickets, heard but not seen, filled the air with a cacophony of sounds. Though there was still a chill that forced them to wear warm sweaters, Spring was in full swing.

Bernchal walked over to them, slapped a quick high five to Silas's waiting hand and plopped down on the grass next to Shane, nudging her softly with his good shoulder. She peeked open one eye and smiled.

"You have a decision to make," he whispered.

"A decision?" she repeated, turning to face him. She sat up, crossed her legs and waited.

"Yeah. About what comes next."

She eyed him, curiously. "How's that?"

He turned to face Silas and replied. "If you want to keep fighting. Because I'll fight alongside you," he said softly, turning back to her, his eyes burning through hers. "Till my last breath, Shane, I'll fight next to you."

She smiled sadly, but said nothing, so he continued.

With a slightly more chipper tone, he added, "Or do you want to pick up, take the kid and get out of this God-forsaken place? Start over on a tropical island where no one knows us and no one cares."

She considered his words, his declaration, for a moment and watched him, his hazel eyes expecting and hopeful; her dark eyes peaceful.

"Well then," she said, reaching for his hand and feeling his knuckles with her thumb.

Their fingers intertwined and he gave her a small squeeze as he waited for her response.

She locked eyes with him and smiled.

The End

The official revolution lasted five years.

The size of the rebellion grew and more Americans still alive and still willing to fight for their country emerged.

In the end, the very same women that had been stolen, broken and trained, were the very ones to take back their world, take back their power, and take back their children. They joined forces with other rebels, other soldiers and officers that had somehow survived, other military stationed around the world that had held out hope for a return to their country to make things right. Together, they defeated the remaining militia leaders and soldiers and reclaimed their country.

In retrospect, it only took sixty-six months to wipe out half the population of the United States, destroy its government and turn its remaining citizens into killing machines.

When the world began again, all future textbooks and history lessons would paint Yenmor as a radical and his henchmen as savage murderers. At 42, he became the youngest President in the history of the U.S. and the only leader to single-handedly destroy a first-world entity.

The members of the various underground rebellions that rose up in the beginning and continued fighting would eventually be hailed as heroes who fought tirelessly to return this nation to its once former glory.

There was mention of Lieutenant Commander Stephen S. Bernchal of the United States Navy Special Warfare Command in various literature and verbal retelling that was passed down from parent to child, generation to generation for years to come. He was painted as a war hero, doting surrogate father and loving longtime companion.

But there was no mention of Julie Challaw, Sharee Bindi, Betzaida Sinkler or any of the other hundreds of women who were ripped from the arms of their children, tortured and brutalized and enslaved by the government; women who then launched a counter offensive to retrieve their kidnapped children and took down the most corrupt and reprehensible lawmaking system on the planet; women who bled and died for their children and the women and men who fought alongside them.

The history books of the future would make no mention of Shane Milian and what she did to take down Yenmor.

Only the lost children, the kids separated from their mothers and reunited because of their efforts, would come to remember everything.

All that had happened, all that had been lost and all that had been done for them.

Only *they* would remember the mothers that had fought and died so valiantly for them.

Yokairy Tavarez is also author of <u>The "This Is Everything" Collection</u>, a compilation of short stories, as well as <u>The Blue Brotherhood</u>, a crime drama set in New York City.

She is a Paralegal and Child Custody/Visitation Mediator with a twenty-year history in the legal industry. Born and raised in the Bronx, she lived in South Florida for seven years immediately after college and currently resides again in New York with her husband, two children and 12-year old Husky.

For more information, please visit her website at:

www.yokairytavarez.com

Other Titles By

Yokairy Tavarez

The Blue Brotherhood

The "This Is Everything" Collection

The Lost Highway

Redeem Me

www.ingramcontent.com/pod-product-compliance
Lightning Source LLC
Chambersburg PA
CBHW071932130726
47908CB00015B/127